Once upon a time, in a flaming iron-forged forest, a brave
and weary traveler came upon a fork in the road. One trail
led to truth and salvation, the other to damnation and lies...
But which?
You were there. You pointed her towards a path. She chose,
and strode on through the fire.
Does the story end there? Did she get the prince, or the tiger?
No, don't answer. Let me tell you what you're thinking: did I
plan this all along?
Wrong question. Better to ask: did you?
And what if prince and tiger are the same?

~ 1 ~

Come out, you dirty rat-fink villain. I know you're in here.

I crouched in a shadowy corner of the museum, lactic acid and impatience eating at my thigh muscles. Moonlight sprinkled through the curved glass clerestory, falling like stardust over shining glass cases filled with jewels, ancient treasures, dusty artifacts of old. In the case beside my hidey-hole, a glittering diamond-studded figurine winked at me, whispering *Take me! Take me!*

Not me. I'm one of the good guys. Verity Fortune, crime-fighter to the unsubtle, beating holes in things my specialty. I couldn't see the thief I'd come to catch. But I could *feel* him with my augmented senses, like tiny fairy lights glittering beneath my skin…

There. Across the room, the darkness dipped and swirled. I knew it. My mindmuscle itched, eager to kick some villainous butt.

Still, "villain" is relative in Sapphire City. It wasn't as if this dude was planning genocide or world domination. If my tip-off was for real—and I needed a break, the way things had gone for me lately—this was just a greedy little art heist.

Audacious, all the same. Sapphire City Museum—read "swanky art fortress"—is tricked out with the latest in invisible laser *steal-me-and-I'll-fuck-you-up* technology. But for the Gallery—the gang

1

of super-powered lunatics who terrorize our city, led by a lurid pyromaniac arch-psycho called Razorfire—the threat of loot and the promise of violent death are just a turn-on. They pride their cruel, lonely asses on doing impossible things.

Bring it, you thieving Gallery turdball. Whoever this guy was, he'd be no match for me.

My nose twitched, and my secret senses tingled with the sherbety spritz of *augment*... and like a cocky-ass specter, the thief strolled right through the minefield.

Holy crap. He wasn't invisible. Just... un-solid. A glittery, translucent man-shape. His tiny particles danced and shimmered in the silvery moonlight. Glowing with strange inner energy. Eerily beautiful.

For an instant, a foreign gleam knifed through him at waist height. Light scattered in rainbows. The laser system. I winced, bracing for the alarm...

Nothing. No shrieking, no electric shocks, no tiny LED flashing in the corner.

Dude was below the dust threshold. That particle transition dissipated his body heat—which meant no infra-red signature—and reduced his reflective cross-section to negligible. Like a stealth bomber, skipping past radar. The museum's state-of-the-art security system saw nothing but dirty air.

Honestly. How is that fair?

Inwardly, I cursed, sweating inside my shiny gunmetal leather coat. I'm a masked telekinetic crime-fighter, not a Las Vegas stage magician. I'd crawled in here along the ceiling, clinging like a big-ass spider with fingernails and talent, and this dark corner was as far as I could get without alerting security. But this guy could cut to dust any time he wanted and flee, leaving me in laser-surveillance hell.

I couldn't beat him. Could I?

Fact was, I needed this victory. And not only to uphold the law (right, because the law's done so well by me lately) or keep the museum's shiny junk collection intact (rather than spend the money on something useful, like food for poor people) or even just out of principle, because thwarting Gallery villains in their mission of terror and mayhem is what we Fortunes do.

No, I had to prove to Adonis—my righteous prick of a brother and the boss of our crime-fighting outfit, whom I love to death and would happily strangle if it wouldn't prove him right—that I wasn't a liability. That he could trust me again, the way he used to, before… well, before I unwittingly betrayed us all by consorting with our archenemy. If beating some impossibly clever vanishing guy was what it took? Bring it on.

But the thought of clever vanishing guys just made me wince. Don't even talk to me about Glimmer. Glimmer isn't a Fortune, but he's the finest of us, and he *had* been my best friend. Now…

Golden particles glittered, on the move. Mr. Sparkly strode quietly yet confidently, casting no shadow. His ghostly footfalls made no sound. I couldn't even smell him, beyond a tart whiff of the weed he'd been smoking, and that bothered me, too.

See, stinky villains are generally easy game. When you're a gibbering power-mad paranoid with pretensions to world domination? Personal hygiene isn't high on your must-do list. You're too busy going bonkers to care what people think.

It's the clean ones like Sparkly who worry me. The ones who make time for fashion and good grooming. *Body-conscious* means they're at least planning ahead. *Vain*, unfortunately, can mean they've got more brain space than you. If a villain has great hair and smells dreamy? Run. Trust me. Because I *didn't* run, and I got a dead father, a family in exile and months of screaming nightmares for my trouble.

I flexed my mindmuscle, determined to focus. The sinister glittery thief drifted past another glass case, into a pool of bluish shadow. Damn. I'd lost sight of him. I blinked rapidly. Had he vanished? Beamed up to his starship, or something?

My augmented senses sharpened, directional, and homed in. Oh, right. There he was, sparkly again, flitting from shadow to shadow, rematerializing for a few seconds each time he was out of sight. As if his glittery powers didn't last very long and he was recharging.

Whatever. He could be the Energizer Bunny and it wouldn't help him once I got my hands on his thieving Gallery ass. He strolled past a case full of ancient parchments, another stuffed with jeweled funerary ornaments from eighteenth-dynasty Egypt, yet another of antique ivory figurines. In the middle of the room, before a cylindrical glass case, he halted.

Tiny spotlights glared on the item inside. I squinted, trying to get a glimpse.

Looked like… a rock. Lumpy-shaped, like a fossilized seashell, a rusty red-brown color. Was this what he'd come for?

My belly warmed, in anticipation of feeding my hungry power at last. He flexed one glittery hand. Reached for the inch-thick hardened glass… and slipped his hand clean through it. Elbow on one side, hand on the other. Like the glass wasn't even there.

I gulped. That was totally cool.

So how did he not fall through the floor? Gravity isn't advisory-only, even for Gallery show ponies. Could this dude fly as well as sparkle? And how did he make his clothes do that trick? It didn't make sense. Maybe his secret villain name was Logicfail. Why did no one ever *worry* about these things?

Still, no time to puzzle it now. He'd already grabbed the funny rock—and nothing happened. I grinned. Logicfail, my ass. Can't turn *that* to glitter, can you? You're stuck, like honey-stuffed Winnie the Pooh. *Now* what's your plan, smart-ass?

I stretched my mindmuscle, a feline pleasure-yawn, and leapt. *Whee!* Up like a bouncing rubber ball.

He clenched his sparkling fist around the treasure, and *yanked.*

Kapow! Glass exploded, and the thief materialized in a puff of angry gang boy. Young Latino dude, jeans and black tank top, studded dog collar, shaven scalp crawling with prison tattoos. Fist still clenched, gym-built forearm bloody to his elbow and dripping red puddles onto the floor.

I hurtled through the air, slingshotted on a rubber band of mind energy. Tough guy, eh? DNA all over the place, broadcasting his true identity to anyone with twenty minutes and a spectrometer. I liked his attitude.

Umph! I crashed into him and we hit the floor. Fighting, rolling, limbs flailing.

And *now* the alarms went bugfuck.

A siren whooped. Blinding white lights flashed on. Steel security grilles ground down over the exits, *crunch-grr-slam!* We struggled. I aimed a swift punch of force, banging his skull into the floor.

"Goatfucker," he snarled, and scattered into particles beneath me.

I fell *through* him. Slammed into the floor face-first. Shit. The treasure-rock clattered across the tiles into a corner.

His particles swept around me, tingling—steady on, tiger, we only just met—and he coalesced. On his feet, hulking with rage, sweat spraying from his shaven head. "Asshole," he growled, and kicked at my ribs.

I rolled away, grabbing his foot with my power. He fell on his ass, cursing in Spanish. I caught something about an impossible (at least for me) feat of bestial eroticism, and grinned. At least "asshole" and "goatfucker" improved on "bitch" or "whore", this season's must-have snappy put-downs for the discerning sexist-pig villain. Gotta love an equal-opportunity insult. And he wasn't afraid to fight a girl. I could learn to like this guy.

But I'd no time to flirt. Any second now, rent-a-cops with guns would blunder in. I needed to be history when that happened. I grappled for his throat, ready to knock him insensible.

And a third person appeared right next to us, and kicked me in the face.

Not *arrived,* or *coalesced. Appeared.* From nowhere, *eureka!* with a rush of displaced breeze.

My head whiplashed sideways. A broken tooth crunched, and I tasted copper. But no time to care. I was too busy skidding across the floor, and my body slammed into a display case. *Doinng!* The glass and my skull both thrummed with the impact. I blinked, groggy. Who the fuck was that?

A skinny teenage girl, blue dreadlocks straggling to her shoulders. She wore a threadbare camisole top and jeans patched with scraps of plaid. A knotted string bracelet hung on her wrist, the kind of friendship pledge that grade-school kids wear. Her eyes were deep-set, bruised, her pimpled face sickly like a shopping-mall zombie.

And she had a sidekick. An equally scrawny boy, his gangly overgrown legs encased in black jeans. Jagged black-dyed hair with blond roots flopped over his cheek. Wispy unshaven chin, bitten black fingernails. His Yoda t-shirt read DO OR DO NOT – THERE IS NO "TRY". He wore eye pencil, for God's sake. I smelled cigarettes, alcopops, cheap spray cologne.

Just kids. So far as I could tell, they weren't even high. What the hell?

Mr. Sparkly swore and scattered. But Blue Dreads Girl was quicker. And she pulled the very same trick. Dissolved into a metallic cloud of sparks.

I gaped. Impossible. No two augments were exactly the same. Not even Harriet and Eb, my twin cousins, had identical powers... But I had to believe my eyes. Didn't I?

Tornado-like, she chased him, wrapping herself around him, twisting into him, *through* him. The two tangled, buzzing like angry wasp swarms... but Sparkly tired first. He dragged himself free, and slumped to the floor in human form, drained. And the remaining particles swirled into a coiling funnel and remade themselves into Blue Dreads. She laughed and kicked him with her scruffy lace-up boot.

In the meantime, Guyliner had retrieved the treasure and stuffed it into his jeans pocket. I scrambled up, ignoring my aching face. I needed to win that rock. To prove I could still do this, that my lurid sojourn into temporary insanity hadn't crippled me.

6

But Blue Dreads just grinned. Gleeful, a cruel little girl. "Too slow, hero," she gloated, and she and her emo BFF vanished.

Snap! Air slammed into the empty spaces. Gone. Ka-poof. May the Force be with you.

Just like that, I lose.

Shit.

Inwardly, I cringed. I'd wasted my chance. Still, no point crying about it. Sparkly groaned on the floor, limp, and I stumbled over to spend a few precious seconds finding out why Razorfire—because it had to be a Gallery heist, right?—had ordered him to steal a rock. At least that info would be something… and I skidded to a halt, waving my arms for balance.

Twin red laser dots bloomed on Sparkly's chest.

Uh-oh. I glanced down. Another two red dots, hovering over *my* sternum. Nice steady shots, too, barely flickering.

Well, fuckity do-dah.

The loudspeaker started blaring witty commands. "On the fucking floor NOW! Drop your weapons! Hands where I can see 'em!"

Right. Good luck with that. Stupid rent-a-cops, late to the party as usual.

Sparkly tried to rise, but only vomited. Blue Dreads had given him a right good thrashing. I sighed, frustrated. Sparkly, we're just not working out. It's not me, baby; it's you.

I coiled my power around one fist and fired myself at the glass ceiling like a silver-streaked cannonball.

~ 2 ~

Whizz! So far, so good, right?

Wrong. A little Verity-fact that just loomed kind of large: I can't fly.

I'm called the Seeker. I'm telekinetic, which might sound like some kind of psychic horror-film ooga-booga, but forcebending augments like mine are more physics than magic. Sure, I can fling myself through windows, but to do that, I rely on boring everyday things like inertia and centripetal force and the difference between *up* and *down*. When falling time comes? All I can do is hold on, and hope.

On the way up, I pulled my pistol—d'you think I blunder around unarmed? I'm augmented, not stupid—and put two quick shots into the giant clerestory window. *Crack-crack!* Twin starbursts erupted in the glass. I barely had time to stuff the weapon back under my coat before I smashed in, shoulder first.

Boom! The damaged glass shattered. Splinters stung my face, clinging to my hair and all over my clothes. And I hurtled out into the chilly October night.

Skyscrapers, traffic lights, virtual advertising flashing amid swirling searchlights and smoke. Sirens wailed, and distant weapons cracked, a spurt of gunfire. Just another night in Sapphire City: choose your weapon, watch your back, and check your civil rights at the door. That's what you get for electing Razorfire to City Hall. Yeah. Nice one. Hooray for democracy.

I grabbed an exposed metal strut with my power, and pulled. My elastic grip stretched, and contracted like an angry bungee cord, and slammed me sideways into the outside wall.

My breath crushed to a whimper, and for a moment I dangled there, gasping, sixty feet above nothing.

Gradually, I found my breath. Climbed down, hand over hand, along rain gutters and metal joints. Jumped the last twenty feet, landed on my own invisible bouncy castle of force and hop-skip-stumbled to the ground.

Paved garden courtyard, prissy fountain bubbling in the center, iron fence at the far end, and beyond it, the street. Inside, alarms still shrieked, but this part of the wall was opaque. The goons couldn't see me. Heh. Catch ya later, goons. Nice messing with you.

I dusted rueful hands on my swallow-tailed coat. Well, *that* was a bust. Villains: 1, Verity: nil.

But my nerves tingled eagerly, and my muscles hurt with that pleasant ache you get after some tough exercise, or really great sex. I wriggled my thighs, ready for another round. Damn, it felt amazing to use my power again. Adonis didn't let me out alone much anymore, and since that little fiasco a few months back atop the old FortuneCorp skyscraper, Adonis's word was law. I didn't get a say in it. Boy, was he gonna tear strips off me when I got home.

I shuddered. I'm not afraid of Adonis. Not exactly. Too much fond sibling contempt between us for that. Doesn't mean his furious ice-emperor act is something I look forward to.

A homeless guy in an old Nazi trench coat squatted by the fountain on a cardboard sheet. Pigeons pecked for crumbs on the paving around him. He peered at me, scratching his greasy head. "Fuck was that? You a goddamn alien?"

I flipped him a *live-long-and-prosper* salute. "I come in peace, earthling! You seen my spaceship? Thought I parked it around here someplace."

The old dude shook his head sagely. "Nuh-uh. Prob'ly they towed it. Goddamn penny-pinching assholes."

"Too right," I said, but he'd already fallen asleep.

I wiped blood from my chin, spat out a shard of broken tooth, and sucked on my injured tongue. Ouch. Those two mouthy tweens would pay for this.

If I ever saw them again, that was. If I could even figure out who Blue Dreads and Guyliner were. These days, new villains sprouted all over Sapphire City like warts, egged on or chased from hiding or just plain pissed off by our esteemed new mayor's crackdown on the augmented. Insects, most of 'em. Vermin, not worth breaking a sweat over. But these grungy kids with their oddly identical powers bothered me. They drifted in my head, the ghostly remnants of a bad dream.

Especially the girl. Those hollow cheekbones and bruised zombie eyes. Something about her felt *wrong*.

I spared a brief thought for Sparkly, probably cuffed in talent-draining augmentium alloy with blood running from his ears right now. I'd appreciated his talent, his hubris, his glitter-quick reflexes. Our side could've used more guys like him. I even felt a twinge of shame that I'd abandoned a fellow augment to face the heat, even if he was Gallery. Like me, he was just making a living.

But inwardly, I shrugged, his defeat both salty and sweet in my mouth. Shared adversity doesn't make us pals. You make your bed, you die in it, you black-hearted Gallery shitweed.

I peeled off my black leather mask and stowed it in my trouser pocket. Dipped my hands in the fountain, splashed my bloodied face clean. Shook the drips back into my ponytailed hair, and strolled out onto the street.

Cool nighttime air refreshed me. It was late, but traffic still streaked by: silent yellow electric cabs, smart cars, SUVs, a golden stretch Humvee. A kid whistled past me on a scooter. A trolley car rattled along its tracks, lights flickering over the few passengers inside. Late-working office jockeys strode the sidewalk, briefcases and tablets tucked under their arms. A homeless guy wearing a tattered football jersey rattled a paper cup for change beside pasted bills for theatre shows and "occupy" demonstrations and a splurt of all-too-familiar crimson spray-painted graffiti.

BURN IT ALL

Dizziness waltzed in my skull, the giddy specter of half-forgotten fever. Razorfire's catchphrase. What would *he* think of me now? I'd screwed up the simplest job, been taken unawares by a pair of joy-riding boy- band fans. I cringed. Jeez, how humiliating…

Mentally, I smacked myself upside the head. Verity, the only thing he'd care about is that you attacked one of his crew. He's your enemy. He will peel your skin off. Forget him.

Forget him.

Right.

Razorfire's gorgeous scent dizzies me, mint and fire and dark delight, and I can't help but inhale. Swallow, gulp for more, my body yearning to drink him in. His flame licks my bruised cheek, both threat and promise. I flush, mortified. I don't deserve this. I don't deserve him…

Fiercely, I blinked, and the memory splintered and whirled away, leaving only fresh-sliced pain in my temples. Fuck it. The flashbacks of my evil ex-lover—yeah, long and gruesome story—were growing less frequent, easier to banish. But the guilty twist in my guts didn't ease.

Wanna know a secret? It never does. Not for one goddamn second.

Sure, Razorfire tricked me, playing twisted psychological games until my mind snapped. That didn't excuse how I'd acted, or the suffering my twisted infatuation had caused. Adonis had tried to have me treated and it badly backfired. My father and sister were dead, my family in hiding. I had a lot to make up for.

I glanced about for Sentinels, those sneaky augment-detecting gadgets that were bolted to every lamp post in the city these days, or so it seemed. Razorfire's plan since he'd been elected mayor had been inscrutable, to say the least.

In his public persona, he was all *keep the streets safe* and *prosecute to the full extent of the law* and *no tolerance for violent criminals.* Yet every once in a while, he'd climb into his crimson silk archvillain suit and mask, and burn some neighborhood to a smoking ruin. Post threatening videos on the internet. Ratchet the tension higher, let the police department and the district attorney's office take the heat (heh) and generally stir up a furious hornet's nest of violence and fear.

Look, there was a Sentinel: a smug silvery cylinder mounted ten feet up on a building's corner, silently blinking its incriminating red light at me. I flipped it the bird. Detect this, you metal moron.

Across the sidewalk, an office worker in a slim-cut suit did a double-take, and made a move inside his jacket. Sigh. Seriously: a gun? Are they arming metrosexuals now? *Stop, or I'll order decaf!*

I didn't pause. I just pointed into his face as I walked by, and gave him my best Dirty Harry impression. "You really wanna test me, punk?"

He scuttled backwards, dropping his computer case, hands raised in peace. Heh. Must have my angry face on today.

In my pocket, my phone's message tone chimed. Whatever. Probably Adonis wondering where the hell I was. Or Glimmer, texting me a dose of the guilts because he imagined I was drinking myself horny in some seedy Castro Street bar, and of course *he'd* never do anything so grotesquely banal and *ordinary* as get drunk and laid, because he was Glimmer and he was too damn *perfect* and jeez, when did I turn into such a jealous little worm?

I sighed, rubbing the dented scar on my cheekbone. A headache swelled like a tumor deep in my skull, threatening murder. Hell, I wanted a drink and a cigarette, even though I'd never been much of a drinker and I didn't like the smell of tobacco smoke. What I *needed* was food and sleep. I should go home, as far as "home" went these days, now that FortuneCorp were in hiding and Glimmer's secret techno-lair was a crispy barbecue and Sentinels mined half the city's streets into a no-hero zone.

But I needed to salvage something from tonight. Prove I hadn't simply screwed up, hadn't let those villains escape out of carelessness, that my power was reliable and strong. Or hell, I might as well rock on down to Castro Street right now and order a triple brainfuck with a twist of sordid.

Belligerent, I squared my shoulders. I didn't give a moldy fart for Sentinels or cops or vigilante office boys. What were they gonna do, shoot me? I'd survived that before. Anyway, my altercation with Sparkly and the twin tweens had set off every alarm in that building. The entire world already knew I was here.

So I strolled across the courtyard to the museum's main entrance, and kicked the door in.

Crash! Boot mixed with mindmuscle, unstoppable. The revolving door buckled like a crushed beer can. I cracked my neck, satisfied. Damn. Someone fetch me that cigarette.

I hurled the wreckage aside and strode into the tiled lobby, where a weird marble statue resembling a gigantic pink horse turd squatted on a pillar.

A black-uniformed security guard challenged me. I flung up one hand and hurled him against the wall, pinning him under the chin with an invisible grip. His handgun clattered to the tiles. The mega-turd teetered and crashed to the floor, a clatter of broken marble. Oops. Performance art.

"Where's the CCTV, idiot?" Blood pounded in my temples, nearly drowning out the sound of my voice. I was in the clear, unmasked. I didn't care. Let the world look at my scars. Let them see me as I truly am.

Glimmer once told me his mask was his true face. That it wasn't a disguise, but a confession. For me, it's the other way around. My mask is unsullied, fit for public consumption. The face underneath… on my bad days? Not so much. And the physical scars—my souvenir of that hellhole of an asylum, courtesy of my well-meaning asshole of a brother—are the pretty part.

The security guy wasn't dumb enough to play the hero. He jerked his head towards a locked door, his throat bobbing as he tried to swallow.

I let him fall undamaged and stepped over him as he gurgled for breath. Heh. *Dumb enough to play the hero.* There's a lesson we could all learn.

I smashed the security office door open. Old-school video screens, surveillance-camera footage of darkened museum rooms and corridors. In the room where I'd fought the tweens, a battalion of guards and cops and rented heavies were arresting Sparkly and reading him what was left of his rights. From the black-and-bloodied look of his face, they'd left out the "we can't beat the snot out of you while you're restrained" part.

I leveled my pistol at the only guard inside the CCTV room. Chesty young blond, biceps like turnips stuffed up his shirtsleeves. His sidearm lay on the bench. Bad choice, Turnip Man.

His ice-chip eyes widened, and one hand strayed to the can of pepper spray at his belt.

I thumbed the safety off, pulling three pounds on a four-pound trigger. My hands were shaking as badly as my voice. I was weary, hungry, pissed off. "Just try me, moron. See what happened to that window? Imagine what I can do to your skull. We understand each other?"

Turnip Man nodded, otherwise perfectly still, fingers splayed to show he'd surrendered. They weren't paying him enough to die. Sweat trickled down his neatly shaven cheek, and in that moment I hated him utterly.

For being young, ordinary, carefree. For having a regular job, where you went home after work, dumb and happy with your sixteen twenty-five an hour in your pocket, and thought about something else.

For living such a goddamn simple life.

"Good. Then you know what I want." I jerked my bruised chin towards the bank of screens and digital recording equipment. "So get on with it."

Forty seconds later, I was gone.

~ 3 ~

By the time I reached the new FortuneCorp HQ, I was wet, sore and angry, and I reeked of shit.

Sentinels, see. The old ones you could fool with augmentium, the alloy that's resistant to augmented powers. Razorfire strutted around in public for weeks wearing a wristwatch forged from the stuff and no one was the wiser. These improved models? Nuh-uh. At least, not for us. His Archvillain-ness is still getting away with it. Somehow. Fuck him.

Hmm. Right. Moving on from that thought…

Since that night a few months ago, when we lost out to Razorfire big time—he sabotaged his own superweapon, became the city's hero, got himself elected mayor and declared us Fortunes public enemies; if that isn't irony, can me up and call me a sardine—we don't want him knowing where we're holing up. We need to move about out of sight, and a lot of the time that means underground. Sapphire City's sewers date from before the fire at the turn of last century, and they smell like it: greasy brick tunnels, calf-deep in foul flushwater, floating with fat globules and dead rats and discarded baby wipes, and crusted with decades of slimy dripping God-knows-what.

I carried my coat rolled up under one arm, and let my boots take the brunt of it, but by the time I levered up the rusted grate and climbed blinking like a mole into the deserted parking lot by the waterworks, it was two in the morning, I stank like a mediaeval train toilet and my mood didn't smell much better.

Times like this, I wished I *could* fly. Or turn invisible. Or make decent coffee. Or do anything, pretty much, that was useful to anyone anymore.

I slipped unseen into the forest surrounding the parking lot. Fog curled among the tall eucalypts, luminous in the moonlight, wreathing smelly old me with the leaves' disinfectant scent. The city noise faded to a cool murmur. I squeezed stinking water from my trouser cuffs and strode up the hill into the dark. Leaves and soil crunched under my boots. Somewhere a wildcat yowled. A few charred tree trunks lay in my path, black shapes darker than the shadows, and I hopped wearily over them.

At the top of the hill, no lights shone. But I knew the path, and my tongue tingled with the candy-sweet flavor of *augment*. I picked my way through stumps and fallen branches towards our hideout: the derelict asylum.

I'd spent months trapped in here at Adonis's behest, while doctors tried to "cure" me of my little misdirected affection problem. Naturally, I'd escaped and set the place on fire. The concrete-block building was now partly a blackened ruin, but at one end, roof and walls still stood, two stories high.

Had I freaked out when we first came here? Fuck, yes. I'd stalked around with a loaded fistful of power, unleashing on ghosts, jumping at every noise. I was okay with it now. It no longer looked much like the place where I'd been tortured... but sometimes, in the night, I still woke alone in my cold ex-cell to the phantom smells of stewed apple and puke and singed hair, the bright buzz of electroshock, unseen screams grating in my ears.

And Glimmer wondered why I frequented late bars.

I eased the unlocked basement door open, quiet as I could. Inside, a row of caged light bulbs hung, just one in the middle switched on. The old food hall: a stainless-steel serving hatch, steel tables bolted to the green linoleum floor, barred gates to keep the crazies in. No alarm on the door. Glimmer hadn't gotten around to installing one yet. Too busy hacking our cell phones so they couldn't be tracked (good job) and repairing his surveillance kit (from what was left of it, which was pretty much zilch) and rebuilding the data-mining algorithms he'd lost when Razorfire torched his lair.

But my teenage cousin Ebenezer was on watch. Slouched in a plastic chair, playing a game on his tablet. Lank brown hair in need of a wash, dusty trench coat over safety-pinned jeans. His lame left leg was stretched out, still a mite crooked despite endless iterations of surgery and traction, back when the Fortune family were still respectable and Uncle Mike's money could buy that sort of thing. I think Eb secretly likes it that he limps. All part of the package.

Some defects you just can't fix.

Eb blinked at me, short-sighted. One watery blue eye, one brown. "Well, *you* look like you just crawled from a sack of hungry rat corpses."

"Thanks, man. No, really."

"Always here to help." A rare grin, inept, like he didn't care to practice it much. On his lopsided face, it had a kind of evil leprechaun charm.

Eb was the weirdest sibling from a branch of the Fortune family that wasn't exactly noted for being normal, and it wasn't just the limp or the oddball eyes. When he unleashed—which he did more often than was strictly necessary or appropriate—people pissed themselves and cowered into gibbering blobs of *oh-god-let-me-die*.

He'd taken the secret name Bloodshock from a serial-killer character he played on some screwed-up online RPG, and it stuck. He might look like an escapee from the aftermath of the teenage nerd apocalypse, but you do *not* want to mess with cousin Eb.

I believe that allegiance is nurture, not nature. Good versus evil is a choice we all make. But if anyone on our side was born to be a villain, it's this guy.

"You'll go blind looking at that stuff." I ruffled his hair, dodging a punch. What with my Miss Universe face and bubbly personality—and growing up with Adonis and Chance for brothers—I knew how it felt to be the unpopular one. I'd made an effort with Eb ever since I'd forced us all into this charming little camping vacation, and I sort of like the guy. Even if he sometimes makes me want to brandish a crucifix in his direction. "Get a girlfriend. Oh, wait. That'd involve talking to a *real girl.*"

"This isn't interactive porn," Eb insisted. "I'm honing my reflexes."

"Right. When the big-breasted virgin schoolgirl zombies attack, you'll be the first guy I call. Any dinner left?" On cue, my stomach grumbled. My dead appetite had reanimated, at least in part, since my rat-happy sewer jaunt, and I hadn't consumed anything except high-caffeine cola and a candy bar since this morning.

Yesterday morning, that is. Jeez, what am I, twelve? No wonder I'm such a wreck.

Eb nodded towards the darkened kitchen's serving hatch. "Peggy made lasagna."

I rolled my eyes. Of course she did. Adonis's new lady friend was perky, red-headed, domesticated. "Did she bake cupcakes, too? Wearing a frilly apron?"

"Mee-*yeow.*" Eb mimed a cat scratch. "You'd eat it if a *certain person* made it."

"Did I say I wouldn't eat it?" But I dragged the tray towards me a little too hard, spilling tomato sauce on the counter. Glimmer baked the best lasagna on the planet, no exceptions. Glimmer did most things better than everyone else. Especially me.

To be fair, Peggy did everything she could to help out, despite not really being one of us, and her cooking sure tasted nice. Everything about Peg was *nice.* Probably what Adonis said after he fucked her. *That's nice, dear.*

19

Okay, now I really had no appetite. I pushed the tray away. "Maybe later."

"Whatevs." Eb didn't look up.

I slunk upstairs to the second floor, where our bedrooms—read *rusty ex-torture cells*, and yay for that—were. On the landing, Uncle Mike's latest stray cat adoptee hissed at me with a suspicious yellow glare. Poor little bugger looked hungry. "Whatevs," I mimicked as I went by. "You wound me with your disdain, kitty. Lasagna's on the table. My treat."

The dim corridor smelled of old smoke and rust. Steel cell doors lined each wall, stretching into the distance, where the roof had collapsed in the fire and damp moonlight misted in. Light wind whistled through the twisted corrugated iron, *whoo! whoo!*

Electric light leaked from a single door that lay ajar on my right. I tiptoed, trying to creep by unnoticed.

"Where have *you* been?"

Fail. I stopped, folding my arms on a sigh. "Like you don't know."

Adonis leaned in his doorway. Unshaven, his blue eyes bloodshot. His shirt was creased, formerly an extinction-level event for my big brother, who'd spent his life wearing custom suits and diamond cufflinks, wading through rivers of adoring girls on his way to corporate board meetings and glittering charity balls. They write romance novels about guys like Adonis. He's what ordinary women think of as a hot date, and life has gifted him with what you might call a healthy ego. I wouldn't label him *vain*, exactly— he's too pragmatic for that—but let's just say his secret name isn't Narcissus without reason.

His blond hair was ragged, in need of a cut. It made him look a little crazy. And the bruises under his eyes shone darker than usual. He'd been losing sleep. We all had.

"Fine." His voice was hoarse, fatigued. "I know where you've been. So what the hell were you doing?"

"Stopping a crime in progress, since you ask. That okay with you?" But my chest hurt inside, and my hostility lost its luster.

My brother, questioning my good intentions. My fucking *brother*.

He just eyed me, glitter-blue. Accusing.

Christ, I'd no energy to fight with him tonight. "I'm tired, Ad. Can we just get some sleep?"

"Vee…" He touched my arm.

I halted again. "What?"

"We've talked about this. You're not well. You shouldn't go off by yourself and—"

"And what? Do my job? We're crime-fighters, aren't we? How about we fight crime?"

My words bounced off the walls. He frowned, a finger to his lips. Of course, my phone pinged again in my pocket, over-loud.

Shit. I fumbled it to silent to make it shut up. "What?" I whispered fiercely. "Am I gonna wake up the Stepford wife?"

"I'm working. Peg's in her own room." A defiant edge. He knew I didn't like Peggy. I'd never liked any of his long-term—read *longer than two weeks*—girlfriends. None of 'em were worthy of him. It was a brother–sister thing. And ever since I'd murdered our father, and Adonis locked me in the nut house, and I dropped a ceiling on our elder sister, and Adonis shot me and hurled me out a fifty-sixth-story window? Brother–sister things had become a little complicated.

"Sleeping alone? So sad. Does she snore? Or are you just tired of her already?"

"You can talk."

That gloss of disgust took a hacksaw to my nerves. "Screw you, okay? I am *so* over you judging me. At least I tell mine they're losers as soon as I'm done."

An incredulous laugh. "Jesus, Vee. Last day to cash in this month's bitch credits?"

I swallowed, ashamed. Truth was? Seeing him like this broke my heart. He hadn't asked for what had happened to us, any more than the rest of our family had. None of it was his fault.

No. No, it was mine.

21

"She cooked a nice dinner," I allowed grudgingly. He didn't need to know I hadn't eaten any. "And hell, she seems to like Oreos and Bruce Lee movies. I guess there's hope for her."

He rubbed his eyes with thumb and forefinger. "She tries, okay? Give her a chance. It's not her fault she's—"

"Adonis? Everything okay?" A sleepy female voice drifted from the half-closed door.

Adonis sighed, resting his head on the doorframe.

I choked. She *was* in his damn room. He'd lied.

My face burned. Ugly, poison words crawled up my throat. Before I could spit them out, I clamped my teeth and marched away. He didn't call after me. I heard his door click shut. I kept walking, though I itched all over, an army of rabid ants nipping furiously beneath my skin.

I stormed past more rooms: Jeremiah, Ebenezer, Harriet, Peggy, the rest of the stray augments we'd adopted like some stupid special-needs homeless shelter since we holed up here. Jem was coughing, a horrid throat-savaging beast that no doubt we'd all catch before the week was out. I could hear Uncle Mike snoring. Mike, Dad's kid brother, who'd been as civil to me as was humanly possible, considering I got Dad killed.

They don't forgive you, hissed one of the incarnations of me that rattled around in my skull. Since the asylum, I'm like a range of Barbie dolls in there. This one was Nasty Verity, like the ghost of my dead sister Equity with a double shot of spite. *They'll never forgive you. They're just humoring you, until they think of a way to get rid of you quietly, with no fuss. One day, you'll have a tragic accident…*

Viciously, I kicked at the dead leaves littering the floor. Shut your face, Nasty. If Adonis was pissed at me for disobeying him? Fine. That was his right. I didn't care. I didn't even care that my precious big brother was sticking his dick in the world's most boring woman and apparently liked it enough to let her sleep in his *bed*, for fuck's sake.

I cared that he trusted her more than he trusted me.

He'd known Peg a few lousy weeks, and *I* was the one he lied to.

22

Fuck.

A silent scream hollowed my chest, and my mindmuscle burned. I felt like tearing down the broken ceiling to crush us all. The fact that I'd earned his mistrust a dozen times over only made it hurt more.

I reached the door to my room—dark, cold, empty—and hesitated, restless. My muscles watered with exhaustion, my eyes smarted with grit. I needed to crash. But my thoughts howled in wild circles, my power pacing like a caged beast in my belly. My senses had graduated from tingling through prickling to a malicious stinging cloud that wouldn't be silent. Sleep seemed about as likely as a lightning strike.

And I still had business tonight. The memory of those teenage hooligans—y'know, the ones with identical, improbable powers who'd whipped my ass?—wouldn't leave me alone. Who were they working for? What was the artifact they'd taken, and why did they want it?

More to the point: had Razorfire really deployed them against his own guy? And why?

Sure, maybe I was paranoid. Seeing archvillain conspiracies lurking under every rock, every breath of wind and rustle of leaves part of an elaborate plot against me.

Wouldn't be the first time it'd turned out to be true.

I crept to the cell next to mine and pushed on the unlocked door. "You awake?" I whispered.

Dim green glow filtered from a computer screen, throwing the tiny cell into shadows. A cursor blinked solemnly from a window brimming with wingdings code. Schematics and circuit diagrams were stuck to the whitewashed walls with tape and gum. The crumpled bed had disappeared under a heap of silicon hardware, cables, parts of phones; more of the same cluttered the desk, next to coffee mugs and empty cola cans and two unwashed dinner plates.

Glimmer lay asleep at his desk, green light rinsing his face. Head pillowed on one arm, dark hair with an albino splash in front tumbling

23

onto the keyboard. His warm vanilla-spice scent drifted, both comfort and accusation. I inhaled more deeply, like I did sometimes when he wasn't watching. Oyy. Even working nineteen hours a day in a grubby cell deep in the ruins of a sadist's hellhole, he managed to smell like this. If Glimmer were a villain—if he'd even a breath of badness in him, which he didn't—you'd flee from that scent alone.

He looked exhausted, dark stubble stark against his too-pale face. Time was, he'd worn his mask twenty-four-seven around me. No longer. He'd nothing to hide, except that he was young and talented and didn't deserve the shitty deal Razorfire had hurled his way.

I bit my lip. Once upon a time, Glimmer had been my friend. God, I longed to talk the way we used to. Trade insults, give him crap about his hair product. Say, *dude, you'll never believe what happened to me tonight* and have him scoff at me, charm me with his grin and his wise-ass wit. I wanted to be dazzled by his white-knight geekboy brilliance, and hunt criminals together safe in the knowledge that he'd never betray me, never give up. Hell, the jealous part of me wanted to smack his pretty face for being so much better at it all than I.

Compelled, I drifted my palm over his cheek, just a twitch from touching. His breath warmed my hand, and my pulse quickened, shame and loneliness and some deeper compulsion I didn't under-stand mingling like inks in my blood. I could wake him. Stroke that velvety hair from his eyes, take heart from his sweet, crooked smile…

But if I touched him, he might *look* at me.

Instead, I stuffed my hand into my inside pocket and yanked out the DVD of security footage I'd taken from Turnip Man at the museum. Unearthed a pad of yellow sticky notes from the mess on the desk, and stuck one onto the plastic case.

Check out 12:57 am. Who the fuck are these clowns?
xox
V.
P.S. Your lasagna is better.

Quietly, I set the DVD by his keyboard, where he'd see it when he woke. Like he didn't already have enough work to do.

Glimmer's lashes fluttered, and he murmured, immersed in some unwelcome dream. My throat ached. My rude thoughts about him earlier in the night seemed petty and stupid. All his bad opinions of me? They were justified. He was strong, steadfast, a proper hero. Whereas I was unreliable, weak, indecisive, confused about the simplest decisions.

Maybe part of me resented him for making me feel inferior. And okay, maybe another, secret, blushing-girly part would've liked it if he were a bit more jealous about the whole drunk-and-laid thing. He was smart, cute, had a heart of unblemished gold. Any woman would want him.

But mostly, I just wanted my friend back.

I could wake him right now. Tell him how sorry I am for being such a screw-up. Beg him to help me get through this, to be there for me, the way he'd always been since the moment we met…

Bzzz-bzzz.

My phone, vibrating on silent. Shit. It wouldn't give up.

Swiftly, I backed off, and shielded the screen's light with my curled hand. That message I'd ignored a few hours ago, after I'd escaped from the museum guards…

My nerves crackled, ice and fire. The bright letters telescoped, and all else, including time, slipped away.

Confused, firebird?
Let's talk. You know the place.
R.

My throat swelled, throttling me.

Memory swamped me, nightmares of pleasure and passion and utter conviction, both delight and torture. It was unique, singular, terrifying. And I adored it.

I gasped, shivering. I was sweating, my mouth sticky. My hands shook. A junkie denied a fix.

25

Oh, God.

Keep it down, urged Common-Sense Verity, the sensible and incredulous me who still lurked somewhere inside. *It's not what it seems. It's just a learned response. You know that. Fight it!*

Glimmer stirred, a fragrant shadow amongst shadows. "Verity?" he mumbled, slurring. "Whassup?"

My guts hollowed, desperation swimming against a warm velvety undercurrent of desire. Glimmer could help me. I knew he could. *Fight it!*

But I didn't want to.

"Nothing," I murmured, oddly calm. So calm, it should've terrified me. But I was already beyond fear. "It's nothing. Go back to sleep." And I pocketed my phone and walked out.

~ 4 ~

On the bridge across the gateway to the bay, fog spiraled in slow motion, weaving intricate ghostly shapes around the soaring suspension cables. Damp pre-dawn crept chilly fingers up my coat sleeves. Piquant sea air stung my face. To landward, the white halogen spotlights of newly refurbished Rock Island Prison glistened faintly through the mist. Somewhere below me swirled the dark, invisible sea.

I'd walked here, confident, flitting coolly across darkened parklands and Sentinel-free streets. But now, crab-clawed nerves gripped my guts. Damn, I needed to pee. My fingers shook. My lungs wouldn't take in enough air. At my back, a car whooshed by, and I jumped like a startled frog, *ribbit!*

Fuck. My sweaty palms slicked the railing, ripe with fear and anticipation. My senses fizzed, and I glanced over my shoulder, certain I was being watched. But I saw no one.

Deep in the rusty cells of my mind, Common-Sense Verity kicked at the walls and screamed *what the hell are you doing?* The rest of me just felt like a high-school girl on prom night. I hadn't seen him in person for weeks. Suddenly, it seemed so unbearably *long*.

27

This was our place. Always had been, since that very first night, when I'd wept and screamed into uncaring darkness, and he'd come for me. Not my father, not my brothers, but *him*, alone, when no one else would.

And he wasn't here.

My knees watered, like they did when I was small and my father scolded me for some thoughtless mistake. Oh, God. I was too late. He'd already left. I should've picked up that message as soon as it chimed. If I'd displeased him…

Feathers of flame teased the back of my neck. "Hello, firebird."

I whirled, my heart pounding.

And there he stood. Vincent Caine, richest guy in town, lately CEO of Iridium Industries, genius inventor of the Sentinel (among other flashy, ubiquitous bits of kit) and mayor of Sapphire City.

Razorfire.

Not wearing his crimson silken coat, or the rust-blood metal mask that had become the watchword for terror; not even the slate-grey suit and red tie (always red, or plum, or scarlet, jeez, it was like he was *telling* everyone) that he affected in his day job. Just a crisp black shirt and jeans, but still the vision of him swallowed me, a vortex of time and space, and I couldn't breathe.

He isn't superlatively good-looking, not really. More like a sharp, interesting face. No, what Vincent has is *presence*. A cool, effortless composure that flirts with *elegant* and *handsome* as it sashays by on its way to *magnificent*. And after so long apart, it hit me with redoubled force.

But always, it's his eyes that get me. Unholy storm-cloud grey, the cleverest and most dangerous eyes you'll ever see. When he's angry, they're black. When he's utterly furious, they *burn*. Breeze fingered his short bronze hair, wreathed him in mist and dark enchantment. Calm, invincible, untouchable. The perfect picture of power.

They write novels about guys like Vincent, too. The ones featuring mental disintegration and toxic passion that leads to murder.

The awfulicious prospect of his displeasure made me shudder. To be honest, my memory of those heady days was still fuzzy, drunken, trapped in that dark half-world between truth and nightmare. I didn't rightly remember everything that ever happened between us... but I hadn't forgotten his exquisite way with lessons. No, I most certainly hadn't.

Suddenly, I was ultra-aware of the dirt smearing my clothes, the stink in my untidy hair. The scar on my dented cheekbone burned. I should've showered, dressed nicely, fixed myself up for him.

Or not.

I swallowed, parched. "I, er, meant to come sooner. It's just..." Shit. Wrong approach. Never make excuses. *Never apologize, firebird. It's always a lie. If you don't mean it, don't do it in the first place...*

But he just shrugged, fluid. "I know how it is. Museums to rob, chaos to wreak. The diary's always so full." A weaponized smile, loaded as a demon's promise. You can poison small creatures with Vincent's smile. "Oh, and thieves to humiliate. That was entertaining. Seriously. I'm diverted."

The way his lips shaped the word *diverted* made me want to fidget and blush, and mentally I kicked myself in the ass. *Keep it down, Verity. You're here for information. This is a temporary ceasefire, not a date.*

Goddamn it. I'd been doing fine. I'd barely thought of him in weeks, if you could call four or five times an hour *barely*. Barely dreamed of him, either, unless you count the breathless ones where I shudder in firelit darkness and he... well, never you mind. Point is, I was doing okay. Then the bastard flips me a casual text—*one damn text*—and I'm all Stockholm Syndrome. Christ on a cracker.

Stubbornly, I took a step back. "That's sweet and everything, Vincent, but what do you want?" His name tasted minty, faintly chemical on my tongue. I wished I hadn't said it. It made me think of flames. But the question lingered: why had he asked me here? He never did anything without a plan. What new trick was this?

"Well, if you insist on making it all about me..." He slid hands into pockets, a cunning caricature of casual. "I'm just *dying* to hear what you thought of your new friends at the museum. Did you enjoy them?"

My pulse throbbed, a hot warning. I knew those tweens' shenanigans were no accident. Vincent was toying with me. Feeding me lies. I shouldn't play his games...

Then again, I knew them for what they were, didn't I? Lies. Misdirection. If I fell for his bullshit anyway, I'd no one to blame but myself. Right?

Seductive warmth whispered on my skin. I wanted to dive in, revel in the battle, relish his clever traps and gambits. Say *to hell with it* and go with him right now... but part of me shrank like a kiss from maggots at the thought of listening to his toxic words for a moment longer.

I folded my arms, defensive. Like it could shield me from the memory of his quickflame gaze, his strange mint-fresh warmth, his fingers as they clenched between mine...

Keep it business. Find out what he knows, and leave.

"They were surprising, I'll give 'em that," I offered. "Twin augments. I've never seen the like."

"I know! Delightful, isn't it? I confess, I get bored with the same old tricks."

He leaned his elbows on the railing beside me, sleeves rolled up. He has precise, elegant hands. Artist's hands. Lover's hands. His wrist was arrogantly bare, no augmentium wristwatch to shield him tonight. No disguise at all. He really didn't give a damn.

I brushed aside a tendril of treacherous appreciation. Sure, his courage would be admirable, if he wasn't a genocidal psychopath who rated the rest of the human race lower than maggots, except for a happy few of his augmented Gallery minions, and even they weren't worth speaking to most of the time.

He'd had a power-crazed supervillain BFF (of sorts) named Iceclaw, a chuckling maniac with long greasy hair and saber teeth, who froze people's skin for fun. But Iceclaw was dead. I'd dropped him from a forty-foot ceiling and stabbed him in the throat with a shard of broken glass. I still wasn't certain how Vincent felt about that.

I grinned weakly. "Yours, then, are they?"

Great. More Gallery weirdoes to contend with. But my mind stumbled, lost in the fog. By deploying Sentinels, he was dropping his own gang in the shit. Making them feel betrayed and indignant. What was his game? He was manipulating me, I knew that much for sure. But to what end?

Vincent quirked one neat bronze brow. "I'm offended you'd think so. The building was still standing, last I noticed. Wasting such lovely tricks, just to re-home an overpriced rock? And blue dreadlocks? Must be taking style tips from your glimmery puppy dog." He laughed, a starlit ripple of *wrongness*. "I assure you, Verity, that girl's no child of mine."

Sickly, I envied him his certainty. The way he knew without a flicker of doubt what was important. I envied him a lot of things, I guess. I could admit that now. Once, I too had worn that unshakeable confidence. The simple way: just jettison your conscience. No more dilemmas. No more problem.

But those days were gone. I was cured now. I hated the Verity I'd been with him… but I hated it more that in the dark before dawn, when I lay restless and sweating in my cold ex-lunatic's cell, I still burned for what he'd meant to me.

I shivered, hugging myself. "Look, it's nice to see you and all, but I really have to—"

"The girl calls herself 'Sophron'." He studied his perfect nails. "The boy goes by 'Flash'. You saw some of what they can do. From the way they work together, I'd say they're old friends." A twist of sarcasm. Like he could possibly understand what *old friend* meant. "That's enough, I think. It's no fun if I give you all the answers."

Which didn't mean he knew anything. Didn't mean he didn't, either. "Sophron," I mused, intrigued in spite of myself. "What's that supposed to mean?"

"They'll make troublesome enemies, firebird. Dare I suggest caution?"

I snorted, pleased to have caught him in error. "Now why would you use a stupid word like 'caution'? Going soft?"

Fire kindled in his gaze. I didn't see him move, but somehow he was closer, too close, his strange possessive heat mercilessly invading my space and conquering it. Involuntarily, I gasped, and his mint-fire flavor tingled my tongue, sparkling all the way down inside me and resurrecting memories that were better off buried.

"I knew it," he whispered on a smile. "Look me in the eye and make me believe you've changed. I dare you."

Fuck. It wasn't an error. It was bait. And I'd swallowed it whole.

This was what he'd wanted, the reason he'd lured me here. I wanted to punch him and scream *get away from me!* I wanted to fight, to unleash on him, jeez, what a futile effort that'd be. I'd no defense against him, and he knew it. Fucking damn him.

"Come back to me." Insistent, dark with command. "Tonight. Now. Forget this charade."

"No." A whisper, all the denial I could muster. "I can't."

"You *must*. You know you belong to me."

"You're wrong, okay? I don't belong to anyone." My sanity stretched thin, a sheet of rubber yanked too tight. Hit him. Kiss him. Kiss him, *then* hit him. What I couldn't do was back away… because I was too afraid of what he might say.

Even after everything that had happened, I was still terrified he'd think me a coward. That I *was* a coward, for rejecting him. For rejecting *us*. And that frightened me most of all.

"I understand that you're scared. I actually thought I was, too, at first." A besotted smile, almost bashful. "Me, afraid. Can you imagine that?"

Actually, I couldn't, but I wasn't about to let him know that. His unshakeable belief in every insane word he uttered made me cringe. But it melted me, too, deep inside, where I'd locked everything delicious and forbidden I'd felt for him into a rusted little box marked DO NOT OPEN.

See, one thing villains always have over the rest of us is the freedom to follow their convictions. Presuming, of course, that those convictions aren't very nice. For Vincent, emotion—like everything else—is about power, and he exerts it ruthlessly. He offers you every dark and despicable thing you've ever secretly longed for, and watches while you struggle to resist.

I knew all that. And still I couldn't say *no*.

"The way you've gotten to me, Verity, it's… well, it's maddening, really. But we have to face it. We can use it to make us stronger. You can't hide from me forever."

Couldn't I, just? "No, it's over. *We're* over. I have a different life now. I have friends to look out for me." My lips stung. I couldn't stop staring at his mouth. God, I wanted so badly to kiss him. Just once. Just one more time…

"Your 'friends' *despise* you. Not the same thing." He drifted close enough to touch—close enough for those impossible flames of his to wrap our fingers together as one. I held my breath, dying for that explosive heat, the revelation of his body against mine. Almost. Not quite. Goddamn it.

"Come back to me, firebird," he whispered. "You know you want to."

My pulse stumbled. I scrambled for a rational response, when all I wanted to do was roll over and surrender. Whisper his name, let him do whatever he pleased with me. *I will keep cool. I won't lose control. I won't…*

"Vincent, listen," I insisted, shaking. Good start. But what the hell could I say? How do you crack unbreakable conviction like his? "This is all a mistake. Whatever you think there is between us…"

"Whatever I *think*?" His eyes flashed a dangerous gold, and his grip tightened on my wrist, a bright edge of malice. "Shall I show you? Must we cover those lessons again? You know what happens when you disappoint me."

Oh, God, did I.

I trembled, lost. What was I thinking? Reasoning with him was pointless. The magnetism between us was beyond thought, beyond common sense. Oldest story in the book.

I'd *loved* him. And in his warped way, he'd loved me. How could anyone reason with that?

I felt him laugh, a frisson of unhinged delight at the game. His whisper scorched my earlobe, challenging. "Oh, this is precious. Do you surrender? Or must I subdue you all over again?"

I shuddered, and fled.

He didn't follow. Just let me run.

The fog swallowed me, cold and heartless. I didn't stop until I'd passed the end of the bridge, where the fishing pier's lights struggled through curling mist, and sprinted across the freeway into the park.

I collapsed, panting, against a tree trunk. My heartbeat galloped. My skin itched all over, like deathworms wriggled in my living flesh, and I doubled over and spewed my non-existent dinner into the dirt.

My eyes poured and I choked on burning bile. What the hell had I expected? He was merciless, insidious, every move a cunning gambit to kill me or trap me or make me do something I dreaded, all just to prove *he* was superior. To prove he still owned me.

I *knew* that was how he operated. So why had I agreed to meet him? Why didn't I just delete his damn text and go to bed like a normal person?

But I already knew the answer.

We'd been lovers, sure, and that part was incredible. Unprecedented. I could admit that. Still, I'm not a slave to that kind of lust. Sex is great, but it's just sex.

But all the common sense in the world didn't change the awful truth that I'd liked how he'd made me *feel*. Giddy, alive, free from crippling self-doubt and eager to take on the world. Loving Vincent had made me *happy*.

I wiped my acid-ripped mouth. I already had a splitting head-ache, like I'd cracked a machete through my skull, levering the bones apart to let all those black and ugly secrets ooze out. Now my guts hurt, too. I wanted to crawl into a hole, pull dirt over my head and sleep forever.

But I knew how to escape from too much *thinking*. Temporarily, at least… and my nerves twanged bad banjo tunes as I imagined Glimmer's disappointment. Glimmer never said anything, never scolded me outright. He just *looked* at me, with those warm starlit eyes, and lately, I'd been unable to meet his gaze.

Your friends despise you. Vincent's accusation pierced my skull with hot needles and popped my guilt like a bubble.

Fuck it. I yanked my mask from my pocket and tied it on. My damp fingers smeared the leather, and I wiped the sweat away. Vincent was right: my family already scorned me. And so did Glimmer. What did I care if I gave them one more reason?

Because it's always just one more reason. Then another. And another, until the little reasons pile up so high, they smother you. That's how villains are made.

What the fuck *ever*.

Ten minutes later, I stalked down a narrow street in Castro towards a place I knew, an underground dive where masks were just one way people hid from each other. Rats snickered in the garbage at my feet, and I kicked them aside. Down greasy steps, through the rusted door.

Inside, dark shapes hunkered in dim blue light, a snatch of meaningless sounds: music, groans, sobs, vacant laughter. Chains hung from the ceiling in drifting smoke. I inhaled, let the stinking air numb my senses, stumbled up to the bar.

Triple brainfuck with a twist of sordid, thanks, and keep the change.

The guy on the next stool—thin, his once-proud muscles wasting, nice clothes but old and unwashed—clinked his glass against mine, and we drank. Like Glimmer, he bore scars on the inside of his wrist. Unlike Glimmer, he looked ready to try it all over again. Search *human disintegration* and you'll get a picture of this guy.

His phone lay beside him on the bar. One of Vincent's creations, an obsolete model with cracked glass. He wore his wedding ring with that wishful air that bespoke failure and tragedy. Probably carried pics of his estranged kids in his wallet, or on that ancient phone. Too young, I thought as I gulped harsh alcohol, to be so broken.

Aren't we all?

I banged the empty glass down. "Rough day?"

He lit a cigarette, ash flaring. "Fuckin' A."

"Same shit, different year."

"Sing it, sister." He offered me his smoke. Not one from the pack. I took it. What the hell, right? If this was his pick-up routine, I was about the best he could expect.

I inhaled, relishing the horrid gritty flavor, and let my special senses sparkle. I didn't taste augment. Only sour despair. He met my gaze, the wide brown eyes of an animal caught in a trap.

Was that what Vincent saw when he looked at me: prey? An inferior creature, fit only to be exploited or consumed?

I passed the cigarette back. Glimmer's eyes aren't brown, I thought mistily, alcohol already muddling my underfed brain. They're blue. Darkest midnight blue, the shade of the sky beyond stars. I didn't even know Glimmer's real name.

And that was relevant how?

The guy pointed at my glass and signaled to the barkeep for another. He took in my mask, my scarred cheek, let his gaze wander down to my chest. "You got real superpowers?"

Augments, idiot. I didn't bother to correct him. I just grabbed his throat with an invisible fist of force, and dragged him in. "What do you think?"

36

~ 5 ~

By the time I got home, orange dawn slanted through the trees, and I was wide-eyed and popping out of my skin after a gutful of drink and a couple of hours of muttering sleep. I hadn't been followed, or detected by Sentinels. I was pretty confident of that. I was remorseful, disgusted, so furious at myself I could scream, but that didn't make me an idiot.

That guy from the bar—I'd filed his name under *too much information*—had been sweet, and totally on board with my sordid-brainfuck plan, but by the time we'd gotten down to business, he was too drunk to finish, and I'd been too restless. He wept on my shoulder. I threw up in his bathtub. Altogether a fitting experience. I should be satisfied.

But I wasn't.

Birds chortled and trilled as I stomped through the forest, and I scowled up at them with half a mind to tear their tree down. "What in hell are you so happy about?"

They didn't answer. Typical. The world's divided into two kinds: happy people, who don't need a reason, and the rest of us, who can't find a reason to save ourselves.

I slouched into the refectory, where the family Fortune (plus assorted hangers-on) were getting stuck into breakfast. Uncle Mike was sitting straight-backed at a table, munching peanut-butter toast and thumbing through messages on his Glimmer-hacked Blackberry. He waved at me, a wry grin on his lined face.

I shrugged, and Mike shook his head in mock scolding. My uncle looked as I imagined Adonis would in thirty years' time: weathered and wise but still handsome, a mesh of silver through his blond hair, his eyes clear with nary a blue twinkle faded. One of those hip older dudes who has to fight off ambitious young tarts with a scythe, if Mike was into that sort of thing, which he wasn't, and for good reason.

Silver anti-conducting *don't-kill-everyone* bracelets glinted around my uncle's wrists. Static electricity crackled over the pale metal, his latent power battling to escape. It's tricky to be a playboy when you're such a lethal weapon.

Mike can fire lightning bolts. He's a menace, really, and it was only good luck for Sapphire City that all those years ago he and Dad decided to fight crime, not commit it. Blackstrike and Illuminatus, merciless scourge of Gallery villains from Oakland to the Bay.

Dad was the eldest, and with his power over shadows and darkness, he'd always been the thinker in their ass-kicking double act. These days, Mike was content just to give advice and let Adonis take charge. One of those rare, lucky people who managed to sustain both an augment *and* a life, or at least he did, before all this happened.

I wondered if Razorfire had ever tried to recruit Mike, and snorted. Good luck with that. Dad had a dark streak—no pun intended—but Mike is one of life's genuine good guys. Not a saint. Just a profoundly sensible man, who instinctively understood the difference between right and wrong.

But as I looked at him, my heart twisted. Mike looked so much like Dad. Except Dad would've speared me on his shadow-licked blue stare, and made some cutting remark about how *some* of his children—he meant Adonis, who aside from failing to marry some "nice girl" and crank out a brood of grandkids could do no wrong in Dad's eyes—could party all night and still show up in time for work.

Dad had loved me. In his distant way, he'd loved us all. Didn't mean he'd put up with our shit.

Thankfully, Adonis hadn't yet made an appearance at breakfast. The smell of baked tomatoes and French toast churned my abused stomach, but it watered my mouth, too, and when Peggy—cooking, of course, apron and oven mitts and all—offered me a plate, I steeled myself and took one.

"Thanks," I muttered, dredging up a watery smile. "You're a champion."

Truth was, my vision still blurred and my head hurt like someone had mistaken my brain for a hockey puck. Peg's existence was particularly infuriating this morning. But aside from a few extra throbs in my temples, politeness cost me nothing.

"You're welcome," Peg chirruped, like she meant it. Perky as usual, in cargo pants and a clean t-shirt, her ginger hair pulled into a cute ponytail. She was one of those stray augments who'd run to us for protection when Vincent got elected mayor, and it took Adonis about five minutes and a flirty smile to latch onto her. Dad would've approved of Peg. A "nice girl". Pretty face, I admitted. Good cook. One of those happy people.

But this was all I knew about her. I frowned. Who was this chirpy cartoon housewife who was screwing my brother? What was her augment, even: baking the perfect soufflé? Did Adonis know? Had he even asked?

Still, unwanted sympathy nibbled my toes. Adonis had high standards, and I couldn't help wondering if she'd heard what he'd said about her last night. *Give her a chance. It's not her fault she's…*

Dumb? Boring? A lousy lay?

She'd definitely heard the part about the Stepford wife. I hadn't exactly been keeping my voice down, and besides, subtlety was never my specialty. She already knew what I thought of her. And sure, Adonis had lowered his girlfriend bar lately. He wasn't exactly

dating celebrities and models right now, the way things were...
but still, as I glanced sidelong at Peg again, my senses stung with
nameless warning.

I found a seat on a table with Ebenezer (pasty-faced, greasy;
situation normal) and Jeremiah (skinny and blond, coughing as
he hunched over his coffee; looked like shit, in fact, damp and
shivering like a waxed yeti) and plonked down my plate, reaching
for the ketchup.

"Nice of you to join us." Eb shoved a clean knife and fork at
me. "Get it out of your system?"

"Screw you, zombie boobs." I squirted ketchup onto my
French toast and forked a slice into my mouth. Didn't look
like Eb had moved since last night, except to pop a few pimples
and swap his dirty tablet game for scrambled eggs. Dude could
use a shower.

So could I, for that matter. My shirt was good and crusty, to say
the least, and my trousers were probably a biohazard. I sniffed the
fug around me and winced. I stank of... well, we all knew what
I stank of. Better attend to that, before...

Flushing, I shrank into my seat. Too late.

Glimmer, fresh from the bath. Black jeans, plain black t-shirt,
same as every day. Even after only a few hours' sleep at his desk,
he still managed to look great. He sat across from me—damn, why
hadn't I picked a table without spare seats?—and gulped from a
bottle of spring water. "Morning, all."

"Hi," I muttered. Munched another eggy mouthful. Waited for
him to say, *Jesus, Verity, you look like hell* or *what's that God-awful
stink?* or *wow, here I was thinking you couldn't sink any lower but
somehow you manage.*

But he just drank his water, then cracked a can of high-caffeine
cola. The white stripe in his hair poked up like a skunk's tail, and
he ruffled it with a tired but cheerful yawn.

Goddamn it. He never *said* anything. Never judged me, at least
not aloud.

40

I pushed my plate aside, appetite MIA all over again. He didn't need to judge. I did enough of that myself. Did that make it better, or worse?

Jem wheezed and barked a cough into cupped hands, ash-blond hair flopping wet over his sharp cheekbones. I grimaced in sympathy. He sounded like a sick Saint Bernard. His pale eyes were running, and his pointy face glowed pink underneath, like he was coming down with the creeping plague.

Glimmer pushed the water bottle toward him. "That sounds nasty. Take it easy, man. Rehydrate."

Jem twitched, and disappeared. Jem's secret name is Phantasm, and he's a lightbender, a trickster of the eye. Disappearing is what he does, and he does it more often when he's angry or confused or feeling just plain contrary. Uncle Mike's kids aren't exactly a well-adjusted bunch, but who am I to point fingers?

Glimmer eyed the shimmering Jem-space archly. "No goodbye? The manners of kids these days."

Ebenezer snickered, ratlike, and gulped coffee. "You spooked him, dude. You know he can't drink that water. He'll freak out unless he counts all the bottles in the shrink wrap first."

"What for?" I contributed, ever-helpful. "There are always twenty-four."

"He knows that," said Eb cheerfully, "but he counts them anyway. Why'd you think he's so antsy?" He leaned towards his big brother and raised his voice. "Hey, you: obsessive-compulsive. I can *see* your twitchy ass. Try harder."

The Jem-shaped shimmer cuffed Eb over the head, making him duck and wince and grab at his greasy hair, and then it slouched away, coughing.

Glimmer ate his Peg-fried tomatoes thoughtfully. "Hey, I saw that thing you brought me last night."

His voice was low and rough, yet sweet, like old bourbon. It took me a second to realize he was talking to me. "Oh, right. The museum. What a bust, eh?"

"Looked like a rough fight. You okay?"

"Sure." Automatic response. "Um… thanks for asking," I added belatedly, amid a searing rush of gratitude peppered with shame. What a bitch. I'd no right to be angry with him just because my own stupid antics embarrassed me.

I checked a sigh. Damn him for being the best friend in the world, when I was such a lousy one in return.

He winked, and I found a smile. Everything was okay. Well, as okay as it'd ever be.

"Haven't had time to do much digging," Glimmer added, "but I know the Latino guy with the glitter. Calls himself *El Espectro*."

"Specter," I supplied. "Nice brand. Unimaginative, but it definitely says *villain*."

"*Pain in the ass* is what it says. He jumped me once in some mansion's bedroom in Ocean Heights, long time ago. Cocky. Typical Gallery sticky-fingers."

"Yeah? What were you doing in the bedroom of a mansion in Ocean Heights, young man?"

"Nothing."

"Right. Same nothing he was intending, presumably. Thought you were above ordinary break and enter."

"Who said I wasn't invited?"

"Eww." I mimed sticking a finger down my throat. "I'm not even gonna ask. So did those storm troopers arrest this Espectro character last night, or just beat him to death?"

Glimmer finished his tomatoes and started on the eggs. He has this enviable ability to munch down food at any hour of the day. "Option A, bless 'em," he said with his mouth full. "They've got him in restraints. He's not going anywhere."

The PD had augmentium cuffs now, courtesy of Razorfire's City Hall. Perfect for banging up your discerning augmented crook. "Did you get a real name?"

"Arrest report says Jesus J. Flores, priors a mile long. Odd one to claim if it's false."

Gallery villains were notorious for taking a beating, pretending to give in and then giving the cops patently false information and smart-ass aliases, like Sawney Beane the short-order cook, or Dougal O'Pooball who works at the sewerage farm. They liked to play games. Still, you had to admire their intestinal fortitude. Sapphire City PD didn't exactly do Miranda warnings by the book these days.

But as usual, Glimmer had squeezed out the good oil. "You naughty boy," I said. "Thought your data-stealing gear was broken."

"It is." A piratical grin. "Depends on your definition of 'broken'. Still a few fakements I can pull."

I reached for coffee, but the jug was empty. Instead, I drank from Glimmer's water bottle. A faint curl of his vanilla-spice scent sweetened my mouth. "How goes the salvage mission?"

When we'd first met, Glimmer was Mr. Techno Nerd, with a secret underground lair full of shiny kit that would make Big Brother jealous. But a few months back, Razorfire torched the place and nearly killed him, and most of Glimmer's stuff was destroyed. He'd begged, borrowed and nicked mismatched bits of gear and had started rewriting his black-art search algorithms, but—a bit like retconning your memories of a time when you did bad things and liked it—the rebuild took time.

"Slowly," Glimmer admitted. "It's a big job. But Harriet's helping."

Just me, or a knot of frustration in that?

I snorted, glad to have something to tease Glimmer about. Harriet was Ebenezer's twin, smart but haughty, her life a teenage melodrama of galactic proportions. "Helping, is she? Or just pouting at you and playing with her hair?"

He tossed crumbs at me. "Whatever, wise-ass. She's good with code."

"Doesn't mean she hasn't got a crush on you."

"She does not."

"Does so."

"Does not… Fine, have it your way. She's a kid. I can take it." He shrugged, and ate his eggs, but I wasn't fooled.

For such a chick magnet, Glimmer is cute and awkward with girls. All I knew was that he used to be married—with a kid, no less—but his wife believed Razorfire's bullshit and broke Glimmer's gallant heart. He wasn't in a hooking-up mood. Maybe he never would be. But I'd bet he was too much a gentleman to embarrass Harriet by saying anything.

Well, I'd never had that problem. Time to have a word with Little Miss Lolita-zilla, before she mistook his refusal to engage for encouragement and started sexting him, or tagging him on naked selfies, or whatever hormone-crazed teens did these days.

I decided to have mercy on Glimmer, for now. "So, what about Huey and Duey at the museum? Seen them before?"

"Nope." Glimmer swallowed his cola. He hadn't shaved, and his olive-tinted throat was dark with stubble. As I'd frequently observed: it was a good look. He passed me the half-empty can. "You?"

I gulped, relishing the sweet fizz. "Never. I, uh, did a bit of digging myself," I added casually, making sure I met his gaze. "They go by Sophron—that's with a P-H—and Flash."

Sickly, I waited for him to call me out, ask me where the hell I'd found that out when he couldn't. I'd have to tell him everything, and I'd cringe and blush and then at last it'd be out there, and no longer this wretched *silence* between us, the kind where you talk all the time but don't ever speak what needs to be spoken…

"Okay," Glimmer said mildly. "I'll see what I can find."

Damn. Thank fucking God. But damn. I swallowed, warm. I still didn't get why Vincent had told me their names. Even supposing he wasn't making it all up to amuse himself… what if I was leading us all into his trap? "Did you see 'em teleport?"

"Yeah. Nice. Why can't I do that? No more waiting at traffic lights, no more splashing through rat-infested sewers…"

I snickered. "Missing the point, Sherlock. They *both* teleported, at the same time. Didn't you see? Slam, blam, no more emo teenagers. Beam me up, Scotty."

"Two people with the same augment? Not possible."

"That's what I thought."

He considered. "Maybe one of them teleported and took the other along for the ride."

"I don't see how. They were on opposite sides of the room. That's one hell of a forcebend."

"Or, they didn't teleport at all. Maybe they just obfuscated and made it look like they teleported to confuse everyone." Glimmer knew his subject. An illusionist himself, he could pull the best mindfuck tricks ever. It still gave me the creeps when he did that *watch-me* thing, even when I knew he was on my side.

But I'd felt the breeze last night in the museum. I'd heard air whooshing to fill the vacuum. They'd moved, and *fast*. "Or maybe we're looking at something new…"

A commotion across the room jerked me to my feet. My thighs hit the table. Plates clattered, and the cola can spilled, along with Jeremiah's half-finished coffee.

Jem thrashed like a grounded trout on the floor, eyes bulging. Drool frothed on his chin, and he shimmered in and out of view, like he'd lost control of his lightbend. The air around him rippled and stung, a malignant haze of *augment* gone wild.

"Jem, talk to me." Frantic, Uncle Mike dropped to his knees at Jem's side. Jeez. I grimaced in sympathy. His kid was having a fit, choking for air, and what could he do? Not a damn thing.

It's the irony we live with every day. I never met an augment who could heal the sick or feed the hungry or bring on world peace. All the special powers in the world can't hide the fact that when it comes to the crunch all we can do is destroy.

People fidgeted, wondering what to do. Peg darted forwards with a blanket, and Mike eased it beneath Jem's head so the kid wouldn't hurt himself. He cradled Jem's half-invisible face, stroking the pale hair as it shimmered alarmingly, now-you-see-me-now-you-don't. "It's okay, son. Take it easy."

"What the hell's wrong with him?" I muttered, aside. "Thought he had the flu."

Glimmer bit his lip. Ebenezer wore an odd expression, like he wanted to feel something but didn't know what. Times like this, I envied him his cluelessness.

Gradually, Jem's convulsions subsided and he fell limp, his breath shallow and fast. Sweat slicked his cheeks. His eyeballs had rolled back, sick pearls shot with crimson. One was leaking blood.

This wasn't any flu I'd ever seen.

"Someone give me a hand." Mike started to lift the boy. Glimmer jumped in and they carried Jem upstairs.

They must have passed Adonis on the way up, because my brother emerged from the stairwell glancing over his shoulder. He looked faded, somehow, his vibrancy rinsed thin. Another sleepless night? He'd looked like that a lot lately. Somehow, I didn't think it was Peg keeping him awake.

"That's not good," Ad said unnecessarily. "Anyone see Jem take anything?"

Everyone shook their heads.

"He was eating breakfast and he disappeared and then he fell," I rattled off. "Could be that God-awful cold he's got. Or he's finally popped a sanity valve."

Ebenezer opened his mouth and shut it again.

Adonis fired him the ice-blue stare of doom he'd inherited from Dad. That part, at least, hadn't faded. "What?"

Eb just grinned his mad-leprechaun grin, because he was socially challenged and had no idea how to show remorse. "We smoked a pipe last night. But I had some too. It can't have been bad stuff."

"Jesus." Adonis yanked his hair at the back of his head, frustrated. "One, you're an idiot. Two, don't ever do that shit in my place again. Three, where did you get it and who gave it to you?"

"No one," insisted Eb. "Some guy. It was just a score—"

"Nothing is 'just a score' anymore." Adonis dragged up a chair and sat. Quietly, Peg brought him coffee and a smile. He had the grace to smile back and whisper *thanks*. "Don't you get it, Eb?" he added wearily. "Anything could be a trap. Everything. It's all just..." He took a long swallow of his coffee—I'd bet on triple-shot latte, three sugars, just how he liked it—and waved a long-suffering hand. "You know what? Fuck it. I don't care. Just buy your sugar candy from Wal-Mart next time, okay? Get a receipt."

Eb flipped him a bug-eyed salute. I swallowed a guffaw.

"Goes for you, too," Ad muttered, too softly for anyone else to hear.

I blanched, guilty. He knew I didn't do drugs, beyond alcohol and caffeine and the occasional sugar binge.

What does he mean? He doesn't know. He can't possibly. None of them can... but the ghost of that forbidden fire-mint scent sprang from its grave, crawling along my skin to make me shiver, and I couldn't help but enjoy it.

Vincent was my drug. And I was a hopeless addict. *Hi, I'm Verity, and I crave being BAD...* Like any prohibited substance, the more it was forbidden, the harder I wanted it, and the more intense my delight when I tasted it at last.

I cracked my neck, resigned. No point crying over what's done. I can't change who I used to be. The important thing was what I did *now*.

I could resist. Go cold turkey, sweat it out, face the heat. Or, I could die. Simple as that.

Simple, my friends, is not the same thing as *easy*.

I shoved hands in gritty pockets. "Well, I'm for the shower—"

"Thank Christ for that," whispered Eb. "You stink like a frontier whorehouse. Who the fuck are you: Calamity Jane?"

I flipped Eb and his slippery grin the finger. "And then let's talk, Ad. We have a situation. Glimmer, you want to fill him in?"

Glimmer shrugged. "Sure. Breakfast in my room, boss?"

I snickered. He always called Adonis *boss*. Partly to annoy him. Partly because he meant it. The two of them had reached a workable truce in the months since I'd dragged Glimmer into our family problems. Glimmer thought Adonis was a talented but corruptible asshole; Ad thought Glimmer a useful if frustratingly honorable idealist. Ad respected Glimmer's opinion; Glimmer respected Ad's authority. Working relationship: go.

Adonis drained his latte. "Thought you'd never ask. When are you going to stop calling me 'boss'?"

"How about the day you aren't giving the orders?" Glimmer arched dark brows. "But don't think it's because I fall for your bullshit charm. I know you only want me for my data."

"Likewise," said Ad. "Those smoky bedroom eyes cut no ice with me, boyfriend. If you drop crumbs in the bed? We are *so* over."

I grinned—they were so cute together—and stomped upstairs to grab shampoo and a towel.

The bathroom, an ugly stainless-steel jail of a place. We'd put up some stalls for privacy, but to me it still stank of ice baths and suffocation and bad memories. I showered with my eyes squeezed shut.

But it did feel great. Hot soapy water sloshed the stains from my body, rinsed my gritty hair, washed away the smells of despair and disgust and shameful deeds in the dark.

If only it were that easy.

Afterwards, I wiped the fogged mirror and dragged a comb through my knots. The roughened scar tissue curling over my cheekbone was reddened, angry. The other eye wore a dark raccoon ring. I looked like I could use a good feed and about a hundred hours of sleep. Situation normal.

Back in my room, I re-dressed in my costume coat—somehow it had escaped the worst of last night's excesses—and fresh jeans, plus my lace-up boots. My only clean t-shirt sported a photo of a gigantic green cactus that wore a scribbled sign reading Free Hugs. I felt better already. My headache was in retreat to a distant battlefield, if not entirely vanquished. Another of Glimmer's caffeine colas and I'd be set. I pocketed my mask and grabbed a banana from my stash (stinky, black and withered, but hey: potassium is potassium) on the way out.

And crashed into cousin Harriet.

Just when I was starting to feel good.

~ 6 ~

"Watch where you're going, can't you?" Harriet bounced moussed locks over one shoulder. She wore an ass-hugging skirt, a stretchy top and bra that made her boobs defy gravity, and enough make-up to blind a badger.

The opposite of me when I was her age. I'd been the angry tough girl in jeans and Doc Martens, and I'd spent most of my time sporting black eyes, getting kicked out of class for swearing, and beating up on a succession of Adonis's snotty queen-bee girlfriends. Yeah, them was the days.

I glanced at Glimmer's cell. Door closed. I sidled closer to Harriet, surreptitious. Heh. I should mysteriously flick my coat open and whisper behind my hand: *Psst! Wanna buy a 'W'?* "Listen, can we have a word?"

Harriet looked at me like I'd suggested we get married. "Right. Because we have *so* much to talk about."

I endured my usual itch to punch Harriet in the face. Skinny, bad-tempered, always ready to fling me an unnecessary put-down, she reminded me of my dead sister, Equity, whom I'd also wanted to deck on a regular basis. Aside from the tragic fashion sense, that is. My sister and I both inherited our late mother's coloring,

50

and Equity had too closely resembled me to ever be beautiful, but at least she'd known how not to look like a cut-rate hooker.

To be fair, Harriet wasn't awash in role models. She'd had no mother since she was a toddler, and like most fathers—fathers who weren't mine, that is—Uncle Mike was a total pushover when it came to his baby girl.

I sighed. "It's about Glimmer."

Harriet scowled, harpy-like. "That's none of your business."

"Is too. He's my friend, and he's not interested in you." I winced. Wow, that came out all gentle and caring. "Look, I don't mean that you're—"

"You know nothing about me, Verity. Where do you get off telling me what to do?" Harriet stared me down, furious, but she kept her voice low. She knew what happened if she got a bit too loud. Warping metal, shattering glass, people screeching and bleeding from the earholes. Not a pretty picture.

"It's not about you, okay?" I whispered fiercely. I couldn't voice-whip glass; I just didn't want Glimmer to hear. "There's a time and a place, that's all. He's trying to work and the way you flirt with him all the time makes him uncomfortable. One, he's too old for you—"

"I'm seventeen, *Mom*." She widened sardonic eyes at me. "I can do what I want."

My mom was dead, too. I sympathized. That didn't mean Harriet could give me lip. "And two," I persisted, "he's got stuff in his past that means he's not interested in hooking up." *With a horny, smart-mouthed infant like you,* I added silently. *Zingg! Take that.*

"Yeah? Like what?" A defiant chin-tilt.

I could've invented something. *His last girlfriend was a serial killer,* or *dude, he's gay, can't you tell?* or even just *sorry, but he asked me not to tell anyone.* But my indignation on his behalf was as gratifying as it was maddening, and my temper flashed like a flintlock. "That's none of yours. Just let him be."

51

"Right. Just because you're too pig ugly for him."

My powermuscle flexed with rage, and I had to bite my tongue. *What the fuck did you say, you vicious little brat?* But the scar on my face stung. I knew how I looked. Everyone knew. Didn't mean we had to trade insults about it.

I gritted my teeth, a salty tang of blood. "Come again?"

"I knew it. You're jealous. And you're, like, *old*. It's so pathetic." Harriet laughed, and it sliced a shrill edge on my nerves like a paper cut.

Oh, honey. Was that a *threat?* "That's bullshit," I said tightly.

"Everyone knows you want him for yourself. Too bad he likes me better. So sad. I win." She pouted, and raised her chin, triumphant. She didn't even know she was doing it. Just one of those teenage-girl things.

But it flared my belligerence afresh, a hot breeze over coals. *Keep it down, Verity, don't do something you'll regret…*

I clenched a fist behind my back and stepped closer, trapping her in my shadow. I was taller, and I made sure she knew it. I hulked. I menaced. I *loomed.* "Grow the fuck up, Harriet."

She edged backwards. "You're not my mother, Verity. I don't have to do what you—"

"Shut your trap for once, and *listen*. Real life isn't a TV bitch drama, okay? Guys aren't prizes you can play for. And real people? They don't have these little contests where they lie and cheat and screw each other over for kicks." Not strictly true in the augmented world, I guess, but my point stood. "So back the fuck off from him, or I'll make you."

"What*ever*." She fixed a sneer on her face, but her chin trembled. She was afraid of me. I liked that.

And I grinned, so she'd know. "Think before you mess with me, girlfriend," I murmured, silk over thorns. "I went bonkers for a while, remember? Madder than a cut snake. Utterly off my rocker. Maybe I still am. If I hear you've been bothering him again… well, who knows *what* I might do?"

Harriet's jaw tightened, mutinous. "Bitch," she muttered—back to boring insults, were we? I had more respect for "goatfucker"—and flounced away.

I popped my neck, satisfied. Hmm. Perhaps I'd handled that poorly?

Whatever. Harriet could have the last word if it made her feel good. So long as she left Glimmer alone.

But her taunt—*everyone knows you want him for yourself*—coated my skin like the guilty stink of a sewer.

I scratched my forearms, irritated. It wasn't true. He was my best friend. I was just looking out for him. Anything else was bullshit. Besides, we all needed to get back to fighting villains—which meant we wanted Glimmer to get on with rewriting his algorithms and fixing his hardware config and praying to the geekboy gods of the dark net. Not wasting time avoiding the advances of an oversexed teenage drama queen.

And even if what she'd said were true—which it wasn't—even if in some twisted mirror universe, I might occasionally wonder what it'd be like to bathe in that delicious vanilla-spice scent, wrap my hands in his glossy hair and pull his mouth to mine—which I didn't—it was still bullshit.

Because he was Glimmer, the white knight. Gallant, courageous, everyone's idea of a hero. I, on the other hand, had murdered innocents. Used my power selfishly. Tried to poison the city to impress a power-crazed maniac.

Glimmer was… well, he was Glimmer. And I was me.

What the fuck *ever*.

But my bones shivered with delightful dread, and I swallowed warm brine. It wasn't embarrassment that Harriet had caught me looking. It wasn't even that Glimmer was so far above me that the idea of us together like *that* was so ridiculous, it bruised some hidden soft spot deep in my heart.

It was what Vincent might say if he got even a whiff that I might be looking sideways at another man. The things he might do to me.

Oh, my. All those breathless, exquisite, excruciating punishments…

I cursed, sweating. Jeez. And if *that* didn't just prove my point. There was *my* Vincent, and then there was normality, the world where he was our archenemy and deserved to die. For my sanity's sake, I had to keep the two sides separated.

I rapped two knuckles on Glimmer's door and walked in without waiting for permission. The lights were on—make that *light*, a single bluish bulb on a cord. My gaze glued itself to that swinging bulb, back-forth, back-forth…

Memories swamped me, that horrid metal chair cutting into the backs of my thighs, that piss-stinking hospital gown, that weighty augmentium helmet bolted around my skull. Electroshock, muscles jerking, fingers clenching and unclenching, the brown stench of singed hair…

I shook myself, dizzy. Was this even my old cell? No clue. No need to freak out.

The museum's fuzzy security footage played on the largest of four computer screens. And my boys: Glimmer, munching on an apple, a long lean shadow in his chair, one foot on the desk; and Adonis, slouching on the cluttered bed, back against the peeling brick wall.

My brother beckoned me in. "About time."

"Shit, did I miss the trailers? Shove over. Where's the popcorn?" I squeezed my butt in beside Ad and peeled my banana, waving it in his direction. Glimmer snickered.

"Gross." Ad made a face. "You really gonna eat that?"

"Bananas are a superfood. It said so on the internet." On the screen, my ex-boyfriend Sparkly—Espectro—was doing his glass-smashing thing, the stolen rock in his bleeding fist.

"Red wine is a superfood," Adonis said. "Smoked oysters in barbecue sauce are a superfood. Bananas are fucking fungus in disguise… Oh, nice trick," he added, nodding at the screen. "Okay, who the hell are these two…? Holy shit. Where'd they go? What's that, a lightbend?"

"Mwash 'gain," I suggested, stuffing my mouth with overripe banana.

"Jesus, Vee, how old are you?"

I swallowed, and burped. "Watch again," I repeated. "Look at the glass splinters on the floor, from the broken display case."

Glimmer skipped the footage back to the instant before the two teen villains vanished. Paused. Played it again in frame-by-frame slow-mo.

One frame, there they were. The next, an elongated blur across the screen, from left to right. Then, gone… and where they'd been standing, the glass debris scattered and swirled into a tiny spiral, as if caught in a little two-teen tornado.

"The air moved inwards." Adonis spoke slowly, trying to take it in. "It's a forcebend… are you telling me they *teleported*?"

I mimed pulling a pistol trigger. "Watch 'em and weep."

"*Both* of them?" Adonis clicked his tongue. "I'm impressed."

Glimmer teetered his chair on two legs. "The blue-haired one is Sophron. The boy is Flash. Pretty much all we know so far." He didn't mention where he'd learned that little tidbit, God love him. Didn't prompt Adonis to ask how I knew.

"Gallery?"

Glimmer shrugged. "Seems reasonable."

"Or not," I argued. "Doesn't seem right to me. Why sabotage Espectro's heist, if they're all working for the same outfit?"

"Rivals?" Glimmer suggested. "Fighting over the loot to impress the big man. Who knows what the hell Gallery clowns do for kicks these days? Maybe whoever menaces the most rent-a-cops each month wins a set of steak knives."

Adonis snorted. "Or they're just crazy assholes. These people don't need reasons. And if they're not Gallery, who are they?"

"Well, I think they're something new." I flipped my banana peel at the bin, and missed.

Glimmer binned it for me. "You are so *lame.* If I were telekinetic, I'd at least make sure I could hit the side of a barn."

"Gee, thanks, Mom." But Vincent's words tickled my memory, persuasive. *That girl's no child of mine.*

In my stomach, the blind worms of my foolishness writhed and stretched their little mouths. I knew it was stupid. God knows, I'd fallen for Vincent's line of bullshit before. I should forget it. Move on.

But I couldn't silence this muttering itch at the back of my brain. The suspicion that while Vincent might lie to beat the devil when he chose? He hadn't lied about this.

And that wasn't just my dark fascination talking. No, what clinched it was the snark about the clothes and the bad hair. Razorfire wouldn't stand for that, not in his house. An issue of style. Even saber-toothed Iceclaw in his greasy leather duds, or snickering Weasel with his scraggly moustaches and rodent incisors: they owned a kind of sicko villain's panache. Sophron and Flash were just… scruffy. Unwashed.

Vulgar.

Not *his* type at all.

From the way they work together, I'd say they're old friends… It's no fun if I give you all the answers… Wasting tricks like those, just to re-home an overpriced rock…

Adonis shoved me, and I nearly fell off the bed. "Whah?"

"There's no audio," Ad repeated, impatient. "What did Sophron say to you, a few frames back?"

"Right after she whipped my ass?" I mocked her whining tones. "'Too slow, hero'. Just getting her gloat on. Listen, what is that rock, anyway?"

"Was wondering that." Glimmer flicked up a fresh browser window showing an art auctioneer's website. "Lot seven-two-nine, 'trans-state granite artifact', whatever that means. Purchased by the museum in an auction… let's see. Nine months ago, for a six-figure sum."

"From who?" Adonis and I spoke together.

Glimmer zoomed in on the text.

"Fortune Corporation?" I snorted. "Dad owned a six-figure *rock*? Please."

Adonis looked as mystified as I. "So whatever it is, we sold it while Equity was in charge. What the hell does 'trans-state' mean? You sure it's just a rock?"

"Looked like one to me. Jeez, did I miss the part where Dad collected crappy art?" But my nerves crawled. Our big sister had sold off Dad's stuff? What for? Wasn't like she'd needed the money. *Overpriced,* Vincent had called it. Like he knew what the museum had paid, and why...

Ad shrugged. "Smells fishy to me. But all our corporate records are cactus, at least until Glimmer can get them back. If he can."

"With your alleged 'encryption'?" Glimmer scoffed. "Spare me. But I gotta scrape the goo off the blacktop first. Someone really did a job on your servers."

Vincent, he meant. Or some slobbering IT savant whom Vincent kept chained to his dungeon wall. These days, he was probably too busy to wreak all the destruction by himself. Outsourced the boring bits.

"Michael might know something about this rock, too." Ad was thinking aloud. "He and Dad were inseparable back in the day."

"Or Espectro," Glimmer added. "He tried to steal it. Maybe he knows what it really is."

"Could be just the six figures Espectro wanted. Still, it's a thought."

"Either way, he's shit outa luck. And so are we." I glared at the video screen, where the spaces that used to be Sophron and Flash cackled at me, triumphant. "Scumbags stole my rock," I muttered. "Not happy."

"So what do we do?" Glimmer grounded his chair and flicked the screen blank. "Write these kids off as Gallery nitwits? Or are we facing a new threat?"

"What, another one?" I echoed glumly, but secretly part of me was delighted at the prospect of fresh asses to kick. "That's a relief. I was afraid we might actually have to stop panicking for a few hours."

Adonis tugged his hair, considering. "Glimmer, can you trawl for more info? Priors, alliances, ideology, anything you can find. Even 'they're just crazy kids' would be useful. I want to know what we're dealing with."

Glimmer flipped him a salute. "Sure thing, boss."

Ad shot him an ironic eye-cross and heaved himself off the bed. "I'll talk to Michael, see what he knows. I don't care what that damn rock is, it's mine, and I want it back."

"That's the spirit." I jumped up, wiping banana-whiffy hands on my coat. I felt good, considering. Rested. Ready for action. "What about me?"

A hard blue-eyed challenge. "You can take it easy."

"What? C'mon, aren't we past this?" But sickness had washed back into my stomach, with added warm seawater, and I knew it was hopeless.

"*This*, as in, the way you've been acting these last few weeks? Breaking things, shouting at people? Not eating properly, drinking yourself blind and playing *pick up the loser*?" Adonis laughed, hollow. "No, Vee. We are very far from 'past this'. You're lucky I don't lock you in your fucking room."

My rage-muscle clenched. It filled me with that slick, tense heat, the kind that groaned and demanded to be satisfied. Oh, God. I held on, tried to breathe slowly, searched desperately for a fiber of *calm*. I wouldn't lose my temper this time. No, I would not.

"Look," I protested, sweating, "the only reason we know anything about these grunge-metal idiots is because of me. Let me be useful. I can help."

"You're right, you can. Go help Peg with the dishes." Adonis walked out, not looking back.

I opened my mouth. Shut it again. Gritted my teeth, and slammed a rage-stuffed fist of power into the brick wall.

Crunch! Mortar crumbled. I'd pulled my punch at the last second, instead of smashing the fucking wall to smithereens. I'd done the *right thing*. It didn't make me feel better.

My eyes swelled with unshed tears. I wanted to run after him and beg him to forgive me. But I feared he never would.

"Goddamn it," I hissed into the silence.

"Hey." Glimmer's voice draped a cool blanket on my skin. "Let him be. He doesn't mean anything..."

"He *does* mean something." Even Glimmer was taking Ad's side, now? "Can't you see? He's determined never to trust me again. How am I ever supposed to prove myself if—"

BOOM! Something above us exploded, and flung me flat on my face.

~ 7 ~

The building quaked. Glimmer dived on top of me, shielding me from anything that might fall... and all the lights in the room popped out. Bulb, computers, everything.

The echo subsided, and together we scrambled up. My ears still rang. I dusted myself off and spat grit. "Okay?"

Glimmer coughed, waving his hands to clear the dust cloud. "Awesome. You?"

"What the hell was that? Lightning strike?"

"With no storm? Not likely." Glimmer grabbed his go kit—pistol, phone, tablet, flash drive—and headed for the door. Dust eddied in his wake.

I trailed after him, but my heart squelched into my throat to strangle me.

Shit. Had Vincent followed me home? Jeez, had I let my guard slip? Gotten distracted by his tricks and given us away? How would I ever live *that* down?

A confused crowd milled in the darkened corridor. Harriet emerged, wide-eyed like a scolded dog. She knew that crash wasn't lightning.

"Okay?" I asked.

Harriet just tossed her hair. "What's going on?"

"Nothing friendly. Stay close." Glimmer was already halfway down the stairs.

In the refectory, dust clogged my nostrils. Peg was directing traffic, making everyone sit down and stay calm, and I was grateful. Most of those we'd taken in were ordinary folk who'd never fought a day in their lives.

Not crime-fighters. Just people who didn't fit in, minding their own business, who happened to have a little something strange or wrong about them. And then one day, they found themselves running and hiding for their lives with a genocidal archvillain in disguise for mayor. Hell, most of 'em probably voted for him. Nearly everyone did.

Peg, on the other hand, had kept her composure. Like she was accustomed to taking charge. Good for her—and right now, good for us, too. But I made a mental note to ask Ad about her later. He wouldn't appreciate my interference. I didn't give a fuck. We were family. She was just an interloper.

Ebenezer, who was sweeping broken window glass into a frosted pile, tossed me an ironic eye-roll. Eb was a scary bastard, but short of a pitched battle? His augment was kind of useless. Mike and Jem, our more conventional warriors, lurked nowhere to be seen. Probably still upstairs, waiting for Jem to revive. Great. Like that'd be any time soon.

"Where's Adonis?" I demanded.

Peg pointed outside. Her cheeks shone pale with worry. "Be careful, Verity. It's not safe."

A distant glaze in her eyes sprang bumps on my arms. Huh? What was her augment, again? But no time to figure her out now.

Glimmer and I ran to the door. He motioned with his pistol, and his silent presence slipped into my head, a sweet-feathered tickle. *Me first. You take the left. I'll cover you.*

I nodded, flushing—gotta admit, I kind of like it when he does that—and eased the door open.

He danced out and I followed, back to the wall. Particles swirled on the breeze. I sniffed, and sneezed on dust. Definitely not smoke. But what…

A skewed metal strut caught the corner of my eye, and I gaped.

The entire eastern end of the asylum had been crushed. Pulverized, like an enormous bare foot had descended from on high and stamped the concrete under its massive heel. All that remained of the last twenty feet of the building was crushed concrete, splintered wood and twisted steel reinforcers, with a garnish of shatter-bright glass.

My stomach tightened. Jesus on a jet ski. Could've been people in there. Maybe had been. Maybe Mike and Jem… but my concern was eclipsed by a guilty flush of relief.

At least it wasn't *burning*.

Disembodied laughter echoed from trees dappled in shadow. Shrill, hollow laughter, straight from an evil fairytale. I shivered. Villains. Nothing if not theatrical.

I spotted Adonis crouched by the kitchen, and he beckoned to me. "Verity!"

I scuttled over to hunker beside him. "What's that God-awful noise? Who does this idiot think they are, the Joker?"

Swiftly, Glimmer checked around the corner, leading with his weapon. He dropped down beside us. "No one. Whoever it is, they're not keen on being seen."

After the museum, and Vincent, and Adonis' implied scolding, I was itching for a fight. "Damn coward. Why are they hiding? *Why don't you come out and face us, you lunatic?*" I yelled the last part, bristling inside.

"Maybe they're shy." Glimmer checked his pistol, a snap of metal slide. "A hit and run, just to piss us off. Make us jumpy."

"Or lure us out," I added. "Do we even know anyone who could do this? Besides, y'know, me on steroids?"

Adonis grimaced. "We need Jem to do a recce."

"He's in no shape."

"Agreed. Glimmer?"

Glimmer tucked his pistol away. "I can give it a shot. Can't guarantee they won't blast my head off. As if you'd be sorry, you heartbreaker."

"And just when we were falling in love." Adonis clapped Glimmer's shoulder and gave me a chilly stare of command. "Vee, stay here."

"But I can help…" I protested weakly, trailing off. Why did I even bother? Adonis could've just unleashed on me, bent me to his will with a wink and a smile. At least he was giving me that much credit.

Like that's supposed to make my house arrest any less frustrating.

Glimmer flicked me an apologetic glance and crept along to the corner, footprints light in the dust. My heart clenched in trepidation, but I resisted the temptation to go all Peg on him. *Be careful, honey. Don't be out too late.*

Glimmer can't make himself invisible, not the way Jem can, by bending light. Glimmer just makes you *think* he's invisible. Which makes him one dangerous mindfuck dude, but it also means he needs to catch your attention first. I've seen him hurl his illusions across a room, a shimmering shockwave of *huh?*—but that was hit-and-miss. His mojo worked best when he gazed into your eyes. *Watch me,* he'd whisper, and next thing you knew…

Not that I'd ever let him unleash on me, not like that. No way. Sad fact is, Glimmer's too much a saint to make me cluck like a chicken, or shave my own eyebrows off, or any of that bad-taste stuff the rest of us would do if we got the chance to hypnotize someone. More likely, he'd pull some do-gooder hypnotherapy moves to suggest I quit drinking, clean up my act and get a steady boyfriend who isn't a power-mad pyromaniac.

Not for the first time, I wondered how far into your brain Glimmer's augment could dig. Could he, for instance, erase memories? Implant new ones? Break my conditioning? Do a bit of sly Vincent aversion therapy?

But the idea of stripping my failings bare like that just lined my guts with cold grease. Glimmer didn't need to see the slimy *things* that wallowed in the cesspit of my mind. It'd… dirty him. Smear him unclean. Tarnish him, somehow.

And that I would not have. Not on my watch, sister.

Glimmer eased his lean frame around the corner. *Can't see 'em,* he murmured in my head. *Just wait…*

Grrrr-ack! The monstrous groan of timber splitting. Leaves rustled *en masse…* and Glimmer dived back around the corner and thudded into the dust.

A massive tree trunk speared into the brick wall six feet away from us. *Boom!* The earth shook. Leaves and sticks flew, a cloud of dirt and ripped bark.

Adonis and I scrambled backwards as one. "Creeping Jesus," I panted as the dust settled. "Who throws a *tree* at people?"

"It's Blue Dreads." Glimmer coughed, spitting dust. "Sophron. Saw her in the forest."

"What about the other one?"

"Flash? No, I didn't—"

That laughter snaked out again, coiling around us. "Now we're getting someplace," the girl called. Her hollow, high-pitched voice rasped, alien. "Miss me, Verity Fortune? Come out and show yourselves, you—"

The rest was obliterated by another tree crashing into the building. Glass exploded, windows shattering.

"How the hell did she find us?" Ad glanced my way, suspicious.

"I wasn't followed," I insisted. "Sewers and shadows, all the way." It hurt that he suspected me, though he'd every right. But a chill clawed beneath my skin, one of Eb's hungry corpse rats chewing on my flesh.

What if Vincent lied? What if Sophron truly was his creature, and in my rank stupidity, I'd led her straight to us?

That's ridiculous, Common-Sense Verity scolded in my head. *If Vincent knows where you're hiding, why doesn't he just burn the lot of you to ash? Why construct this elaborate deception?*

I snorted. Right. You're talking about a man who left me trapped in a lunatic asylum for nine months to get my memory wiped, then pretended not to know me while I fell for him all over again, then tricked me into not only exposing my own augmented family in front of the entire world, but also convincing the city to overlook the fact that he's a hate-drenched maniac and elect him mayor.

Such a man would surely never construct an elaborate deception. What a ludicrous notion. Shut the fuck up, Common-Sense. You know *nothing.*

But on the heels of that thought nipped another, a rabid little rodent with sharp teeth: *it's because he doesn't* want *to kill you.*

So what *did* he want?

But I knew, of course. And it sickened my stomach and tingled my thighs at the same time. *You belong to me,* he'd whispered. *Come back to me. You know you want to...*

"Vee, you with us?" Adonis tugged my arm, yanking me back to reality. Sticks and branches rained on our heads, and we ducked under the cover of the narrow eaves. "Go fetch Michael, tell him we've got a situation here. Ebenezer, too..."

But lightning forked, a rich-smelling *boommm!* of thunder. Mike was already here. Standing by the crushed brickwork, wrapped in an aura of crackling white fire.

Just a small old guy, but he sure looked bad-ass. He wasn't wearing his reflective Illuminatus suit—the one that really made him light up like a blowtorch—but he could've been naked and wrapped in adult diapers and you still didn't fuck with Uncle Mike.

I shook my head like a wet dog to dislodge the clanging in my ears. And that was just a little one.

Razorfire has the flashiest augment in town, naturally. He wouldn't allow it any other way, and until you've watched him slice an office complex in two with a flick of his wrist, leaving a smoking crater of scorched earth and corpses, you ain't seen *weapon of mass destruction.*

But for sheer coolness factor? Mike's gotta run a close second. *Lightning bolts,* people. Fuck, yeah.

Sophron's cackle danced from the forest's shadows. "Come over here and say that, electric. Bring that thing closer and see what happens."

Mike let rip with another bolt. *Ker-ackk!!* A tree split in half and erupted into flame. The stink of smoke and ozone and wet wood showered, and while the explosion still rang, Glimmer dashed over to Adonis and me, and the three of us crouched together. Adonis glanced at me. I glanced at Glimmer. Glimmer nodded. I nodded too.

And as one, we leapt up and sprinted for Mike.

Glass shattered. Concrete crumbled behind us, *blam! blam! blam!* as Sophron slammed the walls with her giant invisible crunching foot, or whatever it was. We dived for cover amongst the rubble.

Smack! I banged my elbow on a broken lump of concrete as I fell, and gasped like a grounded swampfish while the funnies hit my bones.

Mike ducked behind the broken wall with us. He rubbed his silver bracelets together, like a defibrillator, and current arced bright blue, *snap-crackle-pop!* "Jem's sick," he filled us in shortly. "He can't fight. Gotta get rid of these fuckers now and worry about what they want later."

"Agreed." Adonis shot me another dark glance, like everything was *my* fault. Hell, maybe it was, inadvertently. Didn't mean he had to keep on about it.

"Plan?" Glimmer popped his pistol's magazine and checked the chamber. Sure, some augments are bulletproof, or can dodge, or deflect, or whatever. I'm convinced Razorfire evades gunfire on the strength of pure ego. But most can't. So long as you get in quickly? A bullet is still a ninety-five percent solution.

But Glimmer's magazine was half empty. We were running short. Even Glimmer can't conjure more ammo from nothing, and you can't legally buy firearms or rounds in this state without ID. It's black market or nothing, and these days gunrunning in Sapphire City is strictly Gallery.

Me? I'd left my pistol upstairs. Nice move, Verity. A Boy Scout, I ain't.

"Well, we still don't know precisely what their augments are." Adonis grimaced. "And we don't have all day. I say let's shock-and-awe these assholes and find out what they've got."

Like we were free to disagree, or something. Glimmer didn't even bother to speak.

I shrugged. "Sure."

Harriet crawled from the ruins to crouch beside Mike. "Me, too." A mascara-lashed glance at Glimmer. "I want to help Jem."

Mike nodded brusquely. "Okay, I'm in. Just be careful, sweetheart." He ruffled Harriet's hair, making her dodge and scowl.

Happy champagne tingles popped in my heart. Most dads would tear their own skin off before they let their daughter walk into danger. But Mike's no ordinary dad, and Harriet isn't a regular daughter. My family are special, and though I might grumble and snipe and bicker, I love 'em all to death.

Well, maybe not Harriet. But even she's worth a thousand of those normal assholes who hate us and want us kept under control, but scream to us for help when their safe little bubble pops...

Very good, whispered Villain Verity, that scaly, black-twisted snake coiling in my heart. *Nurture that hatred. Feed it. It's what he'd want...*

"Where's Eb?" Adonis breathed deeply and stretched his spine, wincing as the joints popped. My brother's charisma augment works more reliably when he's feeling calm and Zen. When he gets worked up... well, let's just say there's a fine line between an obliging little crush and the sort of obsession that kills.

"He's sneaking around the back." Harriet smirked. Apparently, she liked the idea of Eb leaping out from behind a tree and scaring the living crap out of these idiots.

Come to think of it, so did I.

"Okay." Adonis spoke rapidly, the way he did when he was making shit up as he went along. "Michael, you first, let's flush 'em out. The forest is wet, it shouldn't catch fire, but aim for the ground, not the canopy. Let's keep this covert if we can. When we can see them—presuming we can see them—the rest of us pick 'em off. Glimmer, help Harriet. And everyone watch out for Eb's arc of fire; you know what happens when he gets his hard-on. When you pin one down, yell, and I'll shut them the fuck up. If we can get 'em alive, great. If not? Do whatever. I really don't care. We've got civilians to protect. Verity, you're on shield duty. Just don't tear the fucking building down."

"Screw you." I meant it, too. Why'd everyone have to keep on about that? It wasn't like I'd torn any buildings down *lately*.

Adonis ignored me. "Suggestions, questions, gripes?"

"Yeah. *Screw you.*"

"I'm good." Mike flexed his fingers, testing a sizzle of voltage. For an old dude, he was totally cool. "You," he added, flicking a blue ball of static at Glimmer that made his skunk stripe crackle on end, "with the hair and the face. Make yourself useful and look after my daughter. If she breaks a nail? I'm gonna come looking for you."

"Yes, sir." Glimmer scruffled at his electrified hair, but it only stuck up more.

Harriet blushed a gratifying beetroot shade. "Jeez, Dad, you're such a *nerd*."

Glimmer waved a questioning finger at Adonis. "What about the others, boss? What if the building gets crushed?"

"Peg's taking care of them."

"And what if Peg's on their side?" I retorted, with more bitterness than was really warranted. I was so over being blamed for everything. So I wasn't perfect. God knows, Adonis had made his own mistakes that stormy night at FortuneCorp. Remind me: who almost let the city get drenched in poison gas because he tried to drop Razorfire from a fifty-six-story rooftop? Not *this* scar-faced bad girl.

And—lately, this question had niggled at me, though I couldn't quite finger why—if Adonis was such a golden boy, why had Dad left the company to Equity, instead of to Adonis, whom everyone knew was his favorite son? Had they fallen out? What had Dad known that we didn't?

I didn't say any of that. No one ever asked those questions. Truth was? I didn't want the answers. But for whatever reason, Peg raised my hackles, and I ignored raised hackles at my peril. I'd learned that lesson the painful, bloody way.

"That's ridiculous." A glacial Adonis stare.

"You know what's ridiculous, Ad? Trusting some person you've known for five minutes with our *lives*."

Glimmer touched my arm, forever the voice of reason and *calm-the-fuck-down*. "Verity, let it be."

"What if Peg's a spy?" I persisted. "We've just taken her word for everything. What if she turns traitor? Ever consider that? Or are you too busy thinking with your hard-on?"

Adonis ignored me. "Anything else? Fine. Let's do it. Good luck."

Mike wasn't a subtle fighter. He didn't need to be. He just flicked his wrist and hurled a sheet of lightning.

Ksh-mack! The forest lit up, dazzling sunflash. A tree exploded and fell in a hail of flame.

I jumped up and flung out an invisible wall of force… just in time to intercept another whirling tree trunk. *Bangggg!* It slammed into my shield, jarring my bones right down to my toes. But my eager mindmuscle flexed, and the wall held. I flung the tree trunk harmlessly aside.

I grinned. So far, so fine. But we'd revealed our position now. Attacks would thicken, quicken and slicken. Heh. Good luck with that. They were facing one determined ugly chick. For more reasons than our safety, I needed to get this right.

"Again," Mike murmured calmly, and on a silent count of two I dropped the shield. *Crrrack!* Another sheet of lightning. I dragged the shield back up again. We walked forward.

From the forest, Sophron's laughter echoed louder. Shadows darted in the light of burning foliage.

Silently, I exulted. The stormy ozone tang invigorated me; the thunder thrilled power into my veins. Static from Mike's augment crackled like fireworks in my hair, over my arms. Damn, it felt good to be on the job again. A warm, sweet pain, like stretching muscles that had languished too long. Like massaging a roaring headache into bliss. Oh, my. I totally needed to get out more—but I wouldn't trade this for anything. Was it wrong that this was better than sex?

"You're doing fine," murmured Mike. His face glistened, electric-lit sweat, and his pale eyes glittered with power. "Your brother'll come around. Just take it easy."

"Easy, my ass," I scoffed, but I shot him a grateful glance.

Behind us, Glimmer whispered to Harriet. "How's your aim?"

"Good as yours," came her reply.

"You better believe it, sister. Let's kick some ass, okay?"

Jeez, don't encourage her. I would've rolled my eyes if I didn't know he meant it honestly. People absorbed confidence from Glimmer's trust, his quiet conviction and humble smile. All they ever absorbed from me was aggravation.

I lowered my shield again. Mike lashed out, a glowing spear. *Zzzzap!* Flickering blue light illuminated Sophron. She was crouching by a peeling eucalyptus trunk. Same patched jeans and ragged camisole, the strap hanging off one bony shoulder. The fire flickered around her, close enough to make her sweat. Her ghostly eyes shone, those blue dreadlocks shaking around her cheeks as she laughed.

Icy wire threaded my bones. She was utterly unhinged. Fruit cake packed with nuts. Madder than a shit-house rat.

Her sidekick, Flash, stood behind, one black-nailed hand on her shoulder. Jagged emo haircut plastered to one cheek, dark eyes aglitter. He didn't laugh. Just stared, empty. So Sophron was the master in this little love story, was she? And Flash was just the faithful dog?

Glimmer darted forwards, flinging out one hand. A hemispherical shimmer of confusion erupted, sheeting silently towards the forest like a dome of rippled glass. *Discombobulate!* I wanted to cry out, like a magic word of power. Would it affect Sophron? The stronger your own augment, the more likely you'll be resistant to attack. She seemed pretty powerful. I guess we'd see.

Beside me, Harriet gripped Glimmer's hand to help direct her aim. I covered my ears, just in case she hadn't improved, and Harriet opened her mouth to scream.

Ka-BOOM! A lightning fork stabbed the earth. The ground quaked. Radiant heat sizzled my cheeks, and the tips of my fingers singed and stung. Fuck, that was close...

Oh, shit.

Harriet staggered back, whimpering, clutching her sensitive ears. Blood oozed on her fingers. Glimmer was on his knees, slapping at his burning hair. Mike lay in the dirt. Not bleeding. Not breathing. Hard to do either, when...

I choked on the stink of carnage. Visions of charred flesh and bones. Holy Jesus.

Mike hadn't fired that lightning bolt. Sophron had. And Mike wasn't moving. Or, should I say, what was *left* of Mike.

Harriet shrieked, unfettered.

My eardrums stretched, a spike of agony jamming crosswise through my skull. I yowled, grabbing at my temples. Sounds were muffled, distant, bleeding. Like some erratic silent movie, I saw Adonis—who hadn't even had the chance to do his *love-me* thing— shake Harriet, yell at her, force a hand wreathed with golden sparkles of persuasion over her mouth.

Sophron laughed again. I could *feel* it in my bones, a serpent roiling beneath the earth, ready to burst out and swallow us.

71

Frantic, I tried to crack off my shellshock, force my legs to move, run for her and give her what she deserved… but I just staggered, reeling like a drunken sailor.

My brother cursed, blistering, and unleashed, a fury-blackened cloud of emotional *fuck-you-up* that swarmed through the trees, searching for prey.

But too late. Sophron grabbed Flash's hand, and they vanished. *Ker-snap!* Just empty space and fire.

Well, fuckity do-dah.

Dizzy, I wilted. My muscles were unwilling, my guts shriveling with grief and ultrasonic nausea. Time stretched like lumpy rubber, disjointed. Adonis had Harriet under control, and now she wept in his embrace. Firelight flickered, monstrous shadows danced, the sun seemed far away and gone.

Ebenezer hobbled up, his face sheet-white. He scrambled into the dirt beside Glimmer, who knelt at Mike's side, hands everywhere, trying to do something, anything. Eb's lips moved, imploring his father to stay with him, breathe, open his eyes.

But Mike was gone. One of the few truly good people I knew, who never harmed an innocent or let a villain go unpunished, and never made me feel lower than a worm because I'd failed to do the same.

My eyes burned. I wanted to howl. Sophron had killed him, as easily as she'd swat a mosquito. And then she'd fled, snickering like a naughty little girl… or a coward. Fight unfinished. Score unsettled. Rage unsatisfied.

And somehow, it would be my fault. I was certain of it. My culpability was inevitable, like a storm or an earthquake or the sun one day going supernova. I was responsible for this. And I'd not let it go unanswered. No, I most definitely would not.

My vision swam. Somehow I'd fallen to my knees in the wet soil. I'd been sick. I didn't remember it. I clawed the dirt, forcing it under my nails until they stung and bled. Tilted my face to the uncaring sky, and vowed ugly vengeance.

~ 8 ~

"Verity."

I didn't listen. Didn't want to hear their accusations. The wet ground had soaked into my trousers. My ears rang. Had I been slumped here a minute? An hour?

"*Verity.*" Insistent, a bloodstained hand on my shoulder. "Gotta go."

Dully, I shrugged Glimmer off. "How did she even do that? The lightning, I mean. I've never seen anyone but Mike do that. And the other one can smash concrete. Brilliant."

Acid guilt bubbled and smoked inside my chest. Vincent said he didn't know them. He *said* so. So what did I do? Did I argue, keep it above the waist, think for myself for a change?

No, I went right ahead and *believed* him. Christ on a cheesy cracker, I'm so fucking *stupid*. And now Mike's dead.

"An electric bad guy." Numbly, I giggled, salt and bubbles. "Awesome. Razorfire will be so pleased. Because, y'know, I would be, if I was a *lying archvillain son of a bitch*."

"Keep it quiet," Glimmer hissed. He pulled me to my feet, shook my shoulders. "Get it together. They're back. Can't you hear?"

"Wha...?" The crush of concrete filtered in, dragging me back to my senses. The ground vibrated. Sophron and Flash were

73

pummeling our building again. *Crash!* Another wall fell, coughing up a dust cloud. "Shit. More?"

Adonis strode over. "C'mon, ladies. We can't stay here."

He'd handed Harriet over to Ebenezer, who held his twin's hand, bafflement blanking his pimply face. Eb was wet, I noticed dimly, his clothes stained like he'd sweated a river or tripped over into a puddle. He looked green. Perhaps he'd been sick. Harriet's chin trembled, her eyes dark pools of despair and disbelief. My heart ached, and I wanted to hug her. Cactus. FREE HUGS. Damn it.

Together, we stumbled for cover, one fewer than we'd been when we came out.

We halted at the asylum's far end, beneath low-hanging branches that hid us from view, at least for now. Harriet and Eb leaned on each other, foreheads and fingertips touching, lank dark hair mingling with blond. A single tear shone on Eb's cheek. The twins weren't close. Didn't seem to matter right now.

Behind us, thunder rolled, and another wall exploded, a rain of rubble. Hot metal stink assaulted me, and Sophron's monstrous laughter slithered through the trees, a venomous asp aiming to kill us all.

They weren't gone. Just hiding.

I pulled my hungry mindmuscle taut and ready. "What now, Ad?"

My brother yanked his hair with both hands, smearing it with black dust. "We'll find Peg and the others."

"But this is our home," I argued. I'd been eager for battle before. Now, I thirsted for it. My flesh itched uncontrollably. I wanted to rake my face, scratch my skin raw, let my talent explode. "We can't just let that vicious cow—"

"None of those people can fight, Vee," Ad snapped, as another invisible fist of force hit the asylum, pulverizing another couple of rooms. "They're helpless. We had our chance and we fucked it. You gonna let 'em get killed over a *building*?"

I gripped my mindmuscle and twisted until it squealed and stopped fighting. Ad was right, of course. People before pride. Mike was dead, for fuck's sake. We could fight another day.

Didn't make it any less maddening. "But—"

"Sometimes we just have to admit we're beaten, okay?" He waved at the destruction. "Let her smash the place to splinters, if that's what gets her off. In the meantime? Let's get our people the fuck out of here."

"What about Glimmer's gear?"

"Good point. Nice to have. You volunteering to go back for it?"

"No need," offered Glimmer, "it's the software that matters and it's all backed up." He glanced across the clearing at Mike's charred body and lowered his voice so Harriet and Eb wouldn't hear. "We can't just leave him here, can we?"

"What d'you want me to do, Glimmer? I didn't bring my body bag." A flat statement of fact. "We can come back for him later."

"Jesus, you're cold." Glimmer shot Adonis that accusing midnight stare I knew so well, and I cringed.

But Adonis didn't suffer my doubts. He met Glimmer's gaze, clear and deadly. "We don't have time for this. Don't make me."

My skin crawled. I knew what Adonis had left unsaid. *Don't make me unleash on you.* Right now, it was a fight I didn't want to see.

Glimmer didn't argue. Just shook his head darkly and went to help Harriet and Eb.

Adonis turned his glare onto me.

I warded it off, palms upraised. "What?"

"You know I'm right."

"I didn't say anything," I protested. But grief watered my heart. If I died, would he just leave me here? To be savaged by animals and bugs, my remains washed thin by the rain?

I knew it was stupid. Mike was beyond caring. We'd come back for him as soon as we could. Jem, Peg and the others were very much alive. They needed us. Mike didn't.

But it still didn't seem right.

Lustful Villain Verity laughed. *Let those idiots take care of themselves. They'd abandon you in a heartbeat. In fact, they've already deserted you. Forget them. Your enemies are winning. They're laughing at you. What are you waiting for?*

Rage boiled into my veins. My nails sliced my palms, the pain a drugged needle sliding under my skin. *See?* Villain Verity murmured, her forked tongue licking like a lover's. *Doesn't it feel good?*

My mindmuscle sighed, thirsting for bloody revenge, and in a dark wave of temptation I imagined wrapping invisible fingers around Sophron's neck and squeezing. Tighter, harder, until her eyes popped and spit dribbled from her slackening mouth and oh, God, I'm going to…

"Verity, come on!"

I snapped alert. Sweating, my breath rough and fast. Damn it.

Glimmer waved at me from deeper in the forest, a black-and-white blur. He had one arm around Harriet's shoulder. Adonis and Eb were already out of sight.

One more time, I glanced back at the burning ruin of our asylum. Atop the broken refectory wall, Sophron was sitting beside Flash, swinging her legs. Flash's expression was solemn, but Sophron grinned and waved at me. The flames imbued her blue dreads with an eerie fairy glow.

"Go on, hero. Run!" Her laugh was shrill, mocking. And she turned to Flash and they kissed. Wet, starving, open-mouthed. She dragged his t-shirt up over his head and off. His skin gleamed, pale. Blood trickled from their kiss, smearing down his chin. Her hands groped hungrily over his thin body…

I ran.

We found Peg and the others hiding in a clearing at the bottom of the hill. The afternoon soon grew cold, that chilly spectral fog sweeping in from the ocean to haunt the trees, and the air smelled of encroaching rain.

As I'd expected, Peg had taken charge of our collection of augmented riff-raff. She'd managed to collect blankets and extra clothes, and she had everyone huddling in the shelter of a gigantic fallen tree trunk, where it was dry and warm. She'd even brought coffee, what was left of it, and I allowed a grudging nod in her direction. Credit where it was due.

There sat Grayson and Sal, brother and sister with matching thick glasses and bowl haircuts. Gray had long-wavelength vision, and Sal had this bizarre sense of smell that she claimed could… well, never mind. Bald-headed Ferdy, who we'd found fleeing the cops after he'd accidentally unleashed his plant-withering augment in front of a Sentinel in Golden Bridge Park. Others, whose names I kept forgetting. Someone had to take care of them. I was just glad that most of the time it wasn't me.

But that yapping rat-in-a-dog-suit of doubt wouldn't stop biting at my ankles. Peg was too self-assured. Cute, obedient, organizational skills of Adolf Eichmann on happy juice, and just happens to rock up on our doorstep to cook French toast and fuck my brother?

All too convenient. I'd do some digging, find out what she was up to…

I sighed and swallowed my bitterness. Hell, I was probably just a suspicious jealous-sister-bitch. Likely, I'd discover she was once a trauma nurse, or a pre-school teacher or something, accustomed to dealing with constant crises and herding uncooperative idiots into line.

Adonis pulled Peg aside, and they conferred, low and urgent. I joined Harriet and Eb, who sat desolately in the dirt. Jeremiah twitched in restless slumber, wrapped in a blanket. I could feel the heat pouring off him. His face glowed with perspiration, and every few seconds he'd *fade* to a ghostly Jem-shaped mirage, his light-bending talent haywire. He muttered in his sleep, counting prime numbers. "One forty-nine… one fifty-one… one fifty-seven…"

I squatted and wiped damp locks from his burning forehead. I gripped his hand. It was cold and wet. "He okay?"

Eb shrugged. His mismatched eyes gleamed flat, empty of emotion. Harriet just ignored me and fiddled listlessly with her phone.

Helpless, I shuffled away, sick with how useless I was. Whatever progress I'd made with Eb had been erased. These poor kids had lost their father today and all they had was Adonis (yeah, awesome; I love my brother, but he's not exactly Mr. Empathy) and me.

I gulped, my lungs suddenly too tight. My uncle was dead, and for what? A mocking tease. I burned to text Vincent, say *what the fuck, wise-ass, are you PLAYING with us, come on down here and FIGHT...* Wildly, I grabbed for my coat pocket.

My phone was gone.

I checked again, frantic. Nope. I'd left it behind in the ruined asylum. Shit.

My sweaty fingers slipped on my coat, and I forced my breathing to slow, my hands to relax and stop shaking. A good thing, right? I was better off not talking to him. And his number was probably blocked from this end anyway. He liked best to taunt me when I couldn't taunt him back. Just another way he kept me guessing.

A few yards away, Glimmer sat cross-legged on a mossy log, flicking through stuff on his tablet. I brightened. At least he'd managed to save something. Probably still had his phone in his pocket, and his pistol too. Damn Boy Scout. All I had was my shiny gunmetal coat and attitude. Oh, and a FREE HUGS cactus on my t-shirt.

I wandered over. "Guess this has dented your online sex life big time."

A flicker of smile. "Just a little research. Did you know 'Sophron' was an ancient Greek author?"

"No shit."

"Wrote tragedies for the stage. All that Euripides, 'whom the gods would destroy they first make mad' kind of stuff. Not a fan of happy endings."

"O-kaay." I slouched beside him, confused. Strange name for a teenage madwoman to choose. "But what's it to do with the price of crab chowder? Can't imagine Blue Dreads poring over ancient Greek tragedies in her spare time."

"As it turns out? 'Sophron' also means *truth*."

"Great." My name meant *truth*, too. But I hadn't chosen that one; I'd been given it. Verity, Adonis, Equity, Chance. Truth and beauty; justice and luck. Dad had a weird sense of resonance. Any other kids might have gotten a hard time at school with names like ours, but the bullies at *our* school soon learned that you only picked a fight with the family Fortune once. After that, you kept your eyes down and your smart fucking mouth shut.

I sniffed. "Pretentious, then. Funny, I'd have picked her for angsty love poetry. Those soppy pre-Rabbitites, stuff like that."

"You mean pre-Raphaelites."

"Whatever. Do I look like I paid attention in literature class?" But my bright-forced mood sobered rapidly. When I was a kid, Mom was murdered. Turned to stone by Obsidian, Dad's vengeful archenemy—and during the black weeks afterwards, Uncle Mike had brought us books. Adonis and I had disappeared for days into the adventures of d'Artagnan, Captain Moonlite, Horatio Hornblower. I remembered reading aloud to Chance, our littlest brother. He'd sit on my lap, his plump little fist wrapped around my forefinger, and listen to tales of Frodo and Sam, questing towards Mount Doom. He'd liked the part about the giant spider. Spiders never bit Chance, no matter what he did to them. No crawler was safe in our house for months after that.

In the books, honor gets you everywhere and the heroes always win. D'Artagnan might get his pretty-boy ass kicked occasionally— usually because he's too damn honorable to just kill the guy and get away—but he always gives the bad guys their comeuppance in the end, and the Musketeers never bicker and backstab and hurl each other out of skyscraper windows or into the loony bin.

But when the stories ended, Mom would somehow still be gone, and I'd be the one putting Chance's stubborn spider-slaying butt to bed without her. I'd been eight years old. It was one reason my big sister, Equity, had loathed me so much: she'd fallen apart after Mom died. I hadn't.

Now, I was past thirty, Equity was dead, and I hadn't seen or spoken to Chance for going on five years. No one had.

I choked, my grief at last bubbling up to swamp me. Why did Mom have to die before I was old enough to really know her? And why had I waited until Mike was dead to remember all that? Suddenly, his loss clawed at my heart, unbearable. Why couldn't I have slouched next to him at the dinner table one night and said, *hey, remember those books you gave us when Mom died? That was really cool. Thanks, Uncle Mike. I love you.*

Because we don't, right? We never do. Not until it's too late.

Glimmer was talking. With an effort I lassoed my attention, kept it together. At least for now.

"...doesn't explain how they can do all the things they did," he continued, pretending he didn't know I'd vagued out for a few seconds like a crazy person. "Presumably Flash is the teleporter, with a name like that."

"Seems sensible." My chilled body warmed with gratitude. Glimmer, at least, was still talking to me. Glad to have something to talk about other than Mike and Adonis and what a fucking mess we'd made. "But what about the rest of the powers we saw? If one of 'em can hurl lightning like that, where the hell have they been all this time?"

Glimmer stuffed his tablet away in his pocket. "They're young. Maybe their powers have only just emerged."

"I dunno. Were you a late bloomer?"

"Unfortunately, no."

I imagined Glimmer at high school. A skinny, clumsy Glimmer, hypnotizing people willy-nilly and reading their minds. Heh. Bet all the girls wondered where the hell he'd learned his moves... or was it the other way? Accidents, blushing, inconvenient truths, blurting the wrong thing at the wrong moment, people whispering behind their hands, calling you *freak* and *monster* and *that boy...*

"Neither were my family," I said glumly. "When *we* were stupid mouthy teenagers, I could rip the roofs from cars, and Adonis was unleashing on teachers and other kids' moms for a joke. Imagine the carnage."

Despite our gloomy mood, Glimmer snickered. "Jesus, no. Really? Remind me to choose 'teacher's pet' jokes next time he gives me rubbish."

"Dude, trust me. Ad might be all by-the-book now, but back then he was a menace. Rich-boy jailbait from hell. Ask him about Miss Jankowitz's handcuffs next time he's sunk too many glasses of red." I tweaked a forced smile. "Actually, for your own sake? Don't."

Glimmer unfolded long legs in the dirt. "Still, you've got a point. Sweet kids can turn into monsters overnight. Maybe they're just at that age."

Without a mom, Adonis and I had been at *that age* for longer than most. "Doesn't explain how they've got so many tricks."

"Perhaps they're multi-talented. Just because we've never seen it doesn't mean it can't happen."

"Mmm. Or maybe…" I sat straighter. *Just because we've never seen it…* "Shit. What if there's another one?"

"Huh?"

"We've assumed we can see them all. What if we can't? What if there's one who can hide or move really fast? An invisible one?"

"Or an illusionist," Glimmer added. "It'd explain what happened at the museum, the way they fought Espectro with what looked like his own talent."

"You said 'Sophron' means *truth*, right? Maybe that's the joke. Maybe half of what they're doing isn't even real."

Silently, he met my gaze, and I chewed my lip, troubled. What happened to Mike and our hideout? That was pretty damn real.

But the thought hung around, a stink that wouldn't wash off. Lately, I didn't have the best record with deciding what was real. What if Sophron and Flash were messing with our minds? Making us see things that weren't there. Tricking us into attacking when we shouldn't, fleeing when we needn't, luring us to false conclusions…

Great. How the hell was I supposed to fight that?

Across the clearing, Adonis finished his conversation with Peg. He kissed her and tweaked a strand of her hair. She gazed up at him, smiling like a pretty fool. Inwardly, I snorted. I didn't envy her. Peg was trying to keep her cool, but it was painfully obvious she was besotted with him. Just the way he liked it.

Adonis perched beside Glimmer on our log. "I'll go back for Michael when it gets dark. If anything's left of our stuff—not that there will be—we'll collect it then."

"So where are we gonna go?" I asked. "Not to be Captain Obvious, but we can't stay here."

"I'm working on it. I know some people." Adonis munched a candy bar that Peg must've given him. Caramel coated in chocolate. Just the sight of it watered my mouth. I licked my chops and made wide puppy eyes.

"Jesus," muttered Ad, "get your own girlfriend," and broke off half for me. I tossed half of my half to Glimmer, and we all had a little candy sugar-rush moment together. Aww.

Glimmer ate his piece and shivered in mock horror. "I think my ass just larded up."

"Good job," I grumbled, chewing. "Your skinny geekboy ass could do with some lard."

"Bite me."

"I might if there's no dinner." I licked the last chocolatey smears from my fingers. "What kind of *people*, Ad? Do we know them?"

"People," Adonis repeated. "Dad's friends. Whatever. We're not exactly in a position to be fussy."

"What about Jem? He doesn't look good." I hesitated. "That fit thing? Didn't look like any ordinary flu to me. He could be dying, Ad. What the hell do we know? He needs a hospital, not someone's sofa."

"I can see that." Adonis shrugged, sharp. "I'm open to suggestions."

He was right, of course. How the hell could we go to a hospital, with Sentinels bolted to every street corner? Drag him to the ER and say, *here's our cousin, he's got some weird augmented shit wrong with him, never mind it when he disappears, okay?*

I sighed. "Maybe a pharmacy'll have to do. Get him some antibiotics or…"

"I know someone." Glimmer sounded hesitant. Like he didn't want to speak.

"What's that?"

"A doctor who might be able to help."

Adonis quirked a golden eyebrow. "How much do they know?"

"They know enough."

"Can you call them?"

Glimmer shrugged, not meeting Adonis's gaze. "I can't promise. I wouldn't even suggest it if Jem wasn't in such a bad way. And if it didn't look…"

Room, meet elephant. *If it didn't look contagious.*

Adonis nodded. "Sounds good. Best idea we've had so far. But take care, yeah? We still don't know how these fuckers found us."

The silence stretched, spiked with unspoken accusation.

"It wasn't me, okay?" I burst out. "No one followed me. I was careful."

"You were drunk." Adonis's eyes glittered, a flash away from dangerous. "How careful did that make you?"

"Like you never drink too much." My voice was rising. I didn't care. My stomach knotted, that evil rage-serpent writhing, and I couldn't hold it in any longer. "So I was plastered last night. I'd had kind of a rough day. That doesn't make me an idiot. Give me some credit, Ad. I know the procedure and I followed it."

Glimmer raised calming hands. "Okay, Verity. Chill."

But I was too wild to stop. "Just because you don't like what I do doesn't mean I'm a traitor. And, while we're on the subject, *I* know when to keep my mouth shut. *I* don't let strays follow me home, and *I'm* not the one screwing an improbably perky stranger and telling her God knows what in my own fucking *house*!"

Ouch.

A muscle jerked in Adonis's jaw. Glimmer fidgeted, ready. I waited for the explosion.

But Adonis just stuffed his hands under his thighs, out of harm's way. "It can't be Peg. It just isn't, okay?"

"Why can't it be?" I snapped. "Are you so convinced I'm crooked that you won't listen to common sense?"

"Why are you such fucking hard work all the time? You know what Peg is, Vee? The only one in this miserable outfit who isn't a constant pain in my ass. Present company not excepted."

"Right. I get it. It's nothing to do with the fact that she gives great head."

"Jesus, Verity, I believe it wasn't you, okay?" A fierce whisper, like Adonis didn't want anyone to hear. "And it isn't Peg either. Will you just shut the fuck up about it?"

My mouth hung. I shut it, foolish. He *believed* me?

Warm dizziness swamped me. Relief. Abject, humiliating gratitude.

Adonis believed me. Everything would be okay. Even though I didn't really know the truth and Mike's death could still turn out to be my fault. Even though I'd stood just a few miles from here less than twenty-four hours ago and danced on the edge of committing dark, lustful blasphemies with our archenemy.

My brother didn't think I was a traitor. I'd dodged a bullet.

Better make sure it was the last time.

"Right," I stuttered at last. "Uh. Good. I mean…"

"You stupid fucking bitch." New voice, soft and shrill.

My heart sank. Now what?

Harriet stalked up, her makeup still smeared with tears. She brandished my phone.

I'd assumed it was *her* phone she'd been fiddling with. But it was mine. I recognized that scratched black case. I hadn't left it in the

84

asylum after all. I must have dropped it in the fight, and Harriet found it. That, or the snotty little cow took it from my room...

And with a chilly sparkle of dread, I remembered what was on it. Shit.

~ 9 ~

Frantic, I glanced at Adonis. No reaction yet. Glimmer hadn't spoken, either. Just fiddled with his tablet, like he wasn't even interested.

My thoughts swirled into a merciless vortex. No. No, it was okay. Harriet abused me often enough that her greeting wasn't out of the ordinary. I could still talk my way out of this.

I forced a smile. "Hey, you found my phone. Thought I'd lost it. Thanks—"

Thwack! Harriet hit me.

I staggered, my scarred cheek stinging. Gingerly, I fingered my jaw. Ouch. A proper punch, too. "What the fuck was that for?"

Her gaze shone raw with grief. But triumph, too. She thrust the phone into Adonis's hand. "Look what she's been doing."

"Give that back." I scrambled up, reached for it…

But too late. Adonis swallowed. His fingers clenched white around my phone. And for a moment, he closed his eyes.

Acid bubbled up to choke me. I didn't need to see, of course. I already knew what it said.

Let's talk. You know the place.
R.

He'd even *signed* it. Vincent never signed his messages. He didn't need to. Almost like... he'd known they'd find it.

Like he'd *wanted* them to.

Fuck.

My face burned. My heartbeat danced a lunatic tarantella. Goddamn it, I deleted all his stalkery texts—after I read them about a million times—so no one would find them. I *always* deleted them.

But for some reason, I hadn't deleted that one. Right now, the explanation was a three-way tie between *thoughtless idiot* and *rank stupidity* and *I'm a fucking moron.*

I tried to speak, but my mouth parched. "It's not what you think," I managed at last. Jeez, that was so *lame.*

Adonis's stare was set to kill. "Tell me, Vee, what *should* I think? That your psychofuck archvillain ex-boyfriend is *texting* you because he wants you to meet his new fiancée? Just how dumb do you think I am?"

"So he texted me," I protested, "so what?" My head throbbed hot, lies and misdirections swirling in fog. A moment ago everything was fine. Now, in a flash, Adonis hated me again. I didn't dare look at Glimmer. Didn't even dare to *think* about Glimmer. "I can't stop the crazy asshole stalking me. I don't even read his screwed-up messages anymore. He's always, like, *miss you* or *come over for chips and beer* or *you don't know the power of the dark side* or whatever. I didn't go, okay? I don't know why you'd think—"

Adonis just held a finger to his lips. Like he'd no patience for my lies anymore. Like I'd finally exhausted him with my bullshit.

God knew, I'd exhausted myself.

With a stab of remorse, I remembered how it stung me to the core last night when he'd lied to me about Peggy. A tiny white fib that didn't matter a damn, just to get me off his case, and my heart had howled.

Whereas I'd lied to Ad all along, or as good as. Avoiding the truth, slinking about, not mentioning where I'd been. And my lies *did* matter. Hell, did they matter.

Adonis slid off the log with that cold efficiency that meant trouble, and beckoned to Peg. She came obediently, a whistled puppy.

I scrambled after them, fighting the urge to throttle Peg for being so damn perfect. Exquisitely aware that I was walking away from Glimmer and a mountain of questions he deserved the answers to. "C'mon, let's discuss this like grown-ups. Where are you—?"

"We can't stay here any longer, Peg." Ad ignored me. I might have dropped into a suddenly yawning crevasse. "I'm sorry. You've done a brilliant job, sweetie. Now let's pack everything up. Gray and Ferdy, you can carry Jeremiah. Harriet, take care of Ebenezer. Sal…"

I grabbed his elbow. "Ad, talk to me. Let me explain."

He shook me off. "Sal, can you help with Jem? Find some branches, anything. We need to make something we can carry him on."

"Ad, stop it. It isn't what you think." The pitch of my voice wrenched upwards in desperation. I knew I was begging. I didn't care.

Peg shot Adonis a concerned glance. Her red ponytail had twigs stuck in it. She touched my hand. "Verity, perhaps you should—"

"Back the fuck off, Peg." I shoved her backwards a few inches with a little flick of talent. She'd been nothing but nice to me from the beginning. Right now, I couldn't care less for her feelings. "Ad, I didn't give us away. I'm positive. Talk to me. What are we doing?"

At last Adonis looked at me, and his ice-age chill stabbed straight to my heart. "*We* are leaving. *You're* staying here."

"What? You can't just leave me."

"You're right. Stay, don't stay. I don't give a damn what you do, so long as you don't follow us." Adonis strode away again.

My guts heated, watery. Holy fuck-a-doodle. He was actually…

I dragged him back to face me. "I know it looks bad. But whatever you think I did, I didn't do it." I inhaled, steadying, and focused on what I knew was true. "We met. We talked. He taunted me, I told him to fuck off. We didn't… well, we didn't anything. That's it. I swear."

But we wanted to, firebird. How we longed to…

Gently, Adonis peeled my grip from his arm and squeezed my hand. "You done?"

Dumbly, I nodded.

"Good. Now *you* listen." He cupped my chin, stroked his thumb across the bruise. "I accepted it when you killed Dad, because it wasn't your fault. I understood that. I tried to help you. I even let you get away with killing our sister, because I knew something was wrong with you. You were sick, Vee. A victim. And, hell, I made enough of my own mistakes that week. None of us are blameless here."

His sincerity undid me. I blinked on poison tears. "But I'm better now."

"Yeah, you are." Adonis's expression hardened. "That's the thing, see. Before, you were a victim. Now, you're just a liar and an easy drunk."

The quicksand of my untruths clutched at me, dragging me down deeper. "So I tried to stop you seeing the message. I didn't want to have this argument! But I didn't mean—"

"I gave you every chance to come to me for help. But you just lied, and my sister would never have lied to me. I love my sister." He swallowed, a dry crack in his voice. "Whoever you are? I don't know you. You're his creature. And I can't have you hanging around my family."

I choked on bile. Not *our family*. "But you lied to me, too! About Peg. You said…" My voice trailed off. What a weak, pathetic protest. But bad excuses were all I had.

My brother didn't need to speak. He just watched me understand. Watched me figure it out, and my heart screamed with stupid remorse that had arrived far too late.

I was deceiving my family for *him*.

Adonis was right. It didn't matter that I hadn't let Vincent touch me, or that I hadn't given our location away. I was still his creature, as abjectly as if I'd fallen at his feet and beseeched him to take me back.

Addictions are like that, see. There's no halfway, no *just one drink*. Either you turn your back completely, or you might as well dive in and drown.

In my heart, Childish Verity screamed and banged sticky fists on the wall. *It's not fair!* she howled. I hadn't done anything wrong. Hadn't betrayed our location, or told Vincent anything he didn't already know, or even let him seduce me, though God knew I'd wanted him to. I'd done my best to stop Sophron and Flash at the museum. Mike's death wasn't my fault. It wasn't *fair…*

But Common-Sense Verity suffocated her, indefatigable. *Told you so*, she droned. *No such thing as half a hero, Verity. Make your bed and die in it.*

"I can change." The promise stung like bitter almond cyanide in my mouth. Was that the flavor of hope? Or the poisoned tang of a lie? "I'll stop. I'll never see him again. I swear."

Adonis's gaze dulled with weariness. No longer sky-blue, but the bleak indigo of a ghostly twilight ocean. Skeletal shadows lurked under his cheekbones. He wasn't angry. Just… so very disappointed.

"I don't believe you," he whispered.

And that cracking sound was my heart breaking.

"I'm sorry, Vee," he added. "I truly am. But I meant it when I said I couldn't let you fuck up again."

My chin trembled. I remembered him saying that. Oh, yes. Right before he put a bullet in my chest. My mindmuscle jittered, wary. Should I get ready to run? Fight? Beg for my life?

"I can change." A shrill, hysterical note warped my voice. *Look me in the eye and make me believe you've changed…* "I know I can. Please, just let me prove it. Don't leave without me. I won't let you!"

Adonis's eyes flashed like stars.

My senses screamed, and I tried to dodge, fall back, get out of the way.

But I didn't even manage to hold my breath. Uselessly, I lashed out, but my augment couldn't protect me, not from this… and a cloudburst of shining warmth hit me full in the face.

Glorious sunshine flooded my muscles, bones, organs, sweeter than any drug. My knees turned to custard and I crumpled. My heart melted. Every nerve sang with delight. I was weeping, gasping, exulting with adoration. Adonis had only to say the word and I'd do anything he asked.

Utter, orgasmic bliss. And I wanted to howl in horror.

My brother had unleashed on me. Not just a casual flicker of *do-me-a-favor*, but a full-on missile of captivating power. And no one—not me, not Gallery villains, not anyone—withstood Adonis's talent.

He gazed down at me, enveloped in a heavenly golden halo of *wonderful*. His metallic eyes glimmered. His skin glowed, his hair aflame with glory like an angel. I'd never seen anything so beautiful or terrible.

"Stay here, Verity." His whisper rained on my skin, a godlike benevolence. "Do you understand me?"

Dumbly, eagerly, I nodded. My mouth was watering. Sweat slicked my palms. My flesh ached with the ardent desire to please him any way I could.

"Good girl." He brushed warm fingers over my forehead. I swooned, ecstatic. The blood rushed away from my head. My vision swam. I tried to fight it, to stay upright, but faintness swamped me, a starlit supernova, and the world shimmered to white.

~ 10 ~

Bleary-eyed, I choked on dirt.

Paugh. I spat grit and dead leaves, and pushed up on my hands. My drool had turned the ground into mud. I wiped my face and, fighting a virulent ache in my muscles, scrambled to my feet.

Darkness, thick and leaf-smelling. Only moonlight drifted through the trees, ghostly. Night insects chirped. Somewhere, an owl hooted, forlorn.

Everyone was gone. I was alone.

I stood there, dumb, the empty forest interminable. He'd actually done it. He'd left me.

Well, no point crying over what's done.

Numbly, I dusted myself down and pulled bark from my hair. My stomach rumbled, those mouthfuls of candy bar long since digested. I rubbed dry eyes, fending off a headache. At least Adonis's charisma fuckery had worn off. He hadn't needed to do a long-lasting job. Just enough to get me out of his way. I felt the same about him now as I always had.

Besides, I'd already seen the face of God, and He didn't look like Adonis.

Still, I felt violated, like someone had thrashed around in my skull with a meat tenderizer. When you finally pissed Ad off, he didn't mess around. I felt like I'd been taken for a screaming one-night-stand and thrown out of a moving car onto the turnpike verge with my clothes torn off. Not a feeling I wanted to associate with my brother.

But you know what? I'd deserved his rage. Fling enough shit and you'll get dirty hands. Time I wound up my self-pity party and got on with un-fucking this sorry situation.

Adonis was on the run. With Mike gone, Jem sick, and a bunch of civilians depending on him, I couldn't blame him. But I'd none of those problems now. While Adonis was distracted? Someone had to get rid of this Sophron character and her buddy Flash, before the two of them escalated from hassling crime-fighters to blasting apartment buildings to dust for the fun of it. And someone had to avenge Mike's death.

Seemed that someone was me.

Okay, then. I patted my pockets, taking inventory. One shiny gunmetal-grey coat, soiled. One mask, muddy. One pair of jeans, one cactus t-shirt, sweaty but wearable. One handkerchief, coated in snot. Oh, and two dollars and fifty-six cents change.

Great. Back to stealing, then. Harriet had kept my phone, that traitorous tattletale gadget. So I'd get another, even if it wasn't secure. Filch some change from a café tip jar for food. Find some-where to stay… For a wild moment, the only place I could think of was the guy from the bar last night. Mr. Cry-on-my-shoulder. Heh. Right. Like he'd even recognize me, or let me stay with him if he did.

But the only other person I knew was Vincent. And going to Vincent's—his palatial house atop Ocean Heights, or the eerie underwater-lit high-rise apartment where he sometimes slept when he wasn't burning down buildings or spending nineteen hours a day at his City Hall office or his shiny IRIN techno-lair, raking in a zillion dollars a quarter and plotting the meticulous Rube-Goldberg destruction of his enemies…

Right. Going to Vincent's, in the state I was in? Weepy, weak and vulnerable, fair game for his crafty brainfuck?

Not an option.

Nope.

Don't even think about it.

Well, no matter. I'd figure something out. In the meantime, I'd slept under bridges before…

Leaves rustled in the dark. A moonlit shadow loomed across the clearing, reaching for me. I whirled, a fistful of power at the ready.

"Whoa." Glimmer warded me off with upraised palms, a long, lean shadow in the forest-green night. "I surrender. Take it easy."

Moonlight danced in his dusty striped hair, lighting his midnight eyes with silver. His black t-shirt was speckled with dirt, and by now he sported a genuine two-day growth of stubble. God fucking bless him.

I made some uncomprehending noise. "Wha… What are you doing here?"

He shoved hands into back pockets. "Waiting for you to wake up. You were out cold for hours. I was just about to build us a fire."

A fire. Of course he was. Jesus in a jam jar.

He ruffled his skunk stripe, self-conscious. "What? Did you think I'd just leave you here?"

My heart overflowed. I wanted to kiss him, burst into tears, smack him across his unreasonably good-looking face and demand to know what the fuck he thought he was doing.

He'd heard everything. He'd seen Vincent's text, knew what I'd done. And he'd stayed. When my own brother—and everyone else, for that matter, not that they didn't have good reason—had left me.

A grin splashed my face. A weak, watery one, the best I could dig up, but a grin nonetheless. And I couldn't blot it off.

Glimmer winced. "Ouch. Enough with the sloppy stuff. I'm blushing over here."

Um, I don't think so. He just knew that was how *I* felt. Truly, he was the best friend ever.

"What did Adonis say?" I managed at last, when what I really meant was *I love you, dude.*

"What could he say? He wasn't happy. But even he can't glamour-whip everyone into submission. Just let him try it." A gleam of defiance. "I'm sorry for what happened, Verity. It was uncalled for. I know you must be upset."

Upset, hell. Try grateful Adonis hadn't killed me. "Any clue where they went?"

"Wasn't told, didn't ask." Glimmer sniffed. "Like he'd tell me anyway. Your brother doesn't like me much."

"He does like you. He just thinks you're too damn heroic for your own good." I picked tiny stones from my teeth. "He's right, by the way. You do realize we're fighting this fight on our own?"

Glimmer cracked his knuckles. "Yeah, well, I figured you could use some help. What with, y'know, the way things are for you."

His tone tasted odd, and with a frisson of dread I recalled what he'd said earlier, when I'd realized Vincent had lied to me about Sophron. I'd rambled aloud about it, and Glimmer had hushed me... but he hadn't said *what are you talking about?* or *what do you mean, he told you?* or *are you still seeing that freak on the side, Jesus, what's wrong with you?*

He'd said *keep it quiet.*

Like he was afraid someone else might hear.

"You knew," I accused softly.

A bashful Glimmer shrug.

I trembled, overcome. "How long?"

"A while." He hesitated. "Since just after we moved to the asylum. I suspected, but..."

"Then why the hell didn't you tell everyone?" My voice sliced, harsh. I sounded angry. I wasn't. Just... bewildered. Mortified.

Glimmer just wiped his nose with the back of his hand. "I figured you had your reasons. You're a smart woman. It's none of mine."

My throat ached. Add *so humiliated, I wanted to vanish.*

95

My best friend—make that my *only* friend—knew I was flirting with evil. And he'd let me. Not because he didn't care or was waiting for me to fuck up so he could say *I told you so.*

He thought I knew what I was doing.

Jesus Christ on a cheeseburger. This precious boy *trusted* me. And one day, sure as sugar turned to shit, it'd get him killed.

"You should've said something." My voice quavered, and I raked sweaty palms up and down my thighs. *I* should've said something, but I'd been too afraid to face his reaction. "We could've *talked...* Oh, God." What a fucking *idiot* I am.

I'd acted in isolation, like I always did. Instead of believing he'd be there for me, I just kept pushing him away. Throwing his trust back in his face. No one—not even Saint Glimmer— would put up with that forever. One day, he wouldn't give me any more chances.

Glimmer fidgeted. "I figured you'd tell when you were ready."

Silence. Just crickets chirping in the night and the dark echo of emptiness in my heart.

Screw me for a fool, but I cared what he thought of me. I cared so much, it knifed me deep inside, where I was still torn and aching over Uncle Mike's stupid death and the destruction of our adopted home. But it cut me deeper that one day Glimmer *wouldn't* think of me anymore.

I'd screw up once too often and he'd give up on me. Forget about me, the way you forgot about a bruise that had healed. And the prospect of that oblivion—that non-existence to him, like I'd never been at all—terrified me. I'd do anything to stop it.

Even if it meant revealing the awful truth.

"Well, I'm telling you now." Like dead leaves in my throat, the words choked me, and only a skeletal croak came out. I wanted so badly to pretend this away, to cling to that precious dream world where he believed in me. I didn't want to speak it, make it real. But I had to. "He's still in my head, Glimmer. He texts me and I read it a hundred times. I see his face in crowds and my heart

somersaults. I fall asleep with the taste of him on my lips and I...
I dream about him, I remember the way it was and I..."

"It's okay, Verity." Tranquil, barely audible. "You're not alone."
Just like that.

He didn't try to calm me down, or patronize me by saying *no
problem, everything'll be fine, idiot, what are you worried about?*

My eyes burned. Why the hell did he even give me the time
of day? I didn't know. I just knew I'd spend the rest of forever
trying to deserve it.

And part of me—the sour, jealous, unforgivable part—resented
him for it. For never once making a bad decision, never acting out
of selfishness or spite. For always being the one who helped, while
I was the one with issues—and never asking for anything in return.

But the rest of me just wanted to fall to my knees and pray to
the god of lost causes that, once again, Glimmer was here to drag
me out of the shit pile I'd so willingly dived into.

He didn't come closer. Didn't physically touch me. He knew
I didn't want that, not now. Not while any stray stimulus could
still trigger the memory of *his* fingertips stroking my skin and
his breath burning my lips... but suddenly I could feel Glimmer,
too. A safe, warm, vanilla-scented embrace, invisibly protecting
me from myself.

My lungs ached. I wanted to weep. To hold Glimmer for real,
clutch him close to my heart and whisper the truth, which was
that he was the best thing in my world and every time I hurt him
it killed me a tiny bit inside.

That the hideous reality of my obsession with Vincent didn't
mean I didn't love the hell out of Glimmer, too.

I blinked, dizzy. Whoa. Did I just think that? Or was he creeping
about in my mind? Soothing me, making me feel warm and wanted
so I wouldn't freak out?

Let him, then. I didn't care. I'd just enjoy it while it lasted. It
sure beat being charisma-whipped by Adonis.

Boy, did it.

Glimmer's expression froze a little. Like he realized he'd crossed some line. But he didn't step away or drop his gaze. Too brave for that. "Let's get some rest, yeah? Our problems'll still be there come morning."

I fidgeted on one foot and snorted to cover my discomfort. "Will they? Great. I'm so pleased. What a load off my mind."

He glanced around the clearing. The damp ground was piled with sticks and smelly leaf sludge. Puddles oozed and bubbled in the mud. Frogs peeped. "Nice swamp. I'm all for getting back to nature, but I vote for not sleeping here."

I wrinkled my nose. "Amen. But I'm running kinda low on friends with sofas, and I've got a total of two bucks and shrapnel to my name. Any ideas?"

A crooked, piratical Glimmer smile. "Oh, honey. Watch me and weep."

~ 11 ~

An hour later, I luxuriated in the master bedroom of a swanky fourth-floor apartment by the bay, making snow angels on a white damask coverlet. Tiny chandeliers glittered beneath the mirror-cut ceiling, reflecting like endless stars. The polished wooden floor gleamed, and in the open French windows, white chiffon curtains puffed in fresh sea breeze.

Glimmer emerged from the en-suite shower, a fluffy latte-brown towel wrapped around his hips. Damn. He had lovely skin, smooth and olive-toned, and he was still young enough that he didn't have to work out every five minutes to look lean and well muscled. And that diet of caffeine and computer code sure wasn't doing his body fat percentage any harm…

Okay, fine, so I indulged in a quick stare. One hell of a view. Not that I was, y'know, *looking.*

I made a show of shielding my eyes. "Eww. Dude, put some clothes on."

"Why?" He rubbed another towel in his dripping hair, and his abs did curiously watchable things under that perfect skin. "Not like you haven't seen it before."

"That doesn't mean you have to wander around half naked.

Old chicks like me do have heart attacks, y'know."

He flipped me the finger and ducked back behind the frosted glass screen. It was one of those fancy open-plan bathrooms, with no door and a claw-foot bathtub on a spotlit pedestal in front of the window. Idly, I wondered what he'd do if I burst in there and jumped him. Whipped that towel away and went for it. I might be scarred and beauty-challenged, but I'm not a total loss in the bedroom-games department. He could always close his eyes. Maybe I'd even teach him a thing or two. Heh. Harriet, if you could see me now...

My belly warmed at the thought—and always, secretly, that hot steel needle of fear. *What if Vincent finds out?* "Fuck it," I muttered, mutinous. Vincent didn't own me. Despite what he might believe, he couldn't control my brain. I could think what I liked, and besides, it was apparent that I totally needed to get laid because me fantasizing about Glimmer was doing nobody nowhere any good.

Glimmer emerged, in jeans but still no shirt. Honestly. He walked his cute boy-ass over to the fridge, grabbed two bottles of water and tossed me one. "Anyway, you said this could be my room. I feel violated."

"I lied. This bed is all mine. You can have the guest room." I rolled onto my stomach, wallowing in the squishy quilt. I used to be rich. I'd forgotten how comfortable it made everything. "Besides, chills are crittering up my spine. I think the amorous ghost of Mrs. What's-her-name is haunting you."

He drank deep and wiped his mouth. "She's not dead, idiot. I merely suggested she might like to stay with a friend and let us have her apartment for a while."

"Horny rich widows you've never met before gift you their zillion-dollar apartments a lot, do they?"

A sly grin. "Only when I ask nicely."

"Dude, you could have *married* that lady and lived forever in style. Did you see her face? She thought you were *hot*, baby."

He wrinkled his nose. "I just hypnotize people. Messing with their affections is more your brother's style. Besides," he added, and took another swallow, "perhaps I'm saving myself for the right girl."

O-kaay. I'm leaving *that* one right where it is. He still wore his wedding ring, for fuck's sake. Middle finger, sure, but if that wasn't a wedding ring, I'd eat my mask—with ketchup. A strict no-go zone.

I levered myself from all that lovely squishiness and shrugged off my coat. "My turn in the shower. You better not've used all the hot water. And no peeking, okay?"

"It isn't easy to hold myself back, but…"

"…but somehow you manage," I chorused. "Yeah, yeah. Piss off, pretty boy."

The shower smelled of him, comforting vanilla-spice. I closed my eyes under the hot spray, let it flush the forest dirt and Adonis's scorn from my body and gurgle it down the drain.

When I emerged—no clean clothes, but a shower was better than nothing, and no way could I cram my butt into one of the skeletal Widow Horny's size-zero designer suits—Glimmer was watching TV in the living room, breeze from the open window playing with his hair. T-shirt on now, mercifully. There's only so much ignoring a girl can do.

Barefoot, I wandered over, pulling knots from my wet hair. The place was furnished in faux eighteenth-century glam, with loud embroidered upholstery and glaring polish on the wooden furniture. "What is that, *Augment War Zone*? I told you to cut out the reality shows. They'll rot your brain."

"Shh. Watch."

I squinted at the big shiny TV on the wall. News channel, showing fuzzy selfie images from a video- sharing site. The ticker tape at the bottom read SAPPHIRE CITY TERROR ATTACK CLAIMS FIVE LIVES.

I halted, fingers in mid-comb. I'd know that hollow voice anywhere.

Sophron stood before a ruined building. Dust billowed from crumbling walls, rubble-strewn ground. Reddish afternoon sun slanted left to right. Distant sirens blared, rising.

Her pale face gleamed with that sick smile. Holding the camera at arm's length over her shoulder was Flash. He stared solemnly at the screen, black hair tumbling over one dark-ringed eye.

People yelled, running to and fro in the background. Like they didn't know what the fuck was happening, didn't recognize Sophron and Flash for the culprits. Broken stone columns, steps leading to a carved doorway…

My memory clicked. Downtown, the old City Library. Or what was left of it.

"Shit." I peered closer, trying to quantify the damage from the blurred images. I couldn't spy any bodies. But I'd dropped buildings on people before, in the bad old days. I knew how it happened. The dead would be under the rubble. Along with some live ones, oh yes, bleeding out slowly in agony, their calling voices ever weaker. We wouldn't find them for hours. Days, maybe.

"…and this is what happens." Sophron's hollow, high-pitched little girl's voice. "You can't control augments. You can't keep us down. Treat us like criminals and we'll act like it."

Behind, a fire engine screeched up, and first responders in helmets and smoke gear piled out. Yells, the clank and whizz of hoses and ladders. Blue and red lights flashed.

Sophron just laughed like a punk-ass hyena—*nyih-hih-hih, fuck the po-lice!*—and tossed her lurid dreads. "Gotta go, viewers. So listen up, all you dickheads in City Hall. Take down the Sentinels—every single one—and let us live as free citizens, or we'll destroy one public building every day until you do. You won't know where, you won't know when. Maybe it'll be empty. Maybe it won't. I really don't give a shit."

She leaned her head against Flash's, and they both leaned towards the camera, faces looming large. "They'll try to tell you it's all my fault," she said. "That I did this on my own, that I'm dangerous and insane and deserve to be locked up. But all you normal people out there? You know who's truly to blame." She jabbed a finger over her shoulder. "They are. The ones in charge. The ones who created me. The ones who control you, same as they try to control us. Don't forget that when the bodies start rolling in." She kissed Flash's cheek and flipped the camera a wave. "See ya."

Poof! The pair vanished. The camera clattered to the pavement, reeling images of smoky sky.

The TV picture switched back to the news anchor, a platinum blonde wearing a patently false funereal expression. "Now, we're crossing live to…"

Glimmer muted the audio. "Busy little scumbags, aren't they?"

I slumped beside him on the embroidered sofa. "That was afternoon sun in the vid. When was this? After they attacked us? While you were waiting for me to wake up?"

"Guess so." He didn't accuse—never did—but it stung, all the same.

If I hadn't been dead to it—if I hadn't made Adonis unleash on me and knock me out—we could've been there. Could've stopped her.

Or not. Right now, I had no idea *how* to stop her. No point feeling guilty about not doing something I *couldn't* actually do. Right?

"Still," I admitted, "as far as ultimatums go, you've gotta have sympathy. Flushing the Sentinels down the john sounds like a great idea to me."

"Preaching to the choir, sister. But knocking down libraries with people inside? Not exactly winning hearts and minds."

"Don't bet on it," I scoffed. "These fucking hypocrites love a juicy slice of civil disobedience. This newscast will bust the ratings. So long as it's not *their* grandma getting crushed? They're all for it."

Still, cold fingernails of disquiet traced my spine. *You dickheads in City Hall,* Sophron said.

Like she knew exactly who she was talking to.

103

But I still couldn't carve from my heart the cancerous certainty that Vincent was telling the truth. *She's no child of mine…*

"So what d'you think he'll do?" Glimmer asked. As usual, he knew where my thoughts were heading. How did he even do that? I'd always thought I could feel it when he crept into my head…

But I didn't need to answer. The news cycle had rolled around again, and there was Vincent. Out front of City Hall in the glare of multiple cameras, playing at his mayor act.

I couldn't help but stare. He was mesmerizing. Cool, well spoken, utterly unflappable. And beautiful, damn, I'd seen him only last night, but this was like meeting him for the first time and falling in love all over again.

My treacherous heart fluttered, a shower of warm starlight. Good God, that man's commanding eyes…

"Say it, Verity." His storm-grey gaze skewers me to the spot. I'm a pinned butterfly. Will he release me, or screw me into the kill jar?

It's after dinner. We're sitting at the second-floor window, the lights from the seaside promenade gloating over his coppery hair and sparkling on the rim of my wine glass. He twists a curl of my hair around one finger. Flickering fire licks my cheek, a warning as well as a caress, and my insides shiver and melt. He's so very good at this.

"Tell me again what you are, and make me believe it."

I tremble. My mouth is parched. I'm aching inside, swelling, like my skin's unable to contain what he's made of me. I loathe him. I crave him. Will tonight be the night he finally…? God, the not-knowing is more than I can bear.

It's been twenty-seven days since that first fateful night on the bridge when he came for me. Twenty-seven days of desperation and longing. He kissed me that night. My archenemy, all in one instant blooming into something else, something even more dangerous. It blindsided me in mid-sentence, the illicit pleasure of his lips on mine the shock of my life, and I gasped and inhaled his exquisite scent and for the first time ever (or so it seemed) my soul sparkled truly alive.

Twenty-seven days later, I want him so hard that in his presence I can barely breathe. He knows exactly what he's doing. He's masterful, a consummate torturer of the soul.

But it's so much deeper than physical attraction. To admit I want him is to confess to other, darker secrets: the angry, jealous, murdering kind. I should know better than to test him. I should know better than to venture into his secret world. But night after night, I can't resist, and my desire for him—the lust to embrace all the dangerous things he stands for—scorches like famine in my blood.

Because what he wants—the only thing he'll accept—is the abject truth. And I am so desperately sick of lies.

Still, my voice crumbles. His truth hurts. His truth frightens me. "I can't."

"Try harder." His commanding tone twists my guts. The fact that he does this in public, where everyone can see, just makes it harder to resist. "Don't play. You know what I want. And I'll have it, one way or another."

Blindly, uselessly, I fight. I know I'll pay for it later, he's utterly without remorse, but I fight nonetheless, and a new thought strikes me, so poignant and forbidden that I gasp and shudder, overcome.

I think I want him to fight for me. I want... no, I need... I need to do this the hard way.

I reeled, my cheeks burning. Goddamn it. Did Glimmer see that? Fuck, I was such an easy mark. Just when I thought I was getting over it...

I poked Glimmer, and without comment he flicked the sound back on.

"...tragedy," Vincent was saying, in response to some question. As usual, no prepared statement. A politician's trick, as if he spoke from the heart. He was good at it. "Public safety is our prime responsibility and I promise you, we will uphold it."

Who the fuck did he mean, *we*?

I squinted. Behind him stood Ashton, his personal assistant, whom I'd met at his IRIN office a while back. Nice suit, clean-cut young face, sharp, confident blue eyes. A bit smugger than I remembered. Kid was moving up in the world. Heh. Bet there were lobbyists and political cronies all over the city lining up to do him favors.

Well, good for him. He'd seemed a smart and decent guy, which meant he probably didn't know who he was really working for. Probably. Mark down Ashton as a potential crazy.

Closer—almost *next* to Vincent, and since when did he allow that?—stood a woman in a sharp sage-green suit. Thin as a whippet, with lofty ice-chipped cheekbones and an ash-blond bob down to her chin. Zealous eyes, over-bright like a crusader or a fanatic.

Who the hell was *she*? She reminded me of that head shrink who'd tortured me at the asylum. The one I'd labeled Dr. Mengele. Only... more intelligent. Prettier. Scarier.

Green poison clawed into my guts. Not just good-natured envy, because she was powerful and beautiful and wore smart clothes and nice makeup. This was one-hundred-percent proof, balls-to-the-wall jealousy. I wanted to puke. Scream. Jump through that TV screen and crush her skull with my bare hands.

I pointed, shaky. "Who's that?"

"Which?"

"The ice empress."

"Didn't you watch last week's news? Counselor Mackenzie Wilt, the new deputy mayor."

"The *what*?" No, I didn't watch the fucking news. Vincent was always on it. It was too much like temptation.

"Yup. Just a politician, not augmented. So far as we know."

I swallowed my rage, but it hunkered in my throat like a toxic toad. "So what the hell does he want with her?"

"All I know is, she was some kind of ultra-conservative attorney at a private firm. A mover and shaker, partner at thirty, hit the list for judge but turned it down to take this job. No illegal immigrants, free speech for white supremacists, right to bear assault weapons.

And now Proposition 101, persecuting augments and suspending *habeas corpus*. A real piece of work."

"A hater." I barely got the word out coherently. God, I hated *her*. Look how close they stood. How Vincent said *we* instead of *I*. Like he had a new best buddy. My heart stung, foolish, and I felt three inches tall. No. No way. *I* was his best girl. *Me*.

He hadn't even mentioned her yesterday. Like it was of no consequence that I'd been supplanted. Was this a message? Was he *trying* to hurt my feelings? Because screw me raw, it was working.

"I think the talented Ms. Wilt hates everyone," Glimmer said. "Figures. It's just the kind of fear-mongering, them-and-us, protect-your-family bullshit the good people of this country vote for."

I stared at her, acid scorching my eyes. Vincent had enlisted a virulent, powerful hater as his second-in-command. The man's hubris was beyond astounding. "So what's his game?"

"All part of the joke, I guess. Making him look good to his hater voters while he's playing the bleeding-hearted liberal. He just enjoys proving how monumentally stupid people are."

"And provoking us." A thought whacked me out of left field, and I nearly swallowed my tongue. Did he *know* I'd entertained naughty thoughts about Glimmer? Was he punishing me for daring to think I might have a normal day or two in my life that didn't include *him*?

Ridiculous. Insane. How could he know?

The same way he knows everything else.

"…don't do business with those who practice terror," Vincent was saying. "We won't negotiate with criminals and cowards. Either they give themselves up promptly to the city's justice, or I will hunt them down. That's all, ladies and gentlemen. Thank you." And he strode inside, Ashton in his wake… and between them, Ms. Deputy Ice Queen, swaying her power-skirted hips. Practically at Vincent's side.

Oh, my sweet God. *Did she know who he was?* Was he doing to her what he did to me?

A challenge for him, for sure, to indoctrinate someone like Wilt into his cult. But doing what can't be done turns him on. The archvillain-master-race-brainwash treatment, the ruthless hall-of-mirrors torture, mental disintegration, questions, tests, merciless desire…

Holy shit, is he *sleeping with her?*

Glimmer snorted and flicked the TV off. "'Don't do business with terrorists.' Fuck me, he's got a nerve. Hides in plain sight, surrounds himself with his enemies, invites all and sundry to attack him. I'd have to admire him if he wasn't criminally insane."

I could barely concentrate. I couldn't shake off the images that seared bleeding welts into my soul. Vincent's body on hers, slick muscles working as he does dark and sultry things that make her gasp. The way his damp hair glistens in that reddish firelight, a drop of sweat on his shoulder, his long fingers crushing hers into the sheet, her platinum head thrown back in surrender…

"Huh?" I shook myself. But the torment didn't cease, and I knew with sick certainty that my defiance was a lie. *He doesn't own me,* I'd told myself. What a bad joke. "What did you say?"

"What do you think his game is?" repeated Glimmer patiently. "Why is he so damn calm? Sure, this Sophron and Flash are powerful, but he could crush 'em in an instant if he felt like it. Hell, he could crush us all in an instant if he felt like it, so—"

"Is this your plan?" My voice strangled. Sweat slicked inside my shirt. My muscles burned, and it wasn't just jealousy or insane memory that plagued me. My guts felt filled with warm salt water, spreading everywhere to soil me, and my face was surely the color of beetroot. I was so embarrassed I wanted to die. "Is this really how we're gonna do this? Because I can't."

"I'm sorry?" He edged back in his seat. Genuine puzzlement quirked his brows.

I jumped up and paced, up down, up down, unable to bear his gaze. My mindmuscle screeched, a trapped rat scrabbling impotently at its cage. I raked my wet hair, rubbed my eyes, cracked my knuckles, but the itch wouldn't cease. "I get what you're doing, okay? But it won't work."

"Verity—"

"I'm grateful as hell that you're here," I blurted out. "Don't for a moment get me wrong about that. God knows, you've saved my life a dozen times and you're probably not finished yet. But I can't take the way you just sit there and pretend nothing's wrong!"

I caught my breath, mortified. That came out a little different than I expected.

Glimmer ruffled his skunk stripe. "Okay," he said at last, "I get it."

"No, you don't. Something's *wrong* with me, Glimmer. In here, or in here"—I jabbed a sharp finger at my heart and then my skull—"I don't know. But th-that…" I stuttered and flapped my hand at the screen. "That *person* comes on TV and it's like I'm *insane*. My blood boils and my brain melts to mush and I don't know what's a memory and what's a dream, or what's not even real at all. And here *you* are, all reasonable and let's-get-to-work, pretending you don't even *notice* that all I can think about is whether he's… jeez, I fucking *hate* it when I *cry!*"

I wiped my face, heedless of the smears. Blinked, in some direction, *any* direction except at him. My skin shrank and tried to take me with it, to suck me into some blessed vanishing vortex where no one would see me ever again. Please, God.

But it didn't work. I didn't vanish. Nope. Still here.

Fucking great. I'm emotional wreckage. He'll think I've finally lost the plot I've been threatening to misplace for months now. He'll pat me on the head and put me to bed with a hot water bottle and a double scotch and Xanax, and next thing I know, it'll be back to the loony bin, with stewed apple custard for dinner and blue-eyed Nazi professors who bolt augmentium helmets to my skull and zap me with electrified wires and say *how do you feel now?*

But Glimmer just bit his lip, his midnight eyes starlit. "Verity…"

"S'okay," I muttered. "Sorry. I'm just…"

"I know what it's like." His voice strained, as I'd rarely heard it, not just pain or regret but distant black rage. He twisted that silver ring around his finger. "I know how awful it is to hold someone in your heart who… who you'd rather wasn't there. How it makes it so damn *hard* to be the person you want to be. And to… to be with other people the way you want."

I'd never asked, I realized dumbly, about his wife. Never invited him to talk about it, like a real friend should. I knew only that Razorfire had forced Glimmer to blow his cover, had poisoned her against him… but had he really? Or had this woman hated and feared augments all along? The poison lurking beneath her skin, a monster in a swamp just waiting to hatch out?

Suddenly, the space between us seemed frighteningly small. And at the same time, impossibly far. "I… um…"

Glimmer stopped his mouth with the back of his hand. Silencing what? A sob? A curse? A mortifying truth? "I'm just saying I understand," he whispered at last. "I won't judge. I can't save you, Verity, only you can do that. But let me help you."

My heart overflowed, burning me inside. God, he was so vulnerable right now that I wanted to weep all over again for him. And *he* wanted to help *me*.

Speechless, I just nodded. *Please, Glimmer. For God's sake. I need you.*

I didn't know if he heard. He just nodded back. And we stared at each other.

I fidgeted, flushing. Was this the part where we… what? Have a big old hug? Or even…?

"I'm wrecked," he said finally, barely audible. "Let's talk in the morning." And before I could speak, he was gone. Into the spare room, the door clicking softly shut.

Shit.

I raked my wet hair, raising vicious tangles that reflected my mood. Jeez, what a *loser* I am. Why can't I ever say the right thing? I've courage aplenty when villains are hurling trees at me or slicing buildings in two with flaming razor whips. So why did talking to Glimmer—I mean really *talking*, not just work talk or giving him shit about his hair—why did it make me want to curl up under the sofa with my thumb in my mouth?

I stalked to my own bed and dropped onto my back on the quilt. I didn't bother to undress. My reflection glared back at me from the ceiling mirrors. Wasted, thin, a shadow of me, my coat spreading out like gunmetal wings.

Let me help you, Glimmer had said.

But how did you help what I had? Mengele and her asylum doctors couldn't cure me. Vincent's conditioning—they say brainwashing isn't real, but they say that about the devil's temptation, too—the piece of him that lived in my head was buried too deep, the scars too permanent. Glimmer, along with everything that had happened over the last few months, had made me *want* to be better, but *wanting* and *doing* aren't the same. Two minutes on the bridge with Vincent and, like an alcoholic sneaking a drink, I'm diving headfirst off the wagon.

I rolled, sweating and restless. I pulled off my coat, threw it aside. Beyond the open windows, moths flapped, lured to their death by siren streetlights. A trolley car rattled by, and the melancholy notes of a saxophone drifted. My solitude gnawed at my bones. I desperately wanted my phone. I'd call my brother and tell him he was an asshole. I'd message Harriet and say *fuck you, you jealous little shrew*. If Vincent texted me right now, I'd...

I gritted my teeth, banging my fists against my temples to jam the crazy back in. How tempting insanity is when you're faced with the bleak, thorny, painful real world.

No. No more.

I wouldn't see him. Wouldn't respond to his messages. Remove the triggers, right? Throw out all your needles or bottles of booze; get the pills out of the house; stop hanging out with your druggie pals. No more obsessing about what he's doing and who he's fucking and what's his plan for world domination this week. If I

111

caught myself thinking of him, I'd stop. Immerse myself in catching Sophron and Flash, and forget him.

Simple—not easy, but *simple*—as that.

And Glimmer could help me.

Determination solidified, a cooling golden shield around my heart. Enough with whining and excuses and *it's all too hard.* I'm strong. I can do this. I'd prove myself worthy of Glimmer's trust—yes, and Adonis's, too—if I had to scrape my own traitorous brains into spaghetti and eat them with a fork.

But what if you're a hopeless case? Common-Sense Verity, ineluctable, her voice echoing into forever. *What if you can't stop? Are you truly prepared to drag Glimmer down with you?*

That stopped me short. I'd risk my own soul in a heartbeat. Hell, I'd done it before, and in terms of self-disgust, I'd already hit rock-bottom the day I realized I'd betrayed my family and killed my own father to earn the love of a monster. I'd nothing more to lose.

But the thought of hurting Glimmer—of *spoiling* him, somehow—spiked poisoned barbs deep into my heart.

I didn't think I'd sleep.

But I did. And, of course, I dreamed.

"But..." I swallow, but my mouth won't moisten. I should know better than to come here. I should know better than to let him dance this midnight waltz in my mind. But each night, he's harder and harder to resist. He's a drug I can't shake. A drunken dream I can't stop having, that maddening impulse to scratch an itch even though your skin's already bloody from your nails.

This is his glass-walled apartment, high above the city where no one can reach us. Where no one can save me but him. A single luminous partition wall gleams, throwing shadows across the carpeted floor. Outside, Sapphire City's lights sprinkle like jewels on blood-soaked snow, and the moon rises, a slim scarlet crescent in the smoke.

It's a heart-stopping view. I barely acknowledge it. I'm too entranced by his storm-dark eyes, the curve of his lips, his stunning grace as he touches one finger to a coppery curl of his hair.

"But what?" That effortlessly arresting tone makes me shiver and yearn. He sits opposite me, across the low table, a silky threat in black and white. His mask lies on the table, a slick of rust-red shine. His crimson coat is draped over the back of the sofa. Without it, his body is strong yet lean, almost too lean. Calculated, as if every ounce of energy he absorbs is burned in the fire of his certainty. A perfectly balanced relationship. Knowing that he possesses absolute, unfailing control of his appetites is one of the easier things I've come to believe.

We're playing chess, glass pieces on a shining glass board. I have no idea where the game's at. I'm too confused, too frightened of my own thoughts and feelings.

God, this is too much. I want to crawl over there and sink into his embrace, drink his fiery kiss, drown in that druglike scent that haunts my dreams. Slip into delirium, so I don't have to think about what the fuck I'm even doing here.

But I know he won't touch me, not tonight. He never does anything without purpose. And right now it suits his purpose to let me suffer.

"But it isn't... I can't reconcile it." Below us, the city lights shimmer in drifting smoke. On the horizon, buildings burn. "The things you do..."

"The things I am," *he corrects gently. He leans forward. Moves a glimmering white piece. I move in return. A faint smile. "Verity, this will go much easier on you if you pay attention."*

"I'm sorry." My guts clench, cold. "I didn't mean..."

"I possess power," he reminds me, ignoring my apology like the waste of time it is. "I exercise it. You can't divorce that from the rest of me and pretend it doesn't exist. When a person wields immense power..."

"Unconscionable power."

He takes a pawn. Pushes it gently to one side of the board. "That's a strange word to use."

"They say you're a psychopath. That you have no conscience." Daring, a challenge. I'm not a pushover. He should remember that.

Those intoxicating eyes kindle, hellfire in storm clouds. "What do you think?"

Unspoken threat slides coolly into my veins. I must tread carefully. I castle my king. I consider. "I think… you choose to have no conscience."

A dangerous, serpentine smile. "Come here."

My heart pounds. Did I speak heresy? Am I to be re-educated, corrected, oh-so-slowly tortured with the ugly reality of my own weakness? God, the way my flesh warms and tingles at that thought makes me ill.

But it makes me sigh, too. Strip away the lies and I'm reborn. There's safety in that. Happiness.

Eager, yet unwilling—dragged by some unearthly force I can't identify—I rise and kneel at his side.

He caresses my hair. One finger, so light I can barely detect it. Too gentle. Too much. I shudder, undone. He strokes my smooth cheekbone, a warm flicker of presentiment, perhaps some secret glimpse of my future. He rests his fingertip on my lips. "You're so beautiful."

For just a moment, I close my eyes. I want to weep. Because I believe him. With all my weak and willing heart.

He kisses me, slow, deliberate but with an underlying hunger that burns in my bones. His mint-fire flavor in my mouth is sweet affirmation of everything I've begged him for. In the heat of his embrace, the cowering creature in the core of my heart withers. Melts, base metal in an alchemist's crucible, and forges into something shinier. Stronger. More precious. We are reality, he and I. We're nothing but truth. This is my reward.

I surrender, my longing for that impure delight stronger than I can resist. He tilts my head back, both hands in my hair, and as our kiss turns darker and more urgent, I barely notice when he reaches past me for the chessboard and makes his final move. Checkmate. And with one sly finger, he topples my king to his death.

~ 12 ~

When I awoke—of course—Glimmer was already up. Yellow sunlight streamed through the curtains, and delicious cooking smells crept up my nose, taunting me with how useless and slug-a-bed I was. I blinked at the bedside clock and groaned. Did that time have a seven on the front? Someone call my attorney. That's cruel and unusual.

I rolled off the bed and stretched, yawning. I'd slept in my clothes again, and my t-shirt was rumpled and sweaty. Guess I'd better steal another. I'd miss prickly old FREE HUGS.

But damn, that was an excellent sleep. I felt reinvigorated, ready for action. Amazing what a good blubbering confession will do for the soul.

I pulled my boots on and wandered into the kitchenette—black marble bench tops, appliances in fresh stainless steel—and grabbed a bottle of juice from the fridge, frowning at the label. "'Breakfast juice'. What the hell is that? Is 'breakfast' a fruit?"

Glimmer pushed a plate of waffles towards me. He wore a clean black t-shirt, from somewhere. It was a little tight. I wasn't complaining. "Shut up and eat, wise-ass. And don't drink that out of the bottle…" He sighed. "Whatever. What've you got against glasses, anyway?"

"Nothing." I swigged again, plonking my butt onto a glass-seated stool. "There's just no need to fill the world with dirty dishes. Waste of effort. Re-use and recycle, all that."

He pointed at a stainless-steel drawer under the bench. "Look: dishwasher. No effort required."

"So? A principle's at stake." I forked waffle into my mouth—hot syrup, butter, perfectly toasted—and nearly drooled on my coat. I rolled my eyes, orgasmic. "God, yes. Dude, you are the best cook ever."

"Great. Another girl who only wants my waffles. Flattery will get you nowhere, you heartless vixen."

"It'll get me more waffles," I pointed out, my mouth still full. "Always has before."

"I feel used. Truly." He hopped onto another stool beside me, nursing a tall black coffee. "Listen, about…"

"Stop," I cut in swiftly, and finished my mouthful, determined to say the right thing for once. My face burned, and my stomach turned to water all over again, but I pushed through. "This is my apology party, okay? I've been an asshole. I shouldn't have lied. I should've asked for your help, and I didn't, and it put us both in danger. I'm sorry, and I promise it won't happen again."

Glimmer drank his coffee. Thought about it. "Okay. No problem."

"Cool."

"Sweet." He finished his coffee and poured more. I dug into my waffles.

And that was that.

"Hey," I added, "I was thinking about what you said yesterday. About why Razorfire doesn't just burn Sophron and Flash to cinders and get it over with?" I sat straighter, pleased with myself. See? I did it. I said his name without melting into a stupid puddle of heartsick adoration. Small victories.

"And?"

"I'm assuming no charred teenage corpses turned up on the news while we were sleeping?"

"Nope. I wondered that too, after his 'I'll hunt them down' speech yesterday. But no one's reporting anything, and it's not like he'd have hidden the bodies, or offed them on the quiet. He'd do it where everyone could see."

"Right. So, either he *can't* kill 'em—which is utterly ridiculous, agreed?"

Glimmer grimaced. "Not that this is the new Vincent Caine fan club? But I'll grant him *ruthless* and *effective*. And he's got resources. If he wanted 'em dead, they'd be ash."

"So it must be that he doesn't *want* to stop them. Which means…

"…that somehow, they're acting to his advantage. Makes sense. But how?" Glimmer drained his coffee and grabbed a green apple. "If he wants destruction, why doesn't he just do it himself? The city's in his pocket. Adonis tried to tell people, remember, and look what happened."

I remembered, all right. Adonis got arrested for his trouble, and Vincent won the election anyway. Not that it'd all been my fault, or anything.

"How does he do it?" I muttered. "He could firebomb City Hall on live TV and they still wouldn't believe he's Razorfire."

"People see what they want to see, I guess."

Oh, yeah. I knew all about that. "So… he wants clean hands, then. He wants Sophron and Flash to wreak the havoc. Maybe it's just a pretext to crack down with the Sentinel program. Let Ms. Nazi Deputy Mayor have her way and hang all the augments from the nearest yard arm."

Glimmer ate an apple slice. "Could be. Or he just gets off on chaos. Whatever, right? We can't waste energy second-guessing him."

"But what if we're playing into his hands?" The idea burned like poison ivy. I'd spent the last few years of my life dancing to his mocking tune, and look what I had to show for it.

"What if we are?" Glimmer said reasonably. "Gotta do what we've gotta do. Stopping Sophron and Flash from tearing buildings down is good work, no matter how you look at it."

I frowned, unconvinced. "Guess so."

"And don't forget that the simplest explanation for his let-'em-be attitude is still that they're Gallery, and he's set the whole thing up from the beginning."

"But it's never the simplest explanation with him."

"Maybe that's what he's relying on."

"Aargh. So what if…" I rubbed my temples, where a familiar, treacherous headache threatened… I shivered. *Bad juju, Verity. Let it be.* "You know what? Fuck it. My brain hurts. Moving on. What's the plan today?"

Glimmer finished his apple, and together we loaded the shiny steel dishwasher. "Well," he ventured, a glass in each hand, "they said one public building each day. What's today's damage?"

"Public buildings, eh?" I dropped my plate into the little slot, *plonk!* Heh. I tried again, just for fun. *Plonk!* Doing everyday stuff was dead cool. "Libraries, offices, monuments…"

"Think about it from Sophron's point of view. If you were an angry teenage psychotic, where would you attack next?"

"Depends what my aims were. Do I attack first responders, looking for maximum shock? A shopping mall or a football stadium for maximum casualties?"

"Or a school," he suggested. "Maximum terror. Threaten people's children and they'll demand action from City Hall. She did seem to have a hate on for that."

"But V… but Razorfire doesn't actually care what people demand. Even if he pretends he does."

"Right. He'll just do what he wants anyway. So…"

"…so what *does* he want?" I banged twin fists against my temples, and the hungry worms in my stomach wriggled and snapped their little teeth. *Hee-hee-hee, Verity, did you think we'd let you forget so easily? Think again…*

My vision blurred, sick. That terrible heat flared in my skull, a glowing ember fanned back into flames, and my mindmuscle twisted, ready to pop out and whiplash someone in the face. *Go on, let it out…*

I ground my teeth. "Fuck it. Why's everything gotta come back to *him*? Why can't he just leave me the hell *alone*..."

A cool, soothing tendril of mindsense wrapped over my heated thoughts. "Verity. S'okay. Chill."

I blinked, and relaxed, *poof!* The heat in my skull faded, blessedly cool and tranquil. Bless him.

Glimmer started the dishwasher. "See? Easy. Your temper is putty in my paws. Putty, I say."

My heart burst, the sticky nectar of gratitude spilling over. "Yeah, well," I grumbled, "don't get cocky, hypno-boy. Just you wait until I *really* get pissed off and we'll see who's putty."

"Bring it on," agreed Glimmer. "Can't wait. I *like* being in the rusty barbed-wire cage match you call your brain. It's so relaxing."

"Screw you."

A grin and no reply. When I resorted to unimaginative insults, he knew everything was okay.

I grinned back, best I could. Fuck, I totally love this guy. "So, now what?"

Cheerfully, he ruffled his skunk stripe. "This morning? Hardware."

"You really do have a one-track mind. Sure, let's get new phones. Those cool IRIN ones, with thought activation and laser-guided weapons and optional virtual bread slicer. Let's get a game console, too. I'd love a few rounds of Kick-Ass Urban Assassin, or whatever—"

"Not for amusement, idiot. For television." He grinned again at my puzzled expression. "Color us clueless, right? We have no idea where our enemies will strike. We could chase around all day eating our own tails."

"Mmm, Glimmer tail. Can I get fries with that?"

"Or, we could let the interwebs do the research for us. There's always some idiot with a smartphone, right? It pops up on the net, we can be there in a few minutes and minimize the damage. That means multiple outlets, portable, in parallel."

He shrugged on a jacket he'd presumably found in the same place as the t-shirt. Short black leather, buckles. Maybe the horny widow had a toy boy, but whoever he was, I doubted he looked cooler in that jacket than Glimmer. "In short," he added, flipping up his collar, "we need a pocket techno-lair. So let's stop standing around chatting, and get ourselves one."

He was already halfway out the door.

I scuttled after him, pulling on my gunmetal coat. "Right. Techno-lair, pockets. I'm on it. Don't just stand there, Glimmer. Slowing me down again."

In the corridor, light from tiny chandeliers gleamed on creamy-painted walls and silver-framed modern artworks. Glimmer grabbed the electric key from the hall table and deadlocked the door. The mirror at the end showed our reflection as we stalked side by side towards the twin glass elevators. Heh. We looked too fucking cool. Switch to slow-mo and cue the theme song. *I'm Too Sexy For My Mask.*

Glimmer waved his hand over the elevator call button, and it glowed red. I straightened my coat and tugged my tangled hair into a ponytail, surreptitiously checking my look. Close up, I wasn't so pretty, but hey: awake, dressed. What more did you want?

"So what's the plan? Smash and grab? A nice augment-armed robbery? Cool. I could use a good shop-clerk thrashing this morning."

"You're such a Neanderthal sometimes. You thrash; I just say 'watch me', and ask nicely." Glimmer flicked a finger in front of my eyes, and they boggled. "C'mon, Verity, keep up."

~ 13 ~

A few hours later, we slouched on the sofa, surrounded by empty boxes and plastic wrap and a dozen brand-new IRIN tablet computers, courtesy of the local department store. I tore the shrink wrap from another one. "Man, this is so cool. Like Christmas, only with good presents and no bickering."

We'd waltzed up to the electronics counter, careless of any Sentinels, and Glimmer had unleashed his *watch-me* trick on the hapless teenage shop assistant. She'd given him everything he asked for, her eyes blank and focused far away. And then he'd snapped his fingers again, and she'd smiled vacantly and wandered off, oblivious and unharmed.

It was creepy just how good he was.

Sure, Adonis could've charmed her into it, but it was kind of embarrassing—not to mention conspicuous—the way his victims gushed and adored. Ebenezer could've done it, too, but not without tears and wailing and a stinky mess on the floor. From Glimmer, persuasion was simple and painless. A user-friendly menace.

I swiped my screen, accessing a video-sharing site. *Ping!* Up it came, quick as you like and in glorious high definition. Sweet.

But the little IRIN logo on the tablet's frame sniggered at me like a mad rat hoarding cheese. I poked my tongue at it.

"What is that, even?" Glimmer eyed me like I'd dropped my marbles down the drain.

I slurped my tongue back in. "Nothing."

But I glared at that cheeky logo again, and it stung me with its evil eye. Iridium Industries. Vincent's corporation. Dude was an engineer, in all that spare time he had between politics and world domination and giving me the creeps. He'd invented whatever chip inside this tablet made it do all the cool stuff, like virtual image projection, instantaneous parallel sharing and optional contact-lens web integration. I half expected him to ooze from the empty box as green mist and coalesce, like fucking Dracula or something. *Velcome to my howse.*

"This one's working," I reported. "Nothing trending so far."

"Give 'em time." Glimmer slotted another tablet with a new SIM card from his little pile. "They've got all day, remember?"

I poked the cards, dubious. "Are these things hacked?"

He looked bruised. "With what, a toothpick?"

"What, you mean you can't secure our comms with mind powers alone? What kind of crime-fighter are you?"

But inside, I squirmed. It was far from impossible that we'd just opened ourselves up to Vincent's secret surveillance. Long-distance mass hypnosis. Ultraviolet telescopic mind control, some shit like that. I wouldn't put it past him.

Still, what choice? Pretty much every device you could buy these days was made by IRIN. They'd cornered the market on cool and flashy kit at a good price, and people lapped it up.

"We'll be safe for a while," said Glimmer. "New phone numbers, new IP. Just don't log on to anything, okay? Use anonymous and guest IDs." He set his tablet on the coffee table with the others. A dozen screens, showing video, news, live blogs, police transmissions, real-time search algorithms for aliases and social media mentions and stuff I didn't even recognize. "Gadget heaven. Don't you feel better?"

"Immediately. Um, what's that one even doing?" I pointed at a screen that flashed through images at high speed. "Scanning for tentacle porn?"

"Face recognition on CCTV, idiot. I cut some pics from Sophron's video. Best I've got."

"Good job. For what CCTV is worth, with people who teleport. Still, gotta try, right?"

"I want to do more research on the Sentinel system, too. Our good buddy the mayor keeps saying it doesn't have surveillance kit hardwired into it, but…"

"But bullshit, right?" I snorted. "Like he'd neglect an opportunity like that."

"His claims stand up," Glimmer admitted. "I've tested it. No transmissions."

"Except for the whole *fuck-you-augments* thing."

"Well, yeah. It's gotta be a passive system. Like a stealth sonar buoy for superpowers. It doesn't ping. It just sits there, waiting, until an augment blunders by." He shrugged, helpless. "But as for what it's actually detecting…?"

"The same thing that augmentium disrupts," I suggested. "That sherbety tingle on the tip of your tongue when someone's augmented… You do get that taste, right? Or is that just me?"

He nodded. "Sure. More like a smell. But no one really knows how augmentium works. No one's managed to isolate the essential energy of augment before."

"Well, now he can," I grumbled. "Great. Why is it always the warmongers who've got the best kit?"

"Paranoia, that's why. This is what these maniacs do. They've got armies of techno-nerds working day and night, inventing neat new ways to fuck up their enemies."

"And to think I've only got you…" My senses prickled. "Hold on. What did you just say?"

"Essential energy? Maniacs? Army of techno-nerds?"

"Yeah, that." My mind stalked and sniffed, slipping back into its old hunting mode. "D'you remember a villain called Weasel?"

We'd fought Weasel a few months back, when we were hunting down the ugly chemical weapon I'd once used to threaten the city, in the bad old days when I was *wrong*.

Glimmer wrinkled his nose. "Iceclaw's sidekick? Ratty little Gallery dude with whiskers and a tail? How could I forget?"

"That's the guy. Remember we overheard him blabbing about the laboratory where they reverse-engineered that weapon? Some team of eggheads who worked for Razorfire."

"Sure. Never could keep his toothy mouth shut."

"Only so many hours in the day, right? Even for Mr. Never-Sleeps Evil Genius. He can't do everything himself. So, if he *does* have an army of mad scientists building augmentium handcuffs and poisonous superweapons...?"

"...then where are they?" finished Glimmer. "Might be a good place to ask questions about the Sentinels."

"Exactly. Razorfire will never tell us anything, but a bunch of boffins with Einstein hair and pocket protectors might." I grinned. "We can be persuasive, after all."

"He could just be doing this stuff at IRIN. He's the boss; the tech-heads there do what he tells 'em. Hiding in plain sight?"

"Could be," I admitted. "But he had to account for all IRIN's research time when he was elected mayor. It's all on the public record."

"He's lied on the public record before. Something to investigate, anyway." Glimmer plucked up a tablet and dictated rapid notes. "Sentinel specs are public domain... check genesis of Pyrotox II weapon... original IRIN patents for cell technology... concept drawings... search off-grid for an in-confidence version..."

I squinted at the last tablet on the table. Wingdings code, plus a glowing green progress bar creeping left to right. "What's that one crunching, baseball stats?"

"It's ripping the layers from Sophron's video upload."

"Right. Good plan. Uh... why?"

Glimmer shrugged, vague. "Just an odd feeling. Can't put my finger on it. Thought she looked familiar, maybe."

I'd already wrung my brain and juiced out a big fat nothing. "Sorry, dude. Can't help. Never seen her before. Maybe another of your bedroom B&E buddies?"

"Mmm. Anyway, worth a look. Also, crawling a few darker sites for more video we haven't seen yet. I'm thinking this might not be their first rodeo, so to speak."

I nodded approval. "Everyone's got an origin story. Villains don't just spring fully formed from nowhere, right?"

"Did you see how they carried on? All that posing and showing off?"

"Kinda theatrical?"

"Yeah. I'm thinking they enjoy being in the public eye—at least, in the eye of the sort of people who might appreciate it."

"What, you mean like a dark net villains' message board? 'Here's the sick shit I did today, post your snuff and torture trophy pics here'?" I made a face. "Yuk."

"No argument here. And if such a site exists, Razorfire's probably on it. But it's worth a try."

"Well, be careful, dude. I saw a lot of fondling going on between those two. You'll probably unearth some gruesome lost-virginity tape." But I shivered, haunted by the memory of Sophron and Flash kissing in the forest amid the ruins of my life. His shirt peeling off, her hands hungry on the pale flesh underneath. Like dead Iceclaw, they were aroused by destruction. Getting off on misery.

Damn it. It just didn't add up. Vincent had used Iceclaw ruthlessly, sacrificed him without hesitation to prove his point with me. And Iceclaw had been Vincent's friend, as much as he ever had any.

These two? He'd give 'em up in a heartbeat. They meant less than nothing to him. All that breathless enjoyment, the touching, the gleeful giggles? It just wasn't Vincent's style.

It wasn't destruction *per se* that got him off. It was power. Control, the sensation of surrender, that exquisite cosmic *crack!* as his victim broke. Inflicting garden-variety misery, on the other hand, was less recreation and more his self-serving duty. His archvillain day job.

My blood chilled and burned. Trophy pics. Surrender. Holy fuck-a-duckling. What if he'd…?

"Verity? You with me?"

I blinked and snapped to. But I could feel my cheeks aflame. "Uh. Listen, um… if you see anything about me on that website…"

"Done." No hesitation. "It's none of mine, Verity. You know that."

"Sure, I just—"

He held up one finger, hushing me. Grabbed a tablet, swiped up the volume. "Listen."

Crackling, raised voices, transmissions that burst and cut out. "What the hell is that? Sounds like shit's hitting the ceiling down there."

"Emergency channels." Glimmer grabbed his kit. "First responders, you said, for maximum shock? That's the frequency for fire department HQ."

Fire. Shit. Sophron and Flash, as they'd promised? Or was it *him*?

I jumped up, checked my pockets. Mask, phone. No handgun, not yet. It'd have to do. Like we'd have a fucking chance anyway, if Vincent had decided to go burning. "So where's the fire?"

Glimmer pocketed his mask, holstered his pistol. "It's not an emergency callout. It's headquarters. The fire department is under attack." A ghostly smile. "Gotta give 'em points for impeccable aim. There's no way our buddy the mayor can ignore that."

Together, we sprinted for the corridor, and hurtled down the indoor fire stairs, the exit door clanging behind us. No time to wait for the elevator.

"How are we getting there, again?" I panted, tripping down the smooth concrete steps. Glimmer used to ride a bike, before it got melted to metal by you know who.

He vaulted over the stair rail, landing at the bottom, half a story down. He waved a silver proximity car key at me. "Widow Swanky's got wheels. I figured we'd borrow. She won't mind."

I followed, from further up, bouncing down on cushions of invisible force and blowing the door open, *bang!* "Right. Bet she travels in style, too. Let me guess: beige Volvo estate?"

We burst into the underground parking lot, where smooth concrete shone under fluorescent lights and blue security lasers flickered around the roll-down steel exit grill. Sleek European SUVs with blackened windows, glossy hybrids, a silver vintage Rolls Royce.

I pointed at a glaring purple smart car the size of a matchbox. "Don't tell me: you hypnotized the un-hippest rich lady on earth."

"Ye of little faith." Glimmer grinned, and a deep-throated engine exploded into life. Lurid green McLaren F1, shaped like a futuristic fighter jet with afterburners, a cool and sexy million bucks' worth.

My mouth watered. "Dude, I take back all the bad things I said about you. You sure can pick 'em."

"I'm aware of that. Look what else I ended up with."

"Screw you. I'm driving."

"The fuck you are."

We both scrambled for the central driver's seat. He beat me, and with a good-natured curse I squeezed into left-hand shotgun. White leather, smooth silver instruments sprinkled with fully optioned flashing lights. I felt like I was reclining six inches off the ground in the cockpit of Darth Vader's tie fighter.

The exit grill was already rolling up. I buckled my seat belt and pulled down the gull-wing door. "Hit it, rock star."

"Yes, ma'am." Glimmer laughed, a kid in a candy store, and jumped on the gas.

Ker-pow! Acceleration slammed me deep into my seat. With a rubbery squeal, we bulleted out onto the ramp, missing the grill by an inch, and took the corner onto the street smooth as silk at sixty miles an hour. The back end barely slid out. Damn, the boy can drive.

Course he can. Jealous Verity, a hungry worm of discontent that crawled in my flesh. *He does everything better than you. Think you're more than hired help? He only keeps you around because you break things when he needs you to. You do the dirty jobs, and he gets to stay perfect...*

Inwardly, I scoffed. Not true. He'd stayed with me when Adonis left me behind. Glimmer was my friend.

Is that what you think? The worm giggled, unhinged. *He stayed with you because Adonis won't stand for his saintly bullshit. If he's so much your friend, why didn't he fight when Adonis unleashed on you? Huh?*

I blinked, stupefied. Well, why hadn't he?

That's right. He likes it up there, on that pedestal where you worship him. The more badly broken you are, the more superior he feels. You're his never-ending ego trip. Ever think of that?

Treacherous resentment seeped into my blood, a warm undercurrent of poison. In my darker dreams? I'd thought of it, all right.

I'd raged at it.

But I glanced across at Glimmer, cool and exhilarated in the driver's seat, fanging it at ninety along Bayside Boulevard with his striped hair poking up like a deranged skunk's tail—Glimmer, the one precious thing that stood between me and destruction—and I throttled my resentment back down.

~ 14 ~

The headquarters of Sapphire City Fire Department is a large oblong building amid the bustle of Market Street where they keep corporate offices and computer systems, plus twenty-four yellow fire engines and their crews. It was already burning when we tore up in our shiny green hero-mobile and squealed to a sonic-boom stop.

I caught my breath, my pulse racing. Now *that* was how you arrived at a crime scene. Conspicuous, sure, but cool's gotta count for something.

We jumped out, and I sniffed the smoky air. My augmented senses tingled… but I couldn't smell mint, or that peculiar not-quite-gasoline scent that signaled *him*. My stomach watered, relieved. Yeah. Relief was what it was. Not disappointment. Not frustration that, once again, I wouldn't get to face him in open battle.

Whatever. Didn't mean we weren't in deep shit.

"Electrical fire," I reported. "No incendiary. Not Razorfire."

Glimmer just pointed.

The entire middle section of the building was crushed. Dust, smoke and flames billowed. Rubble littered the street. Fire crews and police officers dragged injured people and bodies from the wreckage. Blood trails painted crimson in the dust. Ambulances had started to arrive, sirens wailing, and fire engines—the ones that weren't crushed to twisted metal—were raising ladders and unraveling hoses. Men and women wearing hard hats and fireproof coats yelled into radios and cell phones.

"Assholes better not scratch our car," I muttered, as we strode through choking smoke towards the parked police cars forming a temporary barrier to keep back the milling crowd. People videoed with smartphones, texted, jumped on their tiptoes to see. "Fucking vultures. What did I say about civil disobedience? They *love* this shit."

"It's just curiosity."

"Fucking macabre is what it is." I shielded my eyes, searching the leaping flames. Another section of building crumbled. "No water yet. They're setting up for foam. Why hasn't anyone switched the power grid off?"

"Maybe they're trying." Glimmer put his mask on. "Fog of battle, all that."

I snorted as I tied mine, dragging my hair out of the way. "Or maybe someone on high's being obstructive—"

Ka-POW! Lightning struck the closest fire engine, and it exploded.

I stumbled to my feet, power wrapped around my fist... and high-pitched laughter slithered from the smoke to taunt me.

"Hello, hero," Sophron sang. "Glad you could make it."

Glimmer uttered an un-Glimmer-like curse.

Woof! Sophron teleported. Right beside me, a jangle of blue dreadlocks and patched jeans. And kicked me in the kidneys. Hard.

I crumpled. Agony ground huge molars into the base of my spine. Red mist drowned my vision, and my legs stung warm. Fuck, did I just wet myself? A gunshot cracked, deafening. Wildly, I scrabbled for her—but she'd already vanished.

Glimmer dragged me up, pistol in hand. I stumbled, acid bubbling up into my mouth. I spat and groaned as my vision cleared. "Christ in a crackhouse. That hurt."

"Can you run?"

"To beat that uppity grunge witch? I can fucking *fly*."

"Then now would be a good time." He grabbed my hand, and we sprinted towards the burning building.

Beside us, wrapped in smoke, a fire crew wearing breathing apparatus were spurting foam onto the flames like hair mousse squirting from a can... Abruptly, the stream ceased, and the fire crew ran and waved their arms at each other in spasms of *what the fuck?*

Their foam squirter was broken. "Someone's on sabotage duty," I called.

Glimmer pointed at a shadow running along in front of the ruined building. "There's Flash. Must be someone else."

I frowned, remembering my idea that Sophron had an invisible member on her team. I concentrated on my augmented senses, searching through the blinding smoke... and a sniggering giggle pricked my ears.

Snicker, snicker.

Not Sophron. My nose twitched and I smelled...

Blam! Another blast of lightning blew the top of the concrete watchtower off. The ground trembled. "How has she got so many tricks?" I panted, as we ran up what was left of the front steps and crouched in the shelter of a pile of twisted steel and rubble. "What is she, a Swiss Army knife?"

Glimmer wasn't listening. "Block your ears."

I knew better than to argue. I plastered my palms over my ears.

Not a moment too soon. Glimmer let rip with a shimmering shockwave of mindsense. I didn't know what flavor it was. I've seen him put people to sleep, knock them off their feet with dizzy fits, hurl them into a killing rage to put them off their guard. All I felt was a sonar-like *thud* in my skull, like I'd knocked on a piece of wood underwater.

Whatever that was, it popped his eyes wide. "Found her," he reported. "Eleven o'clock high, a hundred feet. Grab my hand."

"Huh?"

He pulled my left hand from my ear, wrapping his fist around mine. "You can go further than I can. Throw this."

And he filled my hand with a burning white starglobe of mindfuck.

What was it? How did he do that? I didn't care. I just flexed my mindmuscle and *threw*.

Eleven o'clock, high. The little flaming sun sailed aloft and went supernova.

Silent starlight shot in all directions, a blinding white firework. So beautiful. I stared, transfixed, watching it fall towards me...

Glimmer hurled me to the ground in his arms. Instinctively, I curled against him. Soothing Glimmery mindsense encircled me, protecting me from whatever havoc we'd just wrought. The starlight shimmered over us, and died...

And Sophron screamed. A bright, unholy howl of agony that faded into silence.

Glimmer still cradled me in a warm bubble of safety. I wanted to stay there. But slowly, I uncurled, on my hands and knees in the dust. "What was that?" I whispered. I hardly dared to ask.

He rubbed dirt from his hair, a grey cloud. "Just a little conscience bomb."

Jesus. I gulped sick laughter, more thankful than ever that Glimmer was on my side. "Nice. Let's go find her."

I jumped up, ready to fight. But a chilly fear finger caressed my spine.

I brushed it off, belligerent. Fuck it. This chick was toast in my griller. Mincemeat in my hamburger maker. A fucking banana smoothie in the food processor of my vengeance...

But my knees shook. Cold sweat soaked my shirt. Jesus, I couldn't do this. I felt like I had when I was eight years old, the night Dad burst in clutching Mom's marbled stone body in his arms. I wanted to curl up in a little ball and weep.

Beside me, Glimmer choked, and doubled over, clutching his middle, and in the midst of gasping for air, I realized what was going on.

An augment. Someone was unleashing on us. And I was crippled with fear. More afraid than I'd been in all my years, and I'd faced the wrath of dozens of villains. My own family. Hell, I'd fought Razorfire at his most furious with more composure than I could muster right now.

Glimmer crumpled on his knees in the dust, spewing. My guts watered and muscles loosened. Oh, Jesus, no…

The air before us shimmered, a haze that solidified into… a girl. Sophron. She'd been there all along. Invisible. Watching us. Goddamn it.

I tried to whip my mindmuscle into action. But I was glued to the spot, limbs rigid and quivering. Fight or flight, hell. I couldn't move an inch. For all my power and determination, I couldn't run right now to save my life. Or Glimmer's.

Blood trickled down Sophron's forehead, ringing her bruised eyes. She'd hit her head somewhere, and her ghostly face was scratched crimson, like she'd raked her nails down both cheeks. The conscience bomb. Glimmer's tricks had hit her, and for a moment or two? She'd been sorry for the terrible things she'd done.

She'd felt *guilt*.

Snap! Flash materialized beside her. His black-dyed hair was caked with dust. Sanguine tears streaked his face, and he'd bitten his bottom lip until it tore. Blood trickled down his left forearm, slicking his fingers bright red.

"Heroes." Sophron's words dripped acid contempt. "Look at you now. Spewing on your knees in the dirt. Where's your famous courage? Where the fuck is *your* guilt, for the lies you feed us all?"

Blindly, Glimmer fumbled for his pistol. Flash kicked it from his hand. I staggered, trying to reach Sophron, but she shoved me with some invisible force, easily toppling me to my knees. Glimmer tried to kindle his mindsense, hurl some glittering spell, but it flickered out in his fingers. Weakly, I crawled towards her on my belly, painfully slow.

Flash pulled a phone from his jeans pocket. Took our picture. Nodded, solemn as usual. No delight there. Just dogged, driven obedience.

Sophron stroked his hair, favored him with a blue-lipped kiss. "You know what? I'm not even going to bother to slaughter the two of you." Her shrill voice raised, calling out to an audience. Naturally, we'd be on video somewhere. "If this is the best you've got, Sapphire City? Then we're *all* headed for hell. See you tomorrow, viewers."

She waved mockingly, and with a dusty *poof!* they disappeared.

I sprawled on my front in the dirt, panting. Dust clogged my mouth. The horrid fear was gone. My limbs and muscles were mine again. But the humiliation still burned.

Glimmer staggered up, coughing. He wiped the mess from his face, spat out dirt and bile. He reached down for my hand, and for once I didn't even try to do it without him. He hauled me to my feet. Glimmer had been hauling me to my feet, one way or another, for as long as I could remember.

Around us, the building burned. Fire crews ran. Medics dragged limp bodies from the rubble. The air hung with smoke and dust.

"Did you see her?" Glimmer didn't sound humiliated, particularly, or angry. Just… tired. "Did you see all the things she can…?"

He didn't finish. Didn't need to. I'd seen it. I knew. Now, we both knew.

"She copied Uncle Mike." I spoke it out loud. It was real. No reason not to. "And Jeremiah. Ebenezer, too. She's stealing our augments, Glimmer. How the *fuck* is she stealing our…?"

I dragged my mask off, wiping gritty eyes. She'd done me, too. Pushed me to my knees with my own augment. Crushed buildings and hurled uprooted trees with it. That whole time at the asylum? She'd been fighting us with our own powers.

God help us if she ever copied Glimmer. Or Razorfire.

"Eh?" I jumped back from a groping hand.

"You okay, ma'am?" A uniformed paramedic, his young face grim. He peered into my eyes, checking for concussion. "Watch my finger. Tell me what day it is."

"I'm okay." I pushed his hand away. Behind him, Glimmer swiftly pulled off his mask. "Really. It's Tuesday, my name's Verity. I'm fine. Just a bystander. Go treat those who need it." I ushered the kid on his way.

"C'mon," I muttered to Glimmer, "she's gone. Nothing more we can do here."

"But…" He sighed and nodded, and we headed unsteadily for the barrier. Nothing more to see here. Nothing to be done, except clean up the mess we'd let her make.

More injured people staggered around like zombies, stained with dirt and blood. I helped a disoriented woman up and pointed her towards the ambulance. She stumbled, bleeding from the head. Glimmer swept her up, carried her, dropped her on the step of the paramedics' truck parked beside that crippled fire engine.

I wiped my nose. It was tingling. I sniffed, twitching. That smell again… wet dog?

No. Wet *fur*. Smelly, giggling, ratty fur.

Gotcha.

"We're fine," Glimmer told the paramedic patiently. "Both of us. We're just…"

"…looking for a friend." I reached beneath the fire engine's front fender. Grabbed a skinny furred ankle, and pulled.

Weasel squeaked indignantly, and thrashed the whippy tail sticking out from a hole in his trousers.

But I dragged him out. "Lookie here. Who's been wrecking fire engines, naughty boy?"

Weasel grinned, whiskers twitching. His big front teeth chomped over his lip, shining white. He wore a smelly button-down checkered shirt with fringes, which looked like he'd stolen it from some fucked-up lumberjack boot-scooting party. "Hello, Seeker. I've so missed your ugly face. Not."

"Likewise, loser. You pining for your boss-buddy Iceclaw? What a shame I killed his maniac ass. You boys must've had such fun together."

Weasel—his real name was buried under years of smart-ass lies—always looked more like a rat to me. Scruffy mouse-brown hair, oversized prehensile ears, whiskery snout of a face. Sharp clawed toes wriggling on the ends of long bony bare feet that poked out from his short trousers. Let's face it: not a class act.

Sometimes, I almost feel sorry for the guy. I mean, what hope did he have of growing up well adjusted? Not his fault he looked like a Looney Tunes reject.

But the asshole Gallery villain part? That was totally his fault.

I winked at the goggling paramedic and pulled Weasel upright, with my fingers clamped tight into the flesh between his neck and shoulder. "Look, I found him. Thank God he's okay. Time to go home, *friend*."

And I frog-marched him towards the hero-mobile, a startled Glimmer in my wake.

"What are we doing, again?" Glimmer whispered as we strolled, insouciant, avoiding eye contact.

"Not you as well." Weasel scowled, and tried to run. I didn't let go. He kept struggling. "Great. I like you guys *so* much. You're so *nice* to me. Ornery pair of assholes…"

"He's working with Sophron. He might know something." Last time we'd met, we'd tied Weasel up and left him to explain a truckload of chemical weapons to the cops. He'd gotten off lightly, thanks to some slippery lawyer tricks, but he'd still done a couple of months in shiny new augment-proof Rock Island Prison for illegal substance trafficking. Not the first time I'd sent him down. He didn't exactly count us among his best buddies. "We'll just have a friendly little chat. You like chats, don't you, Weasel?"

"Hands off me, you two-faced psycho bitch. I ain't telling you jack." Weasel wriggled, a mouse in a cat's jaws. I cuffed him over the head with a fist of talent. He aimed a reproachful glance at me, and started singing off-key. "I know a bear who you don't know…"

"Changed sides, have you, scumsucker?" He kept singing and kicked at my ankles. I dodged. "Joined the rebel alliance? The Emperor won't be happy with you."

He twirled his tail in one hand and skipped a few steps, kicking up his heels. "Yogi, Yogi bear… Yogi, Yogi bear…"

"You're an artist, Weasel. True musical genius." We reached the F1, which now sported a coat of dust, and I grabbed Weasel's skinny wrists and bound them behind his back with the bottom half of his shirt, which I tore off with a satisfying *rrrip!* The fabric felt greasy, loaded with grime. I wrinkled my nose. "Jesus, you stink. Ever hear of a shower?"

"Yogi, Yogi bear…"

I frowned. Luggage compartment didn't look big enough. Hmm. Surely I could stuff his scrawny carcass in if I shoved hard enough…

Glimmer waved a scolding finger. "Seat."

Goody-goody. I sighed and pulled up the gull-wing door. "Get in, freak."

Weasel just kept singing, scratching one ankle with his toe claws. "Yogi's got a girlfriend bear…"

I hooked my foot around his calf and shoved him inside. He bounced up and down as I fought to strap him in. "Cindy, Cindy bear…" He aimed a lightning-quick bite at my hand.

I barely evaded it. Fuck, the little squeezer was fast. Those teeth could chew through steel. I clocked him under the chin, hard enough to snap his jaws together. "Shut it, ratbag. Want me to tape your mouth shut?"

At last, I jammed the clip into the buckle and yanked the belt tight as I could. Shrugged off my coat and wrapped it around his head, so he couldn't see where we were taking him. Gross. It'd totally need a wash now.

"Fuck you, hero trash," he sang inside, without breaking his tune. "Cindy, Cindy bear…"

In the driver's seat, Glimmer sighed. Weasel's store of dirty ditties was legendary. "Tell me he's not gonna sing all the way home."

"I imagine he is." I climbed in on the left and pulled the door shut. "We *could* tape his jaw shut," I suggested over the bear-flavored din. "Or I could just punch him until he shuts up. Or, stuff a…"

"No, it's okay." Glimmer shot me a dark glance, as if he wasn't sure whether I meant it or not. "I'll just drive louder."

~ 15 ~

Half an hour later, I had Weasel's wrists cable-tied around the toilet in Widow Swanky's guest bathroom. His skinny bristled legs poked out on the sand-colored tiles, clawed toes twitching in time with his God-awful singing. The window was frosted, the door closed. He'd never identify this place.

I yanked the coat from his head. "Rise and shine, pissface."

Weasel bristled his whiskers. "You suck," he announced, breaking off his song in the middle of a verse. "No, really. I mean it. You *totally* suck. All my life, I've had bastards like you kicking my ass. Think you're special? Go screw a pig's head."

"Nice." Behind me, Glimmer folded his arms. "Give him a glass of water, why don't you?"

"He does sound a little croaky. Must be all that musical talent." I filled a glass and tipped water into Weasel's mouth. He clamped his lips together, but his buck teeth got in the way and he swallowed, spluttering.

"There." I wiped his whiskery chin, satisfied. "Don't say we're not nice to you, furry. Now talk."

"About what? You ain't asked me anything. Christ, you people are so dumb."

"Keep the wise-ass remarks to a minimum, and this will go easier on you." I poked him in the belly. "Sophron. Who is she?"

He squirmed, crunching his toes. "She's my mom."

Heh. Ticklish, was he? I poked again, hunting for his ribs. "Wise-ass," I warned.

"Honest. She's my *mommy*. Popped me out her butt one night after munching too much curried egg… wahh!" He screeched and wriggled as I tickled him harder. "No fair. Stop it. Wahh! Okay, okay, ease up. I'll talk. Just stop it, you bad woman! Ah!" And he burst into hiccoughing laughter.

I backed off, disgusted. "Don't know what you're so cheery about. You're a traitor, Weasel. A rat fink snitch. When Razorfire catches you, he'll strip your flea-ridden skin off with his fingernails."

A glint of darkness crossed Weasel's beady eyes. He was still giggling softly, but sweat popped on his forehead.

Gotcha.

"And he will catch you, Weasel," I added, inspired. "Don't think I won't leave you super-glued to a lamp post out front of City Hall for him to find."

His face greened, but he sneered. "I've done time, bitch, thanks to you. General population. How d'you think that went down for me? Think you can scare my furry ass?"

"Maybe not. But *he* should scare you, Weasel. He really should. Don't think for a moment it'll be quick. I should think he'll take his sweet time. Make an example of you."

"Or what, hero?" Weasel sounded weary. Sick of being beaten up and used. "You'll kill me anyway. Might as well go out in screaming Technicolor."

I glanced at Glimmer, who shrugged. I crouched by Weasel's side. "Let's do a deal. You tell us what you know, and we'll… let you go. Anywhere you want. No strings. You scuttle off into the night, never to be seen again. Razorfire never needs to know."

Hope lit across his face, and just as quickly died. "Don't believe you."

"Your options aren't exactly myriad," Glimmer pointed out.

"Sorry, gimp, don't buy it. Why would you just let me go?"

I grinned. "Because it's her we want. You're insignificant, Weasel. Just fly dirt on our windshield."

"Great. Thanks for nothing. And what if I don't talk?"

"Lamp post, glue, flayed upside down with a rusty scalpel dipped in lemon juice. Your choice."

Weasel wriggled his cable-tied wrists. Sighed, resigned. And beckoned me closer with a twitch of his nose.

Cautiously, I leaned in.

He whispered, a waft of smelly rat breath. "It's Sophron. I couldn't help it, okay? It just happened. I'm... well, I'm in love with her."

"Uh huh." I supposed it was possible.

He nodded, licking his incisors eagerly. "She's my girly-friend. I found her on the internet under *crazy blue-haired bitch* and it was love at first sight. She sits me on her lap and feeds me grapes, and her skinny brother sucks my dick." He cackled, delighted. "Bite me, Seeker, you weak-assed coward. I am *not* a snitch. And you don't know *jack*."

He spat at me. *Splat!* A blob of Weasel-spit hit my cheek.

I recoiled and slapped him, *crack!* A mix of hand and invisible force. His skull clanged against the toilet. He shook himself and spat blood.

Had I broken one of his back teeth? I didn't care. I wanted to smash the rest of them, too. Crush his face in my fist, hear the bones break and yell *don't you call me weak, you rabid little squeezer...*

Glimmer pulled me aside. "Ease off, Verity. C'mon."

I shook him off, itching. I'd let Weasel bait me too easily. I knew that. He wasn't afraid of me? Fine. My ego could take it. But it stung me like crazy that he might be braver than I was. That he could brush off with a shrug the monsters that haunted my dreams.

I'd threatened him with Razorfire's vengeance, and he'd just *laughed* at me.

141

Glimmer prodded Weasel's leg with one boot. "So Flash is her brother, is he?"

Weasel blinked. "Never said that."

"Yeah, you did. Too busy being a wise-ass to stop your mouth running off?"

"Maybe I'm just leading you where you want to go, pretty boy."

A smoky Glimmer smile. "I don't think so, girlfriend. Frankly, I don't think you're clever enough to fool me."

"That a fact?" A sullen gleam of challenge in those beady black eyes.

"That's a fact. So how d'you know they're related? Didn't act much like brother and sister for mine. Looked to me like they were in *lurve*. How'd you feel about that?"

"Never said nothing." Weasel licked his bloody lip, gazing at the ceiling.

"C'mon, man," Glimmer coaxed, "I'm good cop, okay? You know how this works. We can sit here all day with lots of blood and howling, or you can give me something. You like Sophron, right? You like her a lot."

Weasel blew bloody bubbles around his teeth. But his face was dark, reddened.

"See," Glimmer persisted, "I'm asking myself why a stinky little no-friends squeaker like you—no offense—would desert the Gallery for a pair of punk-ass rogue villains."

"Who says they ain't Gallery?" But Weasel's gaze slipped, and respect for Glimmer's wits warmed me yet again.

"Unless," Glimmer continued, "something's in it for Weasel. Something he wants badly enough to risk Razorfire's wrath. So now, I'm asking myself: what does Weasel want more than anything?"

Weasel stared, and his snickering died. "Oh, screw you. You didn't. You mind-reading motherfucker…"

Glimmer gave a gentle shrug. "I just grab what's out there in neon lights, dude. Sorry."

"Enough, okay?" Weasel licked his chops and glared balefully up at us. "All my life, there's been people like you, or Razorfire, or the rest of those smug assholes. Even Deck despised me, and he was supposed to be my friend. 'Weasel, you ratty bastard loser, go buy the milk or mop up the blood or scrub the goddamn john.' Need a sewer pipe chewed through? Call Weasel. You think I *like* chewing sewer pipes, you fucking idiots? You think I enjoy scraping up everyone's messes?"

The tip of his pink nose glistened wet, and his eyes glittered, rage and tears.

"So what, you trying to get in Sophron's pants? You really think a stinky no-dick rodent like you has a chance?" I winced at my own brutality. But no time for sympathy with villains. I tried to keep in mind that I'd seen Weasel giggling like a fiend with his good buddy Deck—Iceclaw, in case I'd forgotten—over the idea of drenching the city in deadly nerve gas and killing thousands of people. Weasel had commissioned the ugly stuff on Razorfire's instruction. He'd done time for manslaughter. He wasn't a nice guy. "So sad. What a pity Flash got there before you."

"Shit in your gutter mouth," Weasel spat. "You're not worthy to speak her name. She's *polite* to me. She says *please* and *thank you*. She doesn't look at me like I'm slime." He stared straight ahead, mutinous. "So piss off, with your safe little lives and your normal-looking faces and your heroic bullshit. You know nothing about misery or loyalty. A scumbag I might be, but I won't snitch on the only person who's ever shown me an inch of fucking *respect*."

All he'd ever wanted. Just someone to treat him like a *person*. And we'd ridiculed and despised him, called him a freak. Just like everyone else.

"Go right ahead," he added carelessly, "leave me for Razorfire if you want. Let him torture me to death. Because, you know what?" He hawked blood onto the tiles, defiant. "I don't actually *give* a shit."

I crouched and grabbed his chin to make him look at me. No way would I let him clam up now. "So, what's the sorry story, now Razorfire's gone all politics and is feeding the Gallery to the muncher? Are you the only Gallery turncoat? I don't think so. Is Sophron collecting her own gang? Who's she got on her side?"

Cold, Weasely silence.

"So she is, then. Where does she hole up?"

Just a *fuck-you* twitch of whiskers.

"Where?" I demanded. "Tell me."

A shrug.

"Where are they planning to strike next?"

Weasel's shoulders hitched again, and a snort bubbled from his nose. He wasn't shrugging. He was giggling. Cocky little runt was *laughing* at me.

I grabbed his throat. "Where are the eggheads you told us about?"

"Up my ass. Ha ha! Itchy little fuckers, too."

I shook him, digging my fingers in. "The think tank where Razorfire builds his weapons. Where is it?"

He laughed aloud, unable to hold it in any more. Great guffaws, his skinny belly heaving. "Weapons?" he wheezed. "Please. You really don't know jack, do you?"

My mind reeled. They weren't making weapons? "Then what?"

He choked more laughter, his eyes streaming. "You stupid whore… no, you're less than a whore, Seeker. Whores I can respect. It's business. But you? You're just a lab rat, same as the rest."

"What d'you mean?"

Wet crimson giggles bubbled from his nose. "Think you're so special? Lab fucking *rat* is what you are. You let the boss man fuck with your *brain* this whole time, not to mention whatever else he's been fucking. And what've you gotten out of his sick little games? Not one goddamn thing, that's what."

My blood fried with impotent rage and before I could think, I'd summoned a sizzling fistful of talent and jammed it up his nose.

He struggled, spluttering blood. I shoved harder, deeper. He couldn't breathe. He thrashed, a wet muffled sound coming from his chest. "Where is it?" I screeched. "Tell me, you murdering turd-brain, or I'll jam this so far down your throat you're shitting bricks."

Glimmer flung me backwards, ripping my grip free. I tumbled onto my back, gasping. "Back the fuck off," he hissed. "Jesus, what's gotten into you?"

Weasel was laughing and panting at the same time. Bloody phlegm flecked his whiskers. I scrambled up, reeling. My lungs burned. My mindmuscle howled at me to dive in, grab him, throttle him until his eyes popped…

Glimmer yanked me into the living room and slammed the bathroom door shut after us.

"What the hell was that?" Tight-lipped, pale, his midnight eyes burning violet.

My mindmuscle whiplashed, and a mirror on the wall shattered. "He was gonna tell me," I spluttered. "He was. Just let me…"

"You nearly killed him! We don't do torture, Verity. We're the good guys. Remember?"

The compulsion I'd felt with Weasel in my grip—the vicious rage-bright need to shove that fistful of force deep down into his body until he stopped wriggling—returned, salted sharp with guilt. "Right. Because you're so damn virtuous, Glimmer. What d'you call what *you* just did to him? A friendly chat?"

"I call it *interrogation*. I tricked him into talking. I didn't try to suffocate him."

Sickly, I laughed. "Give me a break. You guilt-bombed a socio-path today, for fuck's sake. Retrofitted a guiltless girl with a conscience, after all the things she's done. In what universe isn't that torture?"

"That's different." Glimmer's stare didn't even flicker. "She did those things, not me. If she can't face it, so much the better. Maybe she'll think twice next time."

His certainty—self-assurance I'd sure as shit never have again—hacked my flesh raw. "Oh, so *mental* torture is okay, but whacking Weasel upside the head is such a damn crime? That shitweed has

145

tried to kill us more than once. Exactly how nice to him do we need to be?" I was practically yelling now. My nerves thrashed and sparked, out of control. Fuck, I needed to calm down before I broke something.

Glimmer let out a steadying breath. "Look, I don't…"

"You know what? Keep your righteous bullshit." My whole body itched to explode. Fuck, he was so damn *calm*. Didn't even have the decency to lose his temper properly, to jump into the gutter with me and say horrible things back, so I wouldn't feel like such a bitch. "Do you know how *exhausting* it is, just being in the same *room* with you? Must be so nice for you, up there in perfection land. So sorry I don't measure up."

Now I'd hurt him. I could see it, the way he swallowed, tight and controlled. "I never said I was perfect."

"Maybe not," I spat, "but you sure as hell act like we all should *think* it."

Silence.

Venom stung, bitter and horrid on my tongue. I wanted to spit it out, unsay what I'd said. I rubbed my eyes, fighting that crippling headache all over again. "I'm sorry. I didn't mean—"

"It's okay." Distant. Cool. Like he didn't care.

Clearly, it wasn't okay. Whatever cohesion had developed between us—whatever bond we'd forged over the last few harrowing days and weeks—I'd just shattered it. "Glimmer…"

He just opened the bathroom door. Flipped a knife from his pocket, cut Weasel free, and pulled him out.

Weasel came, stumbling and snorting bloodied laughter. "Know what it feels like, don't you, being the gutter-dweller?" he called to me over his shoulder, as Glimmer hauled him to the front door. "Enjoy it, Seeker. Hope you fucking choke on it."

The door slammed, and I was alone.

Fuck.

~ 16 ~

Numbly, I mopped up the mess in the bathroom. Tossed the bloodied paper towels in the trash. Took yet another shower, rinsed the smoke and bruises from my body.

I banged my forehead against the tiles, let the water flow through my hair. The walls cackled, shuddering inwards to crush me. Great work, Verity. What a perfect day you've had. Got thrashed again by the upstart villains who killed your uncle. Said horrible things to your only friend. Let a grimy little Weasel-assed bad guy taunt you into a killing rage.

Because that's all it was, right? I just lost my temper for a bit. I would've pulled it together. I wouldn't really have suffocated Weasel.

Right. You keep telling yourself that. The spiny hate-serpent in my guts uncoiled, spiteful. *What if Glimmer doesn't come back? Who'll drag you back from the precipice then?*

I dried myself. Dressed. Smoothed my Weasel-smelling coat, tied my wet hair back and tried not to think about what I'd do if Glimmer was really gone. If today was the day he finally realized I wasn't worth bothering with, and decided not to put up with my shit anymore… and cold wind howled through an empty hollow in my heart. Facing this alone seemed worse than impossible. Without him—without his unerring compass for right and wrong—what was the point of any of it?

In the living room, our collection of tablets glistened on the table, doing their thing. Listlessly, I swiped my thumb across one, leaving a smeared fingerprint on the plastiglass. The screen flashed bright, scrolling through pages of mentions and updates and pingbacks. Bitches sure were trending now.

Glimmer had left all this gear behind. Hadn't even taken his phone. Dared I hope it meant he was coming back?

Either that or he just couldn't stand my company for an instant longer.

Suddenly, the close air stifled me. His damn vanilla-spice scent was on everything. Like an accusing fingerprint, smearing the glass of my life.

Christ, I had to get out.

I grabbed the magic marker from its magnet and scrawled on the fridge-door note board.

Thank you for coming back.
I'm sorry for what I said. I'm sorry for everything.
Let's talk.
V.

If he did come back, that is. If I ever saw him on friendly terms again.

Let's talk.

The phrase sickened me. Exactly what Vincent had texted to me. Entrapment. Lies. A lure to drag me back in, like a hooked fish on a line.

Was that what I was doing to Glimmer? A lie to trap him into forgiving me, so I could abuse him all over again?

The old headache flared between my temples, cold yet burning with threat. Weasel was right. I was the gutter-dweller in this relationship. And no matter how I wanted to, I couldn't heave myself out.

Couldn't forgive Glimmer for not wallowing down there with me.

Maybe, deep down, I *wanted* him to leave me. Just like I'd wanted Razorfire to destroy me. So I wouldn't have to face the truth, which was that while Glimmer might like me, so far as that went, and pity me enough to want to help me… he didn't respect me. He'd never admire me, not the way I admired him. How could he? I'd done nothing to deserve it.

I kicked at the kitchen bench, bruising my toe. The ache felt good, which only made me madder. God, my self-pity was so pathetic. If I wanted so badly to be better, why the fuck didn't I just *try* harder?

I hurled the marker into the sink and stalked out, slamming the door.

For a long time, I wandered, midday sun scorching my eyes. I didn't much care where. All the streets looked the same. Aimlessly, I kicked at litter, leaves, a discarded beer can. A speeding driver beeped his horn and shouted abuse as I wandered across a street in his path. I could've hurled a trashcan after him, but I didn't. Whatever, pal. Do I look like I care about road rules right now?

Along the waterfront, the sun flashed on the sea, scattering jewels to the far shore. Rock Island loomed, for once not wreathed in fog, its squat watchtower forbidding above lines of augmentium-plated razor wire. A solitary boat motored towards the island, doubtless carrying staff or supplies or prisoners for transfer. No one went to Rock Island if they didn't have to.

As I wandered back towards the city, the crowd thickened. Cafés and lunch spots teemed with office workers, stockbrokers and shoppers. Just a normal day. Pigeons flocked on the sidewalks for crumbs. Street performers juggled and ate fire. Beggars shook their paper cups for change. In Union Square, Sentinels beeped and flashed, but in the dense lunchtime crowd no one could see that their cause for alarm was me. I just left a wake of panic and confusion behind me.

Story of my life. A trail of destruction and broken things, while I just sailed on, wondering what the hell happened.

Inevitably, I retraced my steps to the scene of today's carnage. The ruined fire department building still billowed black smoke. Most of the outer walls had been crushed to bricks and twisted metal, the inner honeycomb of the building exposed. Several floors had fallen in, making a crater in the center.

Blue-and-white-striped tape read POLICE LINE – DO NOT CROSS. I ducked beneath it, unnoticed in the to and fro of official personnel. No Sentinels here, not any more.

Inside, the rubble was weirdly silent. On the corner, paramedics and firemen with cranes and metal cutters still searched for bodies.

On the steps, twin bloodstains like sticky puddles. I could see the marks where I'd fallen, where Glimmer had been sick. I poked dully at Flash's dried blood with my foot. He'd bled from the wrist, like he'd cut himself, his fingers painted red. A victorious suicide. Glimmer's conscience bomb.

Glimmer was right, of course. Showing up their failings wasn't above and beyond. Everything they'd suffered was totally on them.

Or was it? I recalled Flash's silent stares, his dogged devotion. Worship for an uncaring goddess. Desperate to do anything to please her, even if she still treated him like scum.

Had Flash deserved the guilt he'd suffered? This was Sophron's party. He'd just followed. Did that make it okay?

I snorted. Fuck, no, it did not. *I was brainwashed. I just did what they told me. How was I supposed to know?* That defense hadn't held water since the Nazis burned six million Jews, and rightly so. Razorfire had manipulated me, sure, but I'd done the killing. It might be ultimately his fault, but I was still responsible.

Think you're so special? Weasel's insults bounced in my head, taunting me. *You're just a lab rat, same as the rest.*

Curious, I poked again at Flash's blood. It had grit mixed in it.

Same as the rest.

Was that what these two were: lab rats? In what kind of experiment?

Did Weasel mean mind games? Was Razorfire dripping his poison into Sophron's ear, just like he'd done to me? Or was it something more… scientific?

The ones in charge, she'd said in her video, were to blame. *The ones who created me.* Was that just a bullshit social engineering excuse? *Don't shoot, I'm a product of the system!* Or did she mean something more?

Hell, maybe Weasel didn't even mean Razorfire. Maybe the little rodent was just bullshitting me, trying to make me lose my temper. It'd worked. He'd gotten what he wanted. I should just ignore him…

I caught a stray scrap of paper sandwich wrapper that blew by on the wind. Dusted it off, rubbed it clean on my pants. Squatted and scraped up a patch of the dirty bloodstain, trying to exclude as much of the dirt as I could.

Blood could be tested. Blood talked. If something was strange about Flash—something *experimental*—we'd find out.

I, that is. I'd find out. There was no *we* anymore.

Carefully, I folded the paper and stuck it in my pocket. I searched the ground for more blood—Sophron's, I hoped—but found nothing. Any stain was long since trampled into the ground…

Ouch. I snatched my hand back. Something sharp had caught my fingertip. I brushed the soil away.

A shard of red-brown stone. Smooth and polished on one side, rough on the other. Sharp edges, like it'd been chipped from something larger.

My fingertip tingled. I inhaled, and my tongue stung with the sherbety sparkle of *augment*.

Shit. Was I under attack? I glanced around, dragging in a clumsy handful of power. Nothing. I saw no one, smelt no one.

I unclenched my fist, but my nerves still jumped. I recalled the seashell-shaped rock the tweens stole from the museum. Dad's rock, the one Espectro had wanted. Same odd, rusty red-brown color. Could this shard be a piece?

If so: who broke it? And how could a rock be augmented? I hadn't noticed, that night in the museum, but then again, the place had been dripping with augment from all sides. I inhaled again, testing. Definitely a tingle.

I straightened, pocketing the shard alongside the blood sample. Cool. My afternoon of wallowing hadn't been a total loss. Now, at least I had something to go on.

But as I ducked back under the tape and slipped into the crowd, icy centipede feet clattered along my spine, and I couldn't help feeling that this was all too easy.

That you know who was leading me on. Were these clues planted for me to find?

I shrugged it off, trying to quieten my twitching hide. Bullshit, right? Look at me, wishing I were so important. No one was out to get me. There were no plots, no secret, wicked plans. I wasn't a target.

Just paranoia.

Right?

~ 17 ~

Twilight fog crept in from the bay by the time I returned to Widow Swanky's. The apartment lay dark and chilly, damp where I'd forgotten to close the window. What an idiot. Lucky for me, no one had broken in and stolen everything.

Glimmer wasn't there.

My scribbled message on the fridge glared at me, unread, as I pulled out the juice. I paused with the bottle halfway to my mouth and sloshed some into a glass instead. It didn't taste any different.

A growl from my stomach demanded my attention. I plated up half a wheel of sticky cheese and a pile of red grapes—only thing we had, besides stuff that I'd need to, y'know, *cook*—and munched as I plonked my butt in front of the array of tablets. They lit up at my command, *sha-zam!* I flicked through one-handed, popping cheese into my mouth.

Video-sharing, check. A dozen different smartphone recordings of the fire department thing. Nothing new there… oh, wait, there's me and Glimmer getting the crap frightened out of us. Lovely. Nothing like looking your best on TV.

Had Adonis seen this? I'd caught no sign of him today. Guess he'd more pressing things on his mind. I swallowed. What had

I imagined: that he'd call to ask how I was? Even if he'd wanted to—which he wouldn't—he didn't have my new number. In any case, something between us had died in that forest. Even that night at FortuneCorp, when he'd shot me, he hadn't unleashed on me, not properly. Just enough to make me lay down my gun. We might be ruthless when dealing out pain to villains, but we didn't unleash on family.

I'd crossed a line with my brother, and I could never go back. Now, I was nothing but an enemy.

I swiped. News, TV specials, social media mentions by the thousand. Link to network footage of Vincent, no doubt giving his stoic mayor's speech about terrorism and not capitulating to criminals. My chin trembled. I burned to tap the link. See his face, outline his shapes with my fingertip on the glass…

I shook myself and swiped past it. Cold turkey, remember?

Next, Glimmer's analysis of Sophron's video transmission. Still calculating, spitting out that wingdings code like digital ticker tape. Guess the vid had a lot of layers. And I wasn't the expert, I reminded myself as I poked at the next tablet. I didn't even really know what he was looking for…

Holy crap. What was that?

Black screen, a single line of centered red text:

WE KNOW WHO YOU ARE

Goose bumps prickled my scalp. *Some sick shit villains' message board.* Had Glimmer's creeping feelers found that secret dark net hole? And how did I get in?

The cursor blinked at me, tempting. Taunting. My fingertips tingled. This page wasn't designed to be stumbled over. This wasn't the world wide web, with search engines and links. An existing member was supposed to give you the address. This was a test. One wrong keystroke and I'd be kicked out, and we'd lose our chance of finding anything about Sophron and Flash, probably for good.

I hesitated, Glimmer's words echoing. *If there is such a site, Razorfire's probably on it.*

Come back to me. Vincent, when we met on the bridge. Had he meant it? Would this secret site let me in if I owned up to being me?

My fingers hovered above the virtual keyboard. What should I say? *Hi, I'm Verity, remember me? Let me see your pretty pictures...*

I squirmed, imagining what those pictures might be. Fuck. I should stay away, leave this dark and dangerous stuff to those with better defenses than I. Playing with fire...

Rattle!

My ears pricked. The corridor outside. A footstep?

Scrape.

Like someone fiddled with the lock.

My secret senses tingled, and such warm relief washed over me that for a moment I couldn't move my legs. If that was Glimmer, I was saved.

I jumped up and ran in an abjectly undignified fluster for the door. I peered eagerly through the eyehole. "Is that you—?"

My throat choked dry. No. No, it wasn't.

I fumbled with the deadlock and opened the door.

Ebenezer stumbled into my arms. I staggered, trying to hold him up. His sweat clagged, cold and thick on my hands. He was weak, shaking.

"Verity..." Eb's breath burned my skin. He coughed, wet. "Help me."

"Jesus, what happened to you?" I scraped damp hair from his face. Sickly white, fiery underneath with fever. His oddball eyes gleamed, bloodshot. Demented.

My stomach twisted. He was sick. The same horrid virus—or whatever it was—that had sent Jeremiah's augment out of control. And I had nowhere to put Eb to keep him safe.

Or to keep everyone else safe from *him.*

155

Better make the best of it. Swiftly, I half-dragged him into Glimmer's room. I pulled the unwrinkled black quilt aside and heaved Eb onto the bed. He'd discarded his trench coat some-where—overheating, probably—and wore only jeans and t-shirt, already soaked. Should I strip him off? I'd nothing for him to wear…

He choked, phlegmy. "Had nowhere else to go. I'm sorry."

"Shh." I tucked the quilt around him and mopped his face with a towel. Fetched a glass of water and held it to his lips. He swallowed greedily, spilling most of it.

My thoughts tumbled, rocks down a precipice. How did Eb even find me? Had he followed us from the fire department scene? Was he even there? I hadn't smelled him.

And why had he come to me, of all people? They all knew what I'd done, Christ, I'd consorted with the enemy and gotten Eb's dad killed. He probably hated me.

"You're fine," I soothed. "Just rest." The lies we tell sick people, like being sick automatically makes them stupid or something. *Sure, kid, you're fine. Let me mop your forehead while you shiver to death.*

Eb coughed reddish phlegm onto the sheet. "I know what you did."

My stomach frothed, salty. "Look, you have to believe me…"

"I was there." His eyelids fluttered closed. "Followed you to the bridge. Heard everything."

My fingers clenched. Holy shit. I knew I'd heard someone skulking in that fog.

"I know you didn't… give us away. Know what it's like to be… suspected…"

I gripped his wet hand. "Eb, what's going on? Why'd you come here?"

"All sick. Jem. Sal. Ferdy. All…"

Chilled needles of dread jabbed my heart. "All of them? Adonis too?"

An exhausted headshake. His dark sweat already blotted the pillow slip. "Was okay… last I saw."

I breathed deep, trying to shake off my suspicions. Well, that was something. Adonis was okay. Maybe it was just a strain of flu, and Adonis hadn't caught it yet. He didn't exactly hang out with Sal and Ferdy, after all. If it was a Gallery plot, the whole camp would be doing the shivery tango by now. Right?

Sure, my inner paranoid hissed. *Unless someone's infecting them on purpose, one by one…*

I snorted. Ridiculous. Who'd bother with Sal and Ferdy? If I were a murderous Gallery villain with a hard-on for the Fortune family—I dunno: Razorfire, for example?—and I wanted to cripple my enemies with the raging shivery snot disease? I'd aim for the big guns. Adonis. Mike…

Who's already dead, reminded the Seekernoid snidely. *Keep up.*

…and Jem and Eb would be next on the list. The scary ones. The warriors.

And me.

But Adonis, Glimmer and I weren't sick, not yet.

Huh?

I recalled the scene in the forest after Mike died. Everyone jammed in next to one another, drinking coffee, talking. We'd eaten in the same kitchen for weeks. Sharing bathrooms, washing clothes together. Jem had been coughing like a sick dog for days now. If it was just flu, we'd all have signs of it, wouldn't we?

And as for Razorfire…

Well, no point denying the truth: it wasn't out of the question that he was possessed by some fucked-up romantic rationale for wanting to spare *me.*

But he despised Glimmer, the puppy dog with the bad hair. And he *loathed* Adonis. Adonis was too much like him.

My mind raced ahead, skipping around obstacles with frightening agility. No, this was something else. Someone did this on purpose. Someone who wanted Adonis healthy, and Jem and Eb sick.

But who? And why?

I re-ran random images from the last few days, searching for something, anything. Adonis in the forest, tossing me half his candy bar and a scowl; in the refectory, chugging his triple-shot latte from an insulated mug. Glimmer in his cell, green shadows on his stubbled cheek, two empty lasagna plates, half-drunk cans of caffeine cola. Ebenezer, chewing Peggy's scrambled eggs on toast…

Eating in the same kitchen for weeks.

My jaw dropped. I shut it again, stupidly. "Eb," I whispered, clutching his hand. "What about Peggy? Is she sick?"

He shook his head and lapsed into muttering, nonsense words and phrases I didn't understand.

Fuck.

My suspicions about Peg reared up and smacked me in the face, and their blows stung with *I told you so.* Peg, always so cheerful and positive. Cooking our meals, fetching us drinks…

Like she had at breakfast that final morning. Was it only yesterday? French toast, eggs, tomatoes… and coffee. The jug on our table. I'd reached for it, but it was empty. Glimmer skipped it, too. He'd had only water and caffeine cola. But Jem was a coffee addict since junior high. Eb had swallowed his entire mugful before I got there, and refilled.

And Peg always fixed Adonis's coffee separately, in a special cup. Triple-shot latte, three sugars. We'd given him shit about it, an eager girlfriend thing.

That cunning cow.

Impotent rage knotted my mindmuscle into a snarl. Why did Peg want to kill us all?

Kill us all. It echoed, *slam!* like a prison door to trap me. I hadn't thought it explicitly before. But what other purpose could this sickness have? If it wasn't fatal, what was the point?

I didn't know. But she'd tested it out on Jem, and when it worked—when he got sick, and stayed sick—she'd let the rest of us have it. If we skipped coffee one morning? No problem. She'd get us another time.

But not Adonis. She'd had dozens of chances to kill him, but she'd abstained. Coveted him. Kept him for herself.

I jammed my eyes shut on images of her lying, besotted smile. Kissing him, making him laugh. Taking him to bed. Fuck me, that was *low*.

Of their own accord, my fingers flexed. Ooh, I wanted to squeeze her perky throat until the spit ran cold and she stopped fighting for air. Bitch had fucked my brother. Slept in his bed, for God's sake. Made him think she *liked* him. And he'd believed her. Shit, *I'd* believed her.

It can't be Peg, okay? Adonis had insisted. *It just can't.*

Not *isn't*. *Can't*. Like he knew something we didn't. Poor Ad. Turns out he was clueless after all.

Now, Ebenezer lay here in Glimmer's bed, shivering and sweating and muttering wild nonsense. I bit my lip. Damn it. Lousy sister I was. Why hadn't I kept on Adonis's case about Peg? Should've *made* him listen to me. But no, I'd given up, written it off as too hard. And now, one by one, they—*we*—were all getting it.

Or was I just listening to the Seekernoid again? Plots under every rock, evil schemes with me at the center. Perhaps it was just… the flu.

Whatever. I didn't fancy sitting here, waiting for Ebenezer's augment to let rip, in order to find out. I'd had enough of being scared shitless for one day. And face it: there wasn't a whole lot I could do for him. I can patch up bullet wounds and scrapes in the best pour-whisky-on-it-and-hope tradition of crime-fighters through the ages. Nothing I can do against some kick-ass virus, or creeping mega-bacteria, or whatever superbug biohazard ugliness this was.

We'd never called that doctor pal of Glimmer's, either. We'd split from Adonis before we got the chance. Oops. For all I knew, now it was too late.

I skipped out to grab some cable ties from the pile we'd used on Weasel, and looped Eb's wrists together. Not too tight, just enough to stop him working free. I rolled him onto his side—fits, vomit, airway; if you've ever drunk yourself stupid, you know the drill—shut the door and jammed a chair under the handle on the outside.

For what it was worth.

But at least I'd hear the commotion if Eb went apeshit with fever and tried to break out. Here's hoping he can't hurl his augment through a closed door.

I hurried to the table, hunting for a phone.

We Know Who You Are

hissed that snide white-screened tablet. *Yes, Verity, we do. We know exactly who you are, and where you are, and* what *you are…*

I ignored it. No time for creepy villain mind games. I grabbed a phone, any phone. Glimmer's, to be precise. Typed Ad's number. I'd text him, tell him I could prove Peg was a traitor…

My thumbs paused above the screen, mid-word. But I couldn't prove it, could I? He'd never believe me, not the way things were. And what if she saw this message first? I'd achieve nothing, except she'd know we were onto her, and might decide it was time to go all bio-warfare on her handsome boy toy after all.

I deleted the half-written message. I could call, speak to him in private. But he'd only hang up as soon as he realized it was me.

I called anyway. He didn't pick up. It just rang out, no voicemail. Maybe he'd ditched that phone.

Shit.

I hung up, disgusted. I'd just have to find proof first. Set some of Glimmer's search engine artistry onto Miss Peggy Perky-Butt. Heh. Let's see how long she remains an enigma cloaked in a puzzle wrapped in a frilly apron *then*.

I glared at the tablets. They glared back, beady eyes taunting me. I sighed. This part would be a whole lot easier if, instead of just having Glimmer's stuff, I had Glimmer. Damn it that he'd left his phone behind. I couldn't even call him and grovel.

Wow. This talent of mine for painting myself into corners was really starting to piss me off.

Not that I just missed the cute little skunk like crazy, or anything. Not that even thinking about him *not being here* made me want to weep, to fall to my knees and smash my own skull against that shiny floor until my ears bled for acting like such a stupid asshole.

They made me cringe, all those wasted weeks when we could have been real friends, if only I'd gotten over myself and my weak-assed problems for long enough to say *I'm sorry.* If I ever see him again? I'm apologizing so fast, he'll barely see me coming.

Evil Serpent Verity snorted, mocking. *Sure. Keep on with your "sorry", hero. And tomorrow, you'll just fuck up afresh. You make the same thoughtless moves, over and again, and expect something different to happen. You know what they call that?*

I cracked my mindmuscle at her like a whip, hateful. I know what they call *you*, snakebitch. Shut the fuck up.

Quickly, I checked the phone for Glimmer's contacts, hoping for anyone who could possibly be a doctor. Call them, say *you don't know me, but I've got these sick augmented peeps, Glimmer said you'd be cool with it, can you help?*

But his contacts list on this new phone was empty. I sighed. Damn.

I picked up a tablet, determined to do something, even if it was pointless. Browser, search engine, go. But what to search? I knew nothing about Peg. Not her IQ, her bra size, her top score on Angry Birds. Zip, zilch, a big sloppy pile of *nada.* Not even a last name.

Peggy. Wow, that'd work. My search-fu knows no equal. *Peggy augment.* Nothing sensible. *Peggy Gallery.* Oops, Guggenheim plus big-breasted nude ladies. No luck.

What kind of name was Peggy, anyway? Irish? Short for Margaret. *Margaret augment. Margaret villain.* Pics of Maggie Thatcher (heh) and the green-faced Wicked Witch of the West. Shit.

I couldn't just trawl the arrest records for assholes named Peggy. I'd be here until Hanukkah. I needed a last name. A family name…

My heart skipped. Family. Augments ran in families.

Yes, they certainly did. The Fortunes were all related. So were Sal and Grayson, the bowl-cut nerd siblings. It was genetic. Brothers and sisters, cousins, fathers and sons… or daughters.

I switched from net search to the DMV. The link was already there and hacked. Bless you, Glimmer.

What if Peg was related to someone we knew? What if…

No. Not possible. Couldn't be. But I tried it anyway.

No *Margaret Caine.*

I breathed cool relief. Too easy. Not that she'd be using her real name if she was related to him. Not that Caine was probably *his* birth name, even.

I trawled my memory for Gallery assholes whose names I knew. No dice on Crook or Flores. I unearthed a Margaret Morven—the last name of Obsidian, Dad's old Gallery nemesis—but she was eighty-six, license suspended for below-par eyesight. I tried the names of a few of Dad's friends. Nope.

Hmm. Pity I didn't know Weasel's real name, though Peggy didn't look like a rodent's relative… oh, wait. Irish. Gallery. Duh.

I typed again, and obediently the screen popped up with a photo drivers' license. And that annoying little face smiled brightly back at me.

Yes. Lively eyes, bouncy ponytail with a few wisps poking out. Who the hell looks perky in their *license photo*, for fuck's sake?

Margaret Ann Finney, that's who. Address in Oakland, no traffic citations or speeding fines (of course). Twenty-nine years old.

Which made her sister—or maybe cousin—to the late, utterly unlamented psycho killer, *Declan* Finney.

Peggy was Iceclaw's sister.

I aimed my forefinger and fired an imaginary pistol at her face.

Well, fuckity do-dah.

~ 18 ~

I sat back, pushing the tablet away. My guts ached, a cocktail of fatigue and sorrow. I didn't feel vindicated, or even triumphant that, for once, I was right and Adonis was wrong.

I just felt heartbroken for him. He'd *liked* her. And she'd betrayed him.

I grabbed a phone and punched in Peggy's number.

Two rings. "Hello—?"

"I'll tear your heart out, you lying little rat."

A swallow. "Verity, is that you?"

"I know who you are, you vicious tart, and I know what you did." I jumped up, my bones burning. "Think you can poison my family without consequences? Think you can *fuck my brother* and get away with it?"

"I don't know what you're talking about."

"Save it, okay? You're only still alive because Ad won't answer his phone. When he does? Your life won't be worth the grease on my finger when I scratch my ass. And don't bother hiding. I'll find you."

I hung up, satisfied.

So what now? I had less than twenty-four hours until Sophron and Flash murdered another bunch of innocents. Not to mention everything else that had piled itself on my plate since. I grabbed a tablet, switched to Notes and dictated a list.

Problems (Tuesday):
2 violent teen troublemakers, whereabouts unknown
1 perky traitor, identified but unreachable
1 sweating fever, spreading and likely fatal
1 asshole brother, won't answer his goddamn phone
1 archvillain, enough said

So far, so bad.

Assets:
1 Glimmer, missing
1 Ebenezer, too sick to get out of bed
1 pile tablets/phone
1 augment, angry

Great. What an arsenal. Good thing I'd kept that $2.56. I dug in my pocket for the evidence I'd collected earlier. Add to assets:

1 pile blood flecks, Flash
1 chip Dad's augmented rock

I dumped them on the table. They sat there, silent and mysterious. I poked the scrunched-up paper. If I wanted Flash's blood analyzed, I needed an expert. There were companies you could pay to do this sort of thing, the kind of genetics labs that were hired to settle paternity suits, or engaged by criminal attorneys and the DA's office.

Two bucks fifty-six wouldn't pay for a DNA analysis. What did I even hope to gain? I needed to *find* Flash, not catalogue his body fluids.

The rock fragment's aura tingled my tongue. I frowned. *Trans-state granite artifact.* What did that even mean? State, as in solid-liquid-gas? It melted? Dissolved? Espectro, that sparkly burglar, hadn't been able to make it do so. Perhaps he could tell me more.

Sure he could, if he wasn't my enemy. And if he wasn't banged up on remand at Rock Island, tighter than an augmentium fish's butt-hole. Damn the PD's new augment-aware procedures. I couldn't get in there, not if I wanted to stay alive. No one could.

I'd just have to think of a way. Villains aren't the only ones who do things that can't be done.

I made a quick search of the police files. Jesus J. Flores, angry young asshole. His steel-studded dog collar glinted in the mug shot, below that bristly scalp and juicy scarlet-bruised face. Arrested, it said, for assault, attempt burglary, vandalize public property, resist lawful detention… and felony murder.

Oops. Must've killed one of those guards. Nice work, Jesus. You just got upgraded to twenty to life, minimum. Maybe they'd trumped up the charges. Didn't matter. Either way, the Gallery better have themselves good lawyers…

An idea sparked. Twinkle, twinkle, just like the little star.

It was fucking insane. I'd get caught. They'd kill me.

Right. Because this day had gone *so* well for me already. What did I have to lose?

Before I could change my mind, I grabbed the tablet and Glimmer's phone, just in case. Glanced down at my outfit. Nope. FREE HUGS would never do. I needed something more corporate…

My eyeballs swiveled towards Widow Swanky's wardrobe, and I groaned, resigned. Trust Glimmer to pick a size zero. Oh, well. I'd just have to improvise.

~ 19 ~

An hour later, I strode up to the reception desk at Rock Island State Prison, tablet tucked under my arm.

Well, I kind of *strode*. More like *minced*, in the ridiculous pointed shoes I'd pinched from Widow Swanky's wardrobe. They went with the suit I'd wormed into, like a fat snake cramming itself into a hose, before I hopped on the last boat to Rock Island for the night. I'd found no trousers I could coax on over my butt, so I'd ended up in a knee-length green pencil skirt and matching jacket that had been designed for some kind of alien stick-figure. Perhaps Widow Swanky shopped at the same boutiques as Deputy Ice-Empress Mackenzie Wilt.

I ground my teeth. Did he actually prefer skinny women? My body was fit and strong, but I was hardly built like a supermodel. I had actual boobs and flesh on my hips. Unlike Mackenzie frickin' Wilt.

Did he *enjoy* all those bones and sharp angles? Dance his glowing twists of fire over them, sink his thumb into the spaces and watch her flinch, taste her flavor, tease quivering reaction from her skin…

Fuck. I shook myself. Snap out of it. This was no time to get all hot and girly.

The long corridor was lined with reflective rivet-studded metal. At the end, the reception desk hid behind a bulletproof Perspex screen. To the side, the visitors' entrance, also bulletproof Perspex. Tiny mirrors glinted everywhere, giving the guards complete line of sight all the way to the front door. They'd refurbished Rock Island in shiny mindfuck-villain style.

In my mind, the walls shuddered and groaned, closing in on me. The long-range Sentinel on the wall blinked its blue light… and remained silent. The light stayed blue.

Heh. Old model. My gamble had paid off. The augmentium handcuff I'd fastened around my left wrist beneath my jacket cuff was chafing my skin red, but it was working. And they couldn't put permanently active Sentinels inside the prison. Too many augmented prisoners. Damn things would go off constantly.

But obviously they thought attack was the best form of defense. Augmentium on an industrial scale was ruinously expensive— Vincent had made sure of that—but they'd broken the piggy bank here. I could smell the rotten stuff, like some evil anti-bacterial mist they'd splashed everywhere to kill germs. Even though my cuff had numbed me, and I couldn't feel my mindmuscle, I imagined it cringing like a sick tapeworm, trying to crawl up its own butt and disappear.

I smiled coldly through the Perspex at the prison guard in his sweaty uniform behind the desk. "Jesus Flores, please."

"Visiting hours are over." The guard scratched his balding head. He was about fifty, paunchy and pale. Not their finest warrior. The rack on the wall behind him bristled with move-alongs, electric whips, cuffs, firearms and canisters of tear gas.

"I'm not a visitor. I'm his lawyer." I pushed my new business card under the barrier. I'd stolen it from a bar, swiped a handful from one of those jars where you leave your card to win a free dinner for two. I'd had to flick through a dozen stockbrokers, business consultants and therapists before I found this one.

Sorry, Macy: no free dinner for you. If ever we meet, it's on me. I just hoped they didn't call her office to confirm. For all I knew, she was a tax lawyer.

He examined the card. "Visiting hours are two until five—"

"My client's charged with a capital crime," I interrupted, in my best smug defense-attorney tone. "He's entitled to meet with counsel at earliest opportunity. This is the earliest opportunity. Or don't Latino prisoners have rights?"

"Miss Fry—"

"That's *Ms.* Fry, thank you, Guard—" I squinted down my nose at his name tag. I was wearing glasses I'd found on Widow Swanky's bedside table, to make me look more lawyerly and distract attention from my scars, and I couldn't see a damn thing. "O'Malley," I finished, and smiled brightly. "Now either you let me see my client? Or I'll bring the Minority Defendants' Anti-Discrimination League down on your ass so hard, you'll think you back-butted a cannonball."

Guard O'Malley sighed, resigned. Probably dealt with a dozen ball-busting minority rights champions every day. I'd just invented the Minority Defendants' Anti-Discrimination League, but he wasn't to know that. Easier just to capitulate and let someone else wear it. At least, that's what I was counting on.

Bless him, he didn't disappoint. An electromagnetic lock clunked and the visitors' door opened. I was in.

Another guard—taller, younger, fitter—led me inside, through the outer defenses into the prison proper. This place dated from the last century-but-one, and they hadn't remodeled completely. It still looked like a bad sixties inmate movie: clanging gates, low ceilings, dog-leg corridors and rows upon rows of bars.

They had, however, upgraded. Surreptitiously, I peered over my glasses as the guard led me inside. Electromagnetic locks, sure.

Video and audio surveillance; black-box cameras high on every wall; laser grids over the ventilation holes, bright lights shining into each corner and crevice. And the unholy, astringent stink of augmentium.

I shuddered. Save me from ever being locked up in a place like this.

We entered the main hall, three floors high with steel catwalks and stairs joining the levels. Outside, searchlights swept by the tall barred windows. The cells—bars in front, some glassed in as well—were all occupied.

Not all the prisoners were augmented, of course. They had to cage the ordinary criminal assholes somewhere, and I glimpsed orange uniforms, tattoos, shaven heads and brutal male muscles. Gang thugs, drug dealers, rapists, killers. Charming. And they were the nice guys. To my left, along a cold bleak corridor, yawned the solitary cells, tiny echoless tombs with no natural light. I imagined the things these good-old-boy guards did to uncooperative cons in there—cons with scary augments that made the guards piss their pants in fear, never a good way to endear yourself to your captors—and shivered.

My heels click-clacked on the hard floor, louder than I wanted. Cons whistled and jeered, yelling crude suggestions. Right. Guess they weren't close enough to see my face. I put on my professional *ignoring-you* expression, my tablet tucked tightly under my arm.

At last, the guard led me into a white room. Bright lights, desk and two chairs bolted to the floor. No watch hole in the door, no window for one-way glass. Just a camera, video only. The private lawyer-stuff room. "Wait here," he said unnecessarily.

I waited. Hmm-mmm, la la la. In a few minutes he returned with Espectro in tow and shoved him into the empty chair. Orange prison uniform, with leg shackles, wrist shackles and chains all augmentium. The bruises on his face still shone, weeping. Dude looked pissed off. I couldn't blame him.

Espectro gave me his dark, arrogant gang-boy eyes, hands in fists on the table. Didn't speak, didn't let on who I really was.

169

He wasn't an idiot. He was charged with felony murder of a law enforcement officer. Any time out of his cell ever again was golden.

The guard chained him to the desk, shoved him again just for fun and walked out. The door slammed and locked.

"Hi." I wiggled cheeky fingers. "Missed you, sweetheart. Been dreaming of me?"

Despite his change of scenery, Espectro didn't look pleased to see me. His fists balled tighter. They'd taken his Gallery ring, and a pale area of skin encircled his finger. "What you want?"

I opened my tablet in case the guards were watching, which of course they would be. "Sophron and Flash. Who are they?"

"*Quienes?* Never heard of 'em."

"C'mon, Jesus. She's got the same augment as you. You must've met her before."

"Oh, her." He grinned. "Still never heard of her."

"Who you working for, sparkles?" I pretended to make notes.

"Who d'you think?"

"Himself."

A shrug. It was no secret. "Sometimes."

"And other times?" I took off my glasses, waited through a few moments of silence, and sighed. "Look, I didn't sashay all the way in here crammed into this fuck-awful suit just to gaze upon your pretty face. Not that you're pretty anymore, incidentally. Those cops really did a job on your eyes. You'll have scars. Probably a good thing. You know what happens to handsome young boys in here—"

"What's in it for me?" Chains rattled as he wiped his nose on his shackled forearm. "Why the hell should I talk to you? You gonna get me out of this place? Keep me off death row?"

"No."

"Then—" He repeated the same bestial insult from the museum, topped with a fuck-you grin.

I grinned back, letting a little of my crazy seep out. "As fun as that sounds? I'll pass. Look, glitter boy, you know me, right? You

170

know who my friends are." Emphasis on *friends*, and one *friend* in particular. "D'you think lethal injection's the only thing I can threaten you with?"

He flipped twin middle fingers at me, belligerent.

"Why, Jesus, I'm stung by your attitude. I'm here to help you. Cover up your pathetic little mistakes. That loot from the museum, for instance. Himself won't be happy you lost that."

A shrug.

"Think *he* can't get at you in here?" I snorted. Weasel had laughed off my threats, because he honestly didn't care if he lived or died. This guy? No such protection. "Death row? Shit, you'll be begging to check in there by the time he's finished."

He just looked at me. Lifted his shackled hands. And laughed.

The sound of resignation and helplessness. I leaned forward, urgent. "I can help you," I lied. "Steal it back, make sure he gets it. Soothe his temper. Make him understand it wasn't your fault. I just need you to tell me what it is and where they are."

"Fuck you." But his forehead glistened, fresh sweat. I'd made a dent.

"You know who I am, right?" I persisted. "He listens to me. What's the rock, sparkles? Why does he want it?"

"You're so thick with the big man? You ask him." But his bruised gaze skittered, uncertain. Everyone had heard the stories—oh, yes, and seen the pictures, too, no doubt, on that creepy message board I was yet to hack into—but Espectro still wasn't sure which side I was really on. Whether I was Razorfire's disciple or his enemy. For once, the confusion was an advantage.

I laughed, sinister as I could muster. "Lesson one, dude: if you want to live, you do *not* present the big man with problems. You provide him with solutions. Let me help you do that, and you might actually remain *compos mentis* for long enough to die from a smooth, easy lethal injection." I flipped my tablet shut and drilled him with my coldest stare. "Instead of, y'know. Slobbering custard down your shirt for the next forty years in whatever solitary hellhole of a nut house they'll lock you up in once he's finished shredding your mind. Hard to hold the spoon when you've gnawed your own fingers off at the knuckles."

Espectro ground his teeth. "Don't know, okay? I just steal the shit he tells me."

"C'mon, man. Credit where you deserve. You got this gig in person, right? You actually talked to himself, face to face?" A shot in the dark. But Espectro was talented. Spirited. Had a sexy augment. Just the kind of ally Vincent enjoyed.

He nodded, wiping his nose again. "He wanted it for some *collection*. Said it was special, and he'd been waiting for it to come on the market for a long time."

Emerge from the Fortune vaults, he meant. I frowned. Didn't recall Vincent having a collection of anything, unless you counted homicidal minions or red ties. Inwardly, I ached. I'd never asked Uncle Mike what the deal was with this rock. Another opportunity missed.

So Dad dies, and suddenly here's the International Rock of Mystery in a glass case for everyone to see… or to steal. Who'd sold the piece to the museum, and why?

Glimmer hadn't yet scraped the data from the ruined FortuneCorp archives. But I'd stake my chips on big sister Equity, who'd taken over the company after Dad died. Ditching Dad's prized possessions was just the kind of insensitive, *I'm-the-boss-now* shit she'd pull.

"So how's he paying? What's your end?"

Espectro coughed and spat dark phlegm. "C'mon, y'know you don't ask that. You just take what comes, and hope you're still alive at the end."

True enough. Only a brave or monumentally stupid villain asked Razorfire *what's in it for me?* People had lost body parts that way. "And you've no idea what 'trans-state artifact' means?"

"Not a damn clue." His growl broke into a wet choke, and his face reddened. "Do I look like a fucking professor?"

My nerves prickled. Coughing, sweating, his dark eyes blood-shot… "Dude, are you feeling okay?"

He said something rude in Spanish.

"Don't suppose you know a woman called Margaret Finney?"

"Sure," he muttered indistinctly, wiping his nose. "Peggy. Deck's sister. Redhead, great tits. What d'you care?"

Fuck me. Espectro had the disease. Soon, like Jeremiah, he'd be coughing his lungs to pink soup and throwing an involuntary glitter fit…

Only he wouldn't, would he? My stomach curdled. He was shackled in augmentium. He couldn't turn to glitter even if he wanted to. Couldn't use his augment at all. Like my mindmuscle while I wore this handcuff: his power was trapped.

Immovable object, irresistible force.

I didn't want to see how that might turn out.

"Okay, cool. You'll hear from me." I stood hurriedly, unable to meet his eye. Nothing I could do to make him better. No way I could help him. He was a villain. I shouldn't care. Right?

"Hey," Espectro called as I banged on the door for the guard, "Seeker."

I glanced back.

"You really his girlfriend?" An incredulous gleam lit his blood-shot eyes. Like it was the loopiest fucking idea he'd ever heard.

I swallowed sticky bile. "Some of the time."

A laugh that turned into a spluttering cough. "Fuck me. You got balls, *senorita*, I'll give you that."

Damn. I wanted to help him. Apologize for leaving him behind for the cops, promise I'd do everything I could. Get him a doctor, a lawyer…

But the guard was already unlocking the door.

I minced back through the prison, those stupid pointed shoes pinching my toes. Wild thoughts fought and clawed in my skull. So Razorfire wanted the mystery rock for his *collection*, did he?

Wasn't about to let a pair of upstart villains swipe it from under his nose, then. No way.

I don't care what that damn rock is, it's mine, and I want it back. And that was Adonis, who compared to Vincent was Mr. Reasonable. No, Vincent would never let Sophron and Flash get away with this. They had it coming, big time.

So why was he holding back? I didn't know. But something told me he wouldn't be for much longer… "Huh?" I tried to focus. "Sorry, what?"

The prison guard eyed me oddly as we reached the outer door. "Get everything you needed, Counselor?"

"Oh. Right. Yes, thank you, for the moment. I'll be in touch with my client again later this week." Might even call him a real lawyer. "Please see to it that he's transferred to the infirmary," I improvised, giving the guard my best simper of potentially carnal gratitude. "I'll be applying to the court in the morning, but I recommend you don't waste time. If I'm not mistaken, Mr. Flores has the stomach flu. You don't want that in general population."

"Sure, I can have him checked out." The guard hesitated. "Next time, okay your client conference with visits coord first, can you? Makes paperwork for us when you guys show up after hours."

Tit for tat. I blinked innocent lashes. "I'll certainly do that. So sorry for the inconvenience."

"No problem." The guard unlocked the outer door, fumbling with his electric keys. For an instant, his gaze wandered downwards, then up again. He did a double-take. And froze.

My blood stung cold. The loose half of my augmentium hand-cuff had slipped, and now it tumbled down over my hand. In plain sight.

Oh, well.

I smiled wider. Let the handcuff key slip into my other hand. "It's a lifestyle thing," I whispered. "Can't wear the collar in court, y'know. You into it? Because it can be really intense—"

In a blur, I unlocked the cuff and yanked it off. The guard's hand flashed to the electric whip at his belt. Whoa, Sundance. Dude was fast.

But not as fast as me.

I dived for the door, hip and shoulder, knocking the guard flat. *Boom!* The Perspex was bulletproof. It didn't break. But the door was already ajar. It burst open and I tumbled out onto the lobby floor.

Behind the screen, Guard O'Malley swore and jumped for the weapons rack. Behind me, the Sundance Kid's electric whip erupted. *Zzzap!* Current stabbed the floor, missing me by inches. My hair crackled on end. The Sentinel on the wall flashed red and started to scream.

I ran. Grabbed a coil of power, flung myself against the steel doors. They flew open and I tumbled into the fresh night air. Rolled to my feet—I'd already kicked off Widow Swanky's idiotic heels—and kept running, down the hill towards the froth-lined shore.

Searchlights knifed the mist, sweeping the sharp-wired walls, hunting for me. Guards on the watchtowers readied their weapons, yelled, made radio calls. Alarms howled. Jeez, you'd think a serial killer had escaped.

To them—everyday people, scared witless by Sophron's blood-thirsty antics and Razorfire's relentless terror campaign—we were all killers. All villains just waiting to happen.

I sprinted down the curving path at inhuman speed, past the derelict burned-out buildings from last century, and along the wooden jetty where the boats came in. The mainland shore's lights faded into creeping fog. They looked impossibly far.

No boats at the pier now. Not even a dinghy or an emergency escape craft. Their contingency plan must be from a different pier or the helicopter pad. Shit. I raked my hair. Okay, so my extraction plan (what I'd had of one) sucked from the beginning. It sucked a whole lot worse now.

Cold water swirled, black and frothy in the wind. Waves slapped the pylons, hurled angrily by the growing swell. I kicked at the jetty, frustrated. Like I said: I can't fly.

Luckily for me, I can swim. At this water temperature? Why, I'd have a whole seventeen minutes before I froze to death. And that shore had to be at least an hour away.

Great. Just fucking brilliant.

Searchlights swept closer and the salty breeze wafted the eager barking of dogs—and yes, the *whup-whup* of that helicopter gunship's blades. No time to lose. Hey, I had one advantage that'd buy me time: they'd never believe me crazy enough for this.

Swiftly, I threw phone, tablet and glasses into the sea to die. *Whee! Splash.* They sank into the black water and vanished. Thanks a bunch, Macy Fry, attorney-at-law. It's been fun.

I tore off my too-tight designer jacket—better cold and mobile than warm and drowned—and dived into the hungry sea.

~ 20 ~

I drifted, wrapped in a soft, vanilla-scented cloud. So warm, like the velvet dapple of sunshine on my skin. I smiled and snuggled tighter. My bruises didn't hurt anymore. I felt safe. I didn't want to open my eyes. If only I could stay here forever...

A violent shiver shook me awake.

Fuck. Real world.

Unwillingly, I blinked. Darkness, the low gleam of streetlights on the wooden apartment floor. The wall clock ticked, tiny footsteps over distant traffic noise. Pale sheets, quilt tucked up to my neck, my damp hair curling on the pillow.

I was lying in bed. Naked. And Glimmer—that gorgeous vanilla-spice aroma could only be Glimmer—lay against my back. His arm wrapped around my ribs, hand curled under my breast.

Oh, my.

He stirred, his bare skin whispering on mine. His lips lingered in my hair. "Verity. You awake?"

He was *here*. And God, he was so deliciously warm. Tingly, goose-bumps-all-over warm.

"Ugh," I managed, dazzled. I didn't want to move.

He pushed up on one elbow, a glory of tousled velvet hair and olive-toned skin. He wore jeans, top button undone, revealing a glimpse of smooth hip. No shirt. Good God.

"You're okay. Take it slow." He tucked the quilt around me, brushed back my hair.

"Mmphmbl," I said, when what I meant was *kill me now, before I wake up a second time and this isn't real.*

"Talk to me, and you'd better say something sensible. If you've got brain damage, you are *so* in trouble."

I coughed, coppery sea salt and blood. My insides felt torn, clawed raw. I didn't feel brain damaged. Just… shell-shocked. Bewildered.

"What happened?" I croaked.

"You swallowed enough ocean to drown Godzilla, that's what." His eyes glinted, midnight-blue, his expression stubbornly hard. Then the corner of his mouth curled, a smile fit to melt the devil's heart. "Jesus, Verity. Never hear of hypothermia? What the hell made you think you could swim two miles?"

"Pure talent, I guess." I shivered again, huddling in the quilt. In fragments, I recalled dark, crushingly cold water. Swimming, using my power to drag me along, the blinding attack of searchlights, sand crunching under my nails… and then, nothing.

Hypothermia. He'd stripped me of my wet clothes, warmed me with his body heat. Saved my life, most likely.

Same shit, different day.

"I saw the escape alarms going bugfuck at Rock Island," Glimmer explained, at my no-doubt baffled expression. "Went down to check it out. Found you on the shore. You made it, you moron."

"Not without you, I didn't." I held his gaze, and stupid laughter cracked in my throat. "I don't know what to run with first: the abject gratitude or the thousand groveling apologies."

He shrugged. "You're welcome. And it's okay."

"Don't brush me off, dude. I'm serious."

"I'm not brushing you off. Just shut up and listen." He sat cross-legged atop the quilt, hands fighting each other absently in his lap. "I did some thinking this last day or so. And you were right."

"What?" I pushed up on my elbows, dazed. I couldn't believe this. I'd been the worst friend in the entire world, and now he was...?

"You were right. You're having a hard time and I act like it's all easy for me, knowing what to do." Shadows ghosted across his face. "It isn't easy. Not at all. I struggle, same as you. I'm not trying to show you up, or make you feel bad. It's just... my way."

"I know." I swallowed. Each time he revealed a vulnerable spot I wanted to wrap him in my arms, hold him close, shield his precious heart from this hateful world that wanted to hurt him. Or wrap him in my arms and do something else entirely. Something tasteless and inappropriate that would embarrass the shit out of me afterwards and probably drive him away from me forever.

Or would it? Fuck, I didn't know. I didn't know *what* the hell I wanted. And it wasn't a conflict I should try to resolve with my brain at half mast. Or while I lay here with no clothes on and the sweet echo of his body heat still tingling over my skin.

"I didn't mean those shitty things I said," I admitted. "God, I've been such a stubborn asshole. I don't know how to make it up to you. You're my best friend and I..." A fat ache clogged my throat. Fuck it, I was going to cry again. I *hated* it when I cried. Especially when I was about to say...

"Yeah." Shyly, Glimmer dropped his gaze. Flicked it back up to mine, bright with fresh starlight. "Me, too."

I choked, a tearful eruption that burned. "Shit," I mumbled. Christ on a cheeseburger. What hope did I have against that?

Glimmer passed me the tissues, and I grabbed a handful. "I do have one question, when you're done," he added, putting the box aside.

I sniffed and wiped my face. "Shoot, before I drown."

"Why's Ebenezer tied up in my bed?"

A laugh ambushed me, and I spluttered and had to blow my nose all over again. "He stumbled in here this morning. Don't worry, he's still a virgin."

"God, no." Glimmer shielded his eyes. "Please, no more pictures. But why the cuffs?"

"He's got Jem's sweating disease, didn't you see? Didn't want him staggering off down the street in a fevered fit of scaring the fuck out of people." I tossed the crumpled tissues away. "He looks pretty bad. D'you think we could call that doctor friend of yours?"

"Maybe." He hesitated. "It's a long shot. I never said 'friend'."

"Oh." I sobered, remembering. "I think Peggy's responsible. Did you know her last name's Finney?"

Glimmer winced. "Iceclaw."

"Bingo." I thought of all the meals she'd cooked for us, the coffee she'd made. All the times she'd lurked by Adonis's side, listening in on our conversations, eavesdropping on our plans. Probably reporting to the Gallery the whole time. Bitch.

"Poor Adonis," Glimmer added after a moment.

"Yeah. Poor Ad." I shivered. I didn't want to think about Adonis or Peggy or Iceclaw. I wanted desperately to stay under this warm scented quilt and hide. Wrap Glimmer in my arms, forget all our problems and go back to sleep. Maybe, in the morning, they'd be gone.

Right.

"Onwards and upwards." I stretched my spine with a pop and jumped out of bed, ignoring the protesting twinge in my muscles. Shut up, you big girly-girls. It's always all about *you*. What about me, eh? *I* was dog-tired. I ached all over, bone-deep. My eyeballs stung ragged and my throat felt like someone had curetted it with rusty steel wool coated in salt. But apart from that, I was all good. Don't see *me* complaining.

"While you were out, I went back to the ruined fire department." I stretched my arms behind my back, then touched my toes to limber up. My muscles *hmphed* and their whining dulled to a low grumble, at least for now. "Wanna see what I found?"

"Sure." Glimmer's voice was oddly muffled. "Good idea."

"I scraped up some of Flash's bloodstain. And I found a piece of the museum rock. Like, a chip from it. And guess what? It's augmented."

"Uh-huh."

I glanced back. He was sitting on the bed's edge, his back to me. Like he wasn't even interested. "What?"

"Nothing."

I looked down at myself. Oh. Heh. I cackled like a witch, triumphant. "Now who's bashful, hero? Not like you haven't seen it all before."

He had. More than once. The day we'd met, in fact, when he'd rescued me from a gang of vicious haters and patched up my wounds while I lay unconscious. How was tonight any different?

"Bite me, beautiful," came the reply, and I snickered.

But as I searched for my jeans and t-shirt at the end of the bed, uncomfortable heat bloomed in my belly. I didn't get it. Sure, I looked away when *he* showed skin, but that was because I wanted *not* to, and it embarrassed me. What was his excuse?

Christ. What if he actually *liked* looking at me?

Flustered, I ducked behind the bathroom screen to dress. *Tonight's different because you nearly died. Tonight's different, you fucking moron, because he saved your life and he's just been holding you naked in bed. Give the guy a break. He isn't made of stone.*

Or is he? Perhaps we could find out… and with a jolt of holy-crap, I realized I truly, deeply *wanted* to find out.

Enough. Just don't even go there. Don't ruin it. Don't dishonor all he's done for you.

But a suspicious worm twisted into familiar, forbidden pathways inside my heart. Where was Vincent tonight? What would he have done if he'd known I'd lain freezing to death on that beach?

I dragged my jeans on over my bare butt—the soggy mess my underwear was in? Not a chance—and stared down my blanched reflection in the frosted glass. "Stop it, Verity," I murmured sternly. "Cold turkey, remember?"

My reflection just eyed me back, calm and insidious. Perhaps Vincent *had* known. He'd let me rot in that bizarre asylum for nine months, after all, when he'd known all along exactly where I was and why.

I could never love a woman who needed rescuing, he'd told me once. He respected me too much, he said, not to let me solve my own problems. If I needed his help, I wasn't worthy of him.

But tonight was my own fault. I'd gotten into danger through my own reckless mistakes. My own weakness: the one crime *he* wouldn't tolerate.

I shivered again, longing for Glimmer's lost warmth. I knew exactly what Vincent would do.

He'd let me die, just to prove his point. Then he'd scorch a swathe of the city to ashes in fury, and soothe his broken heart by spending the next twenty years wreaking despotic revenge on my friends.

Vincent's fucked-up brand of desperately romantic. His idea of love.

My palms stung. I looked down. Twin rows of tiny crimson crescents, oozing blood. Just like the flesh in my soul. Torn, bleeding, unable to heal.

Vincent had cut-throat standards, but his ruthless expectation that I'd meet them had made me believe in myself as I'd never done before. Nothing but better than my best was good enough. Only toddlers and puppies loved unconditionally, he said. Just like dogged Flash, striving to placate his goddess: if I wanted his regard, I had to *deserve* it.

And how hungrily I'd yearned for it, back in the day. Did that make Vincent sick? Or just… evolved?

Truth was, back then I'd have done pretty much anything to impress him. Things like blanket the city in nerve gas, and kill my own father, Blackstrike, who'd tried to stop me.

Yet Glimmer's gallant heart overflowed with compassion. He accepted me, weaknesses and reckless decisions and all. He knew exactly what a fuck-up I was, and, without a blink, he'd put his own life in danger to save me.

Did that make him a hero? Or a fool?

My thoughts clanged, ugly barbed confusion against the shining iron walls of my conditioning. A fresh headache speared, threatening vile consequences if I rebelled. I was so fucking *sick* of being threatened.

Do it, then, the headache whispered, sounding suspiciously like Vincent. *If you're so certain of what's right? Make a decision, and screw the consequences. I dare you…*

But my courage quailed, like the feeble, sniveling creature it was, and I yanked on my crusty t-shirt—phew, those Free Hugs were a worse bargain every day—and turned away.

The night was still dark, and that tick-fest wall clock read twenty past three. The witching hour for the late-party crowd. Glimmer was dressed—damn, was I thankful or disappointed?—and I smelled something rich and sweet brewing in the kitchen. Mmm. Best house husband ever.

He held up one of his array of tablets while he poured something from a saucepan into a cup with his other hand. "Get anywhere with this?"

Black text on red, menacing.

We Know Who You Are

I shrugged, shaking off my worries, and despite them, a sunlit cloak of happiness settled around my shoulders. Glimmer had come back to me. The rest of it… well, who cares? It was all a hopeless dream. I had my friend back. That was what mattered. Damned if I'd lose him again.

"Didn't try it yet," I admitted. "Ran short of time. Too busy, y'know, crashing prisons and almost freezing to death."

"Probably just as well. These sites are a booby-trap minefield." He handed me the mug. Hot chocolate, the real homemade kind, dark like cocoa and warm to the touch. "Drink this, and don't complain it's not coffee. Caffeine hits are strictly off limits until you recover. Glimmer's orders."

"Sure thing, doc." I sipped, and my taste buds sighed in delight. A delicious sweet infusion of heat spread inside me. I could feel my deadened nerves springing back to life. Bless him. "God, that's good. So, you're the expert on these web things. Think it's a password?"

"Or an invitation to identify ourselves… wait. Look at this." He plucked up another tablet, the one with the wingdings code and the green progress bar. Where he'd been stripping down Sophron's original video, looking for clues.

The progress bar was full.

I plonked my butt beside his on the sofa. "Cool. What is it?"

"Extra video layer. Must be a codec for this somewhere. Just a sec… yeah. Winner. Check it out." He propped the tablet against a shiny glass vase.

The screen blinked. A window popped up and the video started to play.

A grainy shot of an empty room. Desk piled with books; computer covered in stickers and tribal designs drawn in magic marker. Behind it, a rumple-sheeted bed with an old teddy bear sitting up on one pillow. In front, a shabby grey sofa with sagging cushions. Pale sunlight slanted through a tall paned window to the left, almost out of shot, and dust motes made slow spirals.

The camera wobbled and steadied. And a figure shambled into shot. Skinny legs in denim, black bitten nails scratching his thighs, an emo flop of black-dyed hair.

Flash.

He sat, staring solemnly at the camera, and gave a little wave. "Hey. If you're watching this, you're trying to find us. Hell, by the time you've decoded this, the whole city'll be trying to find us."

His voice—we'd never heard it before—sounded odd. High-pitched and uneven, like a boy's that hadn't quite broken yet. But he looked old for his age. Tired eyes, cheeks hollow and dry. Like a drug addict.

He leaned forward, bony elbows on knees. Scabs and scratches bit his forearms. A fresh bruise crawled black and yellow on his throat, disappearing into the neck of his Yoda t-shirt. "Time's

184

wasting, so I'll get to it. The one who calls himself Glimmer? This is for you."

I sipped my chocolate. "Oyy. The plot thickens."

Glimmer just watched, tapping his thigh absently.

"I figure you're the other one smart enough to find this. The one who'll do something about it. You listening, Glimmer?" Flash glanced around, ensuring he was alone. "Forget the destruction. It's not the point. Well, it is, but there's more. Much more. I'm not who you think, or who I look like. Nothing about this is what it looks like. I can't say much. She'll be back soon… and I think you know who else is watching us. I won't say his name. But you know."

My curiosity sparkled, terrible and wonderful, and I clenched one fist. I knew it. Vincent was behind this. Or at the very least, he'd caused it.

Flash lit a cigarette, ash flaring. He puffed smoke upwards and shook back his lank hair. "Ready to believe? Cool. We haven't been introduced, you and I. I'm Tyler, and I'm seven years old."

~ 21 ~

I blinked, bewildered. Seven? But...

Flash—Tyler—let smoke curl from his lips. "Yeah. I look older, right? That's because I've been artificially aged. My genes have been altered. Though that's not the word I'd choose." He flicked ash. "Butchered, more like. That's what they do in that place: they butcher people's genes. Give them mega doses of hormones and neurotransmitters and retroactive viral reproductive shit and whatever else. I don't know what all the injections are. But they collect augmented kids and they *grow* them. Like in a hothouse. Make them into *us*."

My stomach churned, sick. It was too horrible.

Beside me, Glimmer sat, motionless. Rigid, staring at the screen.

"Who, you're asking? I think you know who." Flash scratched his scabbed forearm, drawing blood. "The same ones who made the Sentinels. Why? Now, *why's* a proper question. They made me; they made *her*. And now she's doing precisely what they designed her to do."

"A weapon," I murmured. But a contrary bug stung in my brain, breaking out lumps. I'd said the word *weapon* to Weasel, and he'd laughed at me.

Like it wasn't weapons they wanted.

"She's angry, she wants revenge," Flash continued. "So do I, man. Believe me. But even more? I want to stop them." Another drag of smoke, deep and urgent. "It's not right. They lie to children. They lie to the parents about a cure. And they're killing us. I'm seven, but my body's sixteen. Next month, it'll be twenty. The month after that?" He butted out his cigarette on the sofa's arm, leaving a blackened burn. "Shit. The month after that, I'll be dead. Think I want to wait around to be eighty, pissing my pants with my teeth falling out?"

He leaned forward, and Yoda's face filled the screen for a few seconds. Flash reappeared holding a pink-filled glass bottle, cracked the top and drank. Vodka and strawberry juice. With a start, I recalled the museum, that sweet jelly-bean smell. Alcopops. It was fucking tragic.

"As for her? She's four, for fuck's sake. Forgive her, for she knows not what she does. I know that one, yeah? They made us read, made us learn shit." Flash laughed, and drank again, finishing off the bottle. "She's nearly drained me. Used my power up, until I can feel… well, it's slipping away. Like it's dying. The more she uses me, the worse it gets. But I'd do it all over again, if she asked." He stared into the camera, hollowed black eyes. "I love her, man. Don't hold it against me. Just find them, Glimmer, before they find you. It's all about you now. They already know who you are. So stop them, before it's too late."

Something—a door?—clattered off-screen. Flash jumped for the camera. "Gotta go," he whispered, his face looming in the frame. "This'll play out to the end over the next few days. You'll see. Don't wait too long. Oh, and one last word of advice? Watch the Sentinels, and stay off the phone." And the recording snapped to black.

I blew out a breath. "Well. D'you believe any of that?"

Glimmer bit his lip, troubled. "It'd explain a few things."

"Yeah. That spooky laugh of hers, to start with. The way she gloats and giggles like a little girl." I shuddered. *Old friends,* Vincent had called them. Cruel, my lover. "If he's only seven, how does he talk like a teenager? And how does he know this secret video encryption stuff? Child prodigy?"

"Kids are quick learners. Maybe the artificial maturation includes brain maturation, and accelerated learning. He said himself he didn't know what all the medications were."

"Could be. He's mouthy enough to be a real teenager. Horny enough, too," I added, recalling their little passion party in the forest. "That chick has him dewy-eyed and drooling. Poor kid."

"And they're both skinny, too. Poorly developed muscle tissue. Could be a symptom of rapid growth." Glimmer shrugged. "Or maybe they just drink too much vodka and subsist on Red Bull and cigarettes. It isn't proof."

"But our 'lab full of eggheads' theory could still hold water, right? They're speed-growing augments." I frowned. "So what's the point of that?"

"Use them as weapons?" Glimmer suggested. "Repopulate the Gallery with loyal disciples, grown to their specifications. Their perfect army."

"Not working too well, then, is it? He's already got a mutiny on his hands." But I recalled what Espectro told me about that museum-piece rock: Razorfire had wanted it for his *collection*.

His collection of what? Rocks? Weird art? Didn't seem likely.

But how about augments? Powers he could use. Like Sophron's, and Flash's. Like whatever that rock fragment was capable of. *Lab rat,* Weasel had called me, *just like the rest…*

I turned to Glimmer, urgent. "Flash said they 'butcher people's genes'. 'They make the kids into us.' What if they're creating *new* augments? Slicing and dicing, using raw genetic material from these children like puzzle pieces…"

"…to make something new," Glimmer finished darkly. "Like the way Sophron can copy others. But how is that even possible? We don't even know what part of an augment is genetic."

"No," I agreed. "But *he* does. He made the Sentinels, remember? Machines that detect the 'essential energy of augment' you talked about? What if he's really found it, and now he can create whatever he likes?" I rubbed suddenly clammy hands on my jeans. "Christ, we're in trouble."

"Maybe. It could all be bullshit, too."

"Yeah. All we gotta do to find out is locate this famous laboratory. Wow. *That* should be a piece of cake."

Glimmer typed rapidly on the tablet. "We don't need to find the lab. Flash already knows where it is."

"So?"

"So let's find Flash and ask him." He swiped his screen. "Ha. Thought so. There's a GPS coord embedded in this. Our good son Flash is leaving us a trail."

"Huh? Why? A trail to where?"

"Uh. Just a sec… yeah. Warehouse apartment block in the old docklands. Less than a mile from here."

We both jumped up. Distant thunder rumbled, an approaching storm. I scrabbled for my coat, Glimmer for a phone—his third or fourth this week, I calculated—and we made a swift exit.

"No way," I grumbled in the corridor. "Pricks have been holed up under our noses this whole time?"

"Looks like. At least we won't have to drive. That lean mean green machine is kind of conspicuous."

"Thought you liked conspicuous."

"With the entire city hunting us? I'll pass."

"That secret vid's a few days old," I reminded as we trotted down the fire stairs. My muscles yelled at me, demanding I cease this idiocy at once and lie down. Heh. Like the concept of *idiocy* had ever stopped me before. "At least as old as the City Library attack. What makes you think they'll still be there?"

"Were you even watching? Flash let us see their place. Zero effort to hide anything. Didn't even point the camera at a blank wall. Dude *wants* us to find him."

We reached the bottom of the stairs. "A traitor's death wish? Great. Nice way to behave, if he's so in *love* with her."

Glimmer yanked the parking lot's door open. "Not so much. It's possible to love someone and still know they should be locked up."

I flushed. "Yeah. I guess so."

Another stormy rumble, louder this time… and in its wake, a massive *crackk!* of exploding steel.

My nerves bristled. That wasn't thunder.

The garage grill rolled up, and I ran halfway up the ramp to sniff the air. Smoke, faint but definite. A whiff of hot-metal ozone, and under it that peculiar, chemical oil-fire scent of…

I looked at Glimmer. Glimmer looked at me. And we jumped into the F1 and he floored it.

~ 22 ~

Thirty-five seconds and three suicidal corners later, he squealed the machine to a halt and we leapt out.

Rusted warehouses in a row, their big sliding doors chained and padlocked. Bladed wire bristled atop chain-link fences. Ahead, spotlights shone on the yellow cranes and conveyors sprouting from the dockside. Opposite, on the boulder-strewn shore, dark waves pounded, flecked with foam.

Flash's warehouse had erupted in flames. Sliced down the middle, easy as a knife through cake, and a chunk of it had been hurled aside to shatter on the road. Remnants of corrugated-iron walls melted and curled, their edges glowing red. Fire roared from the wreckage, fanned by the wind. The stink of hot metal soaked the air bloody. The earth beneath my feet was scorched black, and blobs of melted concrete and steel oozed like lava from the wreckage.

I ran closer, shielding my face. The air stung and glittered with sparks, and my ears zinged with the evil crackle of flames. Wind had swept the fog away and raindrops spattered my face, only to sizzle away in the fierce, radiant heat.

People wandered around, gaping or filming on smartphones.

The street started to clog with traffic, drivers stopping to see what was going on.

No sign of *him*. Apart from the wreckage, that is. But my secret senses licked at the air, searching hungrily, tasting a sweet spritz of triumph.

He'd be here, all right. If he has anything even remotely resembling a weakness? A secret desire that lights him up? Makes him reckless, vulnerable, a prey to his baser instincts? This is it.

Fire.

No point lighting it if you can't watch it burn. And part of me wanted to watch it burn, too.

That little Seekernoid's voice inside me hissed, insistent. *Don't be a fool. Think he doesn't know that? He wanted you to see this. He's making a point.*

Always. But what?

Glimmer grabbed my arm. "C'mon. Sophron and Flash could still be in there."

Do we care? The words bubbled ugly in my throat, threatening to burst out. Those nasty little bastards, wrecking stuff and killing people. Let 'em burn.

But Flash was the only piece of the puzzle we had. We needed him. And hell, saving lives is my job. I'm the muscle, not the jury. They were just kids, after all. Their guilt or innocence is none of my business, their worth as human beings not mine to calculate. Right?

Besides, secretly I *wanted* to go in there. Feast my eyes on what he'd done, exult in it…

"Fire in the hole," I snapped, and I wrapped hot air around my fist and tore down a slab of wall.

Boof! Flame exploded from the gap, a roaring horror. I flung up my shield, covering me and Glimmer both as the fire raged, sucking air into the space I'd made. Sweat beaded inside my coat, and my singed hair ruffled in the draught. When the heat subsided a little, I let the shield fall, and together we edged into the dark doorway.

The warehouse's interior was a pile of ash and smoking rubble. Most of the roof had torn open to the sky. Falling raindrops sizzled to vapor. Flames licked the carnage, orange and scarlet, hurling monstrous shadows. The acrid air choked me, and I covered my mouth.

At the back, a window frame smoked and buckled, the glass panes long since broken or melted to dribbles. "Look," I called, pointing, "same as in the vid."

We scrambled towards it. The mezzanine was still standing. I jumped up on a waft of power, landing in a crouch. My boots crunched on charred detritus, and hot grit stung under my palms.

Flash's loft was still recognizable, having escaped the worst of the damage. The old sofa where he'd sat in the video was blackened, the fabric smoking. On the table, the books had burned, the edges of their pages crumbling to black ash. The computer screen was smashed, the plastic case melted into ink-marbled ribbons.

On the floor, a blackened carcass twitched.

I scrambled to my knees at Flash's side. His clothes were melted and burned, and the flesh underneath was weeping red and black like half-barbecued meat. His hair had caught alight, and now only short blond roots crinkled, showing his pale scalp.

He spluttered, splashing his chest with blood and spit. Still alive.

I clasped his ruined hand. Flash didn't seem to care. He was beyond pain. He blinked lashless eyes and grinned a ghastly red grin.

"We got your message," I whispered. "We'll stop them. I promise." But my heart sank. His burns oozed watery pus. Not a good sign. I'd no rehydration to give him, nothing to ease the pain.

Urgently, I clawed at my brain for first-aid basics. Heartbeat: check. Breathing: check, sort of. Now what? Jeez. Which bleeding bit do I cover first? Where the hell was Glimmer? Probably still searching for a way up.

Flash beckoned me closer, one rawboned finger. I leant in.

The breath rattled in his scorched windpipe. "Case," he mouthed, almost inaudible. "In the sofa. Tell Glimmer…"

"What, Flash? Tell him what?" I shook him gently. "Stay with me, man. Don't let go."

But his chest hitched once more, and he was still. Staring, those bloody eyeballs frozen in place.

Fuck.

I blinked back tears, my throat aching. I felt for him, this skinny kid with his hopeless crusade. He'd been used, as surely as any of us. Sucked dry by the girl he loved until he was nothing but an empty husk built on a skeleton of rage and guilt and sorrow. Just a pawn in some bigger, uglier game.

I folded his hand on his skinny chest. Tugged what remained of his t-shirt over his exposed ribs, garishly white in the ruined flesh. THERE IS NO TRY, read the wise words of Yoda.

Well, this kid had tried. And Razorfire murdered him for it. Wiped him up like a stain.

My mindmuscle jerked, rebellious, and hot rage exploded in my heart. I swept up the table with a roundhouse kick of invisible force and hurled it over the edge of the mezzanine. It crashed to the floor and broke.

Fuck! My teeth crunched a scream to bitter shards. He was just a kid. A baby, for fuck's sake, who happened to have a singular, exploitable talent. Just minding his own business until he was dragged into this.

Why the hell was Flash dead while I was being kept alive?

He was toying with me. And that maddened me more than any poor dead teenager or burned warehouse. I was a rat in a maze, lured this way and that for no purpose other than *his* devilish diversion…

As if on cue, flames dripped from above, an unholy curtain of liquid beauty. I shivered. My mouth sparkled, that telltale chemical scent that meant temptation.

But it also equaled threat. Shit. I scuttled backwards, crablike, my heart pounding.

Razorfire strode along the burning steel rafter, ten feet above my head. Fearless, effortless balance, like an arrogant tightrope

194

walker certain he was too good to fall. His red coat fluttered on swirling updrafts. His metal mask glistened, the rusty red of dried blood. Eager flames licked his footsteps, curling around his ankles in supplication. Behind him, through the broken roof, the night sky glittered, almost eclipsed by a halo of hellish red sparks.

He dropped, landing lightly as a cat in a flare of crimson silk. "Leave that alone," he advised. "You don't know where it's been."

My emotions tumbled, rocks in a barrel. Kill the bastard. Run like a coward. Crawl to my knees and weep.

I tried to yell, spit curses at him, but it withered in my throat. Below us, Glimmer swore, and steel crashed. My thoughts yammered. Had Vincent heard Flash whispering to me? I hoped not. Whatever this mysterious 'case' was, I needed to hide it from him.

Yeah. Because keeping secrets from Vincent was my specialty.

"You've done a poor job, Seeker." Fire kissed his fingertips, curled breathlessly over his wrists. He poked at the wreckage with his toe, and clicked his tongue in mocking dismay. "I'm disappointed. I can't do all the work, you know. Can't swan around all night *burning* things. I've a city to run."

My head whirled, dizzy with ugly choices. I could crack a whip of talent and shove him off the mezzanine. Start a fight. Surely, he wouldn't really kill me, not after all we'd been through? Wouldn't kick me to the curb like garbage, the way he'd discarded Iceclaw and Witch and Weasel and Espectro and…

Yeah. Okay. He totally would. *Think you're so special, Verity? You're already ashes to him.*

But part of me stubbornly refused to believe. Raged against the very idea. Yes, I *was* special, goddamn it. He'd said so. He'd proved it. I'd *felt* it…

"Where's Sophron?" I asked, trying to brush off his taunts, trying not to stare at those clever fingers or inhale that smell that dripped with so many delicious memories. Trying to ignore the splitting pain in my heart when he said *disappointed.* "Did you kill her, too?"

A laugh, chilling despite the warmth that radiated from his body in shimmers. "You're missing the point. Honestly, if I didn't already know how clever you were, I'd think I was wasting my time."

He gazed down at the burning warehouse, a smile curling his statue-perfect lips. Not the cruel, contemptuous smile that had so often paralyzed the city with fear. No, this was his enraptured smile. The one that had made me laugh, made my secret flesh burn, whispered things into my mouth that made me shudder and cry out.

In answer, the inferno glowed brighter, infatuated. The flames flickered in his direction, elongating as if they thirsted for closer contact. As if they needed him, somehow. Fire loved him back. Always had.

I scrambled up, smoothing my dusty coat. "Admiring your handiwork? Vanity doesn't become you."

Dark-fire irony flickered in his eyes. "Of course it becomes me. What's it all for, if I can't gloat a little?"

"So what now? Are we talking, or are you just taking a breather before you roast me to cinders?"

"Where's your puppy?" Ignoring my question. Interesting. "Still clinging like a lovesick barnacle? Oh, look. Thought so."

Glimmer clambered from the smoke onto the mezzanine, hand over hand, having climbed up poles and broken struts to get here. Charcoal dust coated his jeans, smeared his jacket. He scrambled to his feet and drew his pistol, one smooth full-body action. And fired.

Crack-crack! Double-tap from thirty feet away. Gotta love a guy who doesn't waste time.

Razorfire didn't flinch. Didn't even blink.

The bullets sang past him, glittering in warm breeze, and curved harmlessly out the window. Super-heated air, I realized dumbly. Pressure differential. He'd brushed the bullets aside. Dodged a gunshot, just by *standing* there. Holy fuck-a-doodle.

"Try that again." A dark invitation. "Go on. See what happens."

"Can't blame me for speculating." Glimmer didn't lower his aim. But white light glittered between the fingers of his bottom hand, a threat or a crackling warning. My guts clenched. *Fuck, don't throw that. You know you can't beat him. He'll melt you to mist…*

"Verity, you okay?" Glimmer's warm presence slipped into my head, soothing, like a mother waking her child from a nightmare. *Listen to me. Feel me, here with you. You're not alone…*

Razorfire flicked a dismissive finger, and sparks rained. "Separation anxiety. I'm touched. Get lost, puppy, the grown-ups are talking."

"I'm fine." I sidestepped towards Glimmer, unwilling to shift my gaze for an instant. I had to buy time while I figured out what the hell to do. "I talked to your glitterball thief," I improvised. "Lovely guy. Sweet temper."

"Sorry, who?"

My secret senses cried foul. Vincent was petulant. In a mood. Something was up. "Espectro. From the museum?"

"Oh, him." He traced the table's edge, flames trailing from his fingertip. "Hard to stay alive, I'd imagine, with your molecules being torn in two different directions. Glad it's not me cleaning up the mess. Idiotic plan, by the way." Silky steel whetted his tone sharp. "How fortunate you lived through it."

You son of a bitch. My mindmuscle cracked like a whip, furious. I knew it. He'd have let me die. I wanted to claw his self-satisfied eyes out… or fall at his feet and beg him to love me again.

Verity…

Daring, I groped for Glimmer's hand, clasped it tightly, fighting to keep my calm. He was warm, steady. Bless him. But the nightmare world of danger inherent in that innocuous contact made me want to scream for forgiveness. I was touching another man. Holding him. Relying on him.

Razorfire wrinkled his nose. "Oh, please. I think I just threw up in my mouth."

"Espectro used the word 'collection'," I said shakily. "What did he mean? What are you…?"

197

"You know what? I'm not in the mood for confidences." Razorfire's long fingers clenched on a fistful of fiery rage. Sparks exploded in Glimmer's hair, making him duck, and boiling flame sheeted an inch above my head.

I yelped, recoiling… and in a giddy instant, I was on my knees and Razorfire was in my face. "Don't," he spat, an inch from my mouth. "Just don't. You dare to imagine for an instant that you can stroke your puppy's fur and make me jealous? I don't think you understand our relationship."

My heart thudded. I wanted to be sick. I searched my mind desperately, fishing for Glimmer's precious tendrils of strength… nothing. Torn away. Gone. It was just me and *him*.

My courage withered to a crisp. But despite the radiant heat sizzling my eyeballs, I didn't dare look away.

His stare kindled, so dark and warped, and he gave the wildest, most seductive smile in the world. "Kudos for trying, though. I'm stimulated. Seriously. Let's go back to my place and get it over with."

My breath hitched tight. Defiance had saved me, where begging wouldn't. He was playing with me. God, I was so tired of this. I wanted it over. Wanted for once to be on the winning side…

An ugly, tempting thought pierced me, a drug-poisoned needle, and a frosted glass wall in my mind shattered.

If I gave in, would all this carnage end?

My brain reeled, this unpleasant new clarity whacking my balance out of the park. But before I could muster a reply—*you've got to be kidding, you crazy fuck* or *oh God yes please*—sirens wailed on the smoky breeze, rising in pitch as they approached.

He watched me suffer for a moment longer. Gave me his eyes, his dark heat. So many emotions packed into that candid glance. Contempt. Admiration. Desire. Murder.

Then, he shivered, theatrical. "Brr. The city's finest, come to *get* me. Better run. See you soon."

He brushed a fingertip under my chin, a trail of impossible flames. And in a swirl of crimson silk and smoke, he was gone.

I fell to hands and knees and gasped for air. It was like all my oxygen had been sucked away, consumed in that perfidious fire.

Learned response. Pavlov's dogs, salivating at bell's clang. You know it. So fight it.

I gulped, winded. I'd been in love, the way few are ever in love. Didn't change the fact that he was inhuman. Insane. I'd loved a monster.

Was I just being selfish? Clinging hopelessly to ideals I'd never fulfill, in a cowardly effort to redeem myself. Allowing all this destruction and murder, just so I could pretend I was trying to be *good*.

Whatever "good" even meant, for fuck's sake.

Black hypoxic spots swelled before my boggling eyes. What a cruel, thoughtless idiot I'd been. Who the fuck cared about my conscience? If I gave Vincent what he wanted, he'd stop this. I'd save lives.

Or was that just a sick lie? Self-flattering bullshit. Exactly what Razorfire wanted me to think. That classic, twisted villain's mantra: *it's all about me.*

Glimmer swore and thumped me on the back, and my ugly thoughts melted into a puddle of sheer relief that he was safe, that he hadn't been roasted to smoking cinders just to soothe Vincent's ego.

Gradually, I caught my breath. "You okay?"

Glimmer retrieved his fallen pistol and scratched ruefully at his skunk stripe. The ends were crinkled short. "Damn it. That's the second time that psycho has set my hair on fire. Everyone's a fashion critic."

I snorted, glad to brush off my unease with quips. But barbed wire threat still twisted in my veins. Vincent had lost his temper. He never lost his temper that easily. Not unless he wanted to.

So why was Glimmer still alive?

"Be glad that's all he did," I muttered, queasy. "What the hell was that, supervillain PMS?"

199

"You tell me." Glimmer shrugged, distant. Like I'd bruised him somehow.

How had I offended him? What thoughtless shit had I said now? "Thanks, dude," I added, confused. "I needed your help there."

A quick smile, warmer. "You're welcome. I think you're getting stronger. I only had to pull half a dozen muscles to hold you back."

We helped each other stand straight and dusted each other off. The sirens shrieked louder, their pitch leveling off amid the squeal of brakes.

"Seen enough?"

"More than enough. Oh, wait." I turned back and picked up a broken metal shard. Tore into the sofa, scattering ripped cloth and lumps of foam. It took only a few seconds to find it.

A square metal box with a handle on the end, like a safety deposit can or a lockbox. It weighed about five pounds. The surface zapped my fingers, a horrid numb sensation. I recoiled, dark curiosity pricking like a wasp sting on the back of my neck.

Augmentium. I rattled it. Big heavy items clattered inside.

Tell Glimmer. Flash's whisper echoed, fading into the smoke. A dying declaration. He'd had only a few seconds to say something—anything—and he'd chosen this.

But tell Glimmer what? And why augmentium? To protect what was inside… or to imprison it?

Glimmer rummaged in the wreckage of Flash's computer, pocketing a dented hard drive and a few burned books. "You never know," he replied to my raised eyebrows. "Care to take the back door, madam?"

"Took 'em right out of my mouth." Already, those sirens had shut off. Flashlights darted through the smoke, shouts edging closer. Glimmer offered me his hand. I grabbed it, sweet gratitude. He'd been here for me. Saved me. Without him, I was toast.

I flashed him a humbled glance, and the sight of him melted my heart. So brave and steadfast. "Dude, I am so glad you're here."

200

"Me, too." Defensive. Hesitant. Chilly, even. "But promise me something, okay?"

My courage crinkled. "Sure. Anything."

"Don't ever use me as bait again."

I was too stunned to speak.

Bait.

Fuck. I'd needed Glimmer's help a few minutes ago when Razorfire taunted me, and Glimmer gave it. But what if, in my black and secret heart, I'd actually wanted something other than help?

You dare to imagine for an instant that you can make me jealous?

Had I? Did I…?

My face burned, surely ugly red. I didn't know what to say. So I just summoned a twist of force and wrapped it around us, an invisible slingshot. Together, we sprinted for the broken window, and sailed out into the night.

~ 23 ~

When we got home, Ebenezer was sleeping fitfully, muttering feverish nonsense into his pillow. I woke him and fed him water with some double-strength migraine aspirins I found in Widow Swanky's drawer. It was all I had. He swallowed groggily, blinking owlishly at me. His eyes were scarily empty. My stomach coiled, a flicker of his augment sliding like a cold greasy finger in the coils of my intestines. Swiftly, I backed off and shut the door.

Glimmer watched me from the sofa, a keyboard on his lap. Pale dawn streamed in through the gossamer curtains. Outside, birds chirped their irritatingly cheerful song. "How is he?"

"Still alive, if that's what you mean." Eb was my friend. He'd trusted me. Sitting by and doing nothing while his condition worsened made my nerves seethe with my uselessness. But what choice?

Fresh hatred for Peggy Finney frothed in my chest. That perky lying queen bee was responsible for this. She'd tricked Adonis into taking her in, and poisoned us...

A thought glanced off my skull, a brick hurled in a riot. Espectro had the fever, too. But how, if Peggy was responsible?

"Look at this." Glimmer had plugged Flash's hard drive into a shiny black PC he'd scrounged from somewhere—was it Widow

Swanky's?—and the command-prompt window was filled with a list of filenames.

I wandered over, casual. But his accusation in that burning warehouse still raked rusty barbs along my bones.

Bait.

I hadn't intended to provoke Vincent, had I? I didn't *want* to play his games. I'd simply reached for Glimmer when I'd needed help, as we'd agreed. Just because Vincent was bugfuck enough to think I was using Glimmer to make him jealous—that I was *flirting*, for God's sake—didn't make it true.

Right?

"Nice work," I said, determined to forget about it. "What've we got?"

"Most of it's fragmented, so I can't read it. Or the remaining text is scrambled. But there is this." Glimmer typed a filename and hit Enter.

A red window flashed up. Black text, darkly familiar.

We Know Who You Are

"Jackpot." Strange excitement heated my blood. I was torn between wanting to see and cringing away from whatever repulsive content we'd find.

"It's a link to a hidden server," Glimmer explained. "And I can interrogate it for metadata. But—check this—only two registered users." He highlighted a line of code on the original window. "There's *tyler*—I'm presuming that's Flash—and someone called *moreau*. So if it is a message board…"

"…it's a private one." I stared, uneasy. "So, not a villain death-porn site, then. Who's *moreau*? Not the doctor, I'm thinking."

"Maybe it's Sophron. It fits with what Flash told us about the laboratory. In the story, Dr. Moreau was creating monsters on his island."

"If Flash is trying to help us, this could be information about the lab. Maybe he's broken into their files. *Moreau* could be the person who did this to him."

203

"Or someone who's helping him."

"True. Any passwords?"

"Nope. If his system was alive, I could run a key trace. But it isn't, thanks to you know who."

I scowled at the screen's smug message. "How many tries d'you think we get before it burns us?"

"One, probably. But even if we guess correctly, the server can see our IP. It'll know we're not *tyler* and kick us off."

"Great. Can we join as a guest weirdo or something?"

"Sure, we can try. Still only get one go before it kicks us off."

I thought hard. "Remember what you said before? 'It's an invitation to identify ourselves'. So why don't we do just that? This is Flash's party. He knows who we are, it says. So let's confirm it. Maybe that's what it wants."

"Okay," Glimmer said slowly. "Let's play paranoia. But which of us… oh, hell."

"Shit," I said, at the same time. We exchanged glances. We'd had the same thought together, like we did so many times.

It's all about you now, Flash said. *They already know who you are.* And he wasn't talking to me.

Glimmer cocked a dark eyebrow. I shrugged, secretly relieved that for once it wasn't all about *me*. "What've we got to lose? Unless you've got a better guess, go for it."

GLIMMER, he typed, and hit Enter.

The red screen flashed black. And a video popped up.

Same scene: cluttered desk, rumpled bed. Nighttime, a single lamp shining. On the sofa, Flash waved at us, solemn as usual. In the lamplight, his face loomed, cadaverous. He'd lost even more weight, and his skin looked translucent, stretched thin.

"If you're watching this, Glimmer, I'm probably dead and this has started in earnest. I don't have much time, so listen up. Don't trust the Sentinels. They aren't what they seem… actually, they're exactly what they seem. You'll see."

204

What was that supposed to mean? I glanced a question at Glimmer, who shrugged.

Flash wiped his bleeding nose, black-dyed hair flopping over his eyes. "This is all about you, man. I don't know why she wants you. Shit, she never tells me anything and I don't ask anymore. You want to know what's going on? Find Moreau. Moreau's one of them and knows the whole thing."

I bit my lip. Who the hell was this Moreau character? A traitor to the mad-scientist cause, helping Flash stop those cruel experiments? Or was it just part of the trick?

"In the meantime, don't fight her." Flash lifted his thin arms, just bone hung with drooping skin now. "You can't beat her that way. Look what happened to me."

I winced. "Did Sophron do that to him? It looks like he's wasting away."

Flash was speaking again. "Anyway, she won't be satisfied with breaking things for long. She's gonna call him out soon enough. You know who I mean. It'll be messy. So be ready to show her what you're made of." A crash, and outside the window, orange light flickered. Flash smiled, ghostly. "It's started. Moreau, Glimmer. Find Moreau…"

A hiss of static and, abruptly, the video cracked to black.

I gripped Glimmer's arm. "Did you see that? That was firelight."

"It was tonight. Just before Razorfire attacked." Glimmer scraped back his hair. "Call him out, Flash said. Was that what happened?"

"But Sophron wasn't there. Razorfire as much as admitted that. He doesn't make that kind of mistake."

"So if you were Sophron and you wanted to call Razorfire out, what would you do?"

"Attack something he cares about, I guess. Bruise his ego. But how?"

Outside our window, dawn brightened, and a light breeze fluttered the curtains, bringing the salty tang of the waterfront. My fatigue came crashing back. We'd barely rested or eaten in forty-eight hours. But no time to care about that now…

"Oh, hell." My pulse jerked, waking me up. "Bruise his ego. Library, then fire department. All the city's infrastructure. She's working her way to the top."

"And he's gifted her the excuse she's been waiting for," said Glimmer grimly. "He burns her home—"

"—so she'll burn his right back," I finished. "She'll attack City Hall. Today."

~ 24 ~

The big marble and granite edifice of City Hall glistened in early morning sunlight. The gilded dome on the roof glittered with dew. Eerie quiet hung over the paved square out front as we approached. Motorcycle cops patrolled, the usual security precautions, and more uniforms lined the striped steel barricades on the square's edge. Twin lion statues growled down from the frieze above the pillared entrance. The city's motto, carved in Latin: *Shine in adversity*, blah blah, the usual propaganda bullshit. Above the pillars, Sentinels perched on a ledge like ugly gargoyles, ready to pounce on evil spirits.

I *felt* like an evil spirit. A malignant ghost, by my very presence laying a curse on this place. The Ancient Mariner, doomed to spread destruction and sorrow by the creature he'd so thoughtlessly shot down.

Well, the fucking albatross was dead. No point crying over what's done. If Sophron wanted to crush City Hall and bait Razorfire into a fight that could flatten the city to rocks and ash? We'd stop her as best we could. End of story.

For once, at least, we'd arrived first. We were catching up to her. Dared I hope things were at last going our way?

We picked a spot in the park under the sweet hanging fragrance of a row of orange trees. A stray cat stalked by, unconcerned. Litter rattled in the gutter, wafting in the breeze.

The city had barely woken. I didn't care. We'd wait all day if we had to.

Glimmer watched the building, his expression dark. He'd tied a black bandanna over his burned hair—the Dread Pirate Glimmer, somebody fetch this man a cutlass—but he was unmasked. We both were. What'd be the point?

"So here we are," he murmured. "What now?"

"Hell, I don't know. You're the brains in this outfit. Set a trap before she gets here? Our win-loss record isn't too good so far."

"No argument here." He cracked his neck, a crunch of fatigue. "It's occurred to you, right, that Razorfire might be the only one who can beat her?"

I shivered. "Let's pole-vault that pond of piranhas when we reach it, okay?"

"In any case, we should warn these cops, evacuate the building. Even this early, there must be someone in there."

"Think they'll listen? The place is full of politicians. They must get a dozen hoax calls a day." My throat was dry, my eyes gritty. I wished I'd eaten breakfast, or even had a drink of water. Grimly, I flexed my mindmuscle, and it responded, strong and eager but controlled. So far, so good.

"Yeah. But we gotta try." He tossed me his phone. "Call 9-1-1, give 'em a terrorist threat or something. At least get some SWAT and bomb disposal down here. For what it's worth." He hopped over the gutter and walked towards the barricade. Hands in sight, to prove he offered no threat.

I pressed 9-1-1 and hit Call, my eyes on Glimmer. The line rang.

The nearest uniform wasn't taking any chances. He hovered his master hand over his holstered weapon. Sun glinted off his aviator lenses. "Step back. This is a restricted area. Do not approach."

Glimmer kept walking. "I have information. There's a threat against this building—"

Snap! Out came the pistol, two-handed, front-on stance, the way cops do. "Stop, or you will be fired upon."

Now the cop's pals were interested, and suddenly Glimmer had five weapons pointed at him. First, last and only warning. Good dogs, just like they'd been trained.

My call kept ringing. I chewed my lip, impatient. Come *on*.

Glimmer halted, raising his hands. "I don't mean any harm. Come search me if you want. I'm wearing a sidearm and a knife. You can have 'em. Just listen."

At last, my call picked up. "Nine-one-one emergency, how can I assist?"

"Police," I answered. "I'm reporting a bomb threat—"

Crash! Lightning erupted, directly above the dome.

My eardrums smarted. Shit. I dropped the phone and sprinted for the square.

The ground quaked, heaving me off course. Rubble was already falling. Cops scuttled around like maddened ants. Glimmer and I hurdled the barriers together. The stink of burning ozone already sharpened the air. I collected my power and summoned a shield, preparing to hurl us in any direction if attacked.

Bang! Another bolt blasted a lion statue to flying pebbles. And down the jagged white voltage arc surfed Sophron. Like a kid on a slippery slide, arms outstretched, blue dreads streaking in the breeze.

She bounded to the ground, electricity crackling on her fingertips. Above, the dome was burning, and a huge stone fragment broke off and fell through the roof. *Boom!* Bricks and masonry crumbled. The earth shuddered and the façade's columns began to crack and teeter.

Behind us, a helicopter swerved closer, *thwup-thwup!* Police gunship, spiked with assault weapons. I spared a moment for admiration. Brave chopper pilot, flying into an electrical storm. Brave, or a fucking idiot.

209

Glimmer kept running. "Grab her!"

I flashed out my mindmuscle and punched. *Pow!* Sophron flew backwards, slamming onto her back in a pile of broken stone building. The chopper fired. *Tat-tat-tat!* Hail of bullets, pinging off the stones.

Ricochet hell. Goddamn it. I grabbed Glimmer and we tumbled for cover in the dust. Bullets cracked above our heads. "Assholes," I panted. "The least they could do is fucking *hit* something."

Sophron flung out one skinny hand, pointing skywards. An ugly wave of shimmering air erupted, and *whoomph!* the chopper tumbled wildly, a head-over-tail spin. Bullets sprayed. Engines howled, and those slicing blades fought desperately to create lift, to keep the thing airborne.

Sorry. No such thing as a gliding helicopter.

It smashed into the ground like the whirling sack of bricks it was, and burst into howling flame.

Sophron jumped up, unharmed. The evil light of the burning aircraft danced over her face. Her laughter pierced the dusty air. Eerie, hollow, a gleeful little girl's. "Burn, burn," she sang. "Think you can take me, Glimmer? You've got nothing. Now come on out, Mr. Mayor, and let's talk this over."

Glimmer and I crouched, hidden for the moment by a pile of wreckage. "What now?" I said.

He shrugged. "Hit her again. What else've we got?"

"I'm game if you are."

At the square's perimeter—the edge of the mess she'd made— emergency vehicles screamed to a halt. Fire engines, police SUVs, ambulances, their lights drilling through the dust… then, a dark sedan pulled up, its black windows reflecting scarlet flames.

The back door opened, and Ashton jumped out. Immaculate suit, neat blond curls. The perfect PA.

I laughed sickly. Here we go.

Ashton held the door. Vincent oozed out. Mayor's suit, red tie. No mask.

My composure did a clumsy backflip and landed badly. Memory flashed: that stormy night on the roof of the FortuneCorp skyscraper, the last time he'd turned up in the clear to an endgame like this. It hadn't gone well for us.

"What the hell's he doing," I hissed, "giving a press conference?"

Glimmer was focused on Sophron. His fingers weaved a web of shadowy mindsense. "Whatever. Let him draw her eye. But don't get distracted. She's our target."

"Right with you." But unwilled, my gaze followed Vincent. He strode in calmly, surveying the destruction. My nerves wriggled, anticipation and dread. He was on TV in the clear. He knew it. What was his plan?

Sophron bounced, her blue dreadlocks dancing, and clapped delighted hands. "Yay! I knew you'd come."

"Ready?" Glimmer whispered. And without waiting for me, he sprinted for her, full tilt, and hurled a glittering sphere of power. *Boom!* It unfurled, spreading like ripples on a pond, only these were black, ugly throbs of thoughtfuck.

What was it? His sleep trick. Another conscience bomb. Screaming psychosis. I didn't care. I just let rip with a fist of mindforce, and knocked Sophron straight into the ripples' path.

She leapt. Twenty feet, straight up. Avoided the dissipating wave by inches, and at the same time she fired a crackle of blue lightning at Glimmer.

Zap! Frantic, I grabbed him with my power, hurled him out of the way. The lightning stabbed the ground where he'd stood, carving a smoking rut. Glimmer flew across the square and into a broken pillar. He fell, and rolled, and at the sight of the blood on his ripped skin, recklessness stung like an angry wasp at my heart. I jumped up, my mindmuscle thrashing. Screw me raw, if he was hurt, I'd…

"Verity, for God's sake." A hand dragged me back down. I whirled, fists stuffed with angry fuck-off, ready to kill.

Grimly, Adonis held on.

I gaped. My brother was smeared in white dust. Hair, face, shirt, everything, his bright blue eyes blinking out. Blood dripped luridly on his cheek, a cut from a falling rock. I didn't know what to do. Hug him or flatten him? Was he enemy or friend?

I settled for a hug, and damn it if he didn't hug me back. Guilty tears stung my eyes. I pushed away. "Wh-what are you doing here?"

"My job." Adonis shrugged. "We're crime-fighters, aren't we? Let's fight crime."

My heart overflowed, bitter but sweet. I'd rarely been so glad to see him in my life. If that was an apology, I'd take it. For now.

"Truce accepted." I had so much to tell him. But how the hell could I say anything about Peg without alienating him all over again? "Where's everyone?"

"Just me." He didn't elaborate.

I didn't ask. Wherever Jem and Harriet and the others were, they couldn't help us now. "Okay. Let's do this. Any ideas?"

He flexed his fingers. "Same old plan. You hold her down, I'll fuck her up."

"Oldie but a goodie." I stifled a grin. That was my brother.

I glanced around, taking stock of the scene. The crowd was growing, a bunch of idiots milling at the barricade despite the authorities' efforts to hold them back. Cameras flashing, smart-phones held aloft to film. Sophron giggled and tore giant rocks from the rubble, flinging them into the air and watching them smash. Glimmer crawled on bloody hands and knees, catching his breath. Vincent… well, Vincent was dodging flying rocks as a civilian might, with a riot police escort, their transparent shields protecting him from the debris. Honestly.

"Glimmer can help," I added, a kernel of hostility still burning. Easy for Adonis to be nice when he needed me. If he thought I'd simply forgive him and go back to doing as he told me? He could damn well think again. "He's a tough little dude."

"With you for a friend? He must be fucking indestructible." My brother flashed me his smile—no augment, just good old weapons-grade Adonis charm—and I melted, like he'd known I would.

"Asshole," I grumbled.

"That's why you love me."

"Let's go get him, then." And we ran.

Glimmer stumbled to his feet, right as we skidded to a halt beside him. He wiped dust from his eyes, and flexed bruised limbs, testing them. "Fuck it, Verity. That *hurts*."

The warm, fond spot in my heart with his name on it flowered. He could take a beating with the best of them. "You okay?"

"Never been better. I love it when you hurl me into walls." Glimmer winced as he put weight on his left leg, but he flipped Adonis a salute. "Nice timing—"

"Call me 'boss' and I'll whip your pretty-boy ass," Adonis said.

A tired Glimmer grin. "Promises. One day, I'll call you on 'em, you know."

"Dude, if we survive this? I'll even bring the flowers." Ad glanced from Glimmer to me and back again. "Everyone ready?"

I took a steadying breath, my senses aglitter with unexpected hope. Glimmer was by my side. Adonis still loved me, or at least needed me enough to put our differences aside for now. Surely, all was right with the world. "Say the word."

Adonis winked, and for a moment, his old, ironic, *world-won't-know-what-hit-it* self peeked out. "Let's bag us a villain."

And the three of us advanced on Sophron, side by side.

She capered merrily to and fro, hurling boulders and twisted steel at Vincent and his riot-cop buddies. With *my* power, the thieving bitch. Every now and then, she'd let rip with a lightning strike or a shimmer of Eb's feartalent, and someone would burst into flame or crumple to the ground in a melting blubber-ball of terror. Fun for all the family.

The fury in my soul forged hotter, into a steely spear of hatred. That scaly serpent of *bad* coiling in my guts chuckled in triumph. *That's it. Use that hatred. Embrace it…*

But I didn't care. Sophron deserved my wrath. She was wanton, her destruction indiscriminate. Worse than Razorfire, I thought, who at least had the decency to be crazy, with some fucked-up power ideology behind his immaculately planned murderous sprees. Sophron killed on impulse. For *fun*.

Just like Obsidian, the cackling madman who'd killed my mother, just so he could enjoy watching her die. Just so he could relish my father's despair.

Well, Dad and Mike had ended Obsidian, and good riddance. I didn't care if Sophron really did turn out to be a four-year-old forced into a teenager's body. No excuse. She had the mind of an adult now, and she murdered anyway. She deserved nothing less than the ugly end we'd give her.

Because we would kill her, right? Dead. Ended. Not left to the police and the lame-duck legal system, where she might reap the benefit of some idiotic technicality.

Glimmer might have a piece to say about that. Whatever. Accidents happen. They can bill me for the damage later.

With a jagged sweep of force, I knocked Sophron off her feet. *Splat!* Her face planted into the paving, bones snapping. We broke into a sprint. I picked her up, shook her until her limbs rattled, and slammed her onto her back at our feet. Her skull cracked down hard. Blood splattered crimson mess from her broken nose. Suck it up, sister.

Still, she fought to rise. But Glimmer jammed his knee into her shoulder. Grabbed her chin, made her look. His fingertips sizzled with *dizzy* before her eyes. "Watch me," he whispered. "Hush."

She collapsed, eyeballs rolling sickly white, like she'd inhaled some stupefying drug.

Adonis unleashed. Subtle at first, just a mist of faint golden suggestion settling over her body. Sophron thrashed, trying to escape, but her will was bleeding out, as surely as lifeblood from a knife in the throat.

"Breathe, sweetie," Adonis purred, silken as a panther, "that's it. Relax. Let yourself go." The mist brightened, intensifying into a glittering aura. It swarmed over her, invading every crevice. Bright tendrils crawled up her nose, forced into her gaping mouth and down her throat.

She convulsed, a beached fish choking for air. Ruthlessly, Adonis turned his talent on harder. "Let go, sweetie. Don't fight. Just let me…" Her limbs shuddered, and with a strangled cry, she fell limp. Her eyelids fluttered, closing.

I kicked her. No response. Her body just slumped. She'd passed out.

Adonis made a disgusted face. "Eww. Hope it was good for you."

"Not perky enough for you?" I muttered.

"Screw you." No heat in his words.

"Be nice, kids. I love it when a plan comes together." Glimmer tossed me his augmentium cuffs. I bent to reach for Sophron's skinny wrists.

She slammed her forehead into the bone between my eyes.

Doinng! My brain clanged, and the world did a sick, pain-bright somersault. My eyes brimmed. Jesus fucking Christ. Dizzy, I fought to right myself, defend my friends. But I was helpless. I heard her feet scrape as she jumped up, the cruel tinkle of her laughter. Glimmer cursed, and I reeled under another wave of unsteadiness as he hurled a ball of *sleepy*…

Adonis screamed. An agonized, ripped-flesh howl.

Aghast, I dashed water from my eyes, trying to see what had happened. Sophron's evil giggling face greeted me, gloating like a poisoned viper with its fangs sunk into coveted skin.

My brother thrashed on the ground, his mouth bloody with black-glitter froth. He clawed at his face, choking up lungfuls of wet black sparkle, trying to cleanse his system of what she'd done.

She'd stolen his power, stained it black and hurled it back at him. Perverted with rage and hatred. A reverse lovebomb.

All the stuff we'd done to her? It hadn't even made a dent. She'd been *playing* with us.

I stumbled back, flailing, my mind refusing to compute. My thoughts whirled, like a circus dancer in ever-decreasing rings.

What could we do now, against this? What if Glimmer was right? What if everything we had wasn't enough? She had Adonis's power now. She could take over the city. Make them love her, one by one, with a wink and a smile.

Sophron advanced on me. Her sunken eyes glittered diamond-black, suffused with Adonis's distorted power. She was breathing hard and fast. Her fingers flexed hungrily, and her tongue flicked out to coat her lips. Pure relish.

And as I watched, the mess of her broken nose began to heal. Skin and cartilage crawling, reforming, a horrid cyborg dream.

Desperate, I scrabbled for my mindsense. One last defiant blow. *Screw you, witch. You've got no right.*

But she didn't unleash on me. She whirled, and fired her sparkling power in the opposite direction.

Straight at Glimmer.

My heart squeezed in fright, a horror-film shock. I tried to run, hurl something at him, shove him aside, but my mindmuscle just wailed like a frightened animal and I couldn't grab, couldn't control the force. Glimmer staggered, trying to get out of the way.

And with a sulfurous *crack!* that boiled the air like brimstone, a writhing whip of fire sliced the earth from beneath him.

~ 25 ~

Boom! Concrete and rock vaporized, and the rippling air caught fire. Heat blew my hair back, stinging my nose with the chemical-rich scent of incendiary. The melting earth cracked apart, a glowing-edged crevasse like a demon's mouth, and Glimmer dropped into it.

Sophron's glittering missile speared harmlessly overhead. It recoiled in mid-air, snarling, like a snake hunting for lost prey. It caught alight in the superheated air and crisped to a howling cinder. Ash rained on my face.

I screamed.

Sophron snarled and spun, her dirty fingertips aglitter with fury.

With a twitch of one finger, Vincent recalled his flamewhip. A white-hot slice of fire, too bright to behold. It snapped obediently back into his hand with an electric *crack!*

He didn't smile. Didn't lose his temper. Just gazed upon her, calm and perfectly poised. Lethal.

I gasped, winded, searching for air, smoke, anything I could breathe. My mind screeched, that caged lunatic kicking at her cell walls, refusing to swallow what had happened.

Glimmer was gone. Glimmer was burning. Vincent had unleashed, no mask, no costume, nothing. And the world was watching.

What in unholy hell was going on?

But no time to marvel now. Urgently, I dived for the lip of the crevasse. Stretched down into hell, a desperate scoop of all the power I could muster, and *pulled*.

The earth creaked. Dust exploded from the crevasse, searing my eyes, scorching my windpipe. Rocks peppered my face. I fell back, my bangs crinkling into tiny burned coils. And Glimmer's long, lean shape flew out.

Whoosh! Just in time, I thrust out a cushion of repelling force, so he wouldn't break every bone in his body, and he landed beside me, *bounce-groan-flop*.

Flames licked his scorched clothes. I slapped them out and rolled onto my back, coughing. Fuck me, I hurt. But Glimmer was okay. He looked alive, at least... but barbed-wire tears savaged my eyeballs, and my heart erupted with acid vengeance.

If Glimmer was hurt—if *Adonis* was hurt—fuck, if either of them was even *bruised*, I'd do more than lose my temper and kill her. I'd rip her fucking face off and eat it, and *then* kill her. I'd suck the marrow from her bones and spit it out.

My mindmuscle growled like the starving beast it was, and I scrambled up, unholy murder on my mind.

Sophron twisted a blue dreadlock around one finger and chewed on the tip of another, like a little girl. At her feet, Adonis twitched, still in her power. She barely seemed to notice him, and her disdain poured fresh poison into my blood.

Vincent stalked towards Sophron through the fire. No riot police protecting him now. The rubble hissed and spat, and heat haze sizzled around him... but he didn't burn. The flames wreathed him, a luminescent second skin. They *adored* him.

Cruel seduction whispered in my ear. I knew how the fire felt. How it ached, so desperate to please him that it hurt inside, the way a broken heart hurts... only worse, because it's salted with that most horrible torture of all: hope.

I swallowed, a bereft ache in my throat. So redolent with memory, to see him like this. Unmasked, but… alive. His bronze hair burned, alight but not consumed. Latent power crackled over his fingertips, and around one wrist coiled that infamous flamewhip, a snarling white-hot serpent. He was brilliant, fantastic, from another world.

Something cracked inside my chest, and the toxic memory of utter bliss spilled out. He was glorious. So beautiful, it stung my eyes. Like the fire, I longed to fall at his feet and worship him… and it wasn't just infatuation, or even fleshly desire.

He'd introduced me to myself. The real me, that tiny frightened kernel of *self* that hides, lost and alone, deep in your heart, where no one can judge. Lies, expectations, crippling doubts all stripped away… and what I'd found underneath wasn't ugly, but sublime. When I'd loved him, I'd loved *myself*. Vincent made it okay to be me.

Bitter, jealous, rage-ruled, mass-murdering me.

And now here he stood, in the clear. The city's gaze upon us. Was this the final test? The ultimate temptation? Should I jump into the abyss? Or cling to the edge by my fingernails and try one last time to heave myself out into the light?

Vincent glided to a halt, twenty feet from Sophron, amid the burning rubble.

Coyly, Sophron fidgeted on one foot, fiddling with her dreads. "Do you like what I've created? I did it for you. You've taught me so much."

I shuddered. She reminded me of Harriet making eyes at Glimmer. Belay that, girl. You have no idea what you're flirting with.

Vincent just laughed. "Please. Don't even imagine playing that game." Somehow, his words carried over the howling fire. "Let's call this what it is: a pitiful effort to get my attention. Still, I confess, you've inconvenienced me. Last chance. You'd better be sure you want a fight."

Alarm bells clanged an odd discord in my head. He hadn't carved her to pieces when he could have. Hadn't killed us all and strolled away victorious. Instead, he'd chosen to slice the ground from under Glimmer's feet.

Kept Glimmer alive. Thwarted Sophron's designs, inflamed her rage.

Vincent *wanted* to fight her.

Shit. I tried to jump, run, get in first. But my muscles wouldn't move. My tongue wouldn't form a protest. All I could do was stare.

In answer, Sophron just giggled and chewed her fingertip.

Vincent glanced at me, a glitter of heartfelt... something. Gloating? Regret? Challenge? And with an elegant flick of his wrist, he unfurled his favorite weapon. That spitting twist of fire, just a foot long but crackling with threat. Like burning magnesium, so bright it hurt my eyes. "If that's the way you want it."

Sophron just grinned, skeletal, and uncoiled her own.

Vincent grinned back.

I sweated, cold. She'd mirrored Razorfire's power, the way she'd stolen mine and Adonis's and everyone else's. And when she'd copied us? She'd done it just that little bit stronger.

Just like the real one, only better.

Holy fuck-a-doodle.

Swiftly, I glanced around for Adonis. Still trapped, barely breathing. I grabbed Glimmer, shook him. He stirred, and promptly passed out again.

Just me, Sophron and Razorfire. Shit.

~ 26 ~

Vincent unleashed first.

No warning. No telltale expression or grand gesture. He just...
erupted.

Didn't become the unbeaten force of nature he is by giving his
enemies the first move.

Flames howled between him and Sophron, a raging wall of
death. Sophron leapt back, and teleported. *Crack!* She reappeared
directly behind him.

But he was ready. Her face connected with the heel of his hand.
Crunch! Her nose imploded in blood. He followed it up with a
burst of boiling air that set her hair alight.

She screeched, covering her eyes, and hurled a huge broken
slab of marble pillar at him. It whizzed over my head by half an
inch and crashed into the ground where he stood.

Or where he had been standing.

He'd jumped, riding a cushion of warm air. The broken marble
tumbled underneath him, scattering rubble and shards of police
barricade in its wake. On the way down, he slammed his foot into
her head. Hard.

Snap! Her skull whiplashed. She reeled, but still managed to extinguish her flaming hair with a rushing *whoosh!* of oxygen-poor air. Fuck me, she was a tough little thing.

On the square's perimeter, through a pall of smoke and dust, frightened little ant-people charged to and fro, panicking and flailing their arms. I rattled my brain, battling gritty confusion. Epic fight. Best entertainment since Christians vs. Lions. But who the hell was I supposed to root for?

I spared a swift glance for Adonis. Sprawled senseless on the steps. Bloody foam dribbled from his mouth. My stomach twisted, but there was nothing I could do for him right now.

I crawled to Glimmer and shook him. "Could use your help, dude. C'mon, don't just lie there."

Glimmer sat up, shaky, flexing ill-treated limbs. His jeans were charred black in places, and a burn on his forearm gleamed raw. He shook his head to clear it and spat wet dust. "Goddamn it. Enough throwing me, okay? I'm not indestructible."

"Well, we'll just keep pretending you are." I jerked my chin at the battle behind me. "What are the odds?"

"Of it ending in anything but tears? Not good."

"So what do we do?"

Glimmer shook his head, helpless. "Hope they both lose? Just let 'em fight, Verity, and be ready for what happens next. There's nothing else we can do."

Sophron's pasty cheeks glowed with scarlet fury. Her eyes glittered, insane, and she hurled a wave of power at Vincent. My stomach curdled on a whiff of Ebenezer's feartalent.

Vincent just laughed. Utterly without fear. Even Eb can't create what isn't there to begin with.

She tried again. Glittering golden sparks, an Adonis-flavored missile. Vincent set it alight, and black ash rained. Too easy.

But that was merely a distraction. She'd already unleashed her next trick.

Ka-smash! Lightning carved a smoking rut in the ground. My ears split apart. The stormy scent stung my tongue, and dust and smoke blinded me. I waved my hands to clear the air...

A flamewhip struck without warning from the dust cloud like a cackling crimson serpent... and slammed head on into a second, identical one. The two whips clashing, tangling and spitting sparks. Twin flame augments, locked in battle.

The smoke cleared to reveal Vincent and Sophron, joined at the wrist by ten feet of knotted firesnakes. His eyes burned, unholy vengeance. Sweat drops shone on Sophron's face, where her wounded flesh writhed and healed. Fire wrapped her wrist, and her skinny arm quivered with the effort of holding on.

"C'mon, little girl," Vincent invited, "harder. Show me what you've got." A scarlet fireball danced in the palm of his left hand, a giggling little creature hungry to destroy her. He yanked the flamewhip, impossibly strong, inexorably dragging her closer, closer...

Sophron resisted. Behind her, rubble tumbled, clawed by invisible dragging fingers. She scrabbled at the earth for handholds with my stolen power. And still she hurled angry wreckage. Concrete slabs, chunks of marble and brick flew in all directions, crashing into buildings and scattering the panicking crowd.

"Jesus," I muttered. She'd uncanny strength. But Vincent had experience and bloodthirst. And neither of them cared about the destruction they wrought. Glimmer clutched my hand, his face drawn pale. But what could we do? Vincent could brush off our tricks like water. And Sophron...

The earth shuddered with incredible tectonic force. Sophron laughed. The two snarling flamewhips stretched and writhed and knotted around each other, refusing to give way...

Snap! Vincent let go. No warning. No mercy.

Sophron stumbled, off-guard. Suddenly, she was within reach... and Vincent wrapped her waist in his crackling flamewhip, and *pulled.*

I winced, waiting for the stink of burning flesh... but she hit the ground, flailing, still in one piece. He hadn't sliced her in half. No, she'd managed to jam something between her body and his evil flaming garrote.

A glistening membrane of my power.

My anger screeched, thwarted. I wanted to peel that shield from her like sunburned skin. *Stop it, you little turd. That's* mine.

Vincent flicked his wrist. The flame yanked tighter. Sophron yelled and struggled, hurling flashes of whatever random power she could muster. Why didn't she teleport? Maybe she couldn't. Maybe she'd finally worn out poor Flash's stolen augment. But rocks and rubble rained. Golden-black glitter rocketed into the sky like fireworks. Lightning split the heavens.

And still Vincent didn't kill her.

"Fuck, what's he doing?" Glimmer flung an eye-boggling wave of *sleepy* at Sophron. It crawled over her, searching for a way inside. She thrashed it off. He tried again. Same effect. He swore and sprinted for her, but the heat and the flying rubble drove him back. Lightning crackled, and he stumbled back, strangely dazed, like he'd seen something bizarre and ghostly that shouldn't be there.

I grabbed him, held him upright. He barely noticed me.

"You okay? What did you see?"

He didn't answer. Just stared at Sophron, his face white.

Marble walls broke and thundered. Cracks burst in the concrete-paved ground, and widened, travelling at frightening speed. The earth shuddered, an ear-splitting tectonic grinding of rocks, and the mighty edifice of City Hall began to shake apart.

Rock cracked. Power lines burst into flame. Water sprayed from a fractured pipe. My mind boggled. She was tearing the building from its foundations. Preparing to hurl it at Vincent.

To hurl death down on us all. Fuck me, that was some serious power.

Vincent spat a blistering curse and speared a fireball at her. Still, that thin envelope around her skinny body held. And in a flash of incredulous holy-crap that stunned me stupid, it occurred to me that maybe he *couldn't* kill her.

I grabbed Glimmer, frantic. "We've gotta do something."

He shrugged, oddly blank and distracted. Like he was stunned, too.

"She'll slaughter us all if he doesn't finish her off. Christ, there are hundreds of people here—"

"Verity," Vincent commanded across the rock-strewn square, "get over here."

My jaw hung, foolish.

"Now's no time for games." Impatience salted his tone. Behind him, the building tore from the earth, shuddering, roots ripping up like a gigantic stone weed. Smoke and brimstone sprayed from the chasm beneath. "C'mon. Let's put an end to this little worm."

You hold her down, I'll fuck her up, I recalled dizzily, and laughed like a loon. Vincent wanted my help. Needed it. Without me, he'd be crushed.

Sophron was shielding herself with my power, and with that innate resonance on my side, I'd probably be able to break her grip. He knew that. But to defeat her, I'd have to save his life.

On the other hand…

My thoughts warped, shuddering like glass under pressure. For once, he'd nothing spare to defend himself. He was vulnerable. Fuck-a-doodle. I might actually…

But then she'd be free. To vanish, teleport away, destroy more lives tomorrow.

Fuck.

The edges of my mind crumbled, falling away. I'd been in this position before. Saved his life rather than let the city choke to death under a cloud of poison gas. Fair's fair.

But this was personal. This was *his* death we were talking about. Surely, anyone inside City Hall had already perished. The city would survive, at least until tomorrow, by which time I could regroup, think of another plan.

The bottom melted from my guts, and everything familiar inside me dropped out.

I turned wildly to Glimmer, my mouth open but with no words inside. I was speechless. The pain on his face as he watched me agonize was heart-rending. But he just lifted his hands, a helpless shrug. He couldn't help me.

Sophron struggled, fighting for her life. But still her ugly laughter rained ash from the air. "C'mon," she wheezed, "kill me. Or can't you? Pity. I like your style. I'll just have to kill you, and your dumb hero friends, and anyone else I can get my hands on."

"Verity, stop thinking and get on with it." Vincent had resorted to battling her with both hands. He didn't dare step closer. His face glistened with the effort, his feet braced apart on the shaking ground, muscles straining with the exertion of standing still.

Unspeakable decision sank bitter claws into my heart. He couldn't beckon to me. He didn't have to. The glare he shot me was a flaming arrow laced with everything there'd ever been between us. Every breathless, destructive emotion I'd ever felt for him. Hatred. Terror. Brutal, unhallowed passion. And the steel-forged, atom-fused conviction that he was the glorious sun itself, and I couldn't live in a world without him.

My mind jabbered. Common-Sense Verity thrashed and bubbled under, drowning. Surely, the best outcome was that they both perished. Twin villains, gone for good. The gold-plated solution for everyone.

Except me.

If I kill her, he'll survive. If I kill him, she'll escape. As for me…

You can't divorce what I do from the rest of me, he'd once told me. *Love me and you love that. There's no way out. Accept it, or live a lie.*

In this moment, I realized, Vincent was weaker. For once, he'd nothing to threaten me with… except unthinkable loss, versus the irrevocable certainty that to save him was to surrender.

Blinding agony ripped my skull asunder. Screaming, I clutched my temples, trying to squeeze the pain from my body… but it only swelled louder, screeching, dragging iron claws on the blackboard of my soul.

I can't save you. Glimmer's words stung my blood, bitter with truth. *Only you can do that...* but the scarred certainty of Vincent's conditioning wouldn't melt away.

Inside, I howled, fighting it with every shred of courage I could scrounge. *I can't fall for that again. I have to save myself.*

I have to.

My mindmuscle thrashed, one last drunken whiplash of rebellion, and I hurled a shimmering wall of force.

Straight at Vincent.

He staggered, but held his ground. He was fucking strong. But for an instant, his brilliant flamewhip faltered.

Sophron shrieked, triumphant, and flung off her bonds. Leapt to her feet. And teleported. *Krr-ACK!*

But not before City Hall gave an almighty shudder and crashed onto the square like the wrath of God.

Booomm! The earth quaked. Concrete exploded, the shockwave spreading. Cracks split and yawned. Boulders flew. I cartwheeled, flung off my feet, and thudded into the ground in a hail of rocks and dust. I pulled Glimmer close, shielding us with a wall of power.

Glimmer curled around me, protective. Rubble tumbled and stilled. Dust settled. The roar echoed, and faded into silence.

Stunned, we staggered up.

The place looked like a bomb site. What was left of City Hall lay shattered in a huge crater that swallowed half the square, twenty feet deep. Broken steel curled, the remains of foundations and crushed subway trains. A dust cloud wafted heavenward, already spreading like a pall.

Beneath our feet, the concrete was riddled with cracks. Water fountained from split mains, and electricity spat and sparked. I smelled tart leaking gas. This was a fucking fire waiting to happen.

Like it'd matter now.

On the square's perimeter—broken now, the street heaped with rubble—people ran and climbed, calling names, searching for bodies and survivors. Fire engines, police, first responders already on the job. So they should be. They'd had fair warning…

My sprinting heartbeat staggered, exhausted. I gasped for air that suddenly burned bitter with my own betrayal. I'd attacked him. Turned on him when he'd asked for my help…

Glimmer held me back. His fingers trembled, a catch of compassion. "Leave it. Let's go."

I shook him off and clambered over the rocks, stumbling in the wreckage at the crater's edge. The place where Adonis had lain was undamaged but bare. And I couldn't see *him*. Couldn't find any trace of life, not a spark or a lick of that beautiful crimson flame.

I'd pushed Vincent backwards, I recalled in a haze of confusion. He'd fallen…

My guts cramped, and I bent double and spewed hot bile into the dirt.

"Verity, c'mon. You don't want to see." Glimmer pulled me away, gentle but insistent. "Nothing we can do here."

My face burned. I couldn't see for tears. But Glimmer's feather-light touch in my mind—his beloved scent, strength and vanilla-spice—coated my desolation in dull, blessed unreality.

I should be exultant. I'd fought all my adult life for this. It's what my father died for, what countless people had sacrificed everything to achieve.

Vincent was gone. I was free. And all the color had leached out of my world.

Blindly, I let Glimmer hustle me away.

~ 27 ~

Back at Widow Swanky's, I sat on the sofa, but only because Glimmer made me. I'd just stood there, numb and staring, until he'd coaxed me down.

Sunlight poured in the apartment window, colorless, just a useless glare. Even the seaside air smelled bland, like the lifeblood had been sucked from it, leaving only the empty husk of a thing that used to be alive.

Glimmer brought me water. I drank it. Ashes. I didn't even feel it go down.

In the bedroom, Ebenezer muttered, delirious. Dully, I watched from the sofa as Glimmer tried to feed him, give him water. No use. Every now and then a wave of Eb's erratic talent punched me in the guts. I barely felt it. Like everything else, fear seemed irrelevant. Insipid. Not worth bothering with.

The TV news showed the scene. War zone, the crater still smoking, armed police and soldiers taking charge. Bodies being dragged from the rubble. I watched, barely interested. Whatever.

Beside me, Glimmer bit his lip. Didn't speak. Hadn't spoken the whole way home, a mask of shock and despair on his face. But for once his mindsense hid nothing.

His bitterness sprinkled over me, stinging like acid rain. I couldn't feel much else, but I felt that. I struggled for words. "You think I did wrong."

"I didn't say that."

"You think I should've helped him kill her." I choked, and set aside the water glass he'd fetched me. I wanted to be sick again, drown in the sourness of my own defeat. "How can you mean that? I thought you understood."

A glint of midnight-blue ire. "I'm trying here, Verity. I'm giving you space for your broken heart. What more do you want?"

I warded off gnawing confusion. Razorfire was his mortal enemy. How could he say I should have helped? "It was you who told me I need to save myself. Too much of what he did to me is still there! You know that. You've seen it. I can't let him back in, don't you see, not even for a few seconds. I just can't."

"So that means you should leave her alive?" He yanked off his bandanna with a shaking fist and scrubbed his hair wild. "Get some perspective. Sophron is killing people every damn day, while Razorfire is playing at politics and making speeches on TV and doing fuck all. Who d'you think is the bigger threat right now?"

My eyes burned. I'd had exactly the same thought out there on the battlefield. Now, it seemed monstrous. "He's pure evil, Glimmer. I thought we were agreed on that. I won't sell my soul to the devil to win some pointless fight. It's not worth it."

His eyes flashed silver. "The world doesn't care about your soul, okay? Don't be so goddamn selfish."

Resentment charred my heart. I'd killed Vincent. Murdered the man I'd worshipped and adored. And Glimmer had the hide to call me selfish? "What the fuck is *that* supposed to mean?"

"I'm sorry, did I say selfish? How about, you're a damn coward?"

I gaped. His accusation stabbed me cold. It hurt, cruel and bleeding, the way only the truth can hurt, and the fact that I knew it for the truth only made the pain more bitter. Moments ago, I

230

was numb, listless, searching desperately for sensation in a bleak and desolate world where nothing could touch me.

What I'd give to have that back again now.

My fists squeezed tight, and pain stabbed as if I'd crushed thorns. In my mind, blood gushed from my palms. Spilling down my wrists, staining me ragged red. His disdain savaged me. "What the hell is wrong with you?"

An almond-bitter laugh. "With *me*? Take a walk in the hall of mirrors, Verity. You tell yourself you're facing your fears, but you're not. All you're doing is hiding from them."

"Oh, for fuck's sake…"

"Don't keep blaming *him* for your weaknesses. It's so pathetic. This is all on you, okay? If you trusted yourself, even for an instant? You'd have helped him squash her flat." Glimmer shook his head, a mutinous twist to his lips. "I've been there, okay? I know the truth of it. You're not scared of Razorfire. You're afraid of your own heart."

My throat twisted to a pinhole.

I tried to speak. Deny it. Curse at it, destroy it with ugly weaponized words. Beg for Glimmer's forgiveness. But nothing came out. Nothing inside me. Just a cold, empty hollow.

"Fuck." Glimmer let his dark head fall back onto the sofa. Muscles roped in his arms, fists knotting hard in his lap. His skin glistened. As tense as ever I'd seen him. "I'm sorry. That was uncalled for. I just…" He wiped his nose, forced himself to meet my gaze, and the shadowy depths of his eyes brimmed with unspoken fears. "It's been a shitty day. Forgive me."

Silence swelled, taut.

My senses gulped, blind. I'd killed for lesser insults. The old me would have punched him in his pretty mouth for what he'd said. He'd called me on my bullshit denials before, and I'd cursed him raw for a traitor and a liar.

Of course, he'd been neither. Glimmer told the truth as he saw it, and almost from the day I'd met him, he'd known me better than I'd ever known myself.

And the Verity I was now? Here, this moment? She wasn't the old me.

"No." My voice strangled. "No, you're right. I was afraid of… of what I'd do." Stupid laughter spluttered in my chest. Freedom, this willingness to admit your mistakes. A different, painful, bittersweet kind of liberty. "I was so fucking scared I couldn't move."

"Me, too." His lashes glittered, fierce with tears. "I didn't want you to do it."

"Well, neither did I, but we were out of choices right then…"

"Not that." Glimmer's gaze slipped, just for a moment. "I knew you should go to him. Just common sense, right? Enemy of my enemy, all that. But I didn't want you to."

"I know. Neither did I. It's okay."

"No, I mean I *really* didn't want you to." He blinked, a candid flash of silver. "I thought I was cool with it, you know. I thought I understood what it meant to me, this connection between the two of you. I'm like, she's still stuck on the guy and that's okay, I get it, it's none of my business. But when I watched you standing there, with your soul ripped up, fighting to decide what to do… for a moment, I… well, I'd have done anything in the world to keep you from him. Anything. Even if it meant we all died." An incredulous laugh. "So much for my perfection."

You're still perfect to me. I swallowed, and my tonsils felt like plague sores the size of oranges. "Um… I don't understand."

"I'm not entirely rational about you anymore." He shrugged, dark yet fiery. "You've always trusted me to make the moral decisions. Well, now you can't. Not anymore. Just so you know."

Not *rational*? What was that supposed to mean? I trusted him with every fiber of my heart.

Glimmer reached out. I gripped his hand, my vision swimming with confusion and that glorious vanilla-spice scent I'd come to rely on as *home.*

If Vincent was my sunshine, that harsh, beautiful light that wouldn't let me hide? Glimmer was my comfort food. The place

I retreated to when I couldn't cope. Without Vincent, I felt lost, sinking into the mud, the ghost of some lost golden glory. But without Glimmer, I was a worse human being.

Is this how it's supposed to be between friends? Not constant challenge or threat, but...

Glimmer's fingers suddenly tingled my skin, strange. Different. New. God, he was so warm, so safe. He protected me, helped me when I persisted in acting like a buffoon. I'd thought that meant *weak*. But what if it just meant he cared, the way I cared about him?

"Well, it doesn't matter now, does it? He's gone." I tried to dredge up a weak half-smile, but all that oozed out were thick tears.

He's gone. I'd said it aloud. It was real.

Vincent was dead. His rules no longer applied. So why did this—whatever this was—still feel so forbidden?

I sniffed, wet. Crying again. Awesome. What was it, three times this week? But in a wash of warm relief, I knew I didn't care. All that mattered now was this. "I need you. Please don't make me do this alone."

"Never." His bottomless gaze swallowed me. So blue, Glimmer's eyes; that deep midnight shade of the sky beyond stars. Once, I'd thought them black. Once, I'd thought him invulnerable, so strong that he didn't need me, didn't need anyone.

Yes, he was strong, bless him, the best person I knew, with courage and conviction I could only dream of. But he couldn't do it alone. None of us could. I knew that now. And he had no one but me.

My heartbeat quickened. The raw, empty hole in my heart was suddenly more than I could bear. I was isolated, bereft. I didn't want to be alone. God, I wanted...

Daring, I touched his face, tilted it towards mine. "Glimmer..."

"Shh." He squeezed my hand. Kissed it, soft and warm. And gently let it go.

My guts heated, mortified. I wanted to crush my stupid brain to custard and vanish. Oh, fuck no. Talk about misreading the signals. Could I possibly have screwed up any worse? Uh. That's a negative.

"Shit," I said thickly, and wiped my burning face. "Forget it. I didn't mean anything. Um… what now?"

He heaved a deep sigh, cracked his neck, ruffled his skunk stripe. Master reset, Glimmer-style. "We find this Moreau, I guess. We don't have much else to go on. But I have an idea."

"Yeah?" I tried to do the same, get myself together. Focus on the issues, when what I really wanted was to curl up and cry. *Move along, nothing to see here.*

"Just something Sophron said. It could be nothing." He retrieved his tablet, studiously avoiding my gaze. Behind him the TV showed a muted news channel. Destruction, fire engines, body count. Kind of like the carnage I'd just inflicted on our mellow.

Inwardly, I smacked myself upside the head. Great. Top work, Verity. Now he *really* thinks you're falling apart. What the fuck was I thinking? What kind of deranged madwoman makes moves on her best friend—her broken-hearted, utterly unavailable best friend, mind you, not to mention *worst moves ever*—when she's just murdered the love of her life?

The kind who's lost and alone and needs a friend…

My blood curdled. I wanted to claw my eyes out, tear my face off and let it bleed. What an asshole I am. What about what *he* needed? I'd used him to soothe my own despair. Or I would've, if he'd let me. For what seemed like the hundredth time, he'd saved me from myself.

Same fuck-up, different day.

Listlessly, I picked up Flash's augmentium case and rattled it. I had to do *something*. Keep my brain busy, distract it from this awful new reality I was living in. Silence the anguished howling in my heart.

Vincent was gone. I'd never see him again. Never touch him, never feel his heartbeat against mine.

No point crying about what's done.

I'd lived by that mantra all my adult life, ever since Obsidian killed Mom and I was forced to grow up overnight. Get up, dust off, get on with it. But there'd always been an *it* to get on with. What was left for me now?

"Crack on," I told Glimmer dully. "I'll find out what's in this."

No reply. Just an absent, *everything-is-fine* nod. The kind of nod I would totally give to some insane friend who'd just pulled epically tasteless moves on *me*.

I tried to concentrate. Hmm. No point trying to break an augmentium case with my power, I guess. I'd just bounce off, *doinng!* like a rabid rubber ball. I prodded the case with one finger. The metal gave, just a little.

I frowned, my curiosity sharpening at last. What use is an augmentium case that's flimsy enough to break? Unless...

Unless Flash wasn't trying to keep augments out, but stop them finding what was inside?

I wandered into the kitchen and rummaged through the drawers. Spatulas, spoons, whisks, one of those round cheese-grater things you use to cut up weed... ah, perfect. I extracted a meat tenderizer and a pointed stainless-steel knife—hello, hammer and chisel—and set to. A few good whacks and a hole appeared. A few more and I was inside.

Clunk! Jackpot. Three items tipped out onto the bench.

One cell phone. One stuffed bunny rabbit with floppy ears, his brown plush fur old and worn through in places...

...and one rusty-brown collectible six-figure rock. Jackpot.

I poked the cell phone. Not an IRIN model. An old one with a keypad and a tiny dented screen. I pressed ON. Nothing. Battery must be flat. I found the charging jack, but it didn't match mine. I popped the SIM drawer. Disposable card, prepaid credits. Easy to discard or replace.

So why lock your cell phone in an augmentium box? Maybe this was Flash's secret disposable number. Maybe a girlfriend Sophron didn't know about...

I recalled Flash's warning. *Watch the Sentinels, and stay off the phone.* Like he thought a phone might give him away to his enemies somehow. Hmm. I'd fought other villains who had cell phones…

My pulse quickened. Phones, sure. But not IRIN models.

Flash had snapped our photo with a smartphone at the fire department building. I struggled to recall it. Yes, a generic knock-off brand.

My gaze flicked to the kitchen table. Weasel's phone, which we'd taken when we captured him. Same deal: dented smartphone, some cheap Korean brand. Hmm. Last year, before Vincent was mayor, I'd fought a villain called Witch. She'd used a BlackBerry.

So what did it mean that pretty much everyone in Sapphire City had an IRIN phone… except Gallery villains?

Well, well. Perhaps IRIN phones really did have a surveillance chip buried inside, or an ooga-booga mind-control wave generator, or whatever. But it didn't feel like Vincent's style to *tell* anyone. His power had to be absolute. He wouldn't want even his own gang to be immune. Unless…

I sighed. Hell, maybe they just didn't trust him. They were villains, not idiots. Just my paranoia again, right? Anyway, Vincent was gone, his tricks along with him, so what did it matter now?

I turned my attention to the rock. Smooth, rounded, an odd lopsided shape with a few jagged bits at one end. Broken off some statue or carving, maybe. My fingertips found a small rough spot, and I dug in my pocket for the shard I'd found at the crime scene. The edges popped perfectly into place.

Cold spider feet crawled up my spine. First, a chip of stone at the crime scene. Now, the whole thing, hidden in an augmentium box where no one could sense it.

But why did Flash care? The rock was augmented, sure. I could taste it, the telltale sherbety tingle of *weird*. I probed it cautiously with my mindmuscle. Minute pressure pushed back, like pressing on a filled water bomb. It felt… gritty. Organic.

Hmm. What did the rock do, that Flash was so determined to keep it from Vincent's reach?

I tossed the bunny, the phone and the rock onto the table in front of Glimmer. "The plot thickens. Not sure what the bunny's for. Maybe it's catnip for skinny teenage psychos..."

Glimmer didn't reply. He was watching TV... and on the screen, Deputy Mayor Mackenzie Wilt—Mayor Wilt, I supposed, at least for now—was speechifying. A platitude-riddled tirade about rogue powers, crime waves, Sentinels, citywide augment registers and invoking martial law. And the press lapped it up.

Ms. Wilt was a polished orator. She didn't look distraught. Just single-minded. Her pale hair sifted gently on the breeze, and that flash in her green Viking eyes was pure rage. Hatred. A zealot's crusade... but tinged with humiliation and betrayal.

Holy final solution, Batman. Just looking at the ruthless set of her mouth made me want to fumble for a weapon. Either she deserved an Oscar... or she honestly hadn't known what Vincent was. She'd tumbled in free fall into the chasm of his oh-so-reasonable lies, and this morning she'd hit the bottom. Hard.

Sympathy fluttered in my stomach, but ruthlessly I crushed it. Vincent was mine. She'd stolen that. The thieving witch deserved everything that came to her.

My heart ached, bleeding afresh. Viciously, I wiped my eyes. I didn't care if he *was* sleeping with her. I cared that she'd spent hours with him that should've been mine... and now, he'd no more time to share.

More pictures flashed up, of Glimmer and me at City Hall. Apparently, we'd rocketed to the top of the Wilt regime's shoot-to-kill charts. Unholy laughter bubbled in my chest. Great. We'd traded a pretend hater for a real one. This day just got better and better.

But silky satisfaction whispered unbidden over my soul. *I knew it. You're not special, Mackenzie Wilt. He didn't take you into his confidence. You were dirt to him, like everyone else...*

"What the fuck ever," I said shakily, shock still ringing in my bones. "Politicians, always playing musical chairs on the fucking

Titanic. Where's Sophron? That's the real question. What's her next move? And where the hell is Adonis?"

Glimmer didn't reply.

I turned. "Are you even listening to me—?"

My nerves stung. No, he wasn't paying attention. He'd picked up the plush rabbit from the table and stroked it with one fingertip, wearing a strange, faraway expression.

"Hey." I touched his arm, awkward. He'd acted weird since City Hall, my epic idiocy since notwithstanding. Since he'd looked into Sophron's face on the battlefield. Something had changed out there.

He crushed the rabbit in his fist and glanced up, blank, like he'd only just realized I was there.

"You okay?" Idiot question. I tried again. "What's going on?"

"I know who Doctor Moreau is." His hand shook. His forehead glistened. He was sweating cold.

The same ice threaded my veins. "What? Who?"

No answer.

My heart thumped. Shit. He was keeping secrets from me.

Fair enough. He'd every reason not to trust me, after what happened at City Hall. And I'd made way more embarrassing mistakes since then. But my throat ached. The moment I'd dreaded for so long had arrived. At long last, he'd brush me off. Leave me behind…

"You'll see." Glimmer's starry gaze pleaded. Fevered, desperate, like this mattered more than anything that had ever happened to us. "Come with me. Please. I need you."

I choked, overcome. Had I passed some test? I didn't know. But my heart drowned in gratitude that despite his pain—despite the horrid, selfish way I'd treated him—he'd chosen to let me help him.

"Of course I'll come," I blurted. "Jeez, what did you think?"

Glimmer just smiled. Faint and haunted, but it rinsed warm starlight over my soul. So different, he and I. But in some ways, so much the same, it made me weep.

I wiped my lips. I didn't know what else to say. "Umm…"

He stuffed the bunny into his pocket and grabbed his phone and tablet. "C'mon, let's take a ride."

My senses stung, hard like a spider's bite. I froze. "Wait. What was that?"

"Huh?"

"That." My mindmuscle twitched. I took a couple of steps towards the bed, my gaze darting left and right. "Someone's here."

Swiftly, Glimmer pulled his pistol with one hand and lit a crackling ball of silver screw-you with the other.

I pounced, and dragged a kicking figure out from behind the frosted glass screen. Jeans-clad legs thrashed, and a blond ponytail whisked in my face.

I dumped her on the floor, pinning her with a crushing fist of force. "Peggy Anne Finney, you sneaky she-jackal. So pleased you could join us."

~ 28 ~

Peg struggled, wheezing, her slim body crushed by my weight. Desperately, she scrabbled at the sparkling air for her power, and uncanny silvery light glowed from her eyes... but it was only a dim shine that soon flickered out. Nothing like the blinding flash my sister Equity used to make.

"Please," Peg gasped, "I don't mean any harm..."

"Whatever." The memory of my last sight of Adonis—my precious brother, puking wet black sparkles into the dust—made me burn to crush her to pulp. I eased up, all the same, not wanting to repeat my mistakes with Weasel. Peggy had questions to answer. "What are you doing in our place?"

"Let her up, Verity." Glimmer holstered pistol and mindsense both. "Can't you see she's terrified? We don't have time for this. Gotta go."

"She lied to us all." I circled, baring my teeth, a wolf at bay. My knuckles cracked with the effort it took not to tear her face off and eat it. "She deceived Adonis. She poisoned my family!"

"That's ridiculous." Peggy stumbled up and hugged herself, rubbing goose-pimpled arms. Her eyes were reddened, her pretty face puffy. Dirt smeared her usually spotless t-shirt and jeans. A good crying session wasn't too far into her past.

"Right," I snapped, "because you're so fucking *credible* right now. I knew your scumbag of a brother, Peggy. I *killed* him. Want to go look at Ebenezer and see what you've done?"

Her face blanked, incredulous. "What do you mean?"

"Wow. Denial. Great plan, genius. Can we move right along to the begging and wailing? I'm bored."

Glimmer rested a calming hand on my shoulder. Warm, damp, shaking a little. But still it cooled my temper. "What do you want, Peg? We're kind of in the middle of something."

"Adonis didn't come back this morning." She swallowed a fresh sob. "Everyone's sick. I don't know what to do. Please, you have to help me."

"I don't have to do jack shit," I muttered, but my throat ached. Could I help, even if I wanted to? I didn't even know for sure if Adonis was alive.

"How did you find us?" Warily, Glimmer watched her. Good idea. Maybe that little flare of light was the best she could do. But maybe it wasn't, too.

"Adonis tracked you the day the fire department burned."

"Why are we even having this conversation?" I demanded. "She's lied to us all from the beginning."

"Of course I lied!" Defiance sparked in her eyes. "Do you think I'm an idiot? Declan was dead and Razorfire was the mayor. Think he'd give a spit for a weak little girl like me, without Declan to beg me a favor? I heard you were taking in stray augments and I had nowhere else to go. What should I have done, Verity? Stroll up with a smile and say, *hi, I'm Declan Finney's sister, can I stay?* You'd have torn my head off and stuck it on a spike."

Glimmer cocked a single dark brow. "She's got a point."

"Whatever," I grumbled. "Doesn't mean she didn't fuck my brother and poison us."

"I didn't poison anyone." Peg wiped her cheeks, but tears leaked out. "But maybe I should have. You're as bad as the Gallery, the whole cursed lot of you. Declan had his problems, but I loved

241

him, and you're the bitch who murdered him. D'you think I *like* cooking your food and fetching your coffee and sleeping with your asshole of a brother?"

"My point exactly," I retorted. But memory shimmered, an unquiet specter. Weasel, in my bathroom, spitting blood. *Think I like chewing through sewer pipes, you fucking idiot?*

Huh. I'd misjudged enough villains for this week. Hadn't I?

Peg laughed, broken. "You really don't see, do you? I love Adonis so much it *hurts*. You should know what that's like."

I frowned, troubled. "Look—"

"For God's sake, are you blind? I couldn't hurt Adonis even if I wanted to. I let him charm me!"

My jaw slackened. "Huh?"

Her tears ran faster now, but she paid them no mind. "His world had fallen apart. He'd always relied on you and you'd turned on him. He had no one. He needed a friend. Or didn't you notice?"

My nerves wriggled like worms. No, I hadn't. I'd been too wrapped up in my own petty problems. Too busy being furious at him for holding me back to see that Ad was just as lost and alone without me as I'd been without him.

Shit.

Peg wiped her nose. "And I needed a home. So I let him unleash on me. It was… kind of a relief, I guess." Another, wet little laugh. "It makes the whole thing bearable. He's nice when he wants to be. At least he's brilliant in bed."

Pebbles rattled in my mind, filling empty slots. My charming, witty, drop-dead-hot brother, who'd never needed to unleash on a girl to get laid in his life. I'd abandoned him. Betrayed him, no less, as truly as if I'd fed them all the poison myself. And he'd needed a friend so much—a pleasant, uncomplicated, easy friend, who didn't complain all the time, or challenge his authority right when he could cope with it the least—that he'd resorted to trickery.

Now Ad was gone, maybe for good. And I'd never get the chance to hold him and tell him I was sorry, that he was my big brother and I still loved him, no matter the mess I'd made of my life.

My stomach clenched on hot saltwater guilt. *It can't be Peg,* Adonis had insisted. Seems he'd spoken with authority.

But if not Peg… then who?

Glimmer touched my shoulder again, fidgeting on one foot. He wasn't even really listening. He squeezed the plush rabbit in his fist. "Verity, we really need to go."

"Right." I studied Peg, sympathy and killing rage battling fiercely in my blood. She'd done what she had to in order to stay alive. Up to and including sleeping with the enemy. That was admirable, wasn't it? Gutsy?

No. Vincent's disdain, sharp with acid. *It makes me sick. It's weak. Wretched. Wouldn't you rather die than surrender what you are?*

Peg could be lying, I guess. Still a Gallery agent, poisoning us for kicks. Or simply gone rogue with grief, wreaking revenge on me and mine for murdering her beloved psychofuck brother. I'd heard of sicker plans. After all, wouldn't I murder to avenge *my* brother? I'd do anything. Up to and including…

I squared my shoulders, resolved. "Maybe I believe you, Peg. Maybe I don't. Sadly for you, we've got somewhere to be and I don't have time to play Dr. Phil and figure out your shit for you."

Peg narrowed her eyes at me. "So?"

"So, either you can sit still like a good girl while I cuff you to the toilet? Or, we can argue, I can beat the snot out of you and then I'll lock you in that bedroom with Ebenezer, where you can spend the next few hours spewing and pissing your pants when he loses control." I smiled, feral. "Deal?"

It took Glimmer and me forty minutes through half-empty back streets to get where we were going. The main roads were too dangerous. Already, riot police and the National Guard rode in armored vehicles and marched along the sidewalks, setting up striped wooden barricades and unrolling razor wire. As we passed, I saw them grabbing some guy, forcing his face into the ground, clapping him in cuffs. I was guessing the Sentinels in major public areas had been cranked up to maximum sensitivity. Mayor Wilt wasn't wasting any time.

People milled about, uncertain, watching and talking and taking video. No doubt social media was exploding. Shop and café owners peered out their windows, wondering whether to close up and roll their steel shutters down. We passed a burning apartment block, smoke billowing in clouds. No fire engine attended. Emergency services for anything but security would be thin on the ground from now on.

Glimmer drove without speaking, his expression dark and shuttered. But his fingers left damp smears on the gearshifts, and his knuckles were white. The plush rabbit sat on the dashboard, ears dangling.

I couldn't read him and I didn't ask. Curiosity sniffed like a rat in my skull, but I pushed its claws away. Not the time for interrogations, demands, worrying about *my* feelings. Whoever this Moreau was, I'd find out soon enough. Glimmer needed me. I would be there. End of story.

But thrash as I might, I couldn't avoid the black undertow that pulled my thoughts inexorably underwater... to Vincent. Defeated, his frightful power no longer a threat. At long last, the city was rid of him.

It seemed a strange, alien planet we lived on. Like a god had died, and we mortals had been abandoned, to perish frightened and alone.

My throat ached distantly, my eyes strangely dry. But inside, I howled, weeping. I'd betrayed Vincent. I'd killed him. My nightmares would be merciless. What was left of his loyal Gallery would come a-hunting, on top of Mackenzie Wilt's haters and the National Guard and everyone else who despised and feared us. I deserved whatever I had coming.

But I still had one good, honest goal to cling to: whatever happened, I would not betray Glimmer. No way. Whatever fire he strode into? I'd burn right beside him.

Sure, snorted the Seekernoid. *For all the fucking good you'll do.*

At last, Glimmer stopped the car in a quiet street lined with low-roofed offices and corporate headquarters and we got out. Insurance companies, a call center, a store selling used office equipment. Parked vehicles on each side, girl whizzing past on skates, hoodie kid bopping along to his headphones, guy in a boiler suit cleaning a row of dark windows where someone had spray-painted BURN IT ALL.

No police. No Sentinels. Just a few security cameras, black domes glinting in the sun. Heh. Whatever.

The building we'd stopped in front of was single-story with opaque windows reflecting the street. A blue company logo painted on the glass read FARSTAR GM, with a stylized icon of a shooting star. Underneath, it said *Custom Agriculture Solutions For A Safer World.*

I pointed. "A genetically modified food clinic? Is this where Doctor Moreau works?"

"Uh-huh." Glimmer wiped damp hands on his jeans. Breathed in deep, let it out. Wiped his nose. Fidgeting, in fact. Nervous. Was he carrying his pistol? I couldn't tell. "Look," he added, "this could be untidy. Let's not turn it into a fight, okay?"

"Whatever you say." But my fingertips stung in bright warning. I forced myself to keep calm and do as Glimmer asked, instead of saying *dude, you're creeping me out here.* What dangerous foe could we possibly face at a place where they engineered bug-resistant wheat? Mad scientists? Drooling rubber-coated lab assistants named Igor, wielding scalpels and big syringes? Did they have powers? If so, what? Why couldn't we fight?

What the fuck, in short, was going on?

"Hell, she might not even be here," he added, without much hope. My senses prickled again. *She?* Who the hell was *she?*

And then, he smoothed his hair.

No shit. Both hands, tucking his skunk stripe neatly back. Now the alarms in my head really went apeshit. Fuck. I'd *never* seen him do that.

But before I could buy a vowel, he'd tugged open the glass door and disappeared inside.

I hurried after him, my senses poised, tensing my mindmuscle for action... but it was just an office reception lobby. Opaque white security wall with a locked door accessible by proximity card; leafy green plant in a pot; water cooler; white desk below the same blue shooting-star logo. Cool air hummed, the scent of carpet cleaner and coffee.

I relaxed, just a little, my senses still peeled for threats. No one lurked in the waiting room. Only one woman behind the desk. The walls were hung with glossy posters, showcasing healthy organic crops and pesticide-free farms and how they were going to feed the starving millions in the People's Republic of Corruption and Fuckup from a single handful of beans, or whatever.

I snorted, hip-deep in irony. I'm from a high-flying corporate family: I know spin-doctor bullshit when I see it. Odds on these eggheads were manufacturing biological anti-personnel weapons, or gene-splicing new hyper-intelligent species of weeds that could creep underground over state lines and throttle enemy crops on command. A faceless corporate foe can be good fun, but there's a catch: you can't thump 'em senseless. You need real people for that.

So who was the real person behind FarStar GM? I didn't know for certain, but I wasn't offering any prizes for guessing.

Glimmer spoke to the receptionist, and she picked up the phone and made an internal call. I eyed her speculatively. Hmm. Looked more like an admin temp than a scientist. Skinny, short-sighted, possibly not very bright. Probably had a button for that locked security door under her desk.

Apparently, whoever answered the phone said something strange, because the receptionist offered Glimmer an uncertain smile. "One moment, please. Can I get you a coffee while you wait?"

"No, thanks." Glimmer was practically a jitterbug, thigh muscles twitching, fingers folding and unfolding. Christ, does he look like he needs caffeine right now, genius?

I wanted to pet him. Hold him in my lap and soothe him like I might an anxious kitten. Instead, I filled a paper cone from the cooler—bubble, bubble, toil and 10 ppm calcium fluoride—and offered it to him.

He drank it, grateful. "Thanks."

"Everything okay?"

He just crushed the cup and binned it—and the security door in the white wall clicked open.

A slim lady wearing a fluoro-white lab coat walked out. Curling hair spilled over her shoulders, the glossy dark-blood color of merlot. Green eyes like a Disney princess, impossibly large and liquid, in a lovely oval face, her fine brows upswept with an intelligent quirk of character.

Wow.

I closed my mouth, envy soaking my guts. If this was Doctor Moreau, she was ridiculously gorgeous. Clever, too, no doubt. Sexy hips. Hell, I'd just about switch teams for her… but somehow, I doubted my luck. Because she stared at Glimmer, her sweet lips trembling, and her perfect face drained white. And he stared back, deep and blue as space.

"Hello, Nadia." Soft, but not gentle. Oh, no. This was raw. Jagged, broken glass on rocks.

She smoothed her white coat over her thighs. "Ethan."

Ethan? Bewildered, I glanced from one to the other and back again… and sniggering blades of *no-way-never* slashed my heart to bleeding.

This could get untidy, he'd said. Untidy, hell. Doctor Moreau of FarStar GM was Glimmer's ex-wife.

Nadia led us down a long white corridor, past glass-fronted rooms of lab equipment and refrigerators stacked with sample tubes. I followed, bewildered. Glimmer didn't speak. Nobody spoke, and the air fairly crackled with tension. Was I about to hear the full story of what had happened between them?

Suddenly, I was far from certain I wanted to.

Dr. Perfect's office was oppressively tidy. Spotless, in fact, books and DVDs and files in the squarest piles I'd ever seen. Even the pens were corralled in their little jar, lids neatly fitted. Not a fleck of dust on the desk lamp or keyboard. I guess GM scientists need to keep clean. Or maybe just a neat freak.

Either way, I squirmed inside. Glimmer was a bristling barbed-wire grenade. A storm, ready to erupt. My nerves recoiled in dread, stuck in that horrible moment between ripping off a fingernail and the pain. *Any second now…*

She let us in, and we sat when invited. At least, I did. Glimmer didn't sit. He *coiled*, a spring poised to explode.

"This is Verity," he said shortly. "Verity, Nadia."

I flipped a one-finger wave, no smile. Didn't seem the occasion for BFFs. And I didn't fail to notice he hadn't said *my colleague* or *she's just a friend* or anything conciliatory at all.

Fine. I wasn't about to explain. I already wanted to strangle her for whatever she'd done to him. Let her think I was his girlfriend, if it gave him a weapon.

Nadia—a framed certificate in some Eastern European language on the wall read *Dr. Nadia Romaneci*—took her own seat, crossing silk-clad legs that would've done any fishnet stocking commercial proud. Was she the doctor Glimmer had mentioned when we'd wanted help for Jem and the other sick augments?

I winced, my respect for his courage inching even higher. Jeez. That's one tough call to make.

"I, er… wasn't expecting you." Nadia's accent was melodic. She probably spoke three languages. I wriggled. God, this woman would make even Mackenzie Wilt feel inferior. No wonder Glimmer had girl issues.

Yeah, right, Nasty Verity sneered. *It's all about him. Not that you're feeling outclassed right now, or anything. You're looking at the ballpark, and guess what? You're not within ten miles of it.*

"You should've done, don't you think?" Glimmer gave her his quiet, waiting stare. Giving her the chance to speak. But she said nothing.

My heart ached for him. I longed to disarm her, level the playing field... but how? She still wielded power over him. That was obvious, even though I'd gathered she'd burned their bridges forever when she'd discovered his mind-screwing talents. Called him *liar, freak, monster.*

We'd all heard those ugly words. Sticks and stones, right? But to have them hurled at you from the lips of the one you loved...

Glimmer sighed, impatient, and pulled something from his pocket to lay on the desk.

The bunny. One threadbare ear flopped over its little black nose.

Nadia gave a tiny gasp. But my senses sparkled, alert. That wasn't shock, or surprise. More like... resignation. Whatever Mr. Flopsy Bunny meant? Dr. Perfect already knew all about it.

Glimmer! I yelled at him silently. *Watch out!*

But he didn't hear. Wasn't listening.

"Where is she, Nadia?" he demanded. "What have you done with her?"

A lick of those sweet lips. "I didn't *do* anything—"

"Don't pretend, okay?" Glimmer—Ethan? Christ, he'd always be Glimmer to me—leaned forward, gripping the desk, his knuckles white. "Just tell me what you've done to my little girl."

~29 ~

Nadia's pretty mouth hardened. "*Our* little girl. She's my daughter, too."

Oyy.

I gaped, and in my mind, little steel ducks slotted neatly into a row.

She took our baby daughter, he'd told me once. A baby when they'd broken up, that is. When Razorfire had forced Glimmer to reveal his talent and turned them against each other.

Now, the girl would be four. An augmented child, whose mother loathed and feared augments. Whose mother was a genetic scientist whose job it was to create new species…

I swallowed sick laughter. *She's no child of mine*, Vincent told me, that night on the bridge. Emphasis on the *mine*.

Just another thing that Vincent—*who's dead, don't forget*, Nasty Verity sneered, *dead dead dead, and you killed him*—just another crucial little factoid that Vincent had known all along.

Jesus in a fucking jam jar. For once in my life, I had no words. What could I possibly say?

Glimmer snorted, sarcastic. "Right. *Ours*. That's not what you said that day."

"I was angry," Nadia retorted, but her cheeks stained pink. "I was *scared*, Ethan. You lied to me for four years about what you could do. What did you expect?"

"Yeah, you got me. I lied. Because I was afraid you'd react exactly how you reacted. So don't even come at me with that, okay? Just don't."

Her lips tightened. "What was I supposed to think: that what we had was *real*? That I was the only one whose mind you didn't slither about in like a snake? Give me a break."

"I won't have this conversation again. Just tell me what you've *done* with her."

Christ, he was almost in tears. Helplessly, I reached for his hand. He gripped it tightly, slick. Outwardly, he was all but composed, his face pale. But I could feel his mindsense, lost and howling in a chasm of self-doubt and sorrow, and it tore my special senses bloody.

I know what it's like to hold someone in your heart who you wish wasn't there. His words repeated on me with fresh, frightening clarity. This Nadia had disowned him when she found out what he was. Hated him, no doubt poisoned his daughter against him too. And now, the monster who terrorized the city—the villain he was supposed to fight and *kill*, and wasn't *that* just awesome?—was his own *child*.

But part of him loved Nadia still.

I could see it, because I knew what it was like. The way her every word sliced him raw, every meaningful glance a sucker punch. See, it just isn't that easy to cut someone out of your heart. It hurts. The flesh wriggles, striving desperately to escape the blade. And the wound bleeds for a long time. Maybe, it'll bleed forever.

Nadia leaned back, keeping her distance. Controlling their battlefield. "I wanted her to have a normal life. There are treatments available. She needed help."

Glimmer laughed, incredulous. "Treatments. Will you listen to yourself? She's not sick!"

"Look at what she's doing, and tell me she's not sick!" Nadia's eyes burned with dark denial. "A research group from an experimental laboratory came to see me, okay? I checked it all out. This is my field, in case you've forgotten. They'd achieved some amazing pre-publication results. I believed they could cure her. They even took me on as a consultant while she was in the program. It was all legitimate and ethical."

Glimmer caught my gaze and shook his head, disgusted.

I goggled. Experimental laboratory. *Cure.* Jesus on a fucking firespit.

"Well, your due diligence sucks, then," I snapped. "Don't tell me: the program was funded by Iridium Industries. Did you see the news today? See who your *legitimate researchers* really worked for?"

Nadia's gaze shimmered. Only for an instant before she blinked it away. But I knew what I'd seen: guilt.

Barbed wire wrenched tight in my guts. "She knew. Glimmer, she knew all along."

"No. Ethan, that's not true, I swear."

He just fixed her in his stare, a muscle jumping along his jaw.

Nadia looked from Glimmer to me and back again. "Is she one of you, is that it? A freak like you? How dare you bring her in here?"

"Fuck you, okay?" I fought rising rage, those seductive bubbles in my blood that meant trouble. She wasn't a stupid person. How could she be so fucking medieval? God, I wanted to thrash sense into her. Grope inside her skull and rip her stubborn hater attitude out like the shred of useless flesh it was. But I wanted to hurt her more for breaking Glimmer's heart. For that, she deserved far, far worse. "Do you know what you've done? What they're really doing to that girl? How can you want that for your own child?"

"I made a mistake!" Nadia's fingers crept on the chair's arm, nervous. Maybe she had a gun in that drawer. "They lied to me. By the time I discovered what was really going on…"

"Tell me you didn't." The whipcrack in Glimmer's voice made me jump. His eyes glowed with starlight, threatening to burn. "For God's sake, Nadia, he's already destroyed our lives once. Tell me you didn't give her to *him* rather than *let me help you!*"

"I didn't know!" Tears brightened her eyes, too. "I swear, I didn't know it was him until it was too late. I thought they wanted to *cure* her. Not... not *this*."

Glimmer didn't reply. He just snatched up the rabbit and stalked out.

I lurched after him, my vision flashing red. Fuck, I could barely walk in a straight line. My mindmuscle howled for freedom, and my fists squeezed so tight my bones crackled. God's innards, I hated her so much it frightened me.

Nadia stumbled in our wake. "It's you she wants," she called. "She told me."

At the door, Glimmer paused. Didn't turn. Just waited. But I could taste the starry glitter of his heartache. *This is all about you now,* Flash had said. Seems he was right.

Nadia put her hand on the doorknob, to stop us leaving or just to make us wait. Brushed a loose red lock from one beautiful cheekbone. "I visited her, after... just before she left the lab for good. The artificial maturation had progressed. To all appearances she was about twelve. It's amazing, I've never seen anything like..."

She caught Glimmer's dark expression and swallowed. "Well, there was an accident. The other experimental subjects, they... She hurt some of them, she and this boy, Flash. They'd confined her in an augmentium cell and were talking about terminating the experiment because she wasn't cooperative."

I snorted. "Wow, so thoughtful. I'll give 'em fucking *cooperative*..."

Glimmer touched my arm, and reluctantly I subsided.

"I didn't like the sound of 'termination', so I went to try to calm her down," Nadia continued. "She was angry, Ethan, I've never seen such a temper from her. She kept raving about you, how you'd made her what she is, it was all your fault and she wanted to destroy you. I thought it was just rage at being locked up." She dabbed a tissue beneath each of her brimming eyes. "I couldn't bear to see her like that. So as soon as I had the chance, I helped her escape."

"Big of you." Scorn cut my words jagged. "Mother of the fucking year. Pity you didn't think of it *before* they butchered your daughter's DNA."

Glimmer stepped closer to gaze into his ex-wife's face. She was tall; they were almost eye to eye. "And now look what she's doing," he said. Remorseless. Didn't let her look away. Did he want her to suffer? Or just face the truth, the way he must?

"I made a terrible mistake. Forgive me, Ethan. Please." She gazed soulfully up at him, twin pools of shimmering green. Infernally beautiful, the way a siren is beautiful when she lures you to your death. Damn her.

Glimmer's expression didn't change. Didn't even twitch. Good God, the guy really was made of stone. Either that, or he was just screaming inside. Screaming so hard and wild that if he moved even an inch, he'd explode into pieces.

"I should never have let them touch her." Nadia gave a broken little laugh. "How pitiful that must sound, after what she's done. But she's only four. She doesn't understand reason. All she knows is hatred and fear and revenge—"

Glimmer silenced her, a fingertip on her lips. His gaze fell to her cheekbones, her chin, her mouth. It lingered. I waited, breathless. Nadia swallowed, folding her fingers around his… but his mouth hardened, and he yanked his hand back. "If she knows anything about hatred?, She learned it from you."

And he walked away.

"Ethan, stop. I want to help…" She tried to follow.

I held her back, one hand on her chest. Glimmer would want to find Sophron before she called him out again and killed more innocent people. But I'd no idea how, unless Nadia could help us. "That's far enough,'" I said stonily. "Now talk. Why did Flash give us your name? Tell me where she's hiding."

Nadia tried to push by, but I blocked her path. "How would I know?" she snapped.

"Let's see. She's your daughter and this is all your fucking fault. I think you've got a responsibility to know, don't you?"

Again, she tried to sidle by, and again I pushed her, harder this time. Her chin lifted, mutinous. "Get your dirty hands off me, freak."

I shoved her with my mindmuscle, knocking her back a step. "Freak, huh? Let me rephrase. If, and only if, you tell me where she's hiding, I'll let you walk back to your office on your own damn legs."

She stared, her face pale in a cloud of wine-dark hair, and a dark flash of hate oiled her eyes like a snake's. So swift I might have imagined it… then, it was gone, and all I saw was anguish tinged with fear and desperation. The perfect Frantic Mom.

My Seekernoid senses itched. Was she faking it? Or just my overactive imagination?

"I don't know, okay?" she admitted at last. "She didn't tell me her plans. Please, you have to believe me. I want to help. She's my daughter, too."

I winced. Damn it. Part of me wanted to smack her smug hater face and leave her here to suffer. Another, deeper, angrier part wanted to smash each of her perfect ivory teeth into splinters for breaking Glimmer's precious heart, and my fingers itched, darkly eager.

But she was Sophron's mother. We couldn't in good conscience leave her out of this. Could we?

I sighed. Fuck. Glimmer wouldn't like it. Better make sure she's useful, then.

I recalled Ebenezer in our guest bedroom, sweating and showering fear. "You're a doctor, right? You know anything about augmented physiology? Like, treating sick people?"

She eyed me, confused. "Uh… I can try."

"You'd better." I pulled the paper-wrapped sample of Flash's blood from my pocket to show her. "Next question: can you analyze this blood sample, tell us what's wrong with it?"

"Of course. I mean, so long as it's a genetic defect."

Cool. I stuffed away the sample and produced the augmented rock. "Next: any idea what this is?"

A white-coated shrug. "Never seen it before. Looks like a model of a heart."

I squinted at it. I hadn't thought of that. I guess it did, kind of, lopsided with lumpy bits and a rounded point on one end...

Unwanted memory surfaced, a dim reflection on glass. My mother dying in Dad's embrace. Her long dark hair tumbling over his chest, her face marbled with dark granite, one lifeless eye staring.

Dad's old archenemy, the cackling nutbag Obsidian, had turned half Mom's body to stone, and she'd choked and bled and spasmed to an agonizing death. Dad and Mike had dealt with him. But our family was never the same.

Frost crackled my spine. What if this wasn't a model? What if...?

Possibilities unfolded, an ugly pirate map scrawled in blood and marked HERE BE DRAGONS.

No way. It couldn't be. Not in Dad's vault, all this time...

I put the rock away, grim. "Where's this laboratory where the experiments happen? Is it here?"

"No. It's downtown. I can show you. They keep all their research notes there. Maybe they've found something that can help my daughter, some drug or..." Nadia hesitated. "I wanted to search, but my access has been revoked. I can't get in without..."

I snorted, disgusted. "Oh, right, so *now* you want augmented help. Fuck you."

She just looked at me, mute.

I sighed. She was trying, I suppose. If anyone knew about trying to fix unfixable mistakes, it was me.

"Fine," I muttered, "if you play nice, you can come." I grabbed her proximity card from the clip on her lab coat, swiped it and dragged her into the lobby. I gave the surprised receptionist a skeletal grin as I frog-marched Nadia outside. "Don't be alarmed. It's 'take a mad scientist to work day'. She'll be right back."

Glimmer waited by the green machine wearing a stormy, mutinous expression. "You don't talk to him, okay?" I added, prodding Nadia's shoulder. "Don't even look at him unless he looks at you first. You're not real popular in our house. Understood?"

Nadia smiled, a pretty viper's smile. "Wow. Jealous much? I guess keeping him must be hard work, for a woman like you. Did he mess with your mind, too?"

I bristled. *I'll give you 'woman like me', you rude cow. How about a boot in the ass?* But my cheeks burned, and I spun away before she could laugh at me. "Smart mouth for a second-degree murderer. Shut the fuck up."

"Why is she here?" Glimmer didn't look Nadia in the eye. Didn't even acknowledge her presence, apart from his question.

"We need her help." I bundled her into the right-hand seat and crossed to the left. "These assholes at the secret lab might be able to help us stop Sophron—"

"Aysha," he corrected distantly. "We called her Aysha. It means 'life'."

I swallowed, full-fathom five out of my depth. "Look, I don't know what to say. I've got no way to imagine even a fraction of what you're going through. But if Nadia can take us there…"

Glimmer tugged his skunk stripe and palmed his eyes with a sigh. "You're right. It's okay. Bring her." Like she was a pet, or a bag of tools.

Pride and desperate sympathy warmed me with equal energy. I guess he'd had a few years' notice to practice his ice-prince act in case he ever met her again, but damn, he was holding up like a champion. He really was fucking fantastic.

"Thank you." Nadia's face gleamed with worry. Doctor Snarky-Viper had vanished, and only Frantic Mom remained. "I just want to help."

"Right," Glimmer muttered. "Sure. Whatever."

Did he buy into her act? Was he in any state to notice? Hell, maybe it wasn't an act. I didn't know her, I shouldn't judge... but to hell with that, right? She might not be our enemy, but she sure as hell wasn't our friend.

I held the door. Glimmer was jittering, tense, his gaze flitting. "Umm... you want me to drive?" I asked.

He cracked his knuckles, and the ghost of faraway amusement haunted his lips. "Not a chance. Are you crazy?"

"Sure. Didn't we establish that?" But forlorn satisfaction shone weakly on my heart. He'd almost smiled. See, I could help after all.

"This is it?"

Dubiously, I eyed the skyscraper as I hopped out of the car, three blocks from Market Street downtown. Shiny glass windows, revolving doors, brick-edged garden and fountain in the little square out front. "Looks like an office building."

Nadia narrowed her eyes at me. She'd removed her lab coat and her smooth, dark suit gleamed in the sun. "Do you want it to look like Dr. Frankenstein's workshop? Researchers rent office space like everyone else."

Around us, city life carried on. But tension tingled the air, like the smell of distant fire. The crowd was thinner than usual. People eyed each other uncertainly, as if each suspected all the others were armed and ready to pop. A hot-dog seller squirted mustard onto a sausage, one wary eye on his customer's hands. An ironic street musician strummed his guitar and sang "It's the End of the World as We Know It".

Traffic cruised by, slowing for police inspection at the barricades down the street. We'd avoided roadblocks so far, but to go any further, we'd have to walk—and Glimmer and I were in the authorities' sights. If anyone recognized our faces, we were toast.

Snort. Whatever. Do your worst, assholes. We're augmented, remember?

I was already gauging the smoothness of the walls, locations of fire escapes and aircon ducts. We'd broken into skyscrapers the unorthodox way before. I stretched, muscles aching. I felt fatigued, thirsty, overwarm. I needed hot food and sleep. Not climbing, running, dodging gunfire. "What floor?" I asked.

"Seventeen. Ethan, what are you going to do?"

Glimmer ignored her, like he had the whole time. Just gazed up, counting floors. "It's not a public building," he said at last.

"Huh?" I squinted up, sunflash on the windows.

"Aysha said 'public buildings'. This is privately owned."

"You think she won't attack here?"

He shrugged. Calm, wits collected like always. But his eyes burned, a new fanaticism that disturbed me. I could feel the air seething around him, his unquiet mindsense wreaking silent havoc. Whatever darkness lurked in his mind, it ate away at him like acid, and warm excitement mixed a trepidation cocktail in my belly. Glimmer made a dangerous enemy. These boffins better look to themselves.

I touched his arm and whispered so she wouldn't hear. "Do you trust her? Think she's genuine?"

A bruised shrug, helpless. "I can't fucking tell with her, Verity. Not anymore. But what choice do we have?"

I nodded and squeezed his hand in mute solidarity. "You," I ordered Nadia, "stay behind us, and don't get in the way. That's your only warning."

We negotiated the revolving doors. Silver metal lobby, ugly in fine art deco tradition. Reception desk; keycard elevators; security guards, one-two-three-four. I scanned the tenant list on the wall behind the desk. FORWARD RESEARCH LABORATORIES, floor 17.

High in one corner, red lights flashed and a Sentinel screamed.

Glimmer already leveled his pistol at the guards. I threatened with a swell of force, making them stumble, and crushed the desk to splinters behind them. "Cooperate," I yelled over the wailing alarm, "or don't. Your choice."

In ten seconds, we had a keycard. Inside the shining silver elevator, I swiped the card and pressed seventeen. The elevator rumbled up, agonizingly slow. I tapped my foot, impatient. Just before Judgment Day we finally reached the top. The door hissed open.

Dim light greeted us, a single shaft of sunlight through glass bricks. I stepped cautiously into the lobby. Empty reception foxhole, an opaque wall behind it blocking our access, a locked security door. "Why's no one here?"

Nadia glanced about, confused. "I don't know. This is where they kept her. I was here just last week."

Glimmer poked at the keypad next to the locked door. "Can you get in?"

"My access is revoked," she repeated, and tried her code anyway. It didn't work.

I shrugged. "Fine." *Smash!* The wall broke under my mindmuscle, an enormous fist-shaped hole. The dust settled, and we stepped through the crushed plaster, me first, then Glimmer, then Nadia.

White walls, white ceiling, white fluorescent lights gleaming on glass partitions. Each section of the lab was lined with equipment banks, refrigerators, centrifuges, electron microscopes, other high-tech medical stuff I couldn't identify. A faint hot-metal smell twitched my nose. My senses tingled and I reached out feelers… nothing. No augments, no traps.

But I couldn't relax. My toes stung, wary. Something smelled wrong here, and I fumbled behind me for Glimmer, the wall, anything safe.

Bang! Lights erupted, blinding me like a flash-bang grenade. Behind me a huge weight slammed into the quivering floor.

Glimmer cursed. I stumbled backwards... into a cold metal wall. My mindmuscle shrieked and recoiled, a leech from salt. Augmentium. We were trapped.

Nadia's dark laughter raked my nerves with spikes. Her voice rang out, calm and cold, no trace of Frantic Mother now. Just a gloating monster. "You freaks are so *dumb*."

~ 30 ~

Glimmer recovered first. As my vision cleared, he whirled, aiming his pistol at her. Shaking, sweating, but his aim was sure. "Let us go."

"No." Nadia smiled, and it stripped her pretty mask away. Revealing a creature just as beautiful, but monstrous, fanatical, glitter-eyed. "Put that away, Ethan. What will you do, shoot me? I don't think so."

"Don't bet on it." Glimmer always kept his promises. When he said *stop or I'll shoot*, he meant it. But this time, he didn't fire. *Couldn't* fire.

She just waved an indulgent hand. "You wanted to see the lab. Well, here you are. Nice, isn't it? Cost a fortune. The latest and best in everything. But I have extremely rich donors."

"It was you," I accused. "You're running these God-awful experiments. For *him*." Quickly, I backed off, away from the horrid augmentium wall—a security barrier, I saw now, stainless metal gleaming; she must have activated it remotely—and soothed my whimpering mindmuscle. It coiled and shivered like a hunted mouse.

She laughed. "Of course. He made me an offer I couldn't refuse. Science doesn't happen without funding. If you want results, you sometimes have to sleep with the enemy."

The stink of augmentium forced a sick ache into my skull. But Nadia sickened me more.

She'd fooled me? Fine. I was an idiot. I could take the hit for that. But Glimmer...

I darted my gaze left and right. No windows, no other doors that I could see.

But could this whole fucking floor really be coated in augmentium? I doubted it. My mindmuscle was still there, still conscious. But I couldn't see any way out.

"What do you want with us?" Best way to buy time: keep the villains talking.

"Same thing I wanted with all of them: I needed subjects. Freaks don't just crawl out of the woodwork yelling 'pick me!', you know. I had to make do."

Disgust licked my nerves. "So you grew them. You mutilated children. That's real nice."

"I do what I have to. I can't afford to wait for their abilities to grow naturally. I need the mature genetic material *now*. And my patron was most interested in the various side effects of accelerated growth." Nadia walked past me into the lab, unconcerned. Like she wasn't afraid of me.

She was right, of course. Sensible. We wouldn't kill her until we'd figured out what was going on.

Or, I could just tear her smug lying head off and eat it.

I turned to follow her. I didn't want to let her out of my sight. Far in the back, another metal wall gleamed amid the shadows of barred doors. Cages. I shuddered, thinking of the solitary cells on Rock Island. Coated in augmentium, hours and days and weeks shivering in that evil silent darkness...

Glimmer fired at the augmentium screen. *Bang-bang!* Loud in the metal-clad space. Twin tiny dents cracked. That was all.

Nadia laughed again, and it grated, the sincere, misdirected mirth of a madwoman. "C'mon. Think I'd make it that easy? My experiments are resource-intensive, I'm sorry to say. I go through

263

a lot of subjects. I'm always eager for more. And you two are already fully grown. My new serum will be even stronger with your contribution." She unlocked a glass cabinet with a swipe of her card and fetched out a silvery, evil-looking contraption. Cylindrical, festooned with screws and phials. From its side poked a wicked hollow stainless-steel needle, as thick as my finger with an oblique razor-sharp point.

My skin crawled. Great. Sign me up.

"Cranial fluid, you see, from the base of the brain. Of course," she added with a wicked glint of smile, "you'll be dead before I've finished. You'll never see the results. Good news is: the extraction process is lengthy. We've got time to chat! So long as you can keep the screaming to a minimum."

Glimmer holstered his pistol—still careful, despite his distress. "Is that what this is, then? You experimented on Aysha? Your own daughter?"

"Don't you dare lecture me, monster," she growled, her temper flashing out of control. "I wanted to *cure* her."

I gaped. Weasel had told us this wasn't a weapon. Weasel had lied. Or Razorfire had lied to him. Either way, Razorfire was building himself an augment exterminator. So what was his plan? Drag all his enemies into the lab and shoot them up with Nadia's helljuice? It didn't seem flashy enough.

Glimmer stared. "What?"

"Yes, a *cure*," Nadia sneered. "To cut out the filthy disease *you* infected her with. It was all for *her*."

Her words punched him in the face. I saw him recoil. But he didn't falter. "You're an evil woman, Nadia. I thought there was hope for you, but I was wrong." His eyes glittered, a silversnake threat.

Suddenly, somehow, Nadia held her own pistol. Aimed it right at Glimmer, her rage blazing bright. "You won't kill me, Ethan. You're too weak and afraid for that. But don't think I won't kill *you*. Your kind are only good for one thing."

"And what's that?"

A vicious grin. "Spare parts."

I jumped forward, but Glimmer's gesture stopped me. "Put it down, Nadia," he said gently. "You don't want to kill me. Just tell me where Aysha is and we can all go."

A tiny warm sensation feathered the back of my neck. I shivered, aware. He was unleashing. Subtly, softly, imperceptible to anyone who didn't know him. But it was there.

Crack! A bullet slammed the wall behind him. "Stop that," Nadia hissed, murderous. "Just stop it. You make me want to vomit, the whole stinking lot of you. But especially you, Ethan. You played your dirty little game with me for four years. Lied to me. *Raped* me. I can still feel you inside me, your filthy hands touching my body. Was it fun for you, making me *like* it?"

Glimmer's face glistened, greenish. He was trembling. Like he was going to be sick.

Sunflash ignited in my blood. The steel floor groaned and heaved, twisting under the force of my rage. "I'll rip your rotten face off, you evil-hearted—"

"You can't even admit it, can you?" Nadia called, ignoring me. "Even *he* didn't stoop that low. He was honest. He never pretended to be anything he wasn't." Her mouth twisted, ugly. "I refused to believe him when he said there was no cure. And now I've proved him wrong. Aysha *is* the cure, Ethan. I made her and she's going to kill every last rotten one of you."

My mind somersaulted and landed on its feet. Suddenly it all made sense. Vincent wouldn't force us to take his evil augment-strangling serum, or whatever it was. He didn't need to.

Because we'd already taken it.

"That sickness you're so afraid of? It's her. It's what happens when she absorbs your horrid powers. Ha ha! My finest invention!" Nadia spat on the floor at Glimmer's feet. "Death by Sophron. *That's* how you cure augments. And there's no remedy. You'll all die horribly, and good riddance to you."

I cursed, ugly. That explained how Espectro in Rock Island had the fever: Sophron had mirrored his augment at the museum. Ebenezer, at the asylum. She'd mirrored *my* powers at City Hall. Adonis's, too. Which meant...

Glimmer's eyes glittered, not power but tears. "Just tell me *where she is!*"

"All in good time." Nadia sidled up to me, pistol still aimed at Glimmer, and held out one hand. "Rock, please."

"Huh?"

Nadia gestured impatiently. "Are you stupid as well as ugly? I need that augment for my serum. Why do you think I had Aysha steal it?"

My stomach dropped to its death. My mother's face, marbled with granite. Dad weeping over her corpse. He was never the same afterwards. None of us were. And he'd kept this rock safe in his vaults the whole time...

"So it is a heart," I said thickly. "Whose is it, Nadia? Tell me!"

"Who cares?" she sneered. "It's the genetic augment matrix I want, not a shred of dead flesh. Razorfire told me about this Obsidian person. His contribution will be invaluable. Now hand it over before I get upset."

"Fuck you." I folded my arms, and my mindmuscle flexed, too, rabid at being confined. It burned to burst out and strangle her, and I wasn't about to tell it *no*. "You won't shoot Glimmer. You need him for your stupid *serum*, remember? If you want this rock, come get it."

"You're right, I do need him." A supercilious smile made her pretty mouth a horror. "But I don't need *you*." And she flicked the safety off and turned her pistol on me.

Was that supposed to scare me? Please. Like I've never had a gun waved at me before. I frowned. "What about my brain goo, or whatever? Don't I need to be alive for your serum to work?"

"It'll survive without you. Your choice, freak. Die now or die later. How much are a few more hours worth to you?"

The pistol barrel winked at me, a cold black eye. I calculated swiftly. Twelve feet away, no more. Too close to rush her or strike. Too close to do anything.

Fuck.

I swallowed sour defeat. Stuffed my hand in my pocket. And gave her my mother's heart.

My mother's *heart*. For fuck's sake.

But Mom was gone. I'd almost forgotten her face. Was it worth dying for?

No point crying about what's done.

"Just so you know," I hissed, "I'll be taking that back before we kill you."

"Brave words from an idiot at the wrong end of a gun." Nadia took the heart and backed off. My bones stung cold, empty. As if I'd burned a photograph or lost a family keepsake.

Coolly, Nadia laid pistol and rock aside on the white bench. She played with the touch screen on her machine, setting parameters. Unsheathed the horrid needle and raised it to the light. It glinted, wicked. "Now," she said brightly, "who's first?"

A little girl giggled, sweet and poisoned like the chime of an evil fairy's wand. "Mommy, you're so funny."

I whirled, my mindmuscle on edge. A side door, cunningly concealed in the white wall, had swung open, and Sophron walked out. Blue dreads, tank top falling off one skinny shoulder, jeans patched with frayed plaid. Her eyes gleamed, flat and empty.

Nadia hugged her close and kissed her hair. "Hello, baby," she crooned. "Mommy's here. Look what I brought you."

Sophron—Aysha—grinned, chewing on her little finger. Nearly as tall as Nadia, but skeletally thin, her skin stretched too tight. "Hi, Daddy. Did you see the show this morning? It was all for you."

Glimmer stared. "Aysha, please." Hollow, desperate. "You don't have to do this. Whatever she told you, you don't have to."

"I'll do whatever I want!" A petulant pout. Sophron pulled away from her mother, eyeing Glimmer balefully. "You can't tell me what to do. You *left* me."

Glimmer's knuckles crackled white. "I had no choice. I'm sorry."

"No, you're not." Sophron teleported, right into his face. *Snap!* Three inches away. "Your lot are never sorry," she snarled. "You pretend you're so heroic but all you do is tell other people how to live and when to die."

Nadia clicked her tongue, sardonic. "Honey, play nice."

"You could come with us, Aysha," Glimmer whispered, ignoring Nadia. "Please. Leave all this behind."

"How was I supposed to know what to do?" Sophron's voice died, barely audible. "Mommy knows nothing! You were all I had. The only one who could understand what it was like." A grinding sound came from her mouth, teeth cracking. "*And you left me!*"

Glimmer swallowed. His fingers worked unconsciously, as if he longed to stroke her hair. Finally, he gave a helpless, anguished shrug. "You're right."

Sophron frowned. "What did you say?"

"I blamed your mother, but I should have been stronger. I should have helped you, and I didn't." His lashes sparkled with long-suppressed tears. "I'm so sorry, Aysha. I hope one day you can forgive me."

Sophron smiled. A little girl's happy smile, brimming with wonder.

But it wasn't a smile. It was a weapon, sharp and poisoned. And it stabbed Glimmer straight to the heart. Knocked him reeling, though he barely moved a muscle. His expression blanked and melted to pure pain.

"Never," she hissed. "Not *ever*. I hope you die sorry."

A yell burst from my lips, and I fired a cannonball of invisible force straight at her face.

But she brushed it aside. Didn't even blink. The breeze just ruffled her hair as it flew by.

Inside, I screamed, a killing rage. I burned to end her. I howled with the need to bring him peace. But I was helpless. All I could do was stare, as with disinterested serenity that Vincent might have envied, Sophron watched Glimmer break.

His knees buckled. I scrambled to grab him, hold him upright. His sweet-scented hair brushed my face, and my cheek ran warm with his tears. He clutched me, wordless, every muscle trembling.

Sophron sniffed and turned away.

"It's time, sweetie." Nadia was breathing hard, aroused, eyes alight with relish. "Let's finish it. Let's do what I've created you to do."

"Don't listen to her, Aysha," I called. "What d'you think she'll do to you once we're dead? She hates us all, you the most. You'll just be next."

Sophron only tugged her dreads and grinned, unhinged.

My guts shriveled. I needed to pee. She'd kill us. We'd be dead. Today. I didn't want to die today, did I?

But Vincent was already dead. My reason for living—he who made it possible for Verity to exist at all—was gone. I was a worthless thing, not worthy of the title *human being*. And I didn't think Glimmer cared right now if he lived or died.

So fuck it, then. Let's go out together.

I clutched him to me, his beloved cheek on mine. Inhaled the scent of his hair, tasted his ineffable goodness one last time. Imagined for one more precious moment that I was his and he was mine and nothing else on this earth mattered.

But he wasn't. This was here, now, not some perfect dream world. It *did* matter.

"Go on, then," I spat, "kill us and get it over with. I'm bored."

Her eerie, high-pitched laughter crawled. "Oh," Sophron said strangely, "I'm not going to kill him. It's far worse than that."

Nadia giggled, ugly. "That's it, sweetie. Let's extract the brain fluid and then you'll be even stronger and we can finish these freaks off for good."

269

Sophron's eyes flashed bright with rage. "Oh, shut *up*," she hissed. "Who the fuck are you calling *freak,* Mommy? I *love* what I am."

And she swiped the pistol from the bench, and fired.

~ 31 ~

Crack! A bloody rosebud flowered in Nadia's forehead. Behind her, the white wall splashed lumpy red.

Her body wavered on its feet, not realizing it was dead. Then she slumped to the floor. The back of her head was blown off. Just crawling red flesh and bone amid locks of shiny merlot hair.

Sophron teleported. *Boom!* She slammed into Glimmer and me, and we flew into the augmentium barrier and tumbled. Glimmer fell from my arms. I hit the floor. Sophron leapt for Glimmer, crouching over him like a hungry vulture.

My heart pounded, and I scrambled towards him, trying to get there first, protect him, keep her away.

But she didn't grab him. He was just bait.

She grabbed *me*. Lifted me, easily as she might a baby, and hurled me across the room like a bundle of rags. *Slam!* My body smacked into the barred cage door at the back of the room. Bones rattled in my flesh. I lifted my head, groggy, tasting blood… and efficiently Sophron shackled me to the bars. Metal cuffs clicked, the minute sound of death.

"Let her go, Aysha." Glimmer crawled towards us, tried to come for me. Sophron just hurled a glittering golden ball at him, and

271

he reeled, dizzy with confusion and mangled emotions. Sophron had Adonis's power now, and she used it mercilessly.

Furious, I rattled my wrists, but I was stuck fast. Nadia must have left cuffs here for her foul experiments. My mindmuscle howled and whiplashed, still free, and I laughed, incredulous. Steel. They were fucking *steel*.

"You stupid girl. Next time, try augmentium." And I flexed invisible fists, ready to tear the bars down.

"Oh, I wouldn't if I were you." Sophron gazed down at me solemnly, chewing her finger, and giggled, insane. "Boom. All fall down. So sad."

Perplexed, I twisted my neck to see. Wires soldered to the cuffs, copper ends shining. And the wires in turn were soldered to…

My heart sank. Little flashing lights, cubes of Semtex, a stupid mechanical detonator that would've made the Road Runner turn up his nose and ask for something more sophisticated.

Stupid, but damn effective.

"Should've known," I muttered. "Always with breaking things. You've really planned this out in advance, haven't you?"

"Of course. Mommy taught me that. And Razorfire taught me *this*: always give your enemy an impossible choice."

I snorted. "Stay trapped here, or blow myself up? That's not impossible, dumbass. It's fucking *commonplace*. I've made more difficult decisions about what to have for breakfast—"

"But you're missing the point!" Gleefully, she kicked an unresisting Glimmer in the head. His limbs slackened, limp. Black glitter swarmed over his face. Out cold.

My breath felt too warm in my throat, like I burned up inside. "Hurt him again, you nasty little ratgirl, and I'll—"

"Shut up. You're so pathetic. He warned me about you, y'know. Sometimes she gets maudlin and sentimental, he said. He was right."

She heaved Glimmer up, dragging his hair in the dust. Tossed him over her shoulder, impossibly strong. "We'll be going now," she explained happily. "I've got special plans for him. Not *killing* him, or anything boring like that. I want him to suffer way worse. City Hall was just a practice run. I'm going to take away what he values most of all."

My tongue withered, dry. What did she mean? She'd already broken his heart, like her mother before her. "What will you do to him?"

"That's for me to know and you to find out. Ha ha!" She hefted him on her shoulder. "This is where your decision comes in, see? Either you can stay here, and let me do what I want with Daddy and your precious *city*." She spat the word out like a rotten berry. "Or you can break your cuffs and that bomb will go off. Maybe you'll escape, maybe you won't. But there's not just one bomb, see. Pull that wire and you'll bring this entire building down on top of everyone in it."

She snickered, pleased. "See? Lesser of two evils. Kill innocents, or… well, kill more innocents. I really don't care, Verity Fortune. You're the *hero*. You figure it out."

"Screw you," I growled. But my heart sank.

"Bye," she sang. "It's been fun. Pity you're too weak to save him. But don't take too long. Time's burning."

She teleported, and in a rush of breeze they were gone. But not before she'd hurled a twisting whip of fire.

Kerrr-ack! The burning ceiling split, and fell.

I barely flung my shield up in time. *Wham!* Smoking plaster crashed into it, a foot above my head. I hurled it off and withstood another shower of rubble. More and more, dust flying, flames licking higher.

I didn't have much time. Soon, I'd be crushed. Not even I could hold off this kind of weight for long.

My mind scuttled circles, a frightened cockroach. Wreck the building, kill everyone inside, follow Glimmer and probably die trying to save him. Or stay here and let Sophron… what? Wreak more destruction? Torture Glimmer? Kill him? Her snide threat was scorched into my mind. *He'll suffer way more than that…*

She could be lying. Standing outside to watch me suffer and burn. Or the bomb might be a hoax… but I didn't think so. This was real, here, now. I couldn't afford to take the chance.

My thoughts crystallized, starlight and steel. Vincent was dead. Adonis was gone. Only I could stop her. Only I could spare the city her capricious whims. Only I could save Glimmer from her wrath.

For that, would I sacrifice a building full of people?

The impossible choice…

I cracked my neck bones, one by one. Odd calm filtered over me. A zone of lucidity, clear as a glass bellchime, that I hadn't experienced since last I lay sleepy and satisfied in Vincent's embrace.

A tiny, fond smile kissed my lips. Shame on you, lover. You made this one far too easy.

For Glimmer? I'd sacrifice pretty much anything.

Above my head, my shield shuddered, piled with burning debris. Plaster rumbled. My arms were stretched out straight, the cuffs pinning my wrists to the bars. Through the dust cloud, I spied dead Nadia splayed on the floor. Beside her lay my mother's heart.

Worth dying for? Maybe not. But it was all I had left of her. All I'd ever have.

I uncoiled a tendril of mindmuscle. Grabbed the heart, edged it towards me. It skittered across the floor and plopped into my lap. I eased it into my pocket. Told you so, bitch. So sad. See ya. I'm done here.

I curled into a cruciform ball, wrapped myself in a tight cushion of mindforce, and *pulled*.

Bombs roared, and the world exploded.

~ 32 ~

Dizziness, the wild sensation of flight. My shoulders wrenched, agonizing. I tumbled up and down, mixing in a blurred rainbow of fire. The noise pounded my eardrums, louder than the end of the world.

Falling, down and over, plummeting into space... and *boinng!* I bounced, one-two-three, and my body smacked against a gutter.

My lungs squeezed flat. I gulped, winded, my diaphragm spasming... then air sucked in. I panted, catching my breath. Doggedly, I unfolded screaming limbs. Straightened my wretched spine under protest. Stumbled to my feet.

The air stank of ash. The explosion had hurled me hundreds of feet, over the tops of buildings. A few blocks away, black smoke billowed to heaven. Eerie silence stuffed my abused ears, broken only by falling rubble. A city in shock. More dead. More broken streets, buildings fallen, fire.

My nerves stung, ugly with truth. They hadn't seen anything yet.

Wearily, I dusted myself off. Grit made my palms bleed. My pants were torn, my coat gashed. I hurt. My skin stung with tiny cuts. Blood leaked where the cuffs had torn my wrists, and I suspected I'd broken a finger.

That was all.

The greater good. Words I'd wrestled with all my adult life, never finding an answer that satisfied me. Where was my guilt? My anguish, my terror that I'd made the wrong decision, the awful moral dilemma to sink twin hooks into my soul and pull in opposite directions until I tore apart, my heartblood flowing into the dirt?

Where, indeed.

Shouts and heavy footsteps approached. A few streets over, gunshots cracked, and the ground rumbled under the tracks of the National Guard's armored vehicles. Already, the breeze tingled my tongue with the angry, bitter flavor of vengeance.

They'd come for us. Mackenzie Wilt and her cronies would make sure of that. We, augments, who threatened them just by existing. Any of us. All of us.

Despair made curdled milk in my stomach, but my mindmuscle still stretched, overeager, a pleasurable pang. War. The battle he'd always foretold. Pleasingly ironic that he wouldn't be here to see it. Vincent had always appreciated irony.

Fresh steel walls slammed around my heart, salted with that rusty old resentment. The *greater good*—whoever the fuck *they* were—had no right to beg for my protection, then squeal when I provided it in a way they didn't like. They can't saddle me with the tough choices, then expect me to wear the remorse, too.

So fuck 'em. More of them would stay alive today because of me. If they put me in charge? They can't complain when I make command decisions. To hell with guilt. I'd die for my cause. I'd kill for it, too. If they didn't like that, too fucking bad.

And my cause was saving Glimmer. Nothing else mattered. All I needed to know was where she was going.

Armed men in black Kevlar spotted me and yelled. I broke into a run.

The street outside Widow Swanky's crawled with people. I climbed the back wall just in case. Jumped through a window into the stairwell, and sprinted for our door.

I needed to find Sophron and Glimmer, and I had zilch to go on. Back to square one, marked *trawl the internet for clues.* Good thing I already had all the gear.

Fatigue ached in my muscles, and I burned, overwarm. I stank with sweat and dirt. I could use a shower, food, about twenty hours of sleep.

Whatever. I couldn't hide here for long. Adonis, Eb, even Peg had already tracked me to this place. It wouldn't take Wilt's soldiers long to do the same. I needed to grab my shit and find someplace else pronto. Keep moving, or die.

Glimmer still had the keys, so I kicked the door in. *Boom!* Bad luck if the place had an alarm, though somehow I didn't think the alarm-response people would be answering today.

"Peggy, I'm back." The bed was rumpled, my towel from the shower I'd had about a hundred years ago still puddled on the floor. I'd left the TV on for Peg—I know, how thoughtful—and the news channel blared. I tugged the curtains aside and peered out. Firelight flickered in the street from a burning car, and I smelled smoke. Sirens wailed in the distance, a gunshot or two.

The party had started. People danced and yelled and had impromptu punch-ups. Furniture flew from apartment windows and smashed on the road. At the street's end, people were piling up a makeshift barricade of cars, doors, broken tables and chairs.

Heh. Nice bit of civil disobedience. Hopefully, it'd mean the authorities would take a bit longer to find me.

"Peg, you there?" In the kitchen, I grabbed a banana and stuffed it into my mouth. A pang of sorrow seized me at the taste. Boy, I could really use Adonis right now. I missed him, arguments and insults and all. Shit, I missed them all. Even Harriet.

I shoved the bathroom door open. "Wakey-wakey, time to fly…"

The white tiles glared at me, dazzling. Empty.

Peg was gone.

Fuck. Frustrated, I kicked the wall, and pain speared up my toe. How had she escaped? Blood stained the broken cable tie, a few ragged shreds of skin. One end was melted, like someone had held a match to it. I recalled her glowing eyes, that faint radiant heat. Guess Peggy had some power after all. I'd tied her wrists as far behind her as I could without breaking her arms. Jeez, she must have craned her head practically backwards. There's determination for you.

Determination or terror. Guess I must have convinced her I meant business.

I sighed, turning... and a swipe of crimson caught my eye. I blinked. She'd written on the bathroom mirror, letters scrawled with a bloody forefinger.

FIREBIRD

I stared, swamped with heady memory. Vincent's hot whisper into our kiss, our bodies mingling, the sweet ache of our love. *Firebird...*

The name accused me. Taunted me. Seduced me. What the hell did Peg mean? .

Trembling, I stumbled for the spare bedroom, tripping in my haste. "Eb..."

The room smelled rank, of sweat and blood. In the twisted sheets, Ebenezer sprawled on his belly. Face in the pillow, lank dark hair tumbling over one cheek. His lashes and his mouth were crusted with blood.

His ribs weren't moving.

My heart pounded. I scrambled to my knees, felt his lips for breath on my palm. Nothing.

"Eb. Stay with me." Frantically, I shook him. No response. I scrabbled for his pulse. Nothing. And his skin was cold.

He'd been dead for hours. I knew resuscitation would do no good. But I tried it anyway, through hot shimmering tears. Fought to make him breathe, spring his heart back to life, reignite the light in his mismatched eyes.

But I couldn't. None of us can. All we can do is destroy.

I sank back on my heels, strangled by hot grief. I hadn't even known him that well. But I'd tried to make this unhappy, lonely kid my friend. He didn't have many friends. Neither did I. He'd come to me for help, when he had no one else. And I'd failed him.

No point crying over what's done, I'd always said. Well, this was worth crying for.

Worth killing for.

I gritted my teeth, swallowing on fresh sobs. I'd destroy Sophron for this. Hunt her down and put an end to her. And if she'd hurt Glimmer, too?

A black corpse grin stretched my lips. Why, I'd just make sure she died slower.

Somehow, I made my legs obey me. In the living room, the television news blared. The burning skyscraper, updates on the City Hall mess, more sound bites from Mackenzie Wilt. Outside, shouts and gunshots, the zap of electric whips. The sunlight was bleeding with the light of bonfires, and smoke drifted in through the French windows.

Dizziness swept me, tumbling my brain over. Then, it was gone. My throat felt raw, raw like I'd coughed all night. I wiped my forehead and my fingers came away wet.

And deep in my chest, like an ugly flower threatening to bloom… a sick ball of heat.

Fever.

My mindmuscle whimpered, out of sorts, and an awful chill struck deep into my bones. That primal human dread of mortal sickness, an enemy you can't flee or fight. You can only surrender.

Grimly, I pushed the sensation away. Oh, no, you don't. Not me. I've got too much to do to spend time dying.

Better get on with it, then.

I sat, listless, and picked up a tablet. Flicked through a few browser pages. I had no leads. Didn't even know where to begin. Even if I did find her? I had no idea how to win. Every time we'd met, she'd emphatically thrashed the pants off me and mine. I'd nothing to fight her with, no weapon that worked.

But the idea of just waiting for her to attack wriggled my skin like a shedding snake's. Fuck it, I had to do *something*...

I walked to the kitchen, where the remnants of Glimmer's delicious hot chocolate congealed in the saucepan. Vainly, I searched for his scent, warm vanilla-spice... but all I could smell was death.

Dully, I poured a cup of water. Drank. Splashed my face. That damn clock ticked, indefatigable, counting down the remaining seconds of my life. Whatever, clock. Tell someone who cares. On the TV, pictures flashed. A burning building. Army guys running. Street barricades... then another picture. Not Mackenzie Wilt, or grainy smartphone video of the carnage, but...

My cup slipped through my unresisting fingers and smashed.

The floor rolled beneath me, a magic carpet of compulsion, and suddenly I was on my knees, my face an inch from the screen, fingers smearing the glass in my haste.

Vincent was alive.

~ 33 ~

And they'd *arrested* him.

No shit. The news anchor read voiceover on a rerun of the footage from yesterday. "Former Sapphire City Mayor, Vincent Caine, remains in custody at Rock Island this morning after yesterday's shocking revelation…"

In the background, the remains of City Hall burned in their nice new crater. Paramedics and firefighters ran and shouted. And there he was. Triple-cuffed in augmentium, escorted by about five hundred cops with assault weapons. Dust drifted from his bronze hair, and blood trickled crimson from a slash on his cheek.

He didn't speak. Didn't resist or try to escape. But for a second, he tilted his storm-grey gaze to the camera, and I thought I saw him smile.

My heart pounded. I couldn't breathe. Just a silky twitch of the corner of his mouth. Probably no one who didn't know him would've noticed it. Secret, exquisite. Just for me.

The TV flashed back to the news anchor and I was released. Blessed air rushed into my lungs. Tears blinded me, and my heart burst, showering treacherous golden sunshine.

Alive.

We'd been too busy rushing about to watch the news. I hadn't killed him. Hadn't ended it. Hadn't ended *myself.*

But my guts writhed, too, cold and greasy. I squinted in the glaring spotlight of yet another new reality, a fresh iteration of truth and lies.

I'd imagined him so easy to kill. Creeping Christ, who was I kidding? The man could dodge bullets, for fuck's sake. He'd have no trouble surviving a rock fall.

And now, these idiots had locked the most dangerous man alive into a solitary augmentium hole on Rock Island. In the dark. Where the madness lurked.

Laughter withered in my throat. I wanted to dive through that little glass screen to where he was and embrace him, inhale his essence, swoon with his living body next to mine. But I also wanted to run and keep on running.

Fuck me raw. Did I think Rock Island would save me from his vengeance? I'd betrayed him. Tried to kill him because I was weak and afraid. Any lingering respect he bore towards me? I'd shattered it.

The world telescoped, rushing away at dizzy speed. I felt tiny, insignificant, a fleck of fly dust on a wide black empty sea. I wanted to thrash and howl, scream the fact of my existence to the uncaring stars. *I'm still here! I'm real!*

But I was terrified no one would listen.

I'd thought my world had ended when I imagined him dead. But this was far worse. He'd hate me. Scorn me. Discard me for a weakling, no better than the normal scum he despised.

I'd be nothing to him. Which meant I was… nothing.

So what now?

Unsteadily, I sat back, my senses starbursting like crazy fireworks, their message unintelligible and useless. Peggy's bloody writing on that mirror haunted me, a mocking specter that refused to rest. *Firebird.* All this time, she'd been Vincent's minion. Thing was, I'd believed her when she confessed to wanting Adonis's protection. Did she truly flee to us to escape Vincent's wrath after I killed Iceclaw? Or was it just a trick to infiltrate our camp?

Firebird. Vincent, kissing me, murmuring into my mouth, the hot-metal smell of ash on our naked skin. *Firebird.* Striding along the rafter at Flash's burning warehouse, crimson silk flaring, flames licking his bronze-gold hair. *Firebird...*

Christ on a cheesy rissole. This was all a ruse. It had to be. Surely, they'd arrested him because he'd *let* them...

Outside, the soldiers' shouts grew louder. Doors banged. Footsteps pounded on the stairwell outside my apartment door, the metallic clicks and electric hiss of weapons being readied.

Ooh, Wilt's men. Brr. The city's finest, come to *get* me. Better run.

The fact that I was dying—that my family would die, too, horribly, their augments unhinged, and there was nothing I could do about it—seemed unaccountably distant and irrelevant. Hell, maybe I was just being the Seekernoid again. They'd dragged Vincent unconscious from under the rubble. He might be godlike, but he still had a body that needed basic things like air and blood circulation. Not even Razorfire could defend himself while he was senseless. Right?

Hell, I'd better be sure I was right, before I bet my life on it...

Clunk! The penny dropped into place, and dark satisfaction released in my belly. Oh, yeah. Now, I knew what to do. I had a plan.

Shrill, insane laughter pealed from my chest, barely recognizable as mine. I was about to bet all our lives on being *wrong.*

Vincent's city apartment on the fiftieth floor. Dark, locked up, surrounded by armed cops. A crime scene, don't you know.

So I climbed in the window. Simple, with my augment, to break into the apartment upstairs and shimmy down. My breath over-heated my lungs, and every once in a while I shivered violently, sweat beading inside my shirt. I clutched the metal railing, fifty floors above nothing, and my muscles juddered and complained, but they obeyed.

In my current mood? They didn't dare do otherwise.

Beneath me, the nighttime city glittered wildly, backlit with scarlet twilight. Breeze lifted my hair as I unclipped the window sash and posted myself in, feet first.

If Vincent really did know everything? Controlled it all, planned it from the beginning? Fine. I'd damn well ask him, then.

My boots hit the carpet. The vast windows gleamed, that magnificent view redolent with memory. At one end, the bed where we'd slept, fought, made slow exquisite love, had primal sheet-clawing sex of another, blacker sort. The sofa where we'd played chess, sipped red wine with chocolates, talked for hours of dark secrets and fire.

My senses sparkled. Delicately, at length, I inhaled. It hurt my fevered lungs, that deep penetration of air. But his delicious essence washed into me, curling inside my body like the pleasure he'd given me, and contentment warmed me anew. He was here, with me.

The white, glowing partition wall shielded me from the door, where police stalked and paced, weapons ready. But I couldn't afford to linger. Glimmer was in danger. Sophron proceeded with her fucked-up plan while I messed about getting sick, this fever incubating like parasitic larvae in my body. Soon, my mindmuscle would start to wander, a confused creature in pain, looking for something to lash out at…

Time's burning.

Swiftly, I padded to the desk, and flicked my hand over the console switch. It lit up, white light stabbing upwards, a shimmering virtual display in 3D. The cursor blinked, interrogating me with an empty box.

Password time. My fingers hovered over the luminous keys, and I smiled.

FIREBIRD

The letters pulsed brighter, and vanished, and a document sprang out.

284

Schematics. An engineering diagram. I peered closer, squinting at tiny glowing lettering, figures, precise lines and angles, circles and switches and zigzags. I was no expert, but that looked like cell-phone circuitry. Tech specs for some type of chip, and…

I scrolled and turned the schematic, frowning. Tiny claws of memory scratched at the back of my mind. I'd seen this part before somewhere…

I pulled Glimmer's tablet from my pocket and flicked through the files. Ha! I knew it.

This was a diagram of a Sentinel. Newest model, latest upgrades. The specs were public domain, so anyone could build one, just as Vincent had promised his obedient constituency. But this one was different. Why was it integrated with a cell phone like that?

I chewed my bottom lip, making it bleed to soothe me. A Sentinel, integrated with an IRIN cell phone. The kind of phone everyone in Sapphire City carried. And what was this other machine here? The one that looked like some insane Frankenstein wannabe had stitched together a particle collider and a cell-phone tower and some kind of electromagnetic wave generator…

Watch the Sentinels. Flash's warning taunted me. *Stay off the phone.* Like he was afraid it'd give him away to his enemies.

Or do something else to him. Secret surveillance, long-distance mass hypnosis, ultraviolet telescopic mind control.

Deep in my heart, the Seekernoid burst out laughing.

My thoughts clanged, resounding with ugly *told-you-so.* There was no surveillance kit in the Sentinels. No transmission or reception, apart from the augment energy field. Glimmer had said so.

But there didn't need to be. Vincent could collect all the surveillance data he wanted from cell phones. They had transmission, reception, memory. Everything.

And as for what he was transmitting…

My eyeballs swiveled to the weird stitched-together machine, and strange admiration warmed my heart. All the elegance of a

Leonardo da Vinci design, yet... grotesque. An exquisite horror, as only a superlatively arrogant archvillain could possibly imagine.

My fevered pulse quickened. Whatever this nasty-looking machine did? This was where Sophron had taken Glimmer. I knew it. Why else would Vincent have left this diagram for me? He wanted me to find her. This was the answer. It had to be.

All I needed was a location.

Desperately, I scrolled through the document, searching until my straining eyes ached. Deciphering every little notation, scanning for a map, a clue, coordinates, anything...

Damn it. I poked the keyboard, hoping for more files, another message.

Nothing.

I wiped my clammy forehead. Fuck. I had only hours, minutes maybe, before Sophron struck and Glimmer was... well, gone. And I wasn't getting any healthier while I stood here stuffing around. *I needed to know where he'd hidden his creation.*

I'd no time to search the city, building by building. What was left of my life was crumbling to ash, and Glimmer's along with it. *Fuck fuck fuck.* I rubbed stinging eyes. How the hell could I find this goddamned thing? And even if I could, how could I stop it, when the only person who knew how it worked was...

I tugged my ponytail and laughed.

When the only person who knew was locked up in Rock Island Prison, waiting for me.

~ 34 ~

Black, drunken dizziness drowned me, and I reeled.

I'd sided against him at City Hall because I couldn't trust myself to walk so close to the edge without slipping. Floodgates, slippery slope, all that. Shit, I couldn't even read his text messages or meet him for a civilized conversation without breaking out in shivers and sick yearning.

Fuck. I'd tried so hard to be *good*. To live up to Glimmer's heroic example—but all my efforts couldn't change the hideous truth that Vincent's twisted ideology brought me *peace*. And I craved it. All it took was one little mistake.

Just one hit. Like a junkie teetering on the back step of the wagon, ready to fall.

If I'd helped Vincent at City Hall—if I'd taken his hand, struck out at Sophron, helped him win the fight—I'd have been lost. Conquered. Irretrievable.

The truth kicked me in the kidneys, a sheet of bright agony.

This was what he'd wanted all along. Cunning fucker had *planned* this. Got himself arrested and shoved into a solitary augmentium cell, encouraged Sophron to destroy the city and threaten my friends.

All just to prove to me that I needed him.

I could never love a woman who needed rescuing, he'd told me once. Jeez. Had I imagined him helpless? Trapped, unable to act? What an abject, thoughtless fucking *idiot* I was.

He wanted me back. His ego demanded it. And he'd do anything to get me, even blow his cover in front of the entire city and let them lock him up in Rock Island...

Common-Sense Verity snorted. *Seriously?* This was fucking ridiculous. Paranoid. Insane. No way could he have planned all this, right?

Right. Vincent, the hyper-cognitive supervillain mastermind, who thought he loved me. Wouldn't dream of constructing a convoluted scheme to lure me back into his embrace. What a ludicrous notion.

I locked my teeth on a scream. The idea of playing his games slithered cold worms into my blood vessels. *No. I can't, not again. I don't want to.*

But I *did* want to. I yearned so hard I could taste it, mint-fire, a bright and tempting echo of his kisses.

The Seekernoid cackled, a witch stirring the bubbling cauldron of my madness. And every shred of rage or resentment I'd ever felt towards all those normal idiots who loathed me seethed to the surface.

What was stopping me? *Them?* What the fuck did I even *care?* I wanted; I took. End of story.

I struggled, warring serpents of *right* and *wrong* thrashing in my guts. No. That was *him* talking, not me. I didn't mean it...

Stop being so goddamn selfish. Glimmer's accusations flooded back, laced with bitter poison. *You're not facing your fears. You're just running from them.*

I recalled how I'd felt when I crushed that laboratory building—how I hadn't felt much at all—and sick laughter spilled copper into my mouth. Glimmer hadn't meant those things, not really. He was just heartbroken and angry.

But he was right.

God, I'd been so pathetic. Pretended I was facing my fears by admitting Vincent was too much for me, and vowing to avoid him. I'd thought myself so big and brave.

I was just a coward. A bad woman pretending to be good, so she wouldn't have to face the truth.

Vincent was my truth. Always had been. Time I stopped running.

No such thing as half a hero. Well, there's no such thing as half a villain, either. Who the hell was I kidding? I wasn't *good*. I was a deadly weapon, and it was time I started fucking acting like it. Stopping Sophron from breaking things was just a side effect. Collateral decency. The important thing—the only thing that mattered a damn—was that Glimmer was the brightest, best, most precious thing in my world. And he needed my help.

I won't just kill him, whispered Sophron gleefully in my memory. *It's much worse...* and what was more valuable to Glimmer than his life?

Honor. Integrity. The kinds of things a villain could ruin with a cunning, evil trick.

My determination welded, glaring steel, and I ran for the window and climbed out into the crimson-tainted night. Smoke stung my eyes, washing my vision lucid. Whatever filth Sophron had planned? I'd stop her from breaking Glimmer, no matter what it took. Oh, yes. I'd keep him perfect and beautiful, the way he'd always been. I'd kill for that. I already had, back at that doomed laboratory. For him, I'd make any sacrifice.

As for the shreds of my own thrice-rotted honor?

I laughed, and the flame-rich breeze laughed with me. Please. I'll surrender to the darkness in a heartbeat if it means Glimmer will be spared it.

Even if it means he'll never love me.

I borrowed a little motor boat from the quayside—the owner was good with it, after I thumped him unconscious—and sped across the moonlit bay towards Rock Island. The prison's forbidding edifices loomed closer, floodlights splashing the wind-chopped water. Razor-wire coils glittered atop the old stone walls.

The salt-laden air freshened my infected lungs, suffused my muscles with new and bloodthirsty power. No fog to hide me tonight. My boat's shadow skimmed across the waves, a ghostly black me wavering at the wheel.

Last time I'd come here, I'd been in disguise. I smiled grimly. This time, I wanted them to know exactly who the fuck I was.

For about three seconds, before I killed them all.

Only if I had to, of course. No need for unnecessary mess. But I'd do whatever was needed to win. I knew that now. That was Vincent's lesson, the one I'd shrunk from all this time.

Even after all that had passed between us, still I'd denied the truth. I was his creature, and he was mine.

No point crying over what's done. Get up and get on with it. Amen.

Rock Island drew closer. Foam whipped across the waves, piling against the jetty. My senses glittered, feverish and eager. I could almost smell augmentium already.

A quarter mile from the shore, I stopped the boat. Tied it up to a channel marker, and jumped.

Whizz! My slingshot flung me in a high, graceful arc. Stars cartwheeled. Wind buffeted my coat, my hair, stinging my face with salt. And I landed on Rock Island, right on the reception building's roof.

Crrinch! The metal buckled beneath my boots. Stupid alarms wailed. I grabbed a twisted sheet of roof and tore. Rending metal screeched, rivets popping like cracked nuts. I hurled the sheet away and jumped in.

Plaster crumbled, and I landed in a crouch, my torn coat flaring. The shiny metal walls were dented and crushed. Broken bits of building cluttered in my way. I kicked them aside.

Two guards lay senseless and bleeding. Their Sentinel had torn from its mounting and howled unheeded on the floor. My fat buddy Guard O'Malley cowered inside the Perspex security box.

I strode up and punched. The stuff was bulletproof. It wasn't Verity-proof. *Pow!* The Perspex shattered to shards. And my fevered mindmuscle screamed to the stars, exultant.

O'Malley staggered back, blood splattering. I jumped inside and punched him in the face. He fell, senseless. I tore twin black machine pistols from their locks on the wall rack—already loaded, thank you so much—and leaped for the transparent entryway.

This place was riddled with augmentium. Fine. That wouldn't stop a hail of bullets.

As I ran, I laughed. Vincent was so right. There were no rules, not for people like us. If you were prepared to pay the price, you could do anything.

The electrolocked door was in my way. I blew it apart. Kicked it open, dived inside and kept running. *Hold on, Glimmer, my sweet. I'm coming.*

~ 35 ~

Two minutes and a rain of bullets later, I sprinted down the stairs into the solitary wing and slammed the electro-locked door behind me.

Back in the prison proper, guards were no doubt massing to trap me on exit. I'd caught them by surprise. They hadn't had time to arm themselves, to shoot at me or aim properly with their electric whips. My magazine was still half full. And I didn't even have to kill many of them.

See, these prison screws aren't heroes. They work every day in a metal box packed with scumbags who want to eat their skin, and they're not paid enough to let that happen. Certainly not enough to die. If they're too dumb to cover their asses when the pressure's on? Not my problem, folks.

I sneered, scornful, and kicked at the shivering, sweating guard I'd dragged with me. Hypocrites. You lock us up and spout happy bullshit about keeping society safe, but you won't put your own precious asses on the line to make it happen. Where's your justice now, with a gun in your face?

I glared at the low black ceiling, and it glared back, threateningly close. The stink of augmentium crawled up my nose like a salty deathworm waiting to throttle me. This area was ringed with cells, a dozen at least. Shiny metal doors firmly bolted, electric locks impregnable. The cells would be lined with augmentium, too. Keeping the bad guys in.

Not so good at keeping bad guys *out*.

I didn't need to ask which cell. I could *feel* him, like a whisper on my skin, a fingertip tingling up the inside of my thigh. How close he was, a warm, insistent presence in some unknowable dimension. I couldn't see it. I just *knew*.

People say that's what God is like.

I shoved my remaining pistol under my pet guard's chin and marched him up to the control panel. "Open it."

He knew me well enough by now not to ask *which one?* This was our second date, after all. Same whip-happy guy from the other day, the Sundance Kid. Not so cocky with that fucking whip now. I'd torn it from his hands. He was bleeding, limping, spitting though broken teeth.

So I hadn't killed him. Didn't say I'd been *nice* to him. This asshole had locked Vincent in a dark augmentium hole, when in reality he wasn't fit to breathe the same goddamn air. He deserved everything I gave him.

Sundance fumbled with the switch, probably because I'd broken a few of his fingers. I shoved him, impatient. "Today, shitball. And put the lights on."

Wobbling, he punched a code into the keypad. Electric magnets zapped and clunked. Cool. I cracked my pistol's butt over his head, and he slumped. Sorry, Sundance. See ya.

My nerves sparkled. I yanked the bolt back and heaved the weighty door open.

Harsh white light stabbed out, reflecting like a curse from glaring augmentium walls. It was cold inside. Stale air. I blinked, impatient, waiting for my eyes to adjust.

Vincent sat calmly on his bare metal bench. White prison uniform, unaccountably spotless. Hands quiescent in his lap. He wasn't bruised or beaten up, I noticed dimly. They hadn't dared.

He stood, so graceful I wanted to weep. His firedark gaze swallowed me, his uncanny warmth like a caress. My pulse quickened. Softly, he traced one fingertip along my scarred cheekbone. And in the space of one heartbeat, everything we'd ever been to each other rushed back in to drown me.

My blood burned, inescapable hellfire. I'd killed for this moment. Cast aside everything I'd fought all my life to protect. I was cursed. Damned. "God, I fucking hate you."

He leaned closer, daring me. "Prove it."

My rage exploded. I yanked him against me and assaulted him with a kiss.

Our teeth collided. His rich fire-mint flavor ambushed me, tainted coppery with blood, and my reason withered. My gun clattered to the floor. Instead of pulling back like I'd meant to, I kissed him harder. Oh, fuck. Eager, deep, rich with unquenched need and stupid lost time. Everything I'd forsaken when I'd failed him.

I'd failed both of us. But I was here now.

For a few seconds, I took the lead, pushed him against that bleak augmentium wall and took what I wanted. So desperate to get close, to hurt him, make him feel the desolation and fury I felt… but effortlessly, he eased control from my grasp, in that magnificent way he has of *owning* things. His scent made me drunk, his strong mouth on mine demanding not just truth but desire, thirst, desperation. I had no defense, no way to stop wanting him. And before I could gasp or fight or change my mind, it was me against the wall with his fist dragging my hair tight, and I'd wrapped my thigh around him and melted into wet, shuddering surrender.

He felt so real. So alive. All that endless emptiness inside me, screaming to be filled. And I'd no reason to hold back anymore.

A dry sob choked me. I had so much to say. But I didn't want to stop kissing him, so I whispered and kissed at the same time and he didn't seem to mind. "I need you. Please forgive me. I need you so much."

He didn't answer. Already he forced hungry hands under my clothes. My ribs bruised. I didn't care. His thumbs dragged over my nipples, sweet torture. I raked my nails in his crisp bronze curls. Roughly he popped the buttons on my jeans, dragged them away. I wasn't wearing anything underneath. Fuck, he was *touching* me and I was wet and ready for it and my body shuddered and tightened inside.

Jagged lust clawed my flesh. I was going to come right here on his hand. It was too humiliating. Too delicious. "No," I protested, "we can't, not here…"

His lips curled against mine, a toxic smile of challenge. "Don't say 'can't' to me." And he flipped me around, so my cheek pressed against the wall. His naked skin burned mine despite my fever. His voice roughened. "Tell me."

"Now. Do it." That was enough. I helped him, fingers fumbling, and he drove himself into me, hard. "Ah! Fuck, yes."

Again, more, harder, pure sensation that made me cry out. To have him was sweet delirium, utter madness. My tears trickled on the metal wall. Together at last, and no torturous seduction this, but coarse and unpretty. He'd reclaimed me, and it felt…

Too good. Too much. I twisted my head back to taste him, to accept the bruises his mouth made on mine, and in a few more fierce thrusts we came together, shuddering and gasping dark secrets no one alive would ever hear.

Holy shit. I panted, my breath misting the metal. That was… compelling. I was torn between murder and a swoon of ecstasy. Between punching him in the face and dragging his head between my legs for more. I wanted him off me, away, gone. I didn't want him ever to leave me again.

At last, he let me go and pulled back. Raked his thumb over my kiss-stung lips. "So," he said.

And that was *all* he said.

I stared. Gulped. Sweated as I fumbled my clothes back into place. God, he looked hot like this. Breathing hard, his mouth reddened, his perfect hair mussed by my hands. My flesh still ached inside, appalled yet hungry for more. I felt violated, degraded somehow—yet the loss of his touch clawed my wounds open all over again. I wanted to bleed. Say *stop messing around and fuck me again.* Get properly naked, feel his hot mouth on my breasts, make love to him while the world burned.

He wasn't a good person. Nobody's idea of a hero. But he was what I'd chosen. What I deserved. And to remember I was doing this for Glimmer—to save Glimmer from this very same decision—only cut the painful pleasure sharper.

Outside, the commotion escalated. The prison guards were regrouping. We didn't have much time.

I swallowed, hot. Now, we come to the hard part. "I need your help."

"I know." Almost apologetic, not a gloat or a sneer. More like… contentment. I'd acknowledged a simple fact.

Faintness washed me, fever or confusion or just plain stupidity, I didn't know which. But I knew I'd no need to explain. Vincent already knew everything.

"Promise you won't hurt Glimmer," I whispered.

A delighted laugh. "I don't think so. Aren't we past that?"

"But—"

"What's my promise worth to you, Verity? We're enemies, or we're not. Your choice." A scarlet flicker of alloy-suppressed flame in his eyes. "Do you trust me?"

I could, I realized. He'd always be utterly true… to himself. That, I could rely on unto death.

But Glimmer had challenged Vincent's authority. Thwarted his desires, tried to help me change. In a lot of ways, Glimmer had taken what was his. I wasn't sure how Vincent felt about that.

"Okay," I said at last. What choice did I have?

He winked. Swept his beautiful bronze hair back with both hands and stalked panther-like into the corridor.

I followed, one eye on the outer door. Beyond it, guards yelled, their boots thumping. We couldn't go that way. Not without a lot of killing.

Vincent didn't spare a glance for Sundance, who still lay unconscious on the floor. The man meant less than nothing to him. Killing Sundance would serve no purpose. Vincent wouldn't waste his time.

My heart warmed. He didn't murder indiscriminately, my love. Just remorselessly. Not the same thing.

Vincent stretched, and inhaled, fresh air unsullied by augmentium. Dark flame ignited around his fingers, *pop!* He teased it, an enchanted smile on his lips. And his strange augmented paramour teased him back, dancing, winking at him like a seductress.

His lurid augment was dimmed, sure, by the augmentium infesting this place. But he was still powerful, and as I watched him, echoes of our loving shot sweet sensation along my nerves.

I used to wonder if it was just me. The way it felt to use my augment, to show the world what I was. That release, almost orgasmic in quality if not as intense.

But no. Vincent got off on his power, surely as I. He adored it. How it must have pained him, to languish in that cell alone. His fire was the only thing he'd die to protect. Without it, there *was* no him.

I cracked my neck bones, one by one, the combination of the fever and *him* tickling odd sensations in my blood. It felt weird, having him beside me again. Weird, but good. "That's a lot of angry company we've got. Seems your new friends don't want you to leave."

"Yes, well. I'm a people person." Utterly without irony.

"Plenty of augmentium in here, too," I added, a tiny smile of challenge. "You must be tired. Feeling up to an escape?"

A grin, so handsome it terrified me. "Why, firebird, are you flirting with me?"

Oh, God, yes. "That depends. Can you get us out of this place?"

With a sharp *snap-crack!* of ignition, he unwrapped a glittering scarlet flamewhip. "I can now."

~ 36 ~

An hour later, the dark chasm where City Hall once stood stretched before us, ominous like the mouth of hell.

I peered over the edge. Jagged rocks burst from the earth a foot below the shattered concrete surface. The hole stretched down a couple of floors deep to the basement levels. Broken floors and wall fragments jabbed from the rubble, like an ancient ruin half uncovered.

On the crater's other side, rescuers still worked, less frantically than before. The living bodies were recovered, and the authorities had other priorities now. The subway was flooded, the power still out over city blocks. The streets bristled with riots and barricades. Normality needed to be restored.

In the dark, Vincent stood beside me, poised and elegant. No one could see us. We'd returned briefly to his apartment—he'd insisted—and now he wore black instead of the white prison suit. While he changed, I'd fidgeted by the window, unwilling to be near him, not here, where the dark atmosphere hung taut with the memory of the way we'd been. If I got too close, he might kiss me again. Strip me, lick me, make me gasp for him in that merciless way he had. We'd no time for *that* right now... well, maybe we could squeeze in a quick one...

Jeez. For a relationship that *hadn't* actually been all about fucking, I was sure keen on the idea. But I'd felt his gaze searching me, burning with all the time we'd spent apart, the weeks I'd wallowed in denial, and I'd shuddered and looked away.

There'd be nothing quick about it. Nothing easy or forgettable. I wouldn't get away unscathed with what I'd done. No, I most certainly would not.

Now, I squinted into the deep City-Hall-shaped hole, and my vision wobbled with fever-bred vertigo. It was deep. Dark. The lair of a subterranean monster. Dried sweat itched my skin and my muscles ached, the ever-encroaching threat of sickness. "Your machine's down here?"

"Sub-basement four. Still underground." A fluid shrug. "I had all this new office space. Might as well put it to use."

Beneath City Hall? It seemed... too easy. Hardly worth selling my soul for. "And how do we get down there?"

He didn't even bother to answer. Just flicked a sizzling finger, showering tiny sparks. We'd burn our way in. Fine. Good plan. Better hope we didn't crush Glimmer doing it.

I reached out with my augmented senses, feeling for threat... and reeled, staggering with the weight of it. I didn't sense Sophron or Glimmer. I couldn't sense anything except Vincent, and the sheer power of his augment lit me up like fairy fire. Distracting, to say the least. Arousing. A total fucking turn-on, in fact.

I swallowed a dark laugh. Selling my soul. Who was I kidding? I'd lost my soul to this man a long time ago.

I cleared my throat, trying not to look at him, not to notice the fluid way his body moved. I was here to save Glimmer, not flirt with the devil. "What exactly does it do, anyway?"

"It's a supercharged anti-matter superposition generator, optimized for parahuman energy flux, coupled with a remote duplex propagation system and an ultra-EM-spectrum field detector." Effortless arrogance, of the sort that comes with actually being smarter than everyone else. "My own design. Didn't you read the schematic I left you?"

"Right. I must've been absent the day they taught 'wise-ass genius', lover, because I didn't get a single word of that."

An amused flicker of eyebrow. "It's an augment amplifier, Verity. Communicating with a cell phone, routed via a Sentinel. I'd have thought that was obvious."

Oyy. So *that* was why Glimmer couldn't detect any transmissions from the Sentinels. There weren't any—at least, not until you put them next to an IRIN cell phone and activated this… augment amplifier.

Obvious. Right.

He traced my collarbone with one fingertip. "Did I ever tell you I like it when you call me 'lover'?"

Ahem. So did I, damn it. But he was testing me. Seeing what my vow to Glimmer was worth. I wouldn't fall for it. Not this time. Not yet.

Daring, I edged away. "So… you attach someone to this machine and it amplifies their augment? Like… a broadcast? To make it work long distance?"

"I knew you'd be impressed. I call it 'The Infiltrator'."

I snorted. "Seriously?"

"Of course not. Ashton thought that up. Overgrown flair for the dramatic, that boy. Everything's gotta have a name. 'Sentinel' was his idea, too."

I'd wondered how much Vincent's PA knew. "So is Ashton…?"

Vincent just gave a *you-figure-it-out* shrug.

Horrid possibilities unfolded. Sophron, using this "Infiltrator" to spread her talents far and wide. To control people. She had Adonis's augment now. What if she…

Holy shit. What if she put *Glimmer* in the machine? Glimmer was a good guy, sure, but he wasn't harmless. His tricks could be deadly… and what better way to destroy him heart and soul, as she'd promised, than by making him kill?

301

Truth chimed like crystal in my head. Right now, with Vincent at my side? I didn't give a fuck who died. I'd let them all burn, if that's what it took. I cared only for Glimmer's conscience. His honor. His sense of right and wrong. All the good things I no longer had for my own.

I wouldn't let Sophron hurt him. And my own battered conscience seemed an insignificant price.

Sickness rinsed my stomach. Sophron could already be hurting him while I'd fart-assed around deciding what to do. Aysha, that is. His own damn *daughter*. If there existed a more evil, warped scheme to break Glimmer's heart, I didn't know what it could be…

I sweated, feverish, and my brain swelled with hell-fresh vengeance. Aysha was four, for God's sake. Did I imagine she'd dreamed this up all by herself? When Nadia brought her to Vincent's little augment hot-house lab—unwittingly or not—he'd sensed an opportunity. And when it came to vengeance served cold, Vincent never missed a trick.

I'd imagined I didn't know how Vincent felt about my friendship with Glimmer. Well, now I knew exactly what he thought of it. And I was trusting Vincent to help me *save* him.

Christ on a cheesy cracker. How much credit did our history together buy? How deeply did Vincent truly love me? What did that word even mean to him?

Guess I was about to find out.

I turned to Vincent. "What's the range on this thing? How far can it send?"

"Anywhere there's a Sentinel. That's the elegance of ultra-EM flux extraction. Theoretically, the energy is unbounded. Asymptotic degradation. It's quite exciting." Vincent caught my expression. "Oh, come on. I'm expected to build this kind of thing. What's the point of being the archvillain, if I can't plot world domination in my spare time?"

"Planning to use it, were you? Or just feel smug about hiding it right under their noses?"

"Now, that'd be telling. Where's your sense of fun?" Vincent grinned, and unleashed. And hellfire erupted.

Flames howled to the sky, a fiery demon awakened from slumber. The ground rumbled and tore asunder. The heady mint-fire scent of his incendiary speared up my nose and raced around in my head yelling nonsense, like I'd coked up. Deep inside me, muscles clenched hard and released—oh, God—and my mind-muscle lashed and screamed, mad with lust for battle.

I shook myself, eyes watering. Holy crap. I think I just made a mess in my pants.

On the chasm's edge, Vincent pulled me into a kiss. Wild, urgent, his mouth burning mine even through my fever. "I love you, firebird," he whispered, and in that moment, I knew it, for an utter certainty, like death. "Don't make me regret it."

I gripped his hand, and we jumped.

Radiant heat seared my skin. My coat fluttered around me. Ash and sparks rained through the smoke. *Thud!* We landed on a sheer plateau of tilted rock. It felt warm beneath my feet, even through my boots. A drop of my sweat hit the molten edge and sizzled to steam. I dragged freshly crushed boulders aside, clearing our path. Beneath us, in a crack in the concrete basement floor, a broken stairwell twisted down.

As we descended, hot darkness swamped me, playing merry perception games with my senses. I felt dizzy, nauseous. The fever was coming on fast. How long before…

Before I die. If I believed Nadia, that is. Eb was dead. I'd no reason not to believe her. And Nadia said there was no cure. She'd intended to wipe augments off the face of the planet for good. My family would die, and all those other stray augments, too, whom Sophron had copied. Harriet. Jem. Adonis. All of them.

Despair hit me, a sucker punch. But I swallowed it and kept climbing down. I was powerless to stop it. I had to focus on what I *could* save. And as far as I knew, Sophron hadn't yet copied Glimmer.

I'd save him from his mad daughter if I fell dead at his feet doing it. Even if he'd never weep for me, not for the monster I've become.

Would Vincent weep for me? Or would he just shrug and smile, and turn away from my corpse?

I hit a landing and stumbled, banging my head on an over-hanging shard of rock. Vincent didn't catch me. No, he let me catch myself.

I wiped blood from my forehead. Fuck. Pay attention, Verity. This is no time to let your mind wander.

We emerged into a low-ceilinged concrete bunker. Tiny lights gleamed on power conduits encircling the walls. Smoke roughened my breath, the brown smell of electrical resistance, and I waved it away.

In the center, on a glistening glass platform, hunkered a shiny metal machine. Ten feet across, silvery panels forming a perfect twelve-sided geometric solid. A vertical column of white light pierced its middle, flowing upwards to the ceiling, where it splin-tered, bathing the room in scattered rainbows.

On the wall, a white control panel spilled a virtual display, switches and levels and bright diagnostic data. Beside it, a row of television screens showed real-time views of the city. A public square, a shopping mall, Market Street, the bridge turnpike. Experimental subjects. Lab rats for the Infiltrator.

It looked like an alien spaceship console, otherworldly yet… cruel. Precise. Purposeful.

"I know," Vincent murmured in my ear as we sidled around the machine, "gorgeous, isn't it? You're impressed. Admit it."

But I didn't have time to admire it. Wildly, my senses sparkled, and my ears bled with uncanny, high-pitched laughter.

Sophron lounged against the silvery panels, chewing one fingertip. Her dreadlocks gleamed in the rainbow light. She looked… skeletal. Frail, like Flash, her rapid-onset aging catching up with her. But her eyes swirled, brimming with madness and exultation and dark, impossible magic.

And beside her sat Glimmer, a strange metal contraption flattening his black hair. Like a silvery octopus, its eight coiling tentacles gripping his skull.

For a moment, I couldn't move or speak, I was swamped so hard with relief. He was alive. And like a warm breath tickling my neck, I felt Vincent smile.

I kicked myself into action and broke into a run. "Let him go, you—"

But with a negligent wave, Sophron slammed up a wall of my stolen power. *Bang!* I collided with it, staggering back with a bloodied nose. Oddly, Glimmer didn't move. Didn't try to escape.

What the fuck? He wasn't tied down, wasn't senseless. Frustrated, I kicked at her force field.

Sophron laughed. "Glad you finally got here. I was sick of waiting. Glimmer, sweet thing, show her your pretty eyes."

Obediently, Glimmer slanted his gaze up at me, and his midnight eyes glittered gold.

My stomach hollowed. Adonis's augment. She'd charmed him. He was utterly in her power.

"Let him go." The plea hurt my throat. "You've got your own strength. You don't need him. Why play these stupid games?"

A sneer ruined her pretty face, made her into a monster. "Because I want him to suffer. I want him to feel lost and abandoned and worthless." Her voice cracked on that last word. She rounded on Glimmer, tears brimming. An angry, vengeful little girl. "I just wanted you to love me! But you *left* me. You didn't care about me. You were too busy pretending to be a hero. So I'll show the world the sniveling coward you really are."

She strode to the virtual console and poked the switches. The Infiltrator hummed, and its rainbows brightened...

"Hmm," Vincent murmured, "there's a nice trick."

...and with an eye-watering *flash!* and *boom!* the column of light erupted in scarlet.

The metal octopus gripping Glimmer's skull glowed red. His skin burned, his fingers clenching white with pain. But he didn't struggle, didn't fight her off. The air around him shimmered black, a rippling sphere that pulsed and grew.

I watched, aghast. His power was being *extracted*. Sucked out like juice from an orange.

The sphere stretched, contorting, and the burning Infiltrator sucked it up, an uncanny augment magnet. Like a living creature, the machine swallowed and groaned, greedy, dragging in more and more, but feeding a ripple of energy back into Glimmer, too, so the flow would continue…

Blood bubbled from Glimmer's nose. He choked for breath, muscles straining. But still, he didn't struggle.

Sophron ran to the row of TV screens, watching eagerly. The shopping mall crowd milled, the traffic edged along, the people in the park chatted and strolled… and then they paused, glancing uncertainly at each other.

On the turnpike, cars halted and crashed end to end. People jumped out, screaming, and attacked each other. Guys pulled guns and fired. Knives slashed. In the park, people clawed for each others' eyes, kicked and punched and bit like wild beasts, when a minute ago they'd been friends.

Sophron danced, delighted. "Watch me," she said, and giggled.

Fuck. She was broadcasting Glimmer's augment—only this wasn't the *sleepy* or the *dizzy* or the *do as I say*. This was the *rage*. The killing fit, the one he used to make his enemies break their cover, throw them off their guard, make stupid mistakes so he could defeat them.

This time, he wasn't there to intervene. All over the city, everywhere within reach of a Sentinel, these people would kill each other. Tear flesh to shreds, shoot and slash and burn, fight until they died. And when Glimmer woke from his unnatural trance… he'd blame himself.

Red fever misted my vision, and my mindmuscle shuddered, dangerously close to bursting out. Soon, I'd be beyond fighting. It was now or never.

I dragged in all the power I could muster, and hurled myself at the invisible wall.

Rrrrip! It tore, and I burst through and tumbled to the floor. With sick, unholy speed, I scrambled up. Whipped a fat kraken tentacle around Sophron's neck, *ker-snap!* and dragged her off her feet.

Bang! Her face smacked into the floor, exploding in blood. She groaned, stirring. Soon, she'd heal. I held on grimly, trying to cut off her airway. "Vincent, can we turn that thing off? It's killing him!"

But Vincent just watched his machine, entranced, eerie light kissing crimson into his hair. His smile twisted with dark satisfaction. "Excellent. I knew it'd work."

My stomach curdled, cold. If this was the part where he fucked me over for betraying him, he'd chosen his moment perfectly. I struggled to hold Sophron down. "Please. For my sake. Help him."

"For your sake?" Hot glass shattered in his eyes, and fire spilled out. "You should know I don't forget so easily. Puppy dog tried to *spoil* you. For your sake? I should fucking *burn* the little worm."

~ 37 ~

The Infiltrator whirred, screaming, the pitch rising. On the TV screens, people stabbed, tore, chased each other with rocks and shards of broken glass and other makeshift weapons. On the bridge, some guy was ramming screaming people with his Humvee, reversing and running right over them, again and again.

My muscles shook, overwrought with fever and fatigue. I couldn't hold Sophron any longer. The squelching flesh on her face healed, and she tossed me off as easily as she might a mosquito.

I rolled, scrambling up on shaking legs.

But Vincent was already at Glimmer's side, lifting his blood-stained chin with one finger, checking his demented eyes for signs of recognition. "You in there, puppy dog? Such a pity if you can't hear me." He whispered in Glimmer's ear, but it didn't stop me hearing. "You messed with me and mine, you poxy little shit. I can still see your grubby fingerprints on her soul. You're a disgrace to all of us. And I'm gonna make you scream."

"No!" Sophron squealed, grabbing Vincent's shoulder. "This is my party. You said so."

My senses flashed cold warning. She'd *touched* him, without invitation. Surely, he'd scorch her to ash.

308

Vincent just laughed. "Think I'd make it that easy? I created you, little girl. Everything you are, I gave to you. Don't even imagine you can play on my level."

She pouted, a petulant shake of her dreads. "But he's *mine*."

Vincent shrugged, careless. "What the hell, I'm in a generous mood. Want to torture him?" Fire ignited, kissing his fingertips. "Then fight me for it."

"With pleasure." Flame coiled around Sophron's fist, and she hurled his own stolen power at him.

He caught it. Quenched it, a snap of his fingers. "Weak. Try harder."

Sophron howled, a child's frustration, and hurled another fireball. He threw it back in her face. They circled each other, Glimmer in the middle.

Sophron sneered, a mask of hatred. "You're turning on me, too? You're all just afraid of me. You included."

A silky black laugh. "Think you understand me because you've torn down a few buildings? Think you're my equal? *You have no idea what true terror is.*"

Over her shoulder, Vincent's dark gaze caught mine. Flicked towards Glimmer. Back again.

I choked, shattered. *Trust me,* he'd said.

Right. But what choice?

Quietly as I could, trying not to alert her, I crawled to Glimmer's side. My sweaty hands smeared the thick glass floor. His precious face was flushed bright with pain. His glitter-filled eyes streamed, his cheeks wet. But still, Sophron's power held him fast. And still, the black wave flowed from him, sucked into the hungry machine.

"Glimmer," I whispered fiercely, "can you hear me?"

No response. My heart clenched, fearful. I itched to tear that ugly tentacled thing from his head, drag him free. I'd vowed to save him no matter what. But the Infiltrator was still operating. What if it hurt him? What if…?

What's my promise worth to you? Vincent's taunt echoed in my memory. All the vows in the world meant nothing if I *did* nothing. Only actions counted.

I grabbed the octopus and ripped it free.

The Infiltrator moaned, and the rippling black shockwave squealed and popped like an overfilled balloon. *Zzzpt!* In my hands, the octopus crackled, and a sharp electric shock ripped up my arms.

Glimmer screamed. His nose burst crimson. He clawed his ears, his eyes, his face, muscles all over his body spasming in bright horror at what Sophron had done. The sound of his agony stabbed salty blades deep into my heart, and I screamed, too.

But he was free. The glitter masking his eyes had died, revealing tear-bright midnight blue.

"Fucking *bitch*!" Sophron's curse stretched into an unholy shriek that ripped the air asunder. My eardrums juddered, agonizing. The walls warped, metal screeching in protest. A glass panel shattered.

Perhaps she'd stolen Harriet's power, too. It didn't matter. She'd lost her reason and was letting rip with every trick she knew. The air caught fire, a mess of golden glitter and flying objects and jagged blue lightning.

I dragged Glimmer down, shielding him with my body. My augmented senses howled in pain, hammered blind from all sides. It was too much to handle.

Sophron laughed, eerie soprano melody. Electricity arced between her hands, a spitting web of blinding blue.

Vincent stood his ground, a shadow wreathed in crimson. Chaos raged around him and he exulted in it, letting the power flow between his fingers in shimmering waterfalls. Somehow, his voice carried over the noise. "Beautiful. Such a pity you lack respect, little girl. We could have been allies."

"You're so clever? Burn this," she hissed, and hurled lightning.

Swift as a serpent, Vincent *jumped*. Landed neatly on the insulating glass platform. And with an almighty *crack!* the bolt speared the floor, right where he'd been standing.

The metal floor.

The room lit with blinding electric fire. Current crackled up the walls, stabbed along the ceiling and earthed itself through Sophron's body. She screamed and fell, twisting in impossible directions. Joints cracked, the popping sound of muscle fibers breaking.

I goggled, enraptured. Maybe Vincent truly was invincible. Had I thought him truly in danger yesterday, when he fought Sophron at City Hall?

The more powerful your augment, the greater your resistance to attack. And Vincent possessed the greatest power of all. Didn't become the unbeaten force of nature he is by creating enemies greater than himself.

The current spat and died. Sophron choked, spluttering. Her body was tortured, sprained. Her clothes had burned through in the lightning bolt's path, revealing charred and weeping flesh that already started to heal. Still, she struggled to stand, muster her power, defend herself. She was tough. Not beaten yet.

Vincent grabbed her skinny waist and hurled her at me.

I caught her, shoved her into the metal chair, and slammed the octopus onto her head.

Sophron fought, but she was weak now, and grimly I held her in place. The machine growled, guttural, and once again, the air rippled black. Sophron thrashed and screamed, but there was no resisting this. Vincent had made sure of that. And he watched, satisfied, as her power bled away.

Incredibly, Sophron gave a sickly, bloodstained grin. "They'll all... still die," she sputtered. "Made you... kill me... I... still win..."

Vincent just arched that superior, ironic eyebrow—*oh, really?*—and flicked a virtual switch on the console.

On the wall, a power conduit flashed and snapped dark. The TV screens flickered out. He'd severed the link to the remote devices. The circuit was broken, that external outlet severed. Now, her power had nowhere to go.

311

Except into the Infiltrator. And the Infiltrator swallowed it up, exultant.

Sophron's eyes boggled from their sockets. Blood spurted from her mouth. Weakly, she thrashed her arms, trying to summon her augment, any augment.

But nothing happened. The machine had drained her dry. And just as her breath began to rattle—just as the light flickered and dimmed in her eyes—Vincent coolly yanked the octopus away.

The column of light died. The whirring ceased. Sophron slumped in my grip, senseless. Just a small, pale creature, blue hair flopping, her limbs so brittle they might break.

Just a girl.

Dazed, I laid her down. Her eyes had closed, her face slackened in slumber. Her lips dampened as she breathed, their cruelty faded. She looked at peace.

I swallowed. Peace. Right. Just wait until she woke.

Glimmer crawled painfully to her side, stroked damp hair from her cheek. His blood-caked lips moved, making no sound. But I knew what he said.

I'm so sorry, baby.

Mute, I laid my hand on his shoulder. He gripped it. He was shaking. Weeping, maybe. I didn't look. I just let him hold onto me.

Vincent glanced at Sophron, bored. She was just an ordinary girl now. He'd lost interest. "Touching," he remarked, an acid edge on his tone. "What a pity you're both dying."

I sniffed, tasting blood. Heedless, I spat it out. I'd almost forgotten the fever. Eb had died in a matter of days. Jem was probably dead, too, and Adonis. All of them at FortuneCorp, the ones whose power Sophron had stolen, would die.

Glimmer... well, I didn't really know how this machine worked, but I wasn't betting it involved mercy.

A sharp pang seized my guts. She'd mirrored Vincent's power, too. Yesterday, above us, at City Hall.

There's no cure. Nadia's promise rattled like lost marbles in my brain. *You'll all die...*

"Don't play, you son of a bitch." Glimmer's gaze shone afresh, bloodshot still, but silver now with moonlit disgust. "Just tell us what you want."

After all, what's a villain's promise worth?

I looked up, incredulous. And there was Vincent, lounging against the wall, as elegant and un-sick as I'd ever seen him. Hands in pockets and an unapologetic, utterly handsome smile, waiting for me to figure it out.

~ 38 ~

Twenty minutes later, the four of us walked into a brightly lit office across the street. Glimmer led Sophron, who limped along listlessly, uninterested in her surroundings. An empty shell of a girl. She hadn't spoken a word or displayed an emotion. I suspected she never would, and my heart bled. But not for her.

I slammed the office door and locked it. Not a fancy office. Just a room, desk, piles of paper, laptop computers askew. Stacks of boxed files against the walls. Not bad for twenty-four hours' notice. Wasn't easy to relocate your workspace in a hurry. Like, y'know, when someone tore your building from its foundations and crushed it to rubble.

Vincent had the cure for the fever, of course. As if he'd leave that to chance. What he'd demanded in return was simple.

Just a few words in the right ear.

Behind the desk, Mayor Wilt's high-cheekboned face drained white.

"Mackenzie," said Vincent pleasantly, "some people I'd like you to meet."

"Put the fucking phone down," I warned, before Mackenzie could do more than reach for the handset. "This isn't a mass meeting. Do as we say and nothing all that unpleasant will happen

314

to you. But raise the alarm and we *will* make you suffer." I winked. "Just so you know."

Mackenzie let her hand fall. But her eyes gleamed with icy loathing. "Vincent, what have you done?"

Vincent arched elegant eyebrows. "Apart from deceive you? Which, by the way, you made far too easy? Plenty."

Her face spasmed. Shame? Frustration at a political embarrassment? The indignation of a deeper, more personal, betrayal?

Inwardly, I spat into her smug face. She was a hater. She deserved whatever he'd done to her. And I meant *whatever*.

"How did you escape?" Mackenzie's eyes narrowed as she studied Sophron. "Is that her? One of your *friends*?" She spat the last word, venomous as only a woman scorned can be. I swallowed grim laughter. Oh, yeah. She'd had no fucking idea who she was playing with, and he'd taken her to pieces. You had to admire him.

Innocently, Vincent frowned. "Not at all. I think you'll find she's the villain of the piece. Look, you've arrested her! You and our valiant Chief of Police. How heroic. Seriously, I'm teary-eyed over here." Coals kindled in his stare. "That must mean I had nothing to do with it. Which is exactly what you'll persuade everyone. Destroying City Hall? Just a misunderstanding. I've nothing but the city's best interests at heart."

Mackenzie's chin hardened, mutinous. "You're a sick man. How dare you come in here and order me about, after what you've done? I'll destroy you."

"Oh, please. Don't think I can't make you my creature. I've done it once already."

Her beautiful mouth twisted. "I should kill you myself. You're a monster. A freak—"

"Shut the fuck up," I ordered. I was sweating, my muscles fevered and barely under control. Not a good time to insult me and mine. And that word *freak* boiled my blood until I couldn't hold it in any longer, and with a shriek of bottled-up rage I let my mindsense explode…

A hand gripped my shoulder, calming me. Not Glimmer. Vincent. "Mine," he warned softly.

Struggling, I held it in. We were in no position to piss him off.

Vincent ambushed Mackenzie with an eye-watering smile. "As much fun as it is watching you squirm? I really haven't the time to make it elegant, so let's just be blunt. This puppy with the circus-act hair is Glimmer, and he wants a word with you."

Glimmer looked to me, beseeching. My guts chilled. After all we'd been through…

I clutched his hand and whispered. "We'll find another way to get the cure. You don't need to help him."

But we did. I didn't know how else to save us, and neither did Glimmer. I could see it, in the haunted graveyard of his eyes.

Sometimes, to get results, you have to sleep with the enemy.

Glimmer dropped a kiss onto my knuckles. Dried tears still crusted his cheeks, dust still drifting from his ruined hair. He was exhausted, aching, stained rusty red with blood and sorrow. But he wasn't broken.

My throat swelled, burning. Never broken. Not my Glimmer.

"It's okay." The faintest crooked smile. "Facing your fears, remember?"

Because we both had. And we'd come out of this alive, even if we had to sacrifice everything else. He'd do this, not to save himself, but to save my family.

To save me.

I squeezed his hand. Brushed my palm over his cheek. For a moment, he closed his eyes, resigned. And then he sat opposite the mayor. "Ms. Wilt?"

"What?" Mackenzie scowled, her ice-cut chin high.

Glimmer snapped his fingers before her eyes. "Watch me."

Soon—after Glimmer had explained to Mackenzie Wilt precisely what she'd say and do and think—two uniformed police entered on Wilt's orders and clapped Sophron in handcuffs. Double augmentium ones, fresh and gleaming. They were taking no chances, but I doubted they should've bothered. Sophron just stared, lethargic, and let them restrain her. Along with her augment, all the fight had drained away.

Now she was just a girl.

One of the officers eyed Vincent sharply and looked a question at Mayor Wilt. "Ma'am? What about him?"

"He's exonerated, on my order." Mackenzie shot Vincent a grateful glance. "I'll be giving a conference shortly. Tell Chief Paxton to expect a file from my office on her desk in the morning."

"Yes, ma'am. And the girl?"

"Custody, pending mental health evaluation. I imagine a lengthy stay in a high-security treatment facility is in her future."

"Ma'am." The officer took Sophron's arm and led her away.

I sighed, rubbing my eyes. If they decided she was crazy, at least her life would be spared. Glimmer wouldn't need to endure the pain of watching his daughter's execution for multiple murder.

Thank God this was all over with. I was about to fall over from fatigue and fever. All we needed now was this damn cure...

"Wait." Vincent's effortless command presence stopped the officer in his tracks. "A word with the young lady. You can go, Mackenzie."

"Whatever you say." Mackenzie blinked, starry-eyed, and exited.

Vincent smiled down at Sophron, warped. Fireworks exploded in my senses, and I leapt forward...

But he only leaned closer. "I know you can hear me, Aysha. Tell me: how does it feel to be *ordinary*?"

She stared at him with wide, bruised zombie eyes.

"Hurts, doesn't it?" He licked his lips, savoring his moment. "Oh, wait. No, it doesn't. You're numb now. Normal. A slab of worthless meat."

Her eyes rolled, wild. Her lip trembled, and a tear slipped down her hollow cheek.

"I gave you *everything*," he hissed. "Did you forget? Look how easily I can rip it away."

"Enough," I cut in shakily. "Take her out, can't you?"

Vincent jerked his chin, dismissive, and the officers hustled weeping Aysha away. "Powerless, Aysha," he called after her, his malice bright. "Just a rat, like the rest of them. Wouldn't you rather die?"

The door slammed. Vincent laughed in cruel satisfaction.

Glimmer stalked up and hit him. *Crack!* Right across his sharp-cut jaw.

Holy fuck-a-doodle.

Vincent recoiled, as close to shock as I'd ever seen from him. Rubbed a finger gently over the bruise he'd have come morning. Met Glimmer's gaze, a fiery challenge.

Glimmer stared him down, glitter-blue. "If you ever speak a word to my daughter again? I'll kill you."

My blood iced. Surely, Vincent would burn him to crispy crackling. Crush his throat barehanded for such insolence.

But Vincent's smile twinkled, fascinated, and he bent to whisper something in Glimmer's ear.

Glimmer didn't reply. Just folded warm defiant fingers between mine.

Vincent watched a moment, thoughtful. Then he flipped something small and blue into the air with his thumb.

It glittered as it cartwheeled, catching the light. I caught it. A screw-top glass vial, brimming with iridescent blue liquid. The cure.

Or poison. One final trick?

I didn't think so. He'd won. He'd want us alive, to taunt again in future. No point killing us now.

I slipped the vial into my pocket. Nodded my thanks, because I didn't trust my voice. And Glimmer walked me out.

"One more thing."

And here we go.

In the doorway, I halted, squeezing Glimmer's hand. "It's okay. I'll follow you."

Glimmer's grip tightened. I could see he didn't want to let go. But he trusted me. I knew that now. "Be careful," he whispered, and did as I asked. Bless him.

Vincent lounged against the wall and cut me a sharp smile. "Did I say we'd finished our trade?"

I licked dry lips. "What more do you want? He did what you asked."

"Firebird, I'm surprised at you. That was *his* end. Now, I want *yours*."

And he waited. No explanation. Just that hot firedark stare.

My mind stumbled, lost. Glimmer had made his bargain, sacrificed something dear to him. Made a pact with the devil to save my life. But Vincent hadn't asked for anything of mine. I'd nothing precious left to give...

"I met your father when you were still a child," he added, offhanded, as if he'd changed the subject. "Did you know?"

I didn't reply. Nothing Vincent said was ever irrelevant. Where was he going with this? It couldn't be good.

"Really? I'm surprised he never mentioned it." He chuckled. "There I was, eighteen years old, just a superlative genius engineering graduate, burning the odd shopping mall in my spare time and minding my own business, when *poof!* Blackstrike, right in my secret lair. A genuine fan-boy moment. You can imagine how it flattered me when he asked for my *help*."

"What?" I couldn't help but ask.

"I know! He said he knew of my early work, and there was this villain, see, whom he'd had trouble with and wanted taken care of. A bad man named Obsidian, who'd... well, I think you know that part of the story."

My eyes boggled. I'd *thought* I knew the story. *He's lying,* Common-Sense Verity insisted. *Don't listen...*

Vincent's lips twitched. "Well, what could I say? I was eager to impress, and let's face it, Obsidian was a jabbering Neanderthal and no friend of mine. Practically senile. It was time for generational change at the top, so to speak. So your father and I made a deal. An unorthodox trade, to be sure, but needs must. And that night we went hunting. Blackstrike, drunk on the stink of vengeance, and innocent little me. The things we did to that man… well, let's just say Tom Fortune was one cruel son of a bitch when you pissed him off. Seriously. I still get hot thinking about it. I was in *awe*."

Images drowned my breath. My dead mother's mannequin stare, the stone marbling her face. Dad weeping over her corpse, his shadows thrashing black with impotent rage. He'd never told us what happened, that he'd compromised his honor and done a deal with a budding archvillain. All we'd known was that we'd never heard from Obsidian again.

Was this why Dad and Adonis had fallen out? Did Adonis discover Dad's dirty secret?

Of course, it meant more than that, didn't it? All along, amid years of speculation about Razorfire's secret identity, Blackstrike had known who Vincent Caine was. And he hadn't exposed him. Hadn't used the knowledge against him. Hadn't told a soul.

And yet again, I reeled, as what I'd thought were the cast-iron tectonic plates of my world ground asunder and *rearranged*.

When Dad had discovered my dark affair with Razorfire, I'd believed he hated me. Rejected me out of anger, betrayal, disgust.

What if it was guilt?

Vincent watched me, with that tiny smile of satisfaction I knew so intimately. "Afterwards, our deal turned sour. I wanted what he'd promised me, but he refused. He'd changed his mind, he couldn't give it up." A ruthless edge darkened his tone. "It taught me a valuable lesson. If I want what's mine, I take it." His gaze swallowed me, bottomless. "And now, here we are."

I squeezed my eyelids on hot, unexpected tears. Because I knew what he wanted. What my father had promised him, all those years ago. And for once, it wasn't about us.

"No," I whispered. "It's mine. You can't have it."

An indulgent laugh. "You know me, firebird. I never forgive a debt. Even Blackstrike's death at your hands can't erase his obligation." Fire flickered around his wrists, a sultry threat. "I've waited more than twenty years for what he owed me, and *I will have it.*"

My mouth stung, bitter with inevitability. I'd known I wouldn't escape unscathed. Vincent would have his vengeance on me for betraying him, and his twisted love for me—what else could I call it?—wouldn't stop him. He wouldn't spare himself by going easy on me. No, loving me just made his revenge more worthwhile, more sweetly painful for him.

This was who he was. This was the man I'd once chosen to be mine. And try as I might to cut him out, he still laid claim to a burning, treacherous corner of my being.

Defeated, I fumbled in my pocket, and gave Vincent my mother's heart.

Our fingertips touched. Our gazes locked. And my breath caught, sucked away by the fire in his soul.

"Thank you." Just a whisper. So much meaning.

His strange, familiar heat crept over me. So close, yet so far. I could sense his heartbeat, even across the inches that separated us. Too fast for a man who didn't care. Or was he just turned on by victory?

He smiled, that ruthless weapon of a smile, loaded with the memory of everything we'd been to each other, and I knew with dark certainty that he hadn't given up on getting me back.

This wasn't over until he said so. Maybe not ever.

He licked his lips, strangely vulnerable, and my resolve faltered. This wasn't just a game. I had the power to hurt him, and he didn't understand it. Neither did I. But only I ever saw this side of him. All his life he'd walked the world alone, never needing anyone—yet he'd let me in, to gaze upon his soul. As he'd gazed upon mine.

That was what he meant when he spoke of love. Not happiness or sacrifice. Obsession. Unbreakable connection. Unforgettable secrets, shared until death.

Don't run from your fears. Face them.

So what was I afraid of?

My body trembled. I wanted to kiss his beautiful mouth. I wanted to finish what we'd started in that ugly prison cell. Make him mine all over again, lie with him in that precious darkness we alone could share and seal our unholy love with tears.

"I miss you." Vincent tightened his fingers on mine, the warm stone heart trapped between our palms. "Please..."

"No," I said unsteadily, and walked out.

Behind me, as the door clicked shut, he laughed.

~ 39 ~

Glimmer and I returned to Widow Swanky's in the dark of early morning, exhausted and silent. The apartment was safe for us now, thanks to the mindfuck tricks Glimmer had played on Mackenzie Wilt. No authority would arrest us or hunt us down, not if they didn't want the mayor's office crashing down on them like an act of God.

Mind you, even Vincent couldn't erase *all* the evidence. What he'd done at City Hall was all over the internet. People still knew what he was, still hated and feared augments. The murderous spree that Sophron had spawned from the Infiltrator hadn't won us any friends. That mess was still being cleared away, the bodies recovered, the blood wiped up.

But hell, ordinary people had been our enemies since day one. What was new?

Still, as we climbed the stairs, my heart dragged heavy, my lungs weary with the effort of breathing. We were still outsiders. Vincent still pursued me. Nothing had changed. Maybe, nothing ever would.

One ray of brightness had pierced my gloom: a call from Adonis, the luckiest bastard in Sapphire City. He'd survived the blast at City Hall, one of the few they'd dragged from the rubble alive in those first few hours. Ad was tough. Broken bones didn't stop him getting what he wanted. He'd called me from hospital, once he'd awakened enough to convince them to let him near a phone.

Hearing his voice lightened my soul, but our conversation had been punctuated with awkward silences. I hadn't taken the chance to ask him about Dad. I'd told him about the cure for the fever; he'd called Harriet; Harriet had called me, and now Jem and the others had their share. Peg Finney had disappeared, skulked off into the sunset, probably trying to escape Vincent's wrath. Heh. Good luck with that, perky-face. I still hadn't forgiven her for taking advantage of my brother, and I wished her joy of whatever stinking rat-hole she was lurking in.

Vincent's iridescent blue liquid had chilled my blood when the needle went in. I could still feel it, an icy wire of *him* piercing my soul. But Adonis hadn't pressed me on where or how I'd gotten the cure. Like he didn't want to hear me lie. On the other hand, I hadn't pressed him, either, on how he'd escaped death. It seemed uncanny. Had he crawled away before the destruction began? Been protected by some fortuitously falling rubble?

Whatever. In the morning, I'd go to him, and we'd... what? Apologize? Hurl insults at one other? Ad hadn't forgiven me for betraying the family. And though my heart tore in two every time I thought about it, I hadn't forgiven him for unleashing on me. For turning on me when I needed him. Could anything be salvaged from that wreckage?

At Widow Swanky's, moonlight drifted through the lacy curtains. Shadows weaved silken webs. Glimmer didn't say much. Just helped me lay poor Ebenezer out, wash the blood from his skin and comb his lank, dark hair. Eb's soft lashes curled on his cheek, as if any moment they might flutter open. He looked asleep, not dead. Not gone for good, his wise-ass wit and stupid jokes forever silenced. The world would get taken over by big-breasted virgin schoolgirl zombies, and without Eb no one would be able to do a damn thing about it.

I stroked Eb's face and silently said my goodbyes. I'd call in the morning for someone to take care of him. But for what seemed the tenth time tonight, I knuckled away acid tears. Damn it, my eyes were raw from so much weeping, yet it sickened me to my guts what a fucking hypocrite I was. I wasn't a good person. I didn't belong here.

Glimmer kissed Eb's forehead. Touched my cheek, a whisper-light caress of sympathy. God, he had so much to give it over-whelmed me. To lose Eb hurt so deeply it bled, but what Glimmer had endured was so much worse, and I could do nothing to help. Sophron wasn't my daughter. His sorrow wasn't mine to bear, no matter how badly I wished I could share his burden.

My uselessness punched me hard in the guts. I swallowed, fat with tears, as wordlessly he left me.

Soon, I heard the splash of running water. He spent a long time in the shower, steam filtering over the frosted screen, only a small light on the wall burning. I lay on my bed in the dark and let the sound of water rush over me, its constant pattering a reminder of passing time, the healer of all things.

But would this ever heal? Glimmer had given up a little piece of his honor to save me, and I wasn't sure I could forgive myself. And for what? What had I learned, after all the death and destruction was done? Not a damn thing, except what I already knew, which was that I was no one's idea of a hero. And that if I didn't bow to Vincent's steel-forged will, he'd systematically destroy my life—and the lives of everyone I cared about—until I did.

I didn't think I'd sleep. But when next I opened my eyes, the shower was silent. I propped up on my elbows. Moonlight still stretched its fingers in the warm darkness, gloating over the window glass, edging the furniture with metallic fire. It silhouetted Glimmer, slouched in an embroidered armchair by my bed, staring out the window. The fingers of one hand curled next to his chin, the stripe in his moonlit hair shining silver.

"Can't sleep?"

A shake of his velvety head.

I crawled to the bed's edge. "Can I do anything?"

He just looked at me.

Something in that midnight stare made me shiver. Did he know what I'd done? Surrendered so willingly to our enemy, exulted in that dark connection. Let him kiss me, fuck me, whisper warped words of love. Did Glimmer know I'd relinquished my soul?

I hugged myself, suddenly chilled, and slipped off the bed. My feet made sticky prints on the floor. "Look, I'll, uh... I'll leave you alone."

He caught my trailing hand. "Stay. Please."

The raw isolation that roughened his voice threatened to undo me. He'd given me so much, without ever begging anything in return. I couldn't refuse him this simple request now. But I didn't belong here. I didn't want to live with his disappointment. I edged away. "No, it's okay, I..."

"Verity." Glimmer held on. Confused, I pulled back, lost my balance, and all in one moment I was on my knees and he'd slipped from his chair and his fingers curled in my hair, refusing to let me go. He rested his forehead on mine. "Please, don't leave. I can't. Not alone. Not anymore."

And he kissed me. Sweet, trembling, salty with tears.

Gosh. I swooned, my eyes drifting shut. His mouth was so soft, so strong. Exactly as I'd dreamed. Far too soon, he pulled back. Just an inch, his mouth lingering over mine so we breathed the same air. Then our lips met again and this time it lasted longer. A lot longer.

Oh, my. A slowly deepening kiss, the answer to a question still too raw and bleeding to speak aloud. He tasted of anguish and sorrow and bitter loneliness, tainted with the blood we'd shed. But his warm vanilla-spice scent made me drunk, reckless. My lips parted, searching, inviting. When he murmured and crushed me closer, his lean body felt so wonderful against me that I ached, gloriously, my long-shackled desire freed at last. God, he was beautiful, body and soul. Too beautiful for me.

For a dizzy second he terrified me. *I can't do this. He doesn't mean it. He's overwrought. His head isn't right. He doesn't know what he's doing.*

But I'd let him make that decision. He needed me, here, tonight, even if he didn't really *want* me. So I'd be here. I'd let him use me, if that's what he needed. And it didn't even matter that I wanted him desperately, had wanted him without hope for so long that the wanting itself had blurred into dull background noise. An ever-present ache that never died, a beautiful disease of which I'd never be cured.

It didn't matter. Because I'd vowed I'd sacrifice everything for him, even my soul—and that included letting him break my heart.

I fumbled my butt onto the bed. He followed me, still on his knees, and I wrapped one thigh around him and crushed my fists into his velvety black hair while I kissed him. Oh, God. I'd wanted to do that forever. But I couldn't linger on it now. I had his shirt to peel off, his skin to lick, his hard chest to trail my mouth over. His dusky skin glistened from my kiss. He tilted his head back, baring his lovely throat for me to taste, to feel his pulse against my lips. Wow.

He pushed me onto my back, and for a moment I basked in his smoldering gaze. His velvety hair mussed, his lean muscles tight. Sweet anticipation clenched in my belly. Good God, he looked so hot I wanted to cry. And our shared sorrow only sharpened the moment.

Slowly, he bent over me. Kissed me, eased his body onto mine, gave me time to learn his shapes, his weight, his heat. I couldn't help but gasp and surrender. He pushed my shirt up, roamed his mouth over my belly, my bared breasts. My nipple ached in his teeth, so sensitive, and my desire hurt me, it came on so hard. But

327

it was a good pain. I wanted to hold him there forever, drown in him and never come up for air.

But I wanted the rest of it more. I slid my hands over his taut hips, reaching for him. I undid his jeans, and when I touched him he caught his breath. So did I. He was smooth, hot, a delicious temptation. I stroked him, fingertips tingling, and his shudder made me wild, turned the ache between my legs from a pleasurable tension into a matter of painful urgency.

"I want you so much." It tumbled from my lips, unstoppable. Fuck. This wasn't supposed to be about me.

But he didn't mind. He just wriggled his jeans off. It didn't take long to get rid of the rest of our clothes. The glory of lying naked beneath him, his skin gliding on mine, his scent blanketing me… I thought it was utter, incomparable heaven. Until he slipped one finger gently inside me. Oh, fuck, that felt… I clawed his back, arching into sweetest pleasure. I folded my leg around his hips, desperate to feel him, experience that first smooth slide of his flesh into mine.

At last, he eased himself into me. Just a little at first, not enough, nowhere near enough. To have him inside me at last… My eyes stung wet. I was crying again, but that was okay because he was too, his lashes glistening with diamonds.

He kissed me, and I pulled him onto me, into me, moving my hips to welcome him. As we discovered each other, our tears mingled, sweet yet dangerous. He displayed perfect clarity, holding nothing back, learning what he liked and what he liked to do to me, and in my delirium I didn't know whether it was because he'd slipped his mindsense into me along with the rest of him, or just because he was wonderful and I loved him and we were meant to be together.

I didn't care. It was what it was. And if tomorrow, it wasn't anymore? At least I'd have tonight, to revisit forever in my dreams.

My desire sharpened. I needed more. Urgently, I rolled him onto his back. Damn, he was beautiful, all hard muscle and desire-flushed skin, his hair spilling black and silver on the moonlit pillow. His lips were swollen from kissing me, and I kissed them again as I guided him within me to my most sensitive spot. I groaned as my flesh tightened around him. His eyes glittered, wild. I liked him watching me. I wanted him to watch me come. I moved faster. Him and me, together, finally, and it actually hurt, he felt so good... Oh, God. I shuddered with it, crying out, and came apart as he watched me. It hit me hard. More than I'd anticipated, more than I deserved. "Stop. I can't..."

"Verity," he whispered, "you're so beautiful," and I believed him.

I caught my breath, dazed, as I came down. Christ on a fruit-cake sandwich. That was... special. My body still sparkled all over, delicious afterburn. On any other day, I'd call that *fucked into oblivion*. But *fucking* was the wrong word... and I was far from finished. Oh, no.

I relinquished control, let him do what he needed. He rolled on top of me, took me more roughly, deliberately fierce. My vision doubled with delight. Oh, yes, just the way I liked... but who the hell was I kidding? I loved everything he did. Our mingled breath, our lips colliding. His hair slicking my cheek. I slid my palms down his back, digging my fingers into his muscular ass. God, I loved his ass. His hair, his lips, his cock, his fingers that folded between mine now and pinned my hands to the sheet. Everything. All of him.

His eyes darkened to black, his own pleasure quickening. It excited me to feel him enjoying me. I groaned, disbelieving, that delicious tingling heat knotting ever tighter in my belly. Nothing ever felt like this. Surely, I couldn't come again so fast... But I fell over the edge along with him, flying, sweeter and harder than before, and this time it didn't crash so much as fade, exquisite tingles drifting me down to earth.

I lay, dizzy, panting for breath all over again. I didn't want to stop. I wanted to taste him more, swallow him, learn him by heart. But I couldn't move my legs. Perhaps they'd never move again.

I swallowed. So, he'd leave me now. He'd want to be alone. I was good with that.

But he cradled me, lips warm in my hair. Still inside my body, not letting go.

My heart did a crazy flip-flop. Hardly daring to breathe, I folded him in my arms. Settled my thigh around him. Exhaustion crept over me, a warm shroud. I fought it. I wanted to stay awake, in this precious netherworld where Glimmer was mine. Not drown in the dark and ruthless truth of my nightmares.

But eventually, I slept. And I didn't dream.

When I awoke, dawn brightened the sky, the curtains swelling on cool morning breeze. Glimmer lay stretched on his side, watching me. Still spectacularly naked. My sleepy gaze drifted down his long, lean body, savoring that flawless olive skin, the hard contours of muscles. His face, bruised but beautiful, that tiny ever-haunted smile. Those amazing eyes. That fucking fantastic hair.

Well, this was tomorrow. Now what?

"So," I ventured. "Ethan, huh?"

A sweet, apologetic shrug of one shoulder.

I fingered a skunky lock from his forehead. "I like 'Glimmer' better."

"So do I." That voice, rough yet sweet like old bourbon, just like the first day we'd met. I'd thought he'd sounded sexy then. I'd had no idea.

I swallowed, fearful but resigned. "I'm so sorry about Aysha. About everything. I don't know what to say…"

He leaned over and kissed me. I closed my eyes for a moment, overcome. Just a single soft kiss, almost chaste. But it meant the world.

"It wasn't your fault, Verity. You did what you had to." He rolled onto his back, and I snuggled into his embrace, my cheek on his chest.

"Will you try to see her?" My heart shrank at what that girl would have to endure: high-security mental-health facilities, shrinks, endless therapy, questions. After what she'd done? They'd never let her out. Still Vincent's parting shot in her direction—*wouldn't you rather die?*—boomed ominous bells in my memory. A cruelly planted seed, that one. They'd better put her on suicide watch.

"Try? They can *try* to keep me away." Glimmer stroked my hair. I liked how his voice vibrated into my ear. I liked his body naked against mine. Hell, I liked everything.

But my mood darkened a little. I hadn't thought about Vincent this whole time. Hadn't even dreamed of flames, or felt his fiery, accusing gaze on my skin while Glimmer and I…

No. Stop it. It was too soon to give this a name, but whatever it was, it was too precious. I didn't want it tarnished with Vincent's shadow.

Who are you kidding? Think he won't know you slept with another man? Think he won't see it the instant he looks into your face?

But Glimmer had already challenged him, and Vincent just… Shit. I didn't want to break the mood, but I had to ask. "At Wilt's office. What did he say to you? "

Glimmer shifted, tense. "He said, 'I dare you'."

I rested my chin on his chest. "Well, I guess we just dared."

"I guess we did." A dark glance, unreadable.

I sighed and sat up. "Look, I realize that last night was… um… probably not really your thing. It's okay. It was a shitty day and you had the worst of it. I won't give you a hard time."

"I know." He grimaced. "I'm sorry. You know me, always having amazing sex with my best friend and then brushing it off. I get it. It was totally boring. We don't have to do it again if you don't want."

"Fuck, yes, let's do it again," I blurted, before I realized he was teasing me.

Not laughing, exactly. He was too bruised inside for that. But he managed a small, serious smile. "I meant what I said. I don't want you to leave. Don't ever think you don't belong here." He traced one finger along my brow, hesitant, like he turned words over in his head, trying them out before he spoke. "We need to talk about something."

My throat corked. I waited.

He licked bruised lips. "Nadia and I were over a long time ago. Long before all this. But you don't just wake up one morning un-loving someone. The place she once held in my heart... it became a dark, poisonous place, but it was still full, you know? So long as she still inhabited me, I didn't think it was fair to ask you to share."

"Look—"

He hushed me, a finger on my lips. "But Nadia's gone now. She's a ghost and she can't hurt us. You don't have to share anymore."

I swallowed, overcome. To have those words from him was a glorious, improbable dream. But...

"So I know how hard it is to cut someone precious from your heart." He took a careful breath. "I don't expect your feelings to evaporate overnight, if they ever do. But feelings and actions aren't the same thing."

"Um... so what are you saying?"

"I'm saying that what you feel is none of my business—but when it comes to who you're spending your time with? I won't share you, Verity. Not with him."

That unintentional emphasis, the way everyone does. *Him.* Or did I just imagine it like that?

My heart shuddered, torn. *You want me to live a lie!* the bitter part of me screamed. But it wasn't true. Glimmer just needed me to make a *choice*.

There was this—the real world—or there was Vincent. I'd tried so stubbornly to have both. But even in the sweetest depths of my denial, I'd secretly known it was impossible. I just never had the courage to *act* like it.

At my hesitation, Glimmer bit his lip. "I know it's a lot to ask. If you can't..."

"I already told him no." Even as I spoke it, the lie stung my heart. It wasn't a lie. But it was. Or not. Maybe…

Mentally, I smacked myself. Glimmer deserved so much better than my screwed-up doubts. He'd trusted me when I didn't deserve it. I wanted more than anything to deserve it now.

"I told him no," I repeated, more firmly. The idea crystallized, a precious yet fragile jewel in the core of my soul. "I'm not seeing him anymore. It's over."

Glimmer didn't smile, not exactly.

He lit up. Like silvery starlight with hope and gratitude.

Wow. This power I wielded frightened me… and I realized now that I'd wielded it all along. I'd just been too damn stubborn to notice.

But the perilous responsibility I'd just accepted only polished my determination brighter. If I disappointed Glimmer now—if I broke his priceless, irreplaceable heart—I'd never forgive myself. Not ever.

Idly, he twined our fingers together. "So. Breakfast first or shower?"

"Do I get to shower with you?" Half a joke, really. He didn't have to say yes.

"I don't know. Is there room?"

"Well, we could stand really close together." Daring, I added, "And I could kiss you. For, like, an hour. Maybe two. I've got months' worth of secret kissing fantasies to fulfill. Like you didn't know."

A bashful grin, like he couldn't help it, and his cheeks stained pink.

I pointed. "Dude, you're blushing."

"I am not."

"Are too."

"Am not—" He broke off and swiped my finger aside. "Whatever, okay? Have it your way."

"Two hours it is, then. Don't say I didn't warn you." I hopped up, and for a few dizzy seconds, I felt sick. *Over? Not a chance. Not until* he *says so. Maybe not ever…*

But Glimmer steadied me, so warm and safe, and the feeling passed. Together, we crept to the bathroom. Stood under the warm, cleansing water, and held each other. No words, no promises. Just embracing, my head on his shoulder, our lips now and then meeting for a kiss.

Scarred

ERICA HAYES

Harper*Impulse* an imprint of
HarperCollins*Publishers* Ltd
1 London Bridge Street
London SE1 9GF

www.harpercollins.co.uk

A Paperback Original 2016

First published in Great Britain in ebook format by Harper*Impulse* 2016

A catalogue record for this book is
available from the British Library

ISBN: 9780008173173

Automatically produced by Atomik ePublisher from Easypress

Printed and bound in Great Britain